POKÉMON™ ADVENTURES BLACK & WHITE

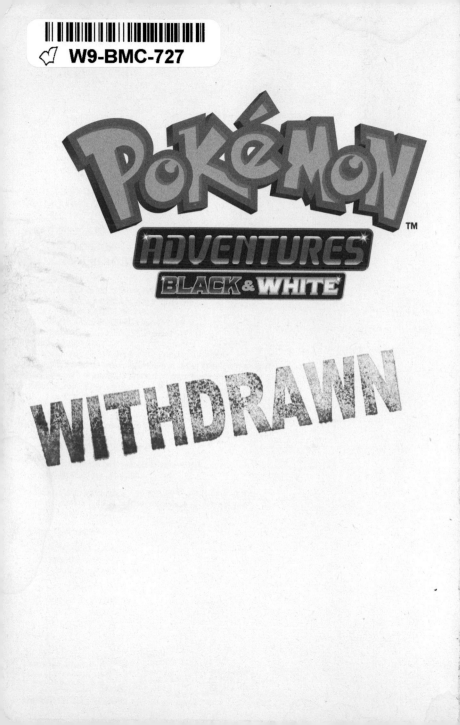

Pokémon ADVENTURES BLACK AND WHITE
Volume 5
Perfect Square Edition

Story by HIDENORI KUSAKA
Art by SATOSHI YAMAMOTO

© 2014 Pokémon.
© 1995–2014 Nintendo/Creatures Inc./GAME FREAK inc.
TM, ®, and character names are trademarks of Nintendo.
POCKET MONSTERS SPECIAL Vol. 47
by Hidenori KUSAKA, Satoshi YAMAMOTO
© 1997 Hidenori KUSAKA, Satoshi YAMAMOTO
All rights reserved.
Original Japanese edition published by SHOGAKUKAN.
English translation rights in the United States of America, Canada,
United Kingdom, Ireland, Australia and New Zealand
arranged with SHOGAKUKAN.

Translation/Tetsuichiro Miyaki
English Adaptation/Annette Roman
Touch-up & Lettering/Susan Daigle-Leach
Design/Shawn Carrico
Editor/Annette Roman

Printed in the U.S.A.

Published by VIZ Media, LLC
P.O. Box 77010
San Francisco, CA 94107

10 9 8 7 6 5 4 3 2 1
First printing, November 2014

www.perfectsquare.com   www.viz.com

POKÉMON™ ADVENTURES
BLACK & WHITE

5
VOLUME FIVE

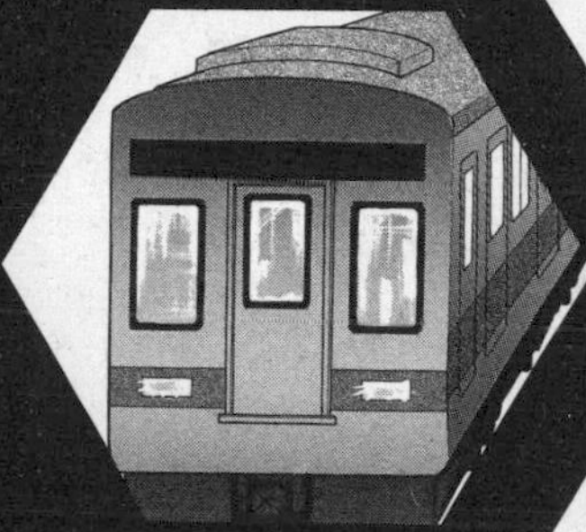

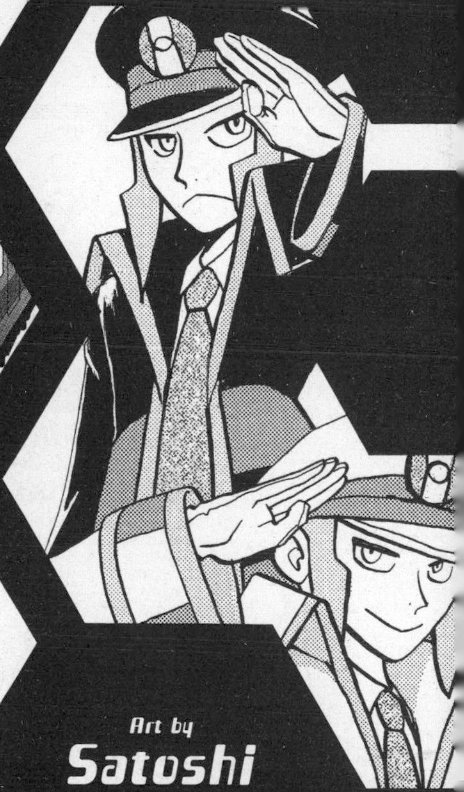

Story by
Hidenori Kusaka

Art by
Satoshi Yamamoto

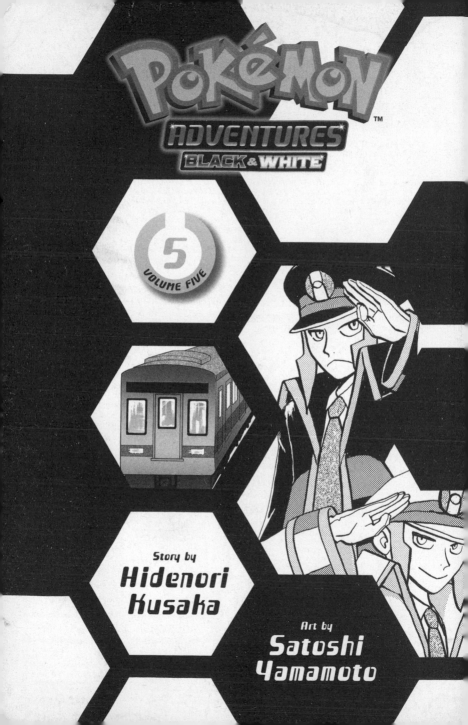

& WHITE

SOME PLACE IN SOME TIME... A YOUNG TRAINER NAMED BLACK, WHO DREAMS OF WINNING THE POKÉMON LEAGUE, RECEIVES A POKÉDEX FROM PROFESSOR JUNIPER AND SETS OFF ON HIS TRAINING JOURNEY TO COLLECT THE EIGHT GYM BADGES HE NEEDS TO ENTER NEXT YEAR'S POKÉMON LEAGUE. ON THE WAY, BLACK MEETS WHITE, THE OWNER OF A POKÉMON TALENT AGENCY, AND ENDS UP WORKING FOR HER. UNBEKNOWNST TO OUR HEROES, AN EVIL ORGANIZATION NAMED TEAM PLASMA IS SCHEMING TO GET AHOLD OF THE LEGENDARY POKÉMON ZEKROM AND THE DARK STONE. WHAT FOR...? AND HOW WILL OUR TWO HEROES GET DRAWN INTO THEIR DASTARDLY PLOT...?!

BLACK DEFEATS NIMBASA CITY GYM LEADER ELESA, AND WHITE'S POKÉMON MUSICAL IS A BIG SUCCESS. BUT N, THE KING OF TEAM PLASMA, SUDDENLY APPEARS AND LURES GIGI AWAY FROM WHITE! IN ORDER TO DEVELOP HER LONG NEGLECTED POKÉMON BATTLE SKILLS, WHITE TAKES ON THE CHALLENGE OF THE BATTLE SUBWAY. BLACK AND WHITE PART WAYS, AND BLACK CONTINUES ON HIS JOURNEY ALONE TO GATHER THE REMAINING BADGES HE NEEDS TO ENTER THE POKÉMON LEAGUE...

A STORY ABOUT YOUNG PEOPLE ENTRUSTED WITH POKÉDEXES BY THE WORLD'S LEADING POKÉMON RESEARCHERS. TOGETHER WITH THEIR POKÉMON, THEY TRAVEL, BATTLE, AND EVOLVE!

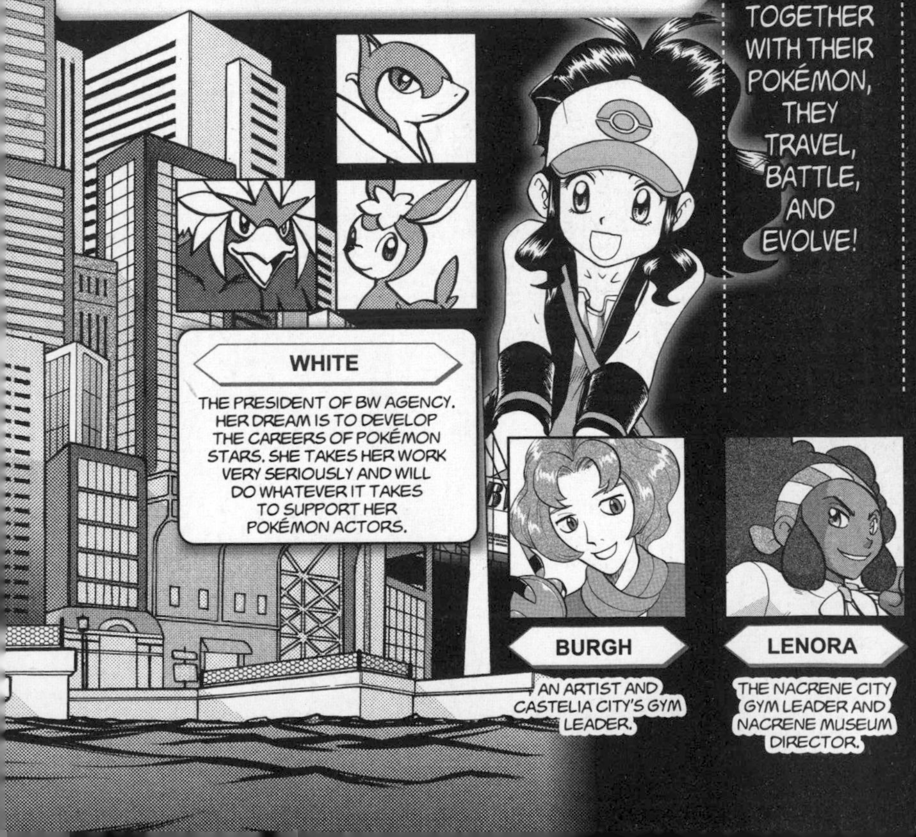
WHITE
THE PRESIDENT OF BW AGENCY. HER DREAM IS TO DEVELOP THE CAREERS OF POKÉMON STARS. SHE TAKES HER WORK VERY SERIOUSLY AND WILL DO WHATEVER IT TAKES TO SUPPORT HER POKÉMON ACTORS.
BURGH
AN ARTIST AND CASTELIA CITY'S GYM LEADER.
LENORA
THE NACRENE CITY GYM LEADER AND NACRENE MUSEUM DIRECTOR.

POKÉMON
ADVENTURES

The Tenth Chapter **10** **BLACK**

PLACE: UNOVA REGION

A HUGE AREA FULL OF MODERN CITIES, MANY OF WHICH ARE CONNECTED TO EACH OTHER BY BRIDGES. RISING FROM THE CENTER OF THE REGION ARE THE SKYSCRAPERS OF CASTELIA CITY, UNOVA'S URBAN CENTER.

BLACK

A TRAINER WHOSE DREAM IS TO WIN THE POKÉMON LEAGUE. A PASSIONATE YOUNG MAN WHO, ONCE HE SETS OUT TO ACCOMPLISH SOMETHING, CAN'T BE STOPPED. HE ALSO DOES HIS RESEARCH AND PLANS AHEAD. HE HAS SPECIAL DEDUCTIVE SKILLS THAT HELP HIM ANALYZE INFORMATION TO SOLVE MYSTERIES.

INGO/EMMET

THE BATTLE SUBWAY BOSSES WHO TRAIN POKÉMON TRAINERS.

ELESA

THE GYM LEADER OF NIMBASA CITY AND A MEDIA STAR.

CLAY

THE MINER KING OF DRIFTVEIL, WHO ACCIDENTALLY EXCAVATED THE MYSTERIOUS DARK STONE.

POKÉMON ADVENTURES

BLACK & WHITE

5 VOLUME FIVE

CONTENTS

ADVENTURE 29
Drawing Bridges 7

ADVENTURE 30
A Stormy Time in the Battle Subway.........................33

ADVENTURE 31
Fight in a Cold Climate..58

ADVENTURE 32
Mine Mayhem..85

ADVENTURE 33
Underground Showdown 111

ADVENTURE 34
Up in the Air..137

ADVENTURE 35
The Battle Within..163

Pokémon™ Adventures
Black & White

PALPITOAD

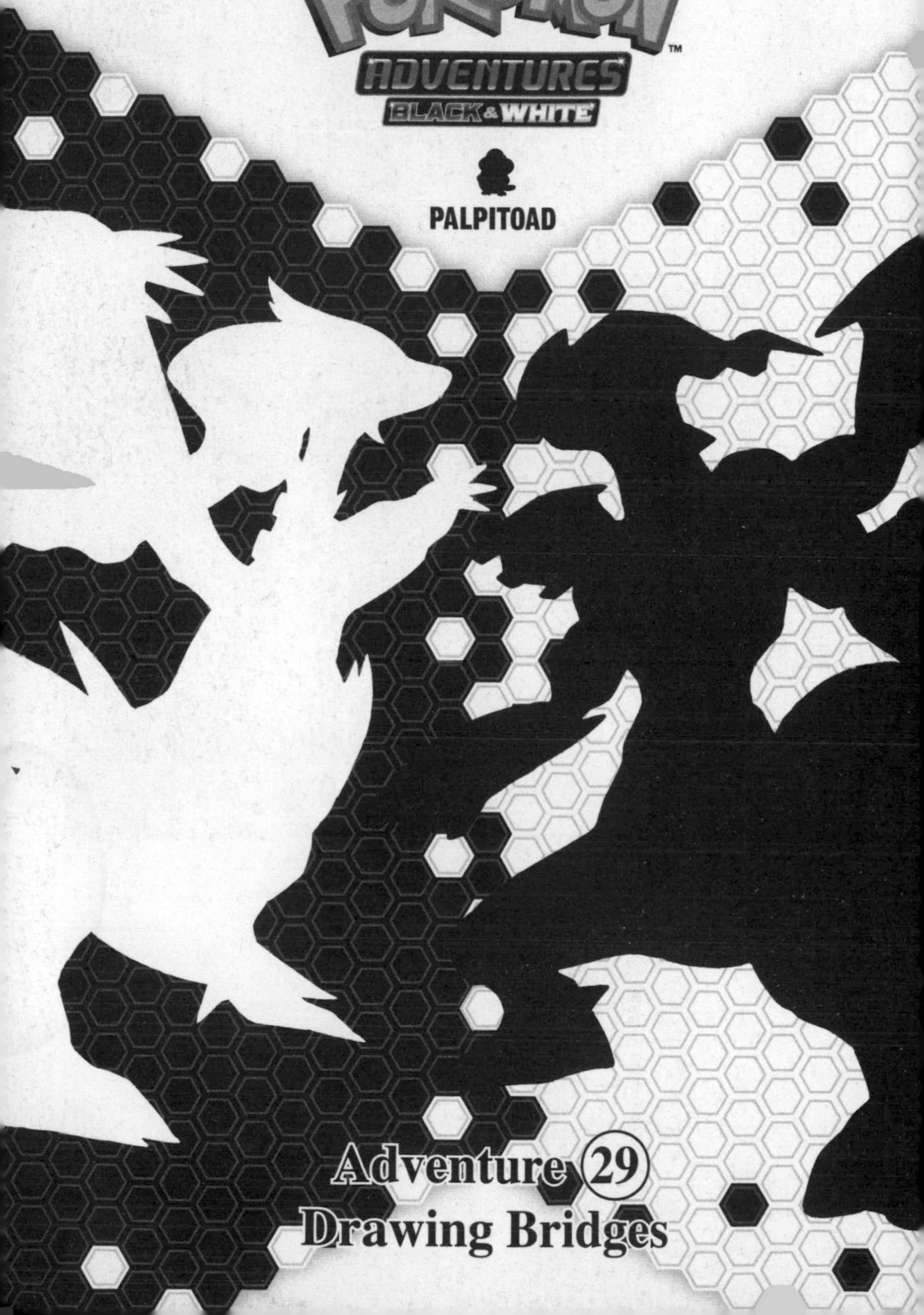

Adventure 29
Drawing Bridges

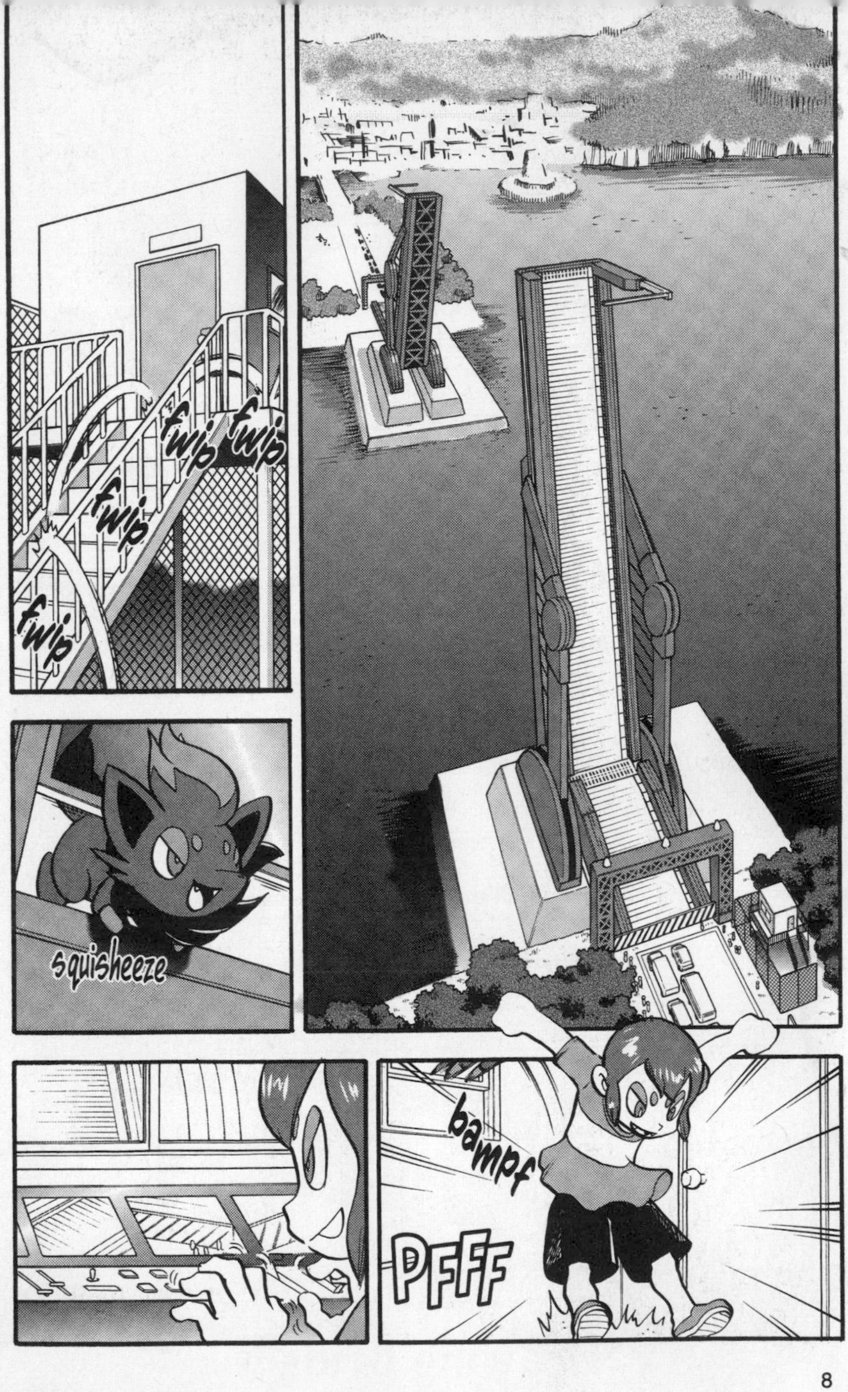
fwip
fwip
fwip
fwip
squisheeze
bampf
PFFF

SIGH... WHAT A HEAD-ACHE.

NOW THAT I'VE DEFEATED ELESA, MY NEXT STOP IS DRIFTVEIL CITY...

AND TO GET THERE, I NEED TO CROSS THIS DRAWBRIDGE...

LIKE I SAID, I'M WAITING TO HEAR FROM YOU. BYE...

OH!

THOSE PEOPLE DON'T LOOK TOO HAPPY TO BE STUCK IN TRAF-FIC.

BUT LOOK AT IT! IT'S BEEN *UP* FOR *AGES.*

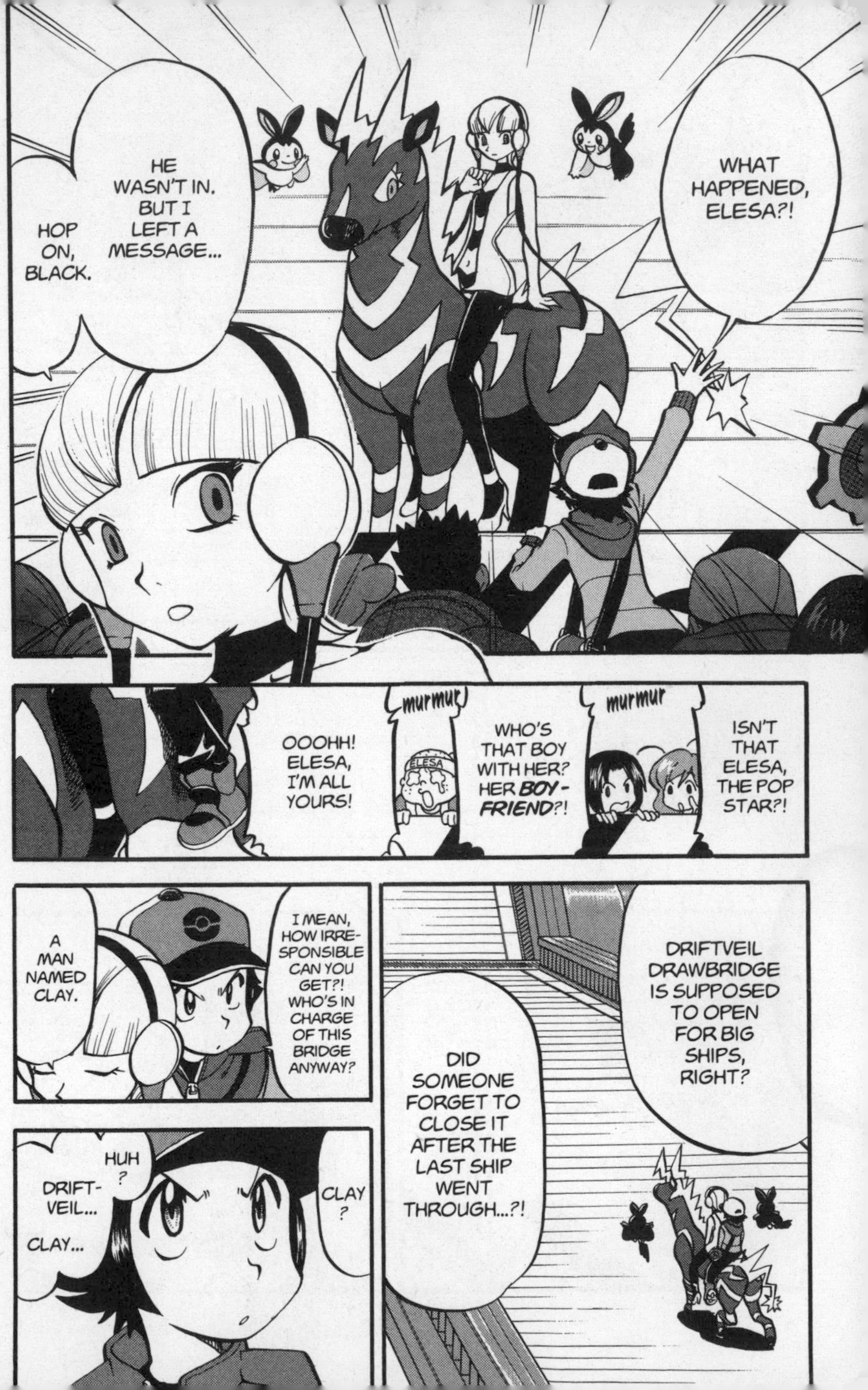
WHAT HAPPENED, ELESA?!
HE WASN'T IN. BUT I LEFT A MESSAGE...
HOP ON, BLACK.
murmur
ISN'T THAT ELESA, THE POP STAR?!
murmur
WHO'S THAT BOY WITH HER? HER BOY-FRIEND?!
ELESA
OOOHH! ELESA, I'M ALL YOURS!
DRIFTVEIL DRAWBRIDGE IS SUPPOSED TO OPEN FOR BIG SHIPS, RIGHT?
DID SOMEONE FORGET TO CLOSE IT AFTER THE LAST SHIP WENT THROUGH...?!
I MEAN, HOW IRRE-SPONSIBLE CAN YOU GET?! WHO'S IN CHARGE OF THIS BRIDGE ANYWAY?
A MAN NAMED CLAY.
CLAY?
HUH?
DRIFT-VEIL...
CLAY...

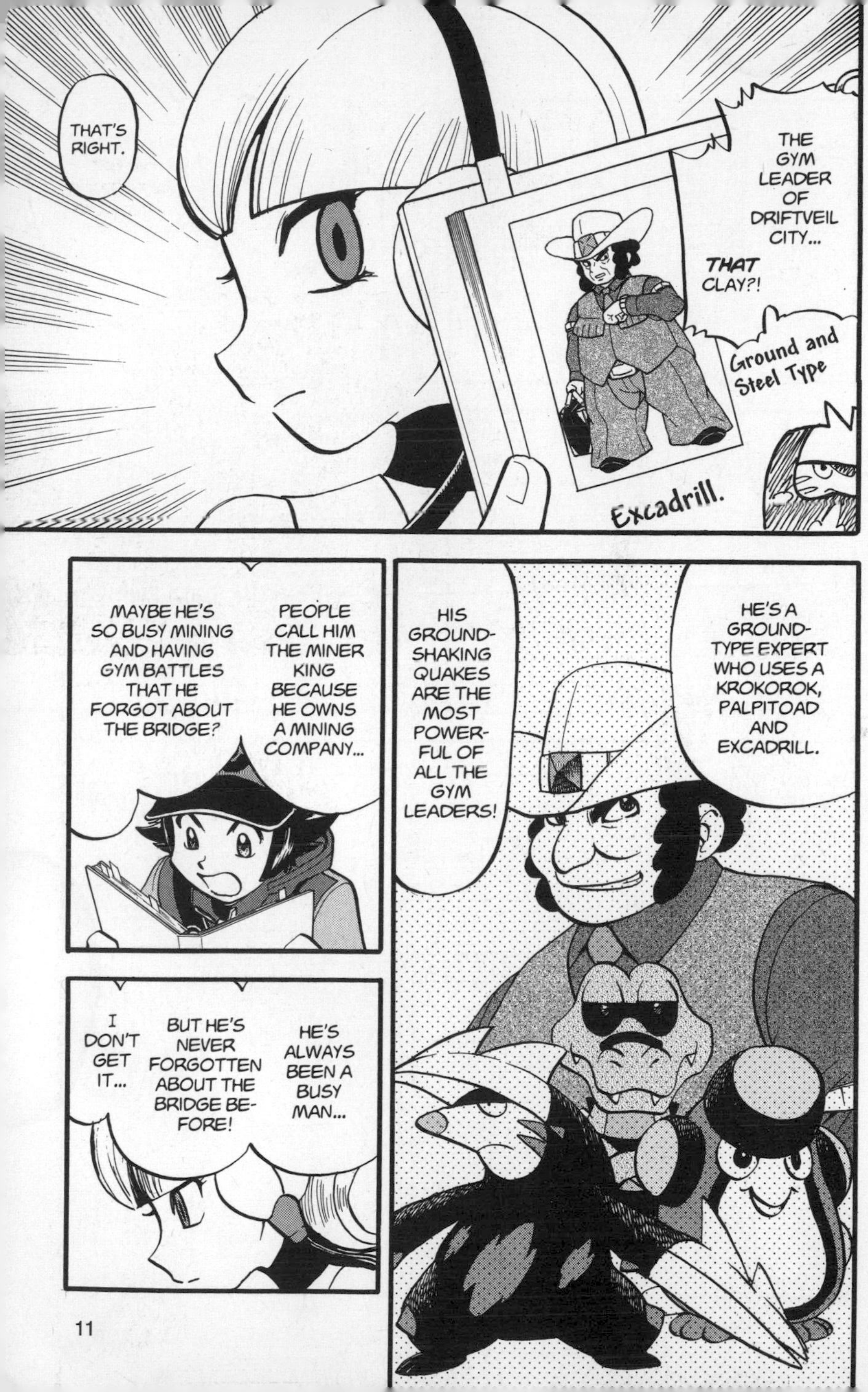
THE GYM LEADER OF DRIFTVEIL CITY...
THAT CLAY?!
Ground and Steel Type
Excadrill.
THAT'S RIGHT.
HE'S A GROUND-TYPE EXPERT WHO USES A KROKOROK, PALPITOAD AND EXCADRILL.
HIS GROUND-SHAKING QUAKES ARE THE MOST POWERFUL OF ALL THE GYM LEADERS!
PEOPLE CALL HIM THE MINER KING BECAUSE HE OWNS A MINING COMPANY...
MAYBE HE'S SO BUSY MINING AND HAVING GYM BATTLES THAT HE FORGOT ABOUT THE BRIDGE?
HE'S ALWAYS BEEN A BUSY MAN...
BUT HE'S NEVER FORGOTTEN ABOUT THE BRIDGE BEFORE!
I DON'T GET IT...

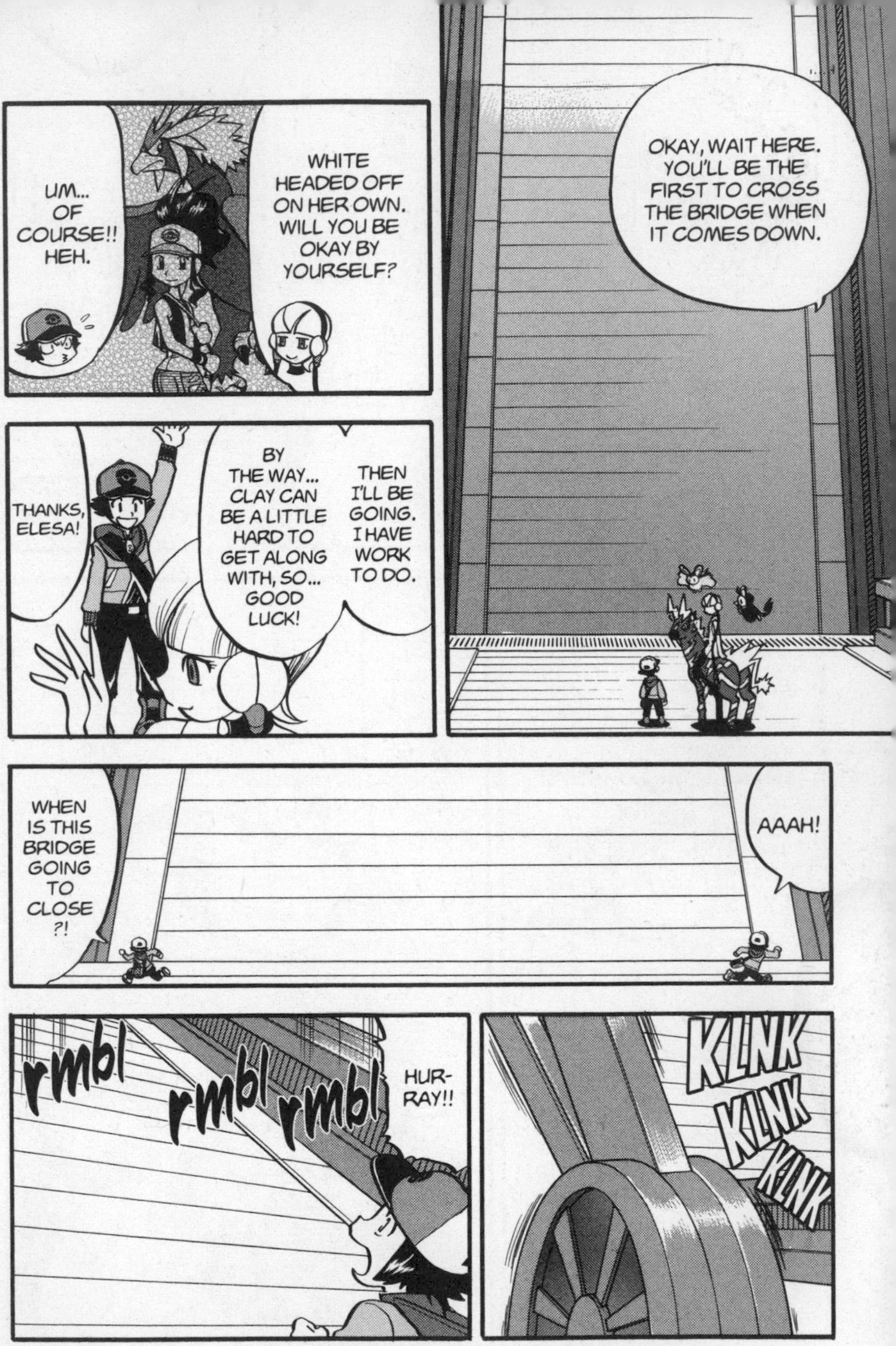
OKAY, WAIT HERE. YOU'LL BE THE FIRST TO CROSS THE BRIDGE WHEN IT COMES DOWN.
WHITE HEADED OFF ON HER OWN. WILL YOU BE OKAY BY YOURSELF?
UM... OF COURSE!! HEH.
THEN I'LL BE GOING. I HAVE WORK TO DO.
BY THE WAY... CLAY CAN BE A LITTLE HARD TO GET ALONG WITH, SO... GOOD LUCK!
THANKS, ELESA!
AAAH!
WHEN IS THIS BRIDGE GOING TO CLOSE ?!
KLNK
KLNK
KLNK
HUR-RAY!!
rmbl
rmbl
rmbl

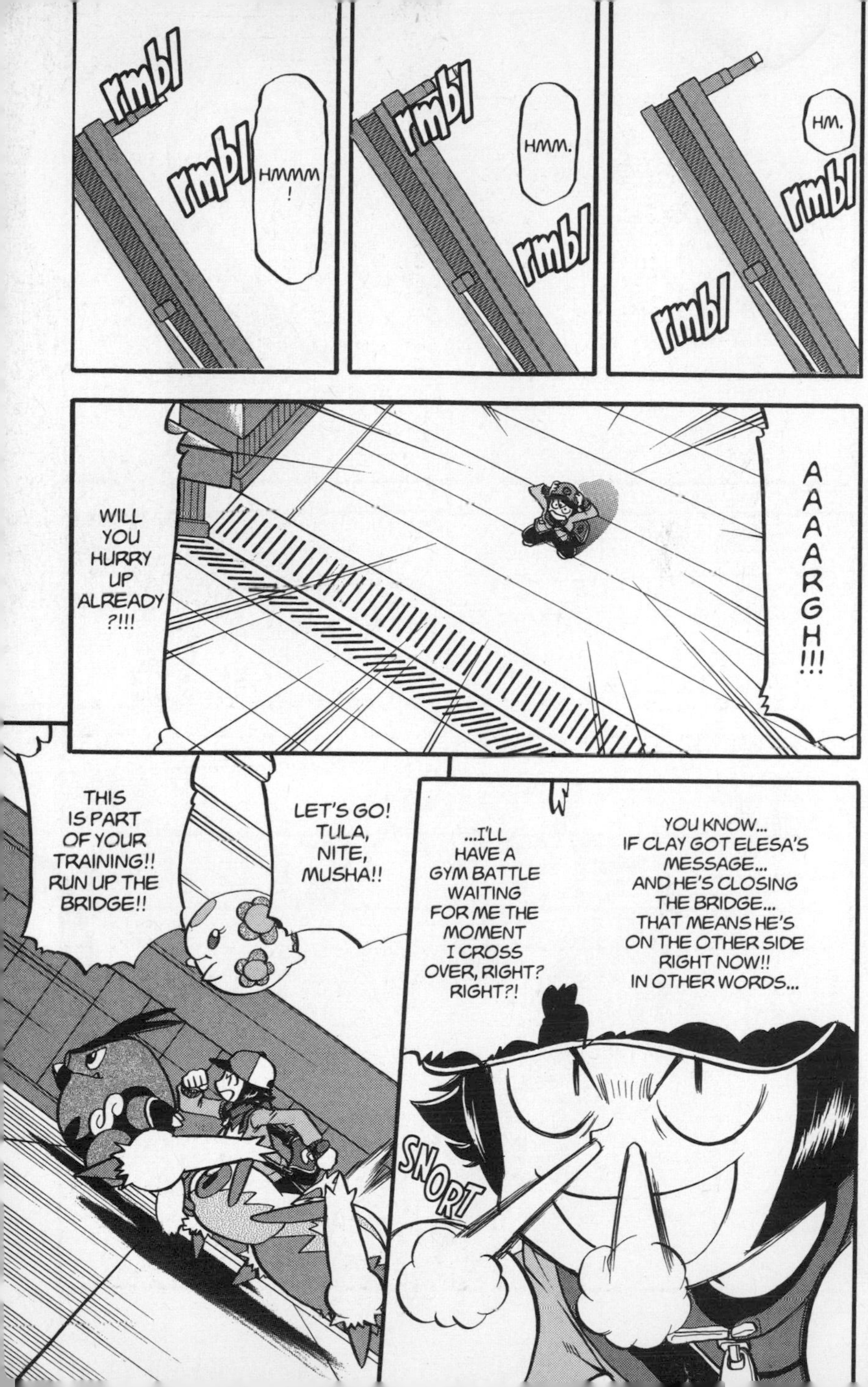
HM.
rmbl
rmbl
HMM.
rmbl
rmbl
HMMM!
rmbl
rmbl
AAAAARGH!!!
WILL YOU HURRY UP ALREADY?!!!
YOU KNOW... IF CLAY GOT ELESA'S MESSAGE... AND HE'S CLOSING THE BRIDGE... THAT MEANS HE'S ON THE OTHER SIDE RIGHT NOW!! IN OTHER WORDS...
...I'LL HAVE A GYM BATTLE WAITING FOR ME THE MOMENT I CROSS OVER, RIGHT? RIGHT?!
SNORT
LET'S GO! TULA, NITE, MUSHA!!
THIS IS PART OF YOUR TRAINING!! RUN UP THE BRIDGE!!

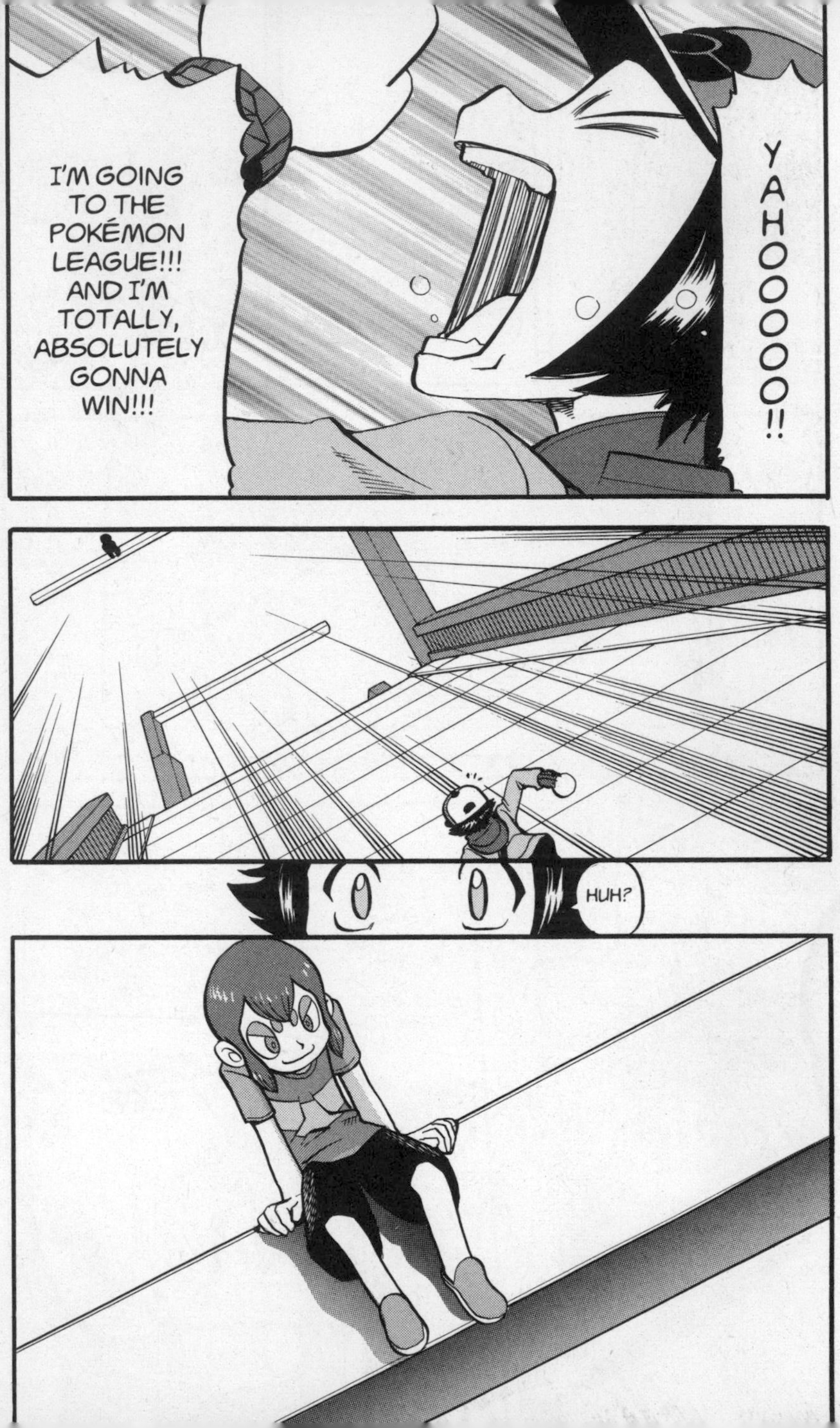
YAHOOOOOO!!
I'M GOING TO THE POKÉMON LEAGUE!!! AND I'M TOTALLY, ABSOLUTELY GONNA WIN!!!
HUH?

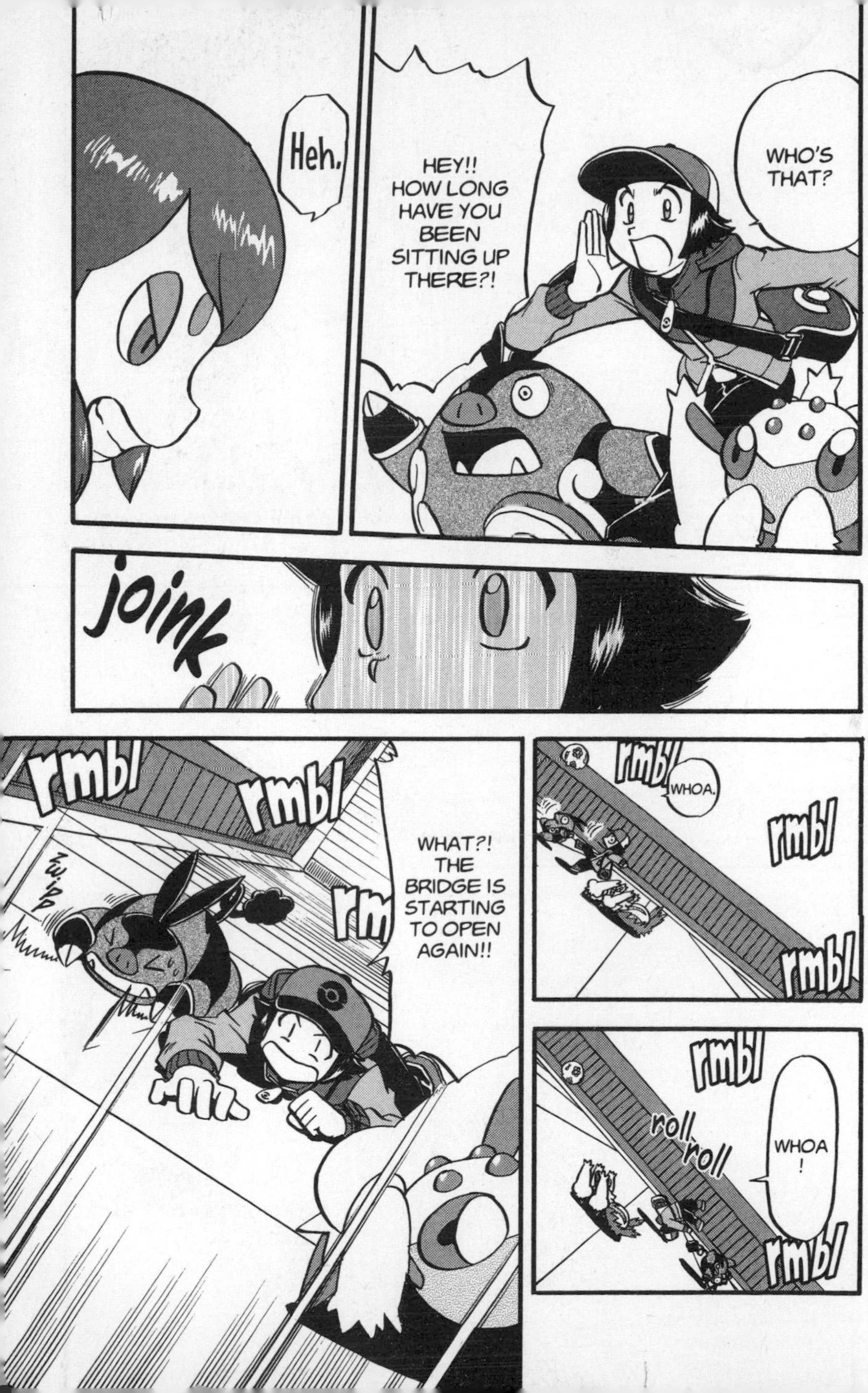
WHO'S THAT?
HEY!! HOW LONG HAVE YOU BEEN SITTING UP THERE?!
Heh.
joink
rmbl
WHOA.
rmbl
rmbl
rmbl
WHOA !
roll roll
rmbl
rmbl
rmbl
WHAT?! THE BRIDGE IS STARTING TO OPEN AGAIN!!
rm
zwipp

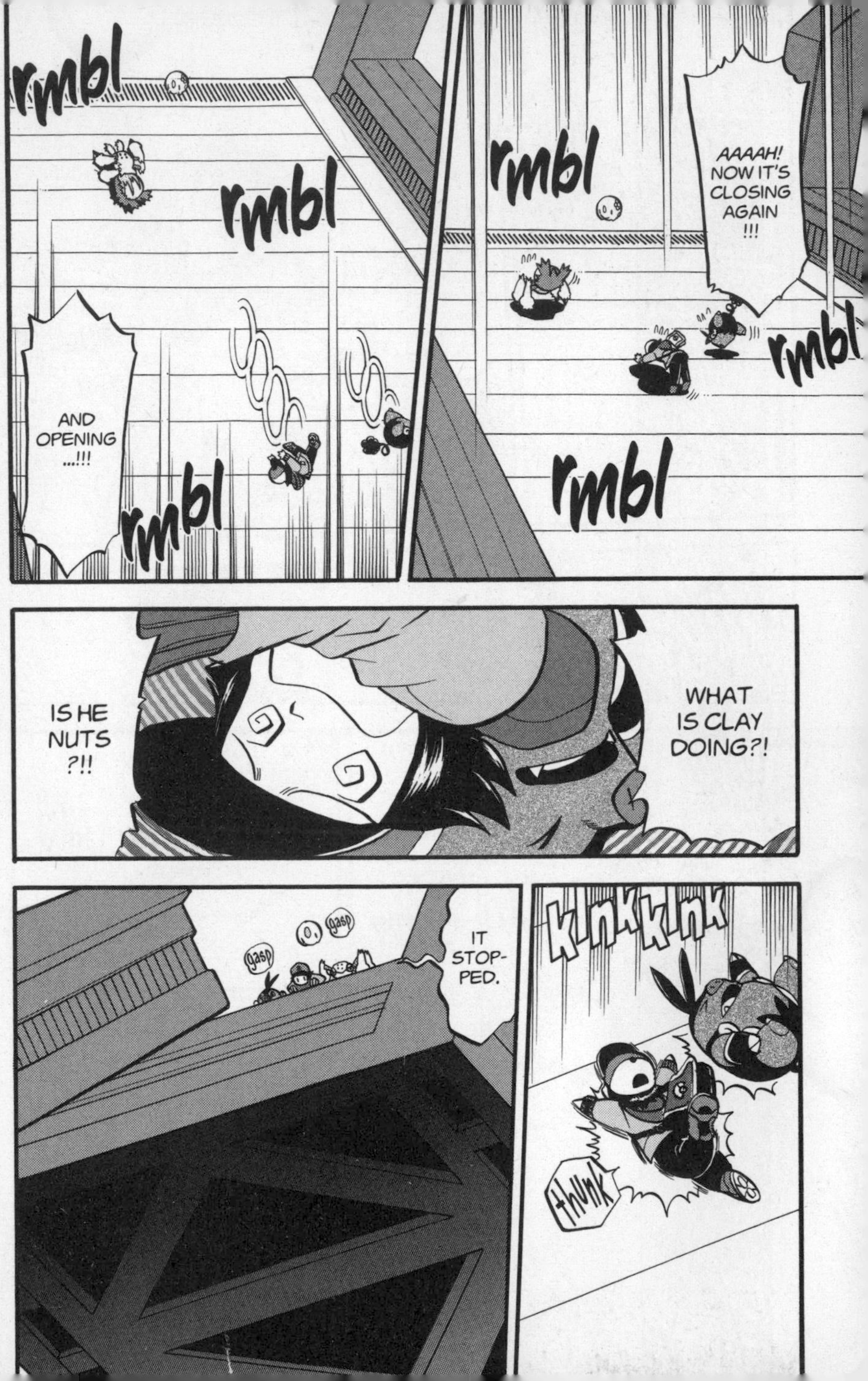
rmbl
AAAAH! NOW IT'S CLOSING AGAIN !!!
rmbl
rmbl
rmbl
rmbl
AND OPENING ...!!!
rmbl
WHAT IS CLAY DOING?!
IS HE NUTS ?!!
kinkkink
thunk
IT STOP-PED.
gasp
gasp

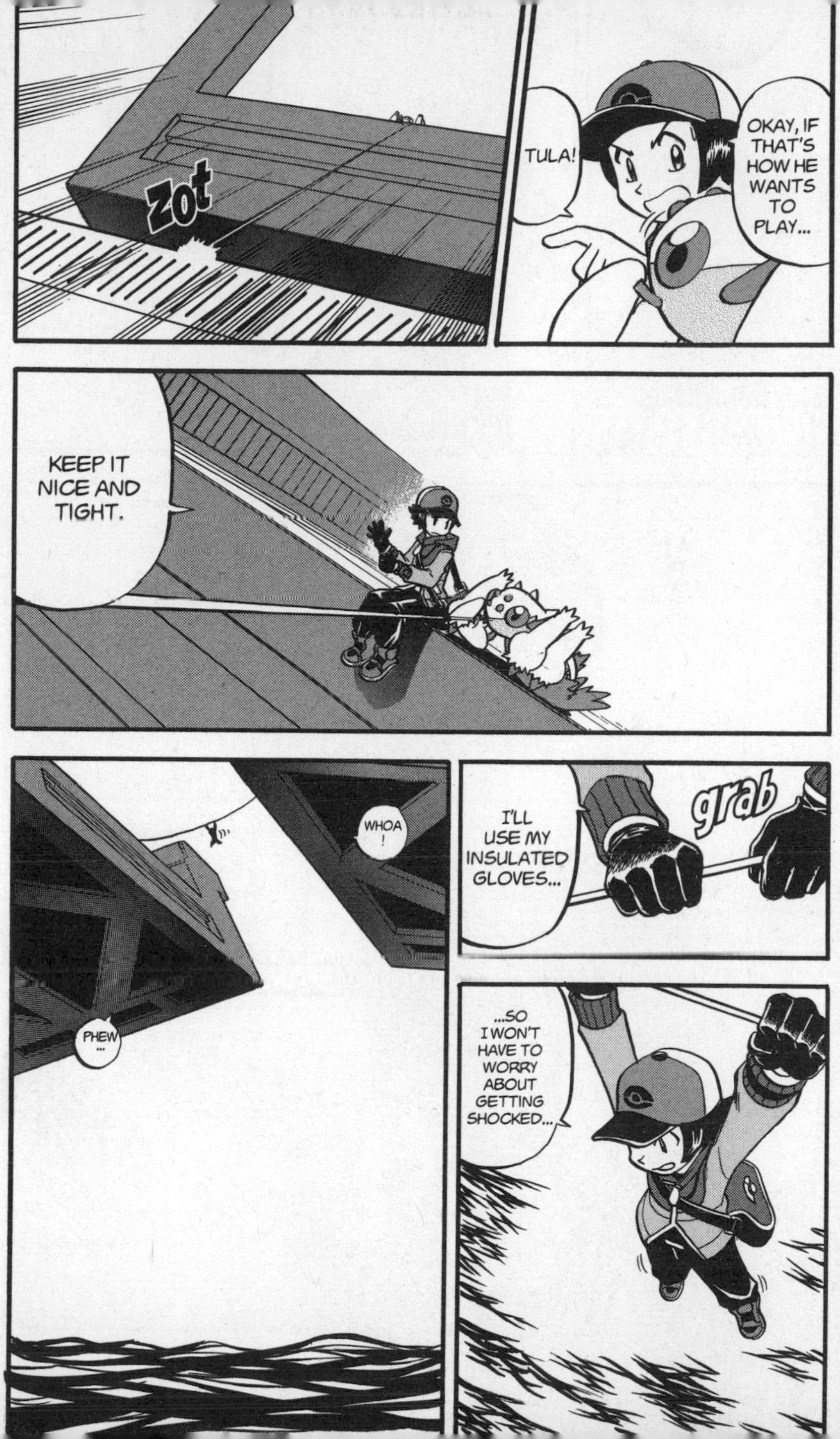
OKAY, IF THAT'S HOW HE WANTS TO PLAY...
TULA!
Zot
KEEP IT NICE AND TIGHT.
grab
I'LL USE MY INSULATED GLOVES...
...SO I WON'T HAVE TO WORRY ABOUT GETTING SHOCKED...
WHOA!
PHEW...

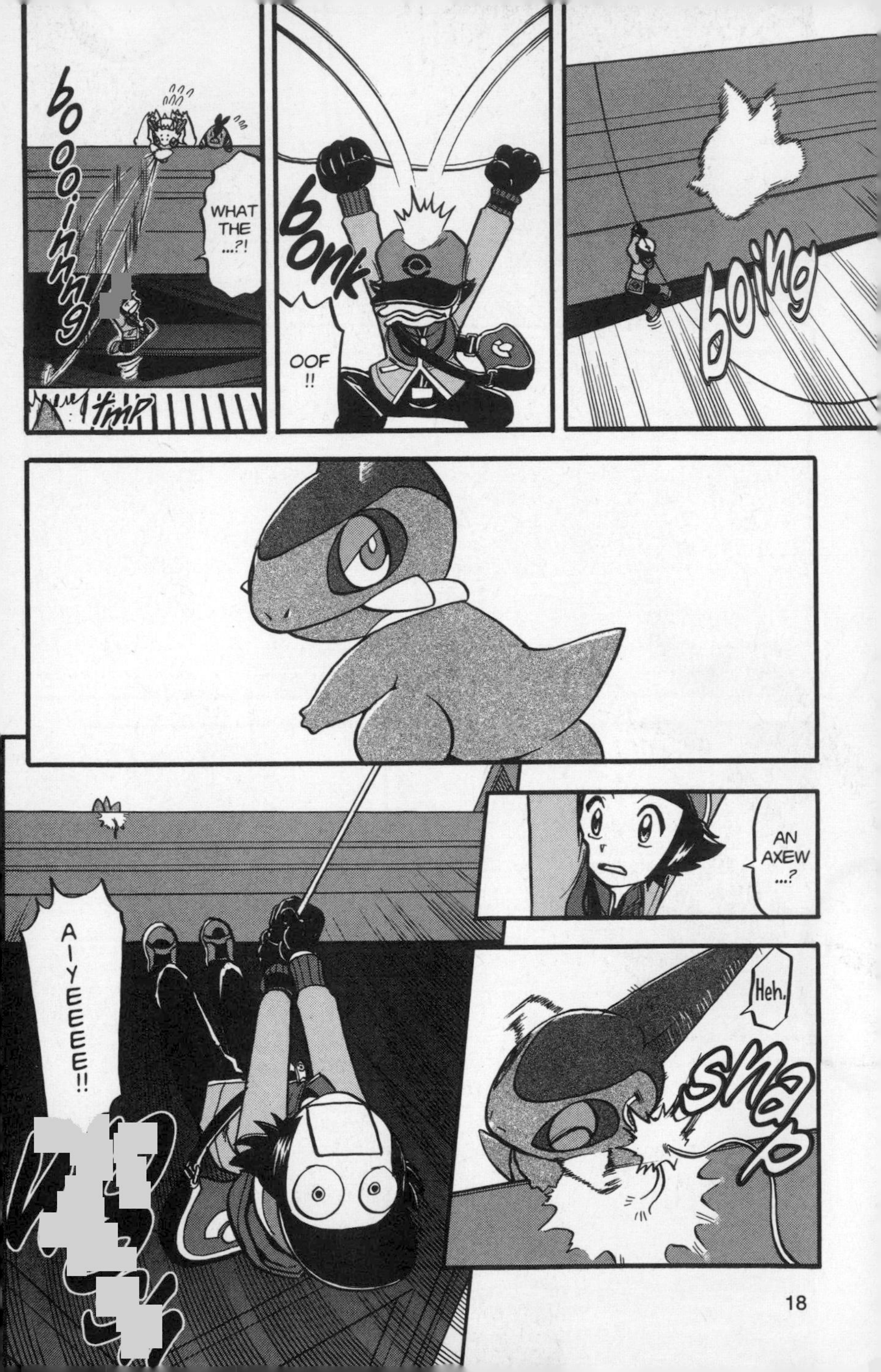
boing
bonk
OOF !!
booooinnng
WHAT THE ...?!
tmp
AN AXEW ...?
Heh.
snap
AIYEEEE!!

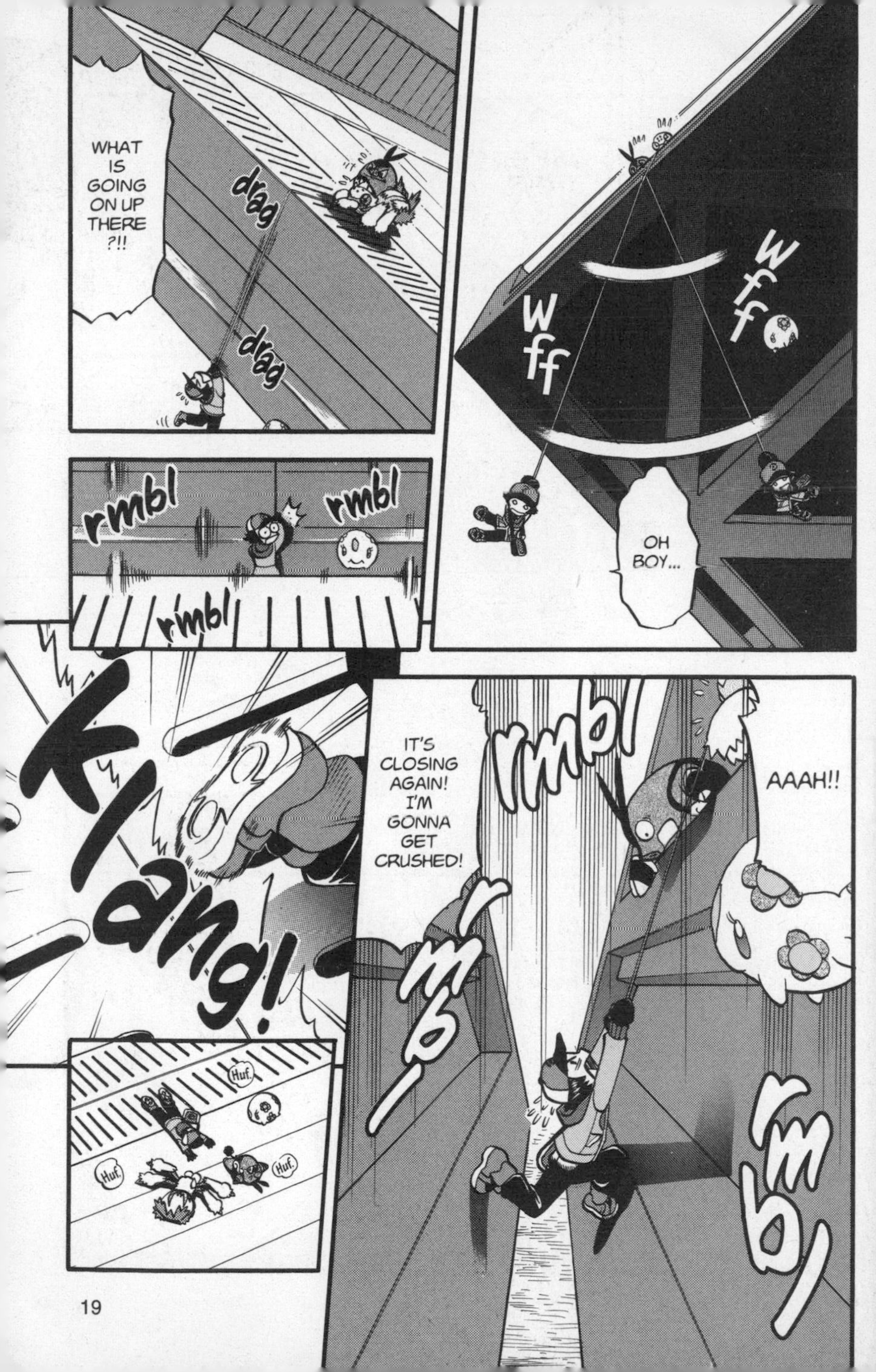
Wff
Wff
OH BOY...
WHAT IS GOING ON UP THERE?!!
drag
drag
rmbl
rmbl
rmbl
rmbl
IT'S CLOSING AGAIN! I'M GONNA GET CRUSHED!
AAAH!!
rmbl
rmbl
Klang!
Huf.
Huf.
Huf.

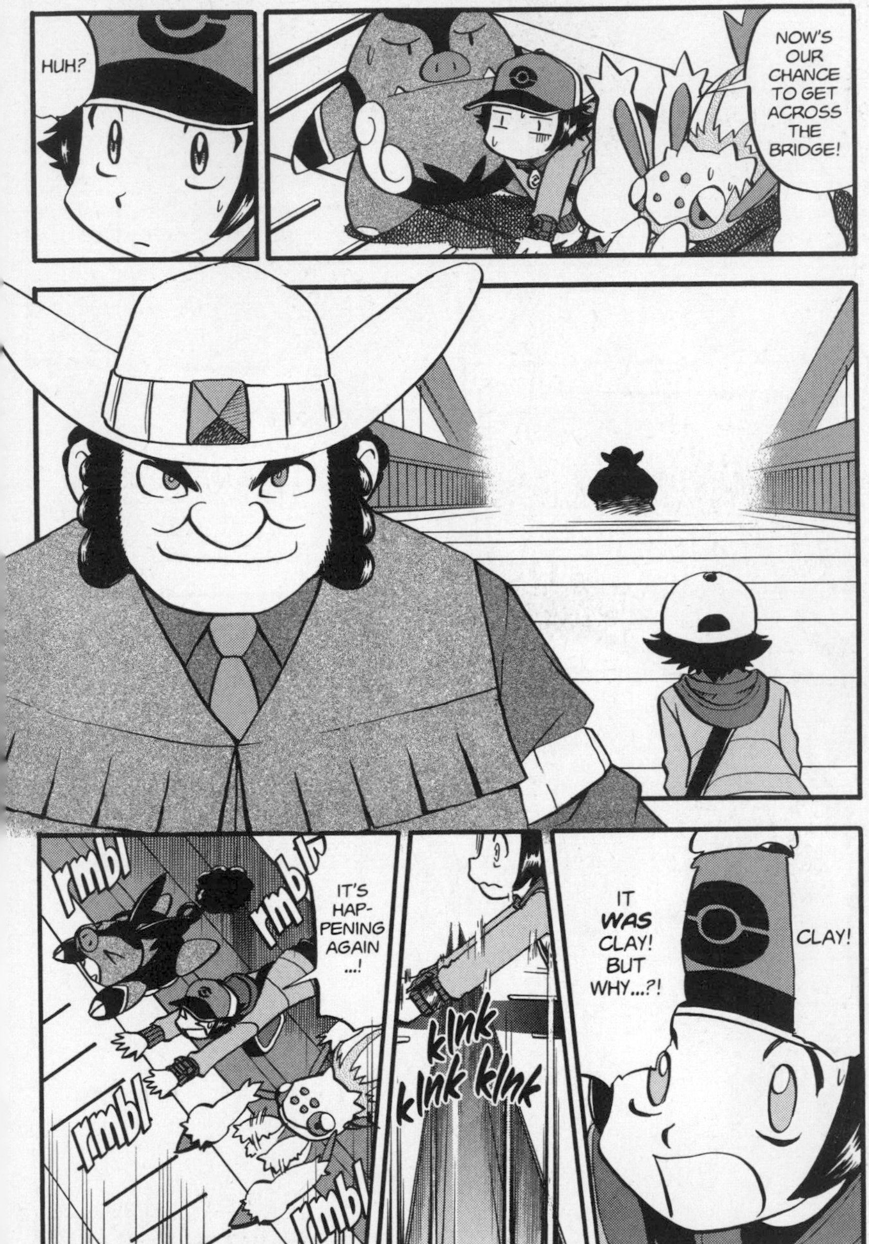
NOW'S OUR CHANCE TO GET ACROSS THE BRIDGE!
HUH?
CLAY!
IT WAS CLAY! BUT WHY...?!
klink klink klink
IT'S HAP-PENING AGAIN ...!
rmbl
rmbl
rmbl
rmbl

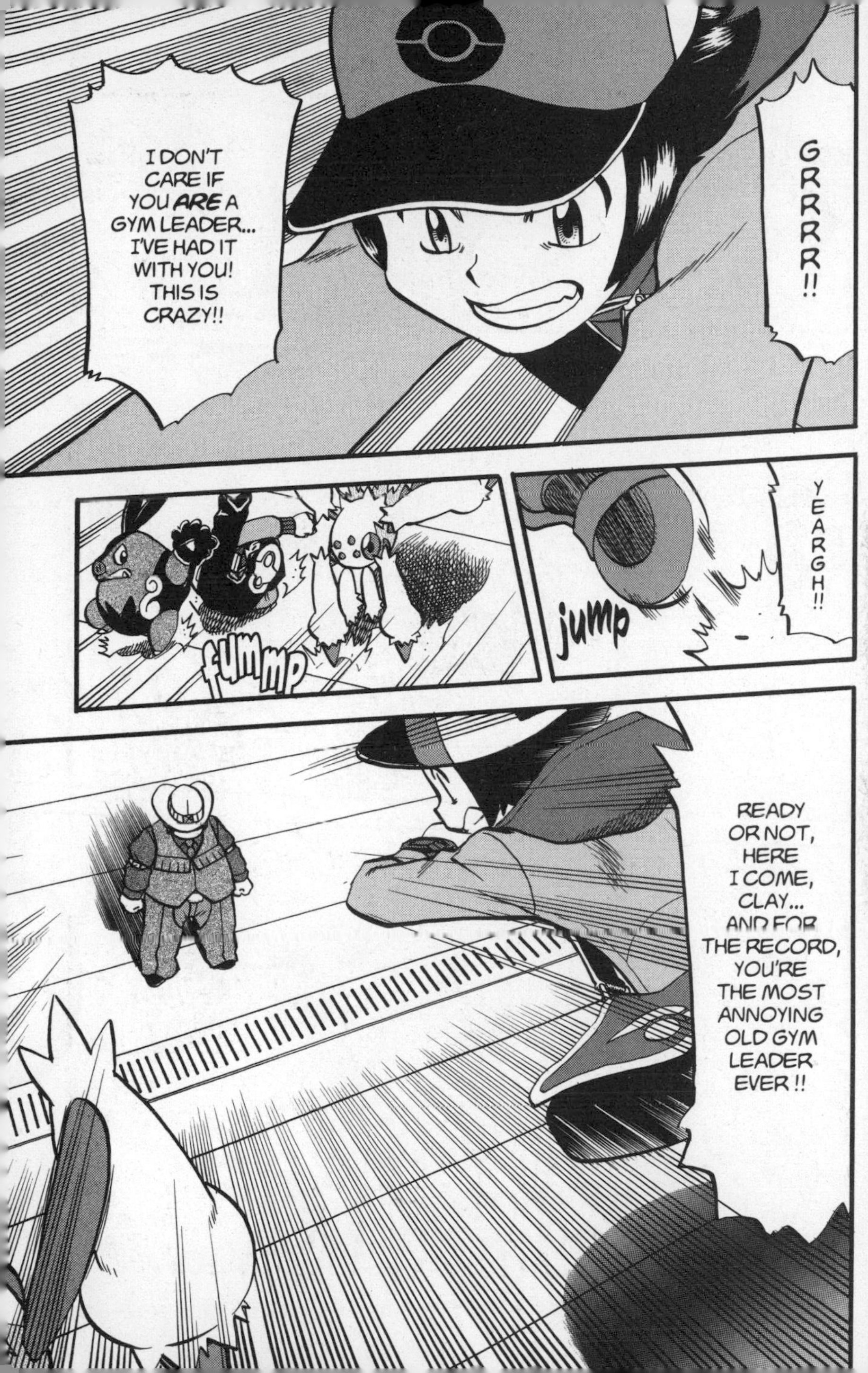
GRRRR!!
I DON'T CARE IF YOU *ARE* A GYM LEADER... I'VE HAD IT WITH YOU! THIS IS CRAZY!!
YEARGH!!
jump
fummp
READY OR NOT, HERE I COME, CLAY... AND FOR THE RECORD, YOU'RE THE MOST ANNOYING OLD GYM LEADER EVER!!

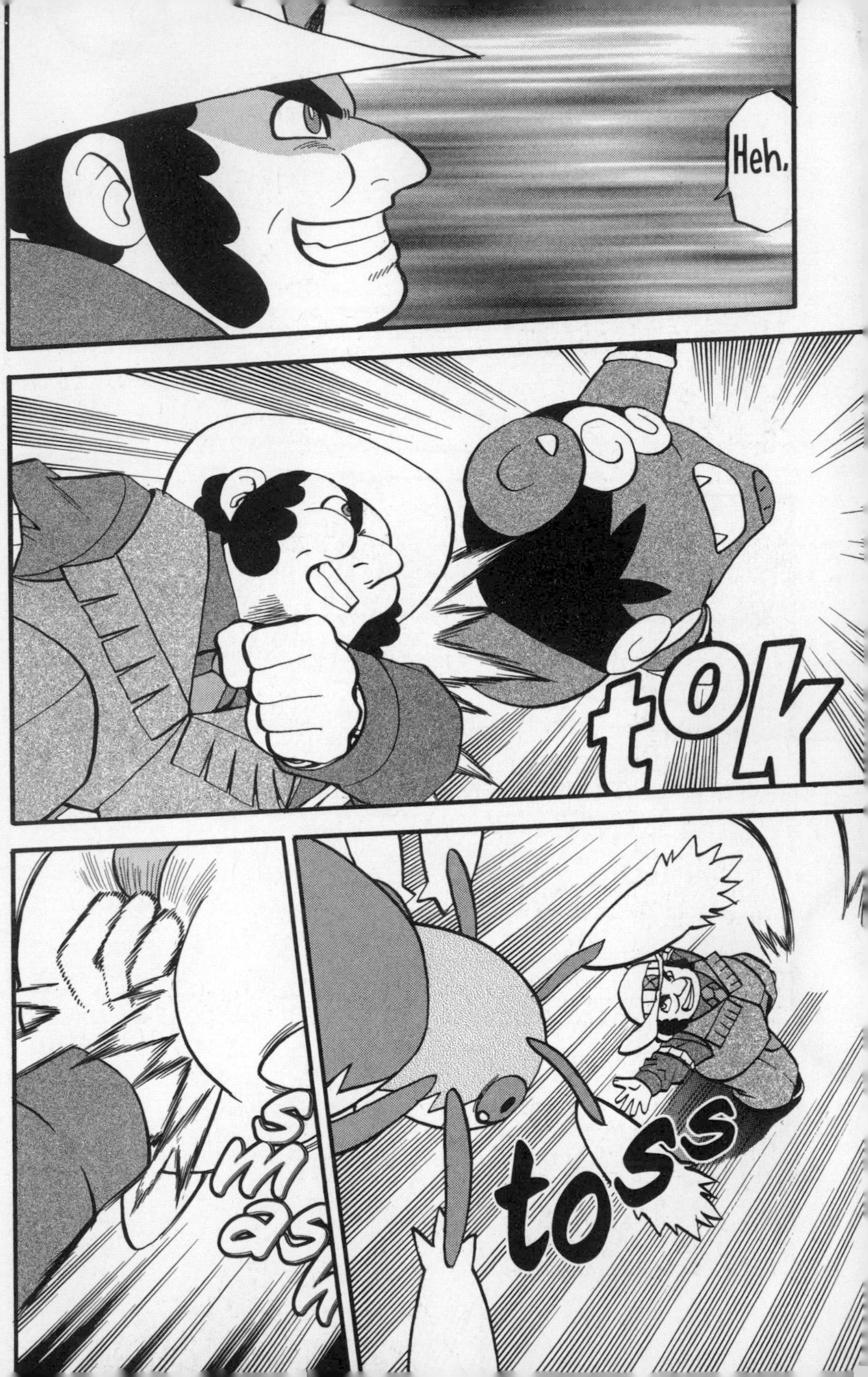
Heh.
tok
toss
smash

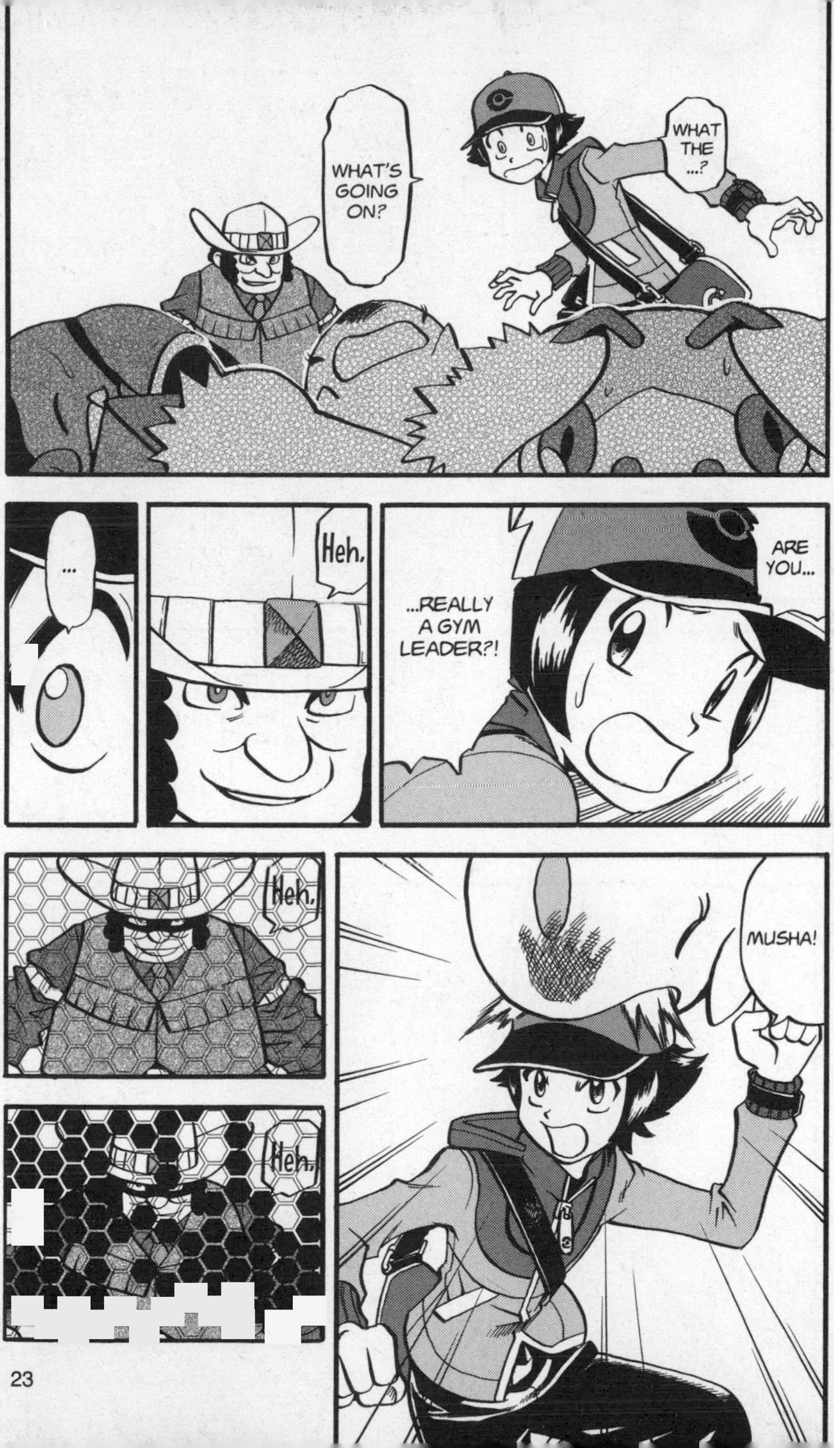
WHAT THE ...?
WHAT'S GOING ON?
ARE YOU...
...REALLY A GYM LEADER?!
Heh.
...
MUSHA!
Heh.
Heh.

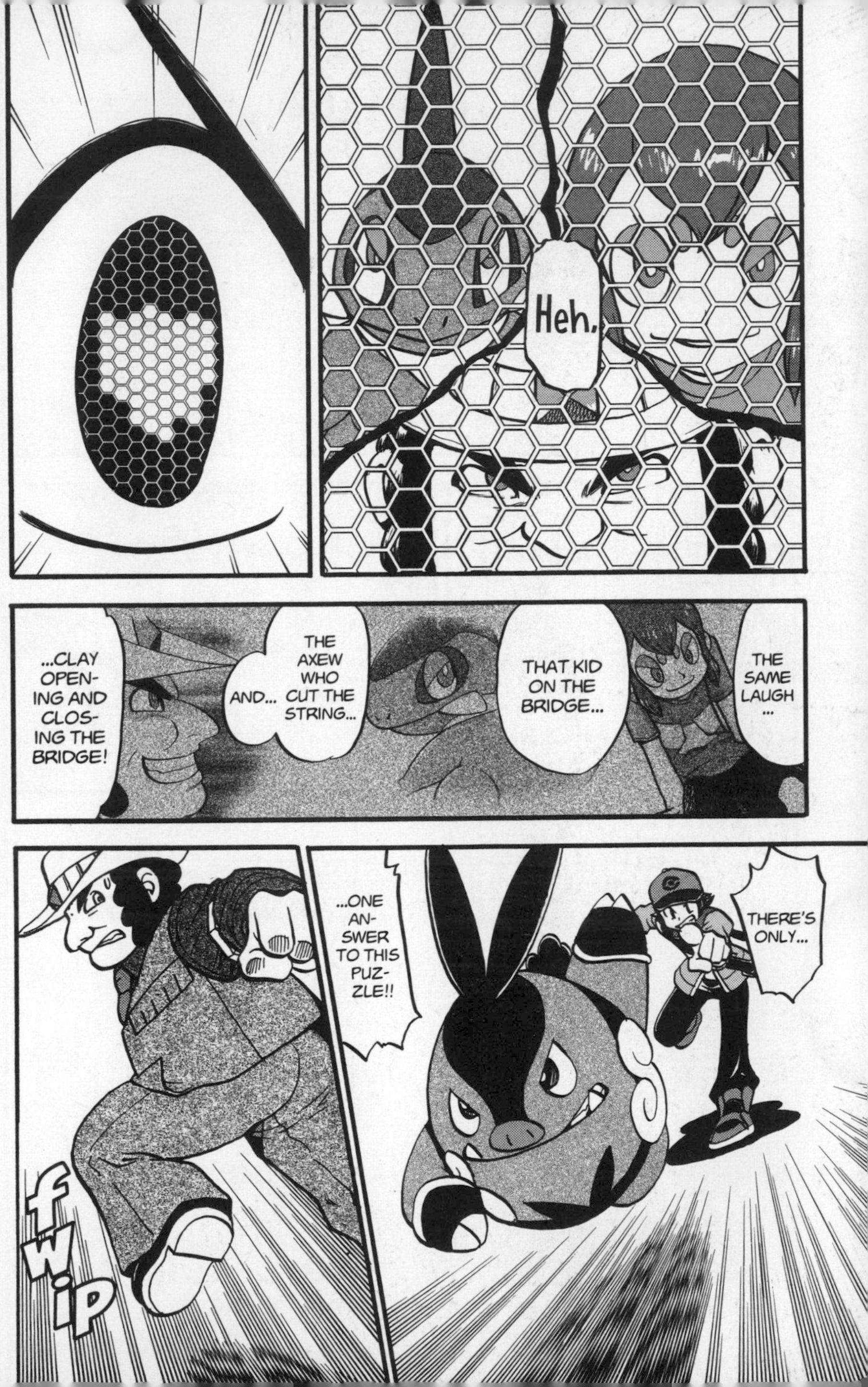
Heh.
THE SAME LAUGH ...
THAT KID ON THE BRIDGE...
THE AXEW WHO CUT THE STRING...
AND...
...CLAY OPENING AND CLOSING THE BRIDGE!
THERE'S ONLY...
...ONE ANSWER TO THIS PUZZLE!!
fwip

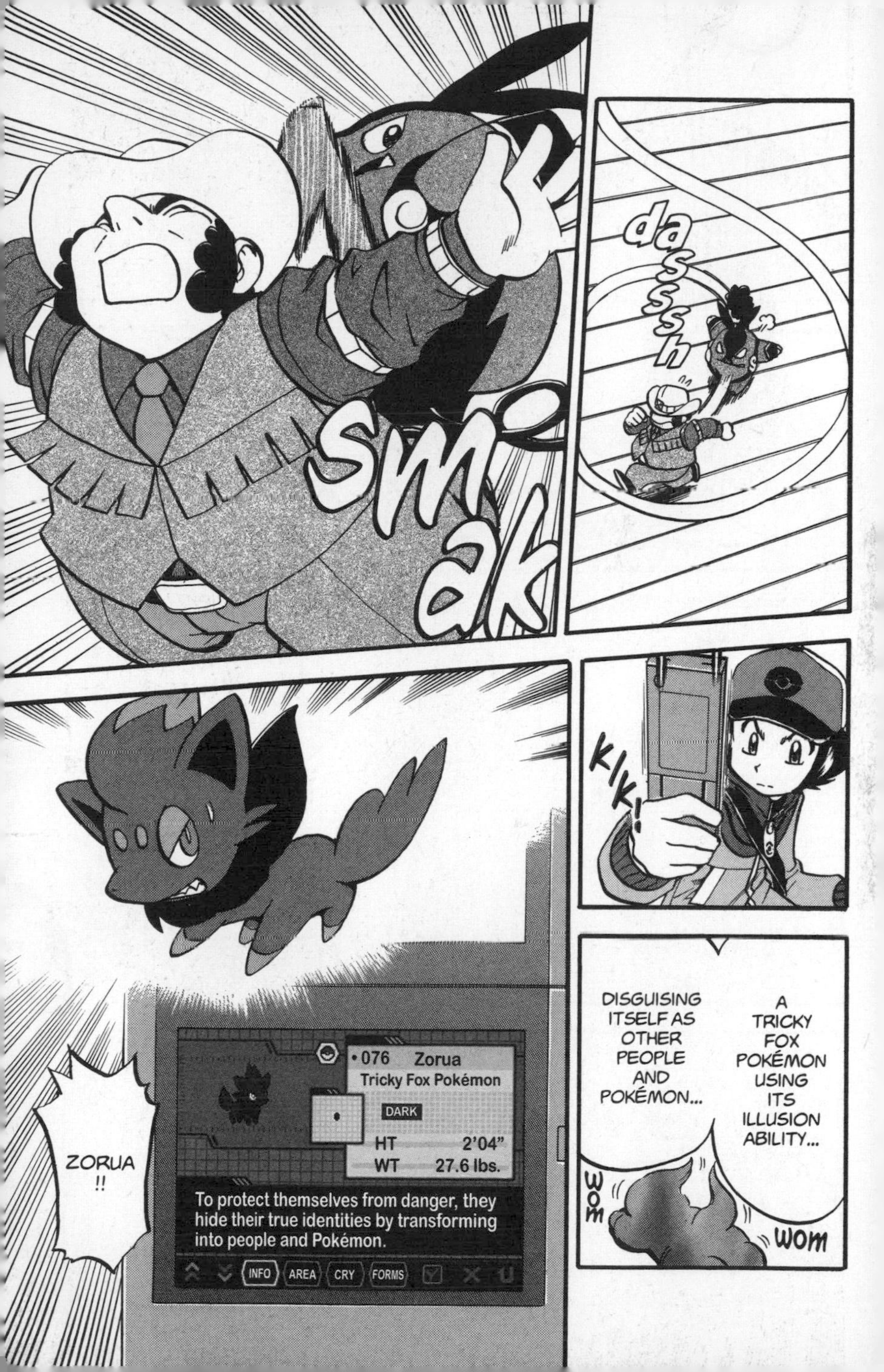
dassssh
smak
K/K!
A TRICKY FOX POKÉMON USING ITS ILLUSION ABILITY...
DISGUISING ITSELF AS OTHER PEOPLE AND POKÉMON...
wom
wom
•076 Zorua
Tricky Fox Pokémon
DARK
HT 2'04"
WT 27.6 lbs.
To protect themselves from danger, they hide their true identities by transforming into people and Pokémon.
INFO
AREA
CRY
FORMS
ZORUA !!

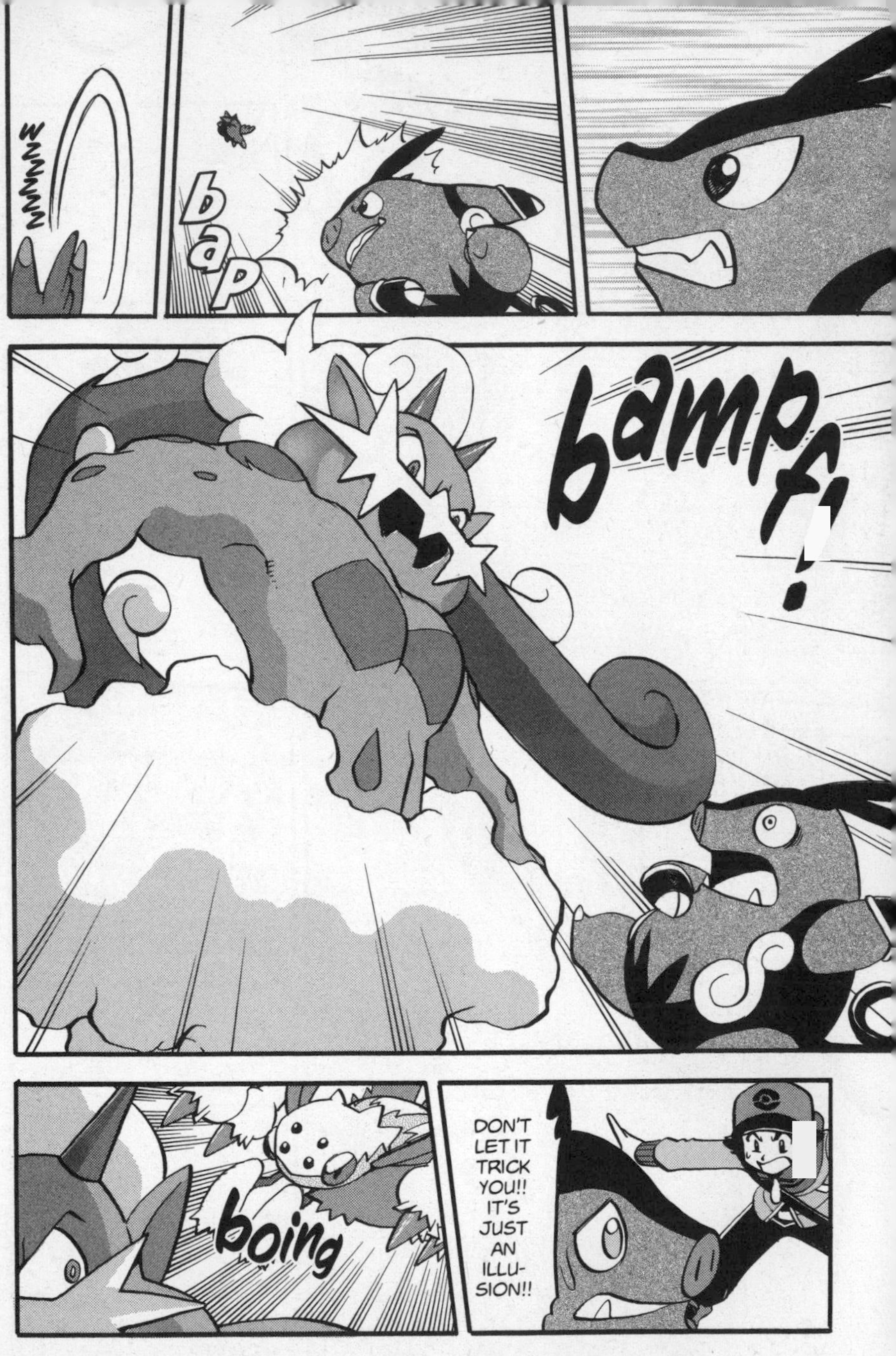
bap
WZZZZZ
bampf!
DON'T LET IT TRICK YOU!! IT'S JUST AN ILLU-SION!!
boing

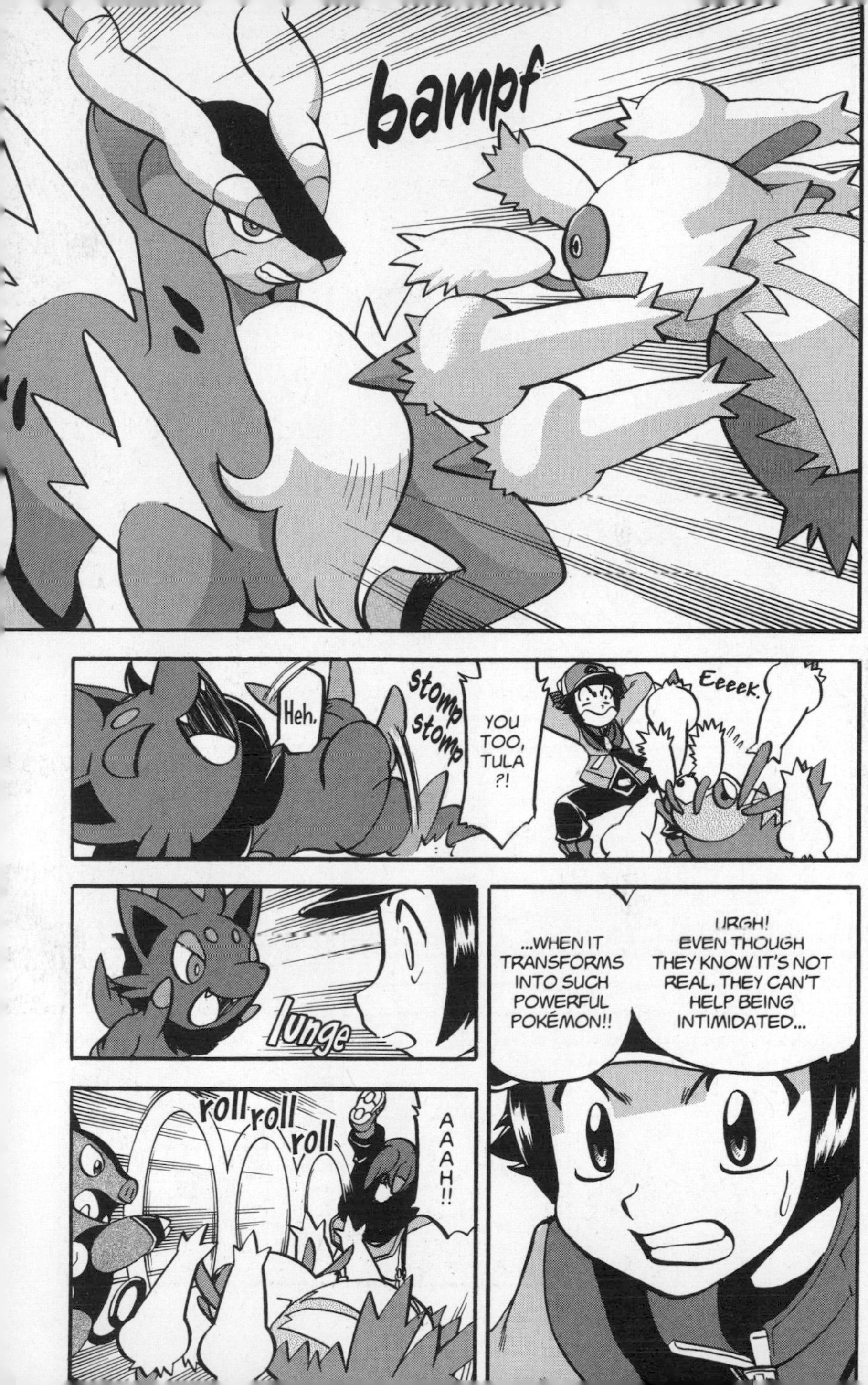
bampf
Eeeek.
YOU TOO, TULA ?!
stomp stomp
Heh.
URGH! EVEN THOUGH THEY KNOW IT'S NOT REAL, THEY CAN'T HELP BEING INTIMIDATED...
...WHEN IT TRANSFORMS INTO SUCH POWERFUL POKÉMON!!
lunge
AAAH!!
roll roll roll

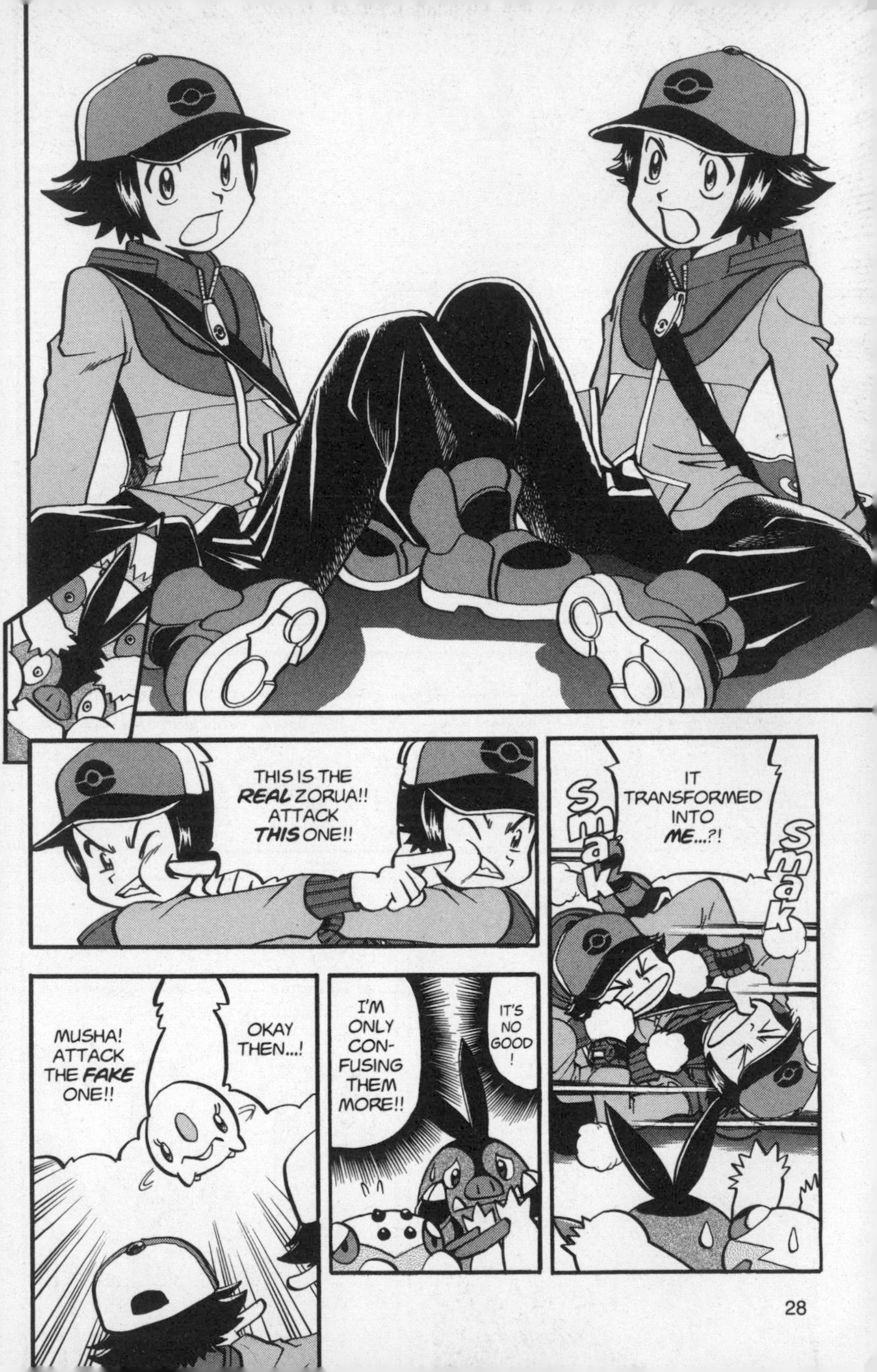
IT TRANSFORMED INTO ME...?!
SMAK
SMAK
THIS IS THE REAL ZORUA!! ATTACK THIS ONE!!
IT'S NO GOOD!
I'M ONLY CON-FUSING THEM MORE!!
OKAY THEN...!
MUSHA! ATTACK THE FAKE ONE!!

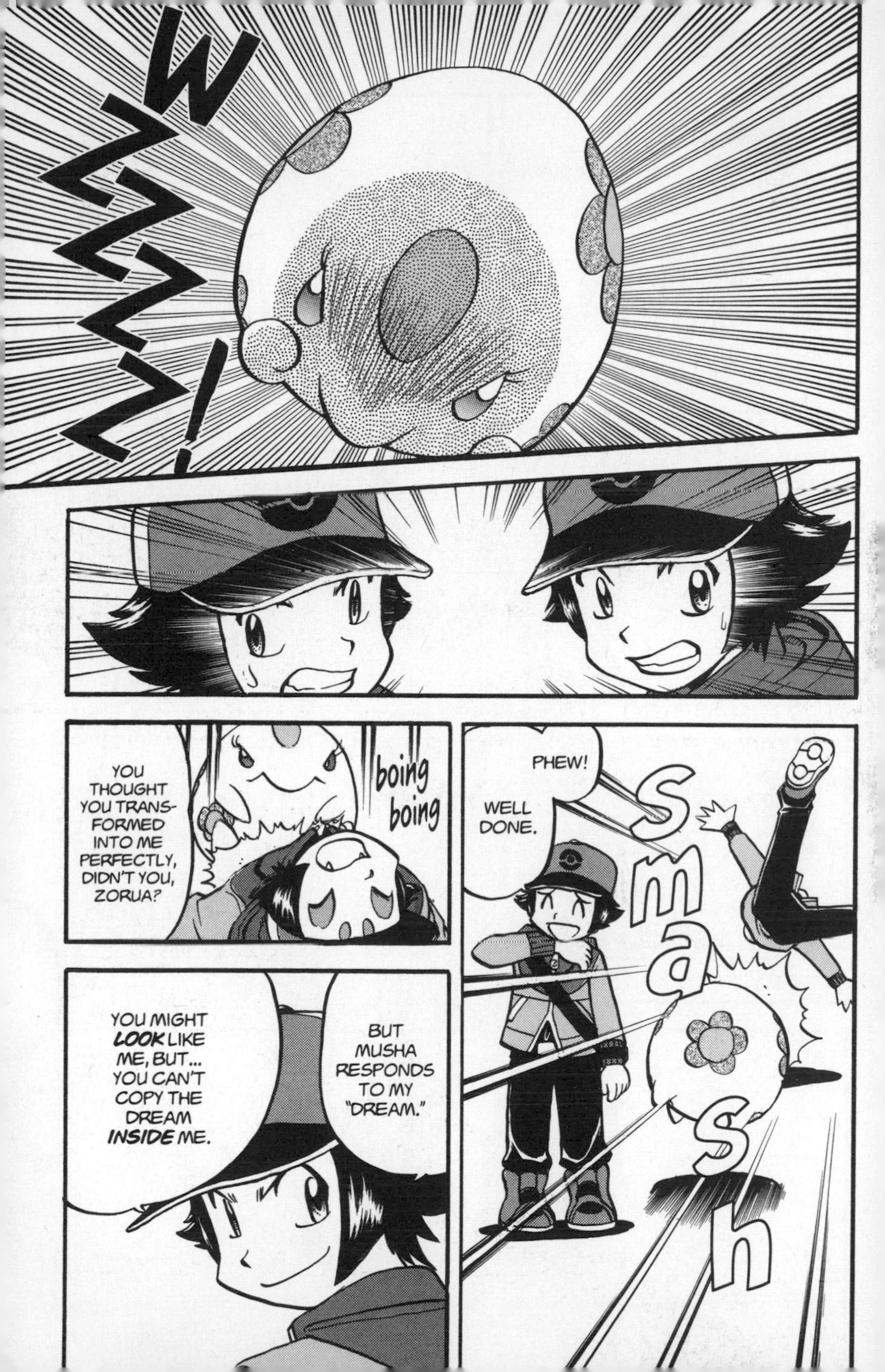
PHEW!
WELL DONE.
Smash
boing boing
YOU THOUGHT YOU TRANSFORMED INTO ME PERFECTLY, DIDN'T YOU, ZORUA?
BUT MUSHA RESPONDS TO MY "DREAM."
YOU MIGHT **LOOK** LIKE ME, BUT... YOU CAN'T COPY THE DREAM ***INSIDE*** ME.

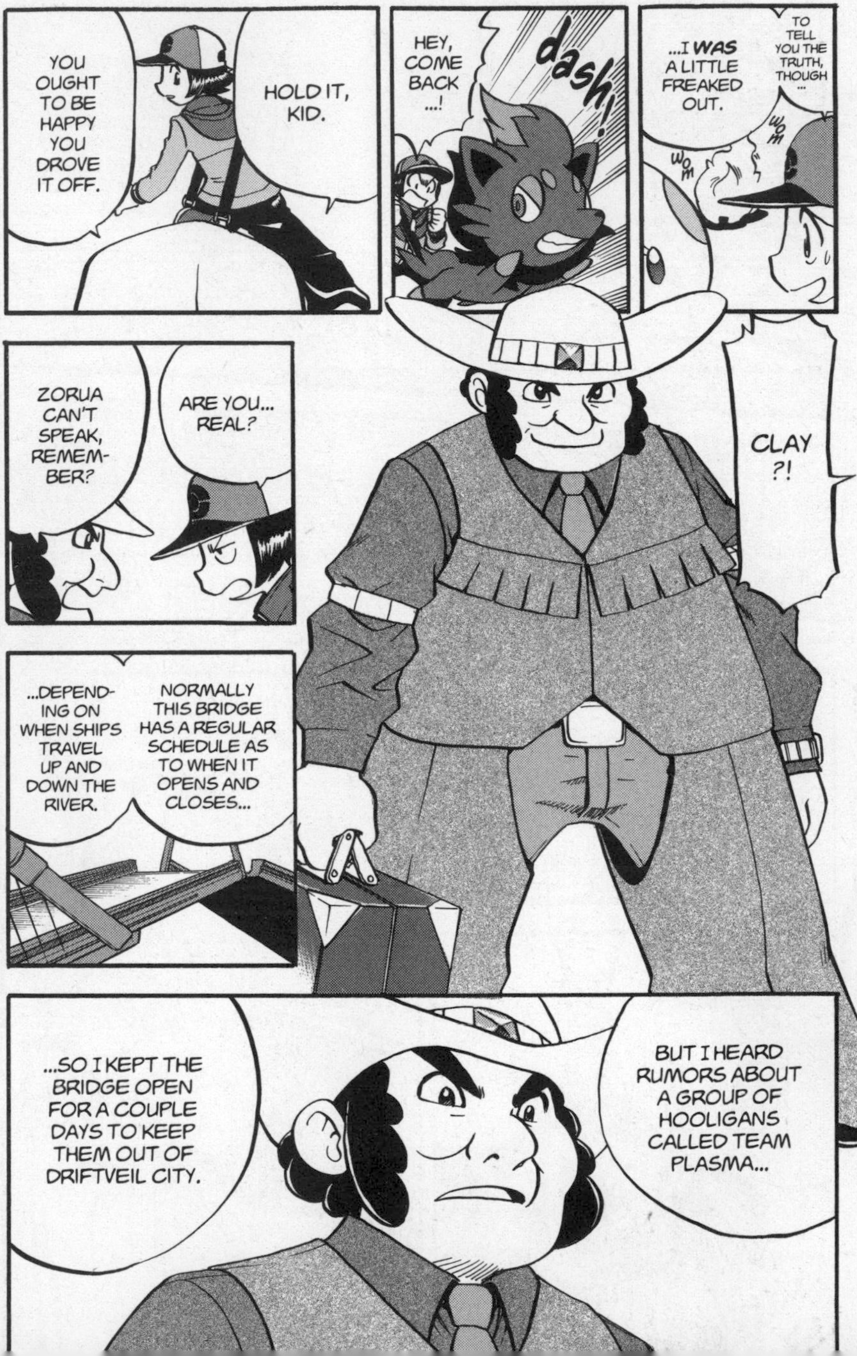
TO TELL YOU THE TRUTH, THOUGH ...
...I WAS A LITTLE FREAKED OUT.
WOM
WOM
dash!
HEY, COME BACK ...!
HOLD IT, KID.
YOU OUGHT TO BE HAPPY YOU DROVE IT OFF.
CLAY ?!
ARE YOU... REAL?
ZORUA CAN'T SPEAK, REMEM-BER?
NORMALLY THIS BRIDGE HAS A REGULAR SCHEDULE AS TO WHEN IT OPENS AND CLOSES...
...DEPEND-ING ON WHEN SHIPS TRAVEL UP AND DOWN THE RIVER.
BUT I HEARD RUMORS ABOUT A GROUP OF HOOLIGANS CALLED TEAM PLASMA...
...SO I KEPT THE BRIDGE OPEN FOR A COUPLE DAYS TO KEEP THEM OUT OF DRIFTVEIL CITY.

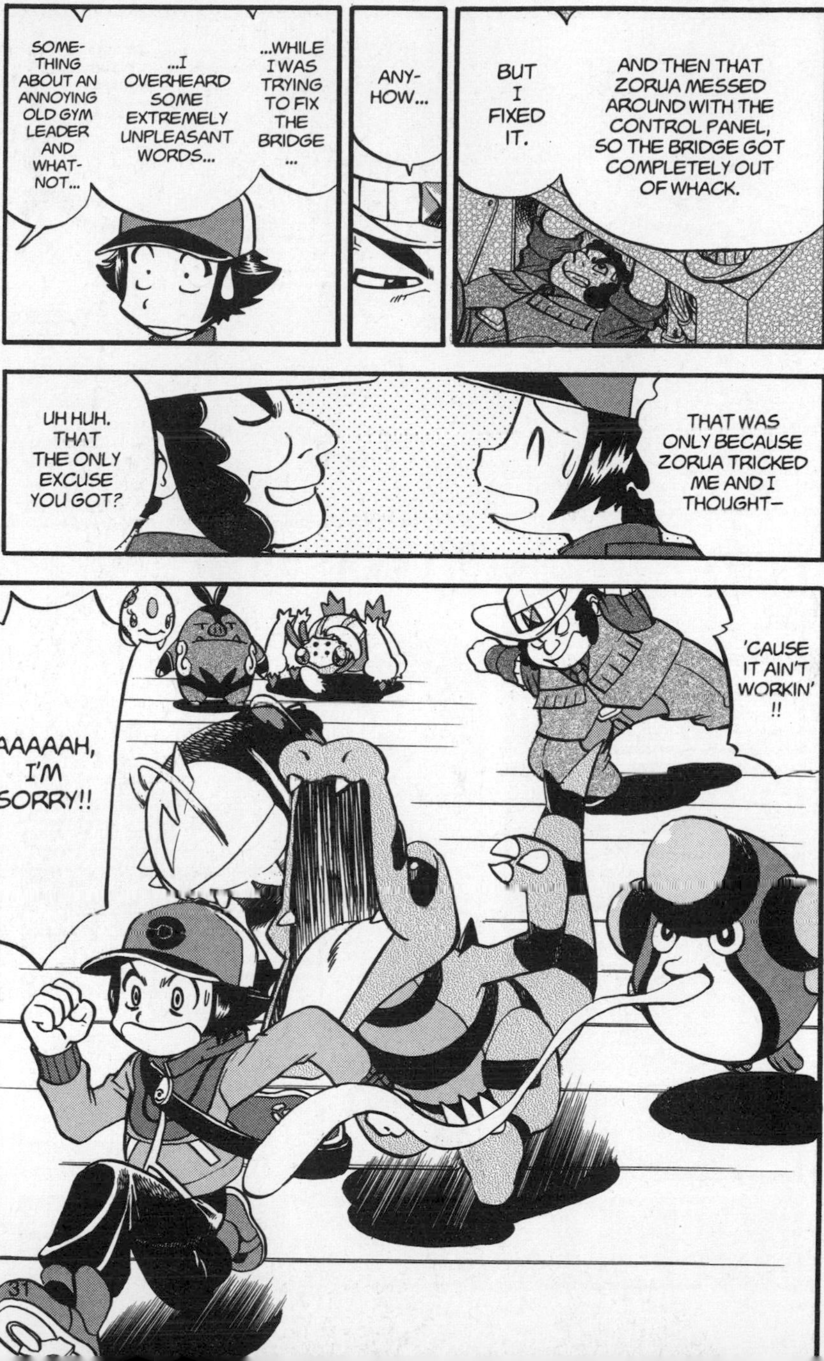
AND THEN THAT ZORUA MESSED AROUND WITH THE CONTROL PANEL, SO THE BRIDGE GOT COMPLETELY OUT OF WHACK.
BUT I FIXED IT.
ANY-HOW...
...WHILE I WAS TRYING TO FIX THE BRIDGE ...
...I OVERHEARD SOME EXTREMELY UNPLEASANT WORDS...
SOME-THING ABOUT AN ANNOYING OLD GYM LEADER AND WHAT-NOT...
THAT WAS ONLY BECAUSE ZORUA TRICKED ME AND I THOUGHT—
UH HUH. THAT THE ONLY EXCUSE YOU GOT?
'CAUSE IT AIN'T WORKIN' !!
AAAAAH, I'M SORRY!!

ADVENTURE MAP

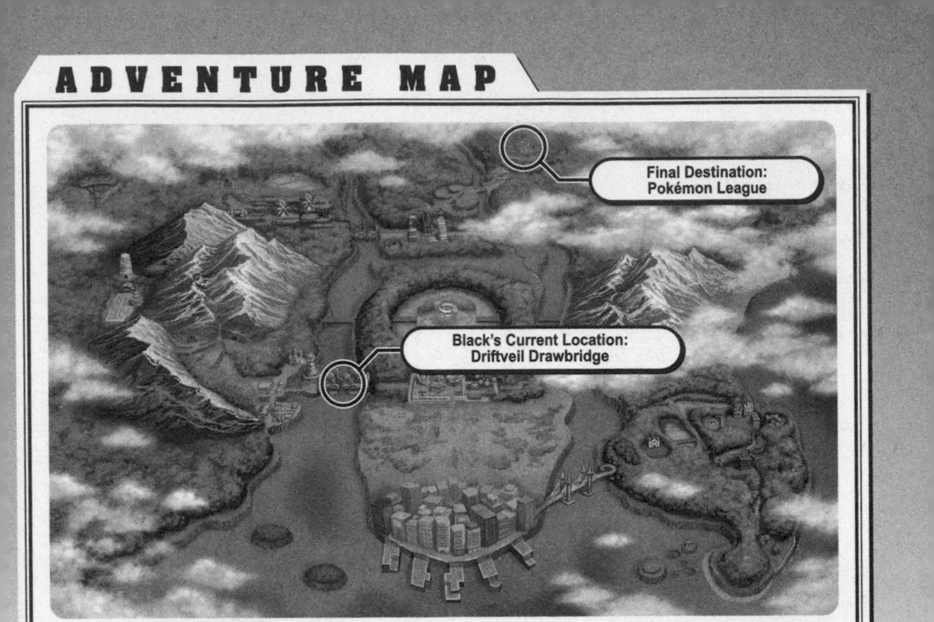
Final Destination:
Pokémon League
Black's Current Location:
Driftveil Drawbridge

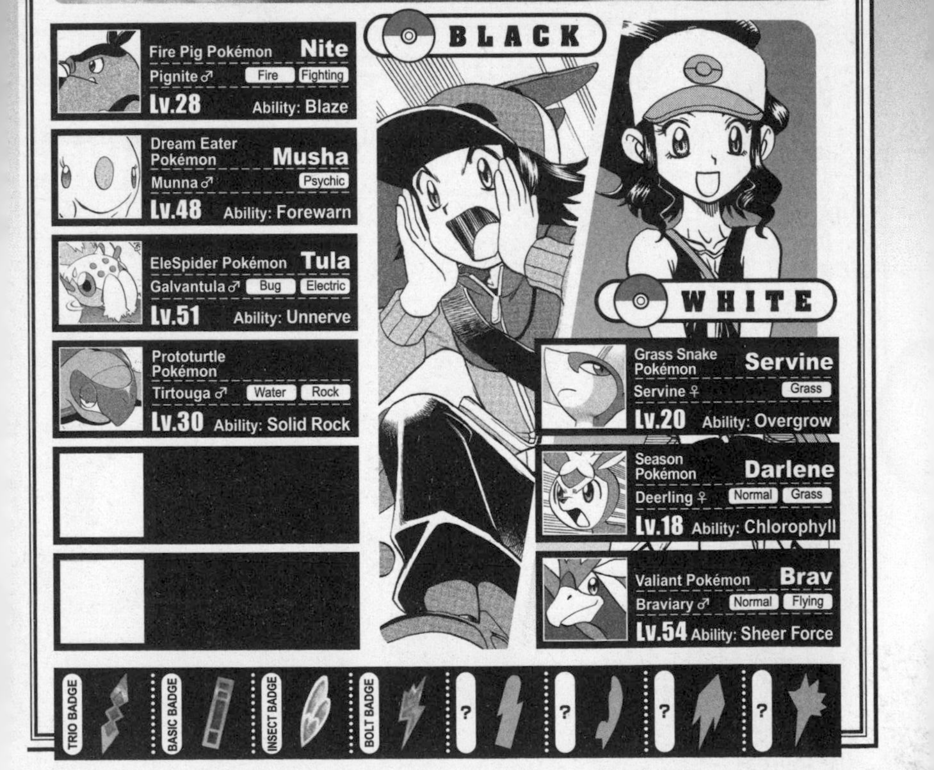

BLACK

Fire Pig Pokémon **Nite**
Pignite ♂ Fire Fighting
Lv.28 Ability: Blaze

Dream Eater Pokémon **Musha**
Munna ♂ Psychic
Lv.48 Ability: Forewarn

EleSpider Pokémon **Tula**
Galvantula ♂ Bug Electric
Lv.51 Ability: Unnerve

Prototurtle Pokémon
Tirtouga ♂ Water Rock
Lv.30 Ability: Solid Rock

WHITE

Grass Snake Pokémon **Servine**
Servine ♀ Grass
Lv.20 Ability: Overgrow

Season Pokémon **Darlene**
Deerling ♀ Normal Grass
Lv.18 Ability: Chlorophyll

Valiant Pokémon **Brav**
Braviary ♂ Normal Flying
Lv.54 Ability: Sheer Force

TRIO BADGE | BASIC BADGE | INSECT BADGE | BOLT BADGE | ? | ? | ? | ?

POKÉMON™

ADVENTURES

BLACK & WHITE

TORNADUS/THUNDURUS

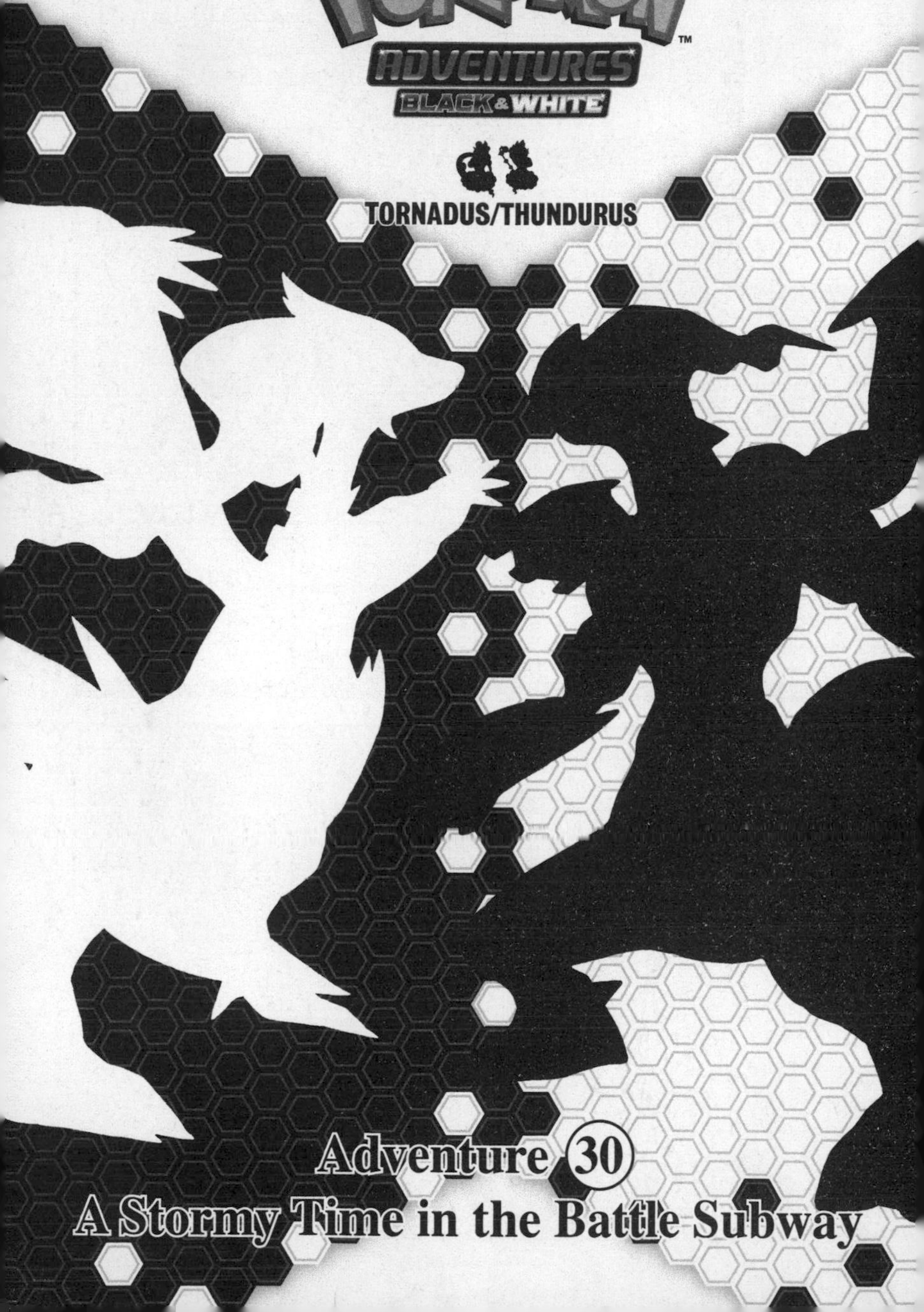

Adventure 30

A Stormy Time in the Battle Subway

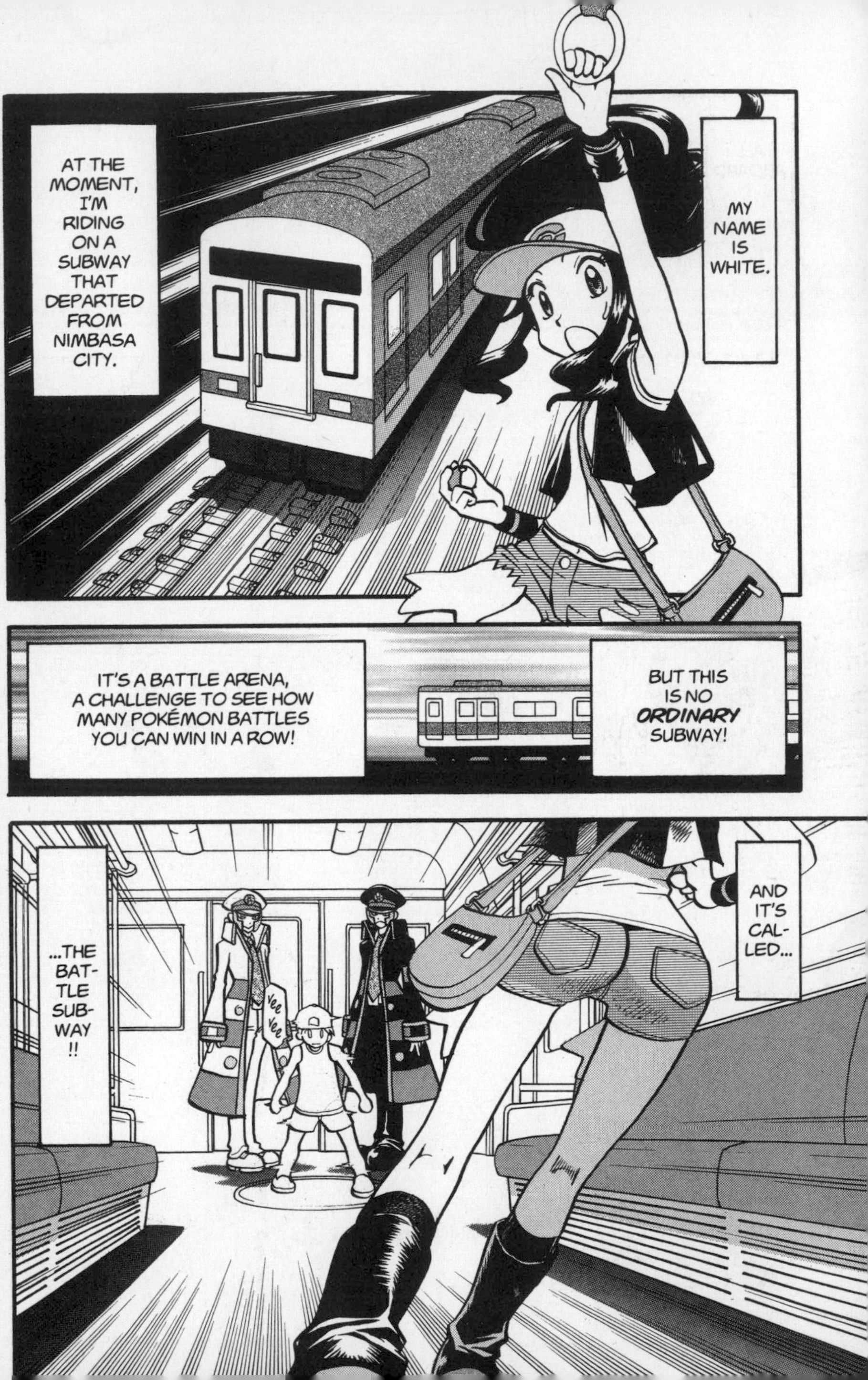
MY NAME IS WHITE.
AT THE MOMENT, I'M RIDING ON A SUBWAY THAT DEPARTED FROM NIMBASA CITY.
BUT THIS IS NO ORDINARY SUBWAY!
IT'S A BATTLE ARENA, A CHALLENGE TO SEE HOW MANY POKÉMON BATTLES YOU CAN WIN IN A ROW!
AND IT'S CAL-LED...
Vee Vee
...THE BAT-TLE SUB-WAY !!

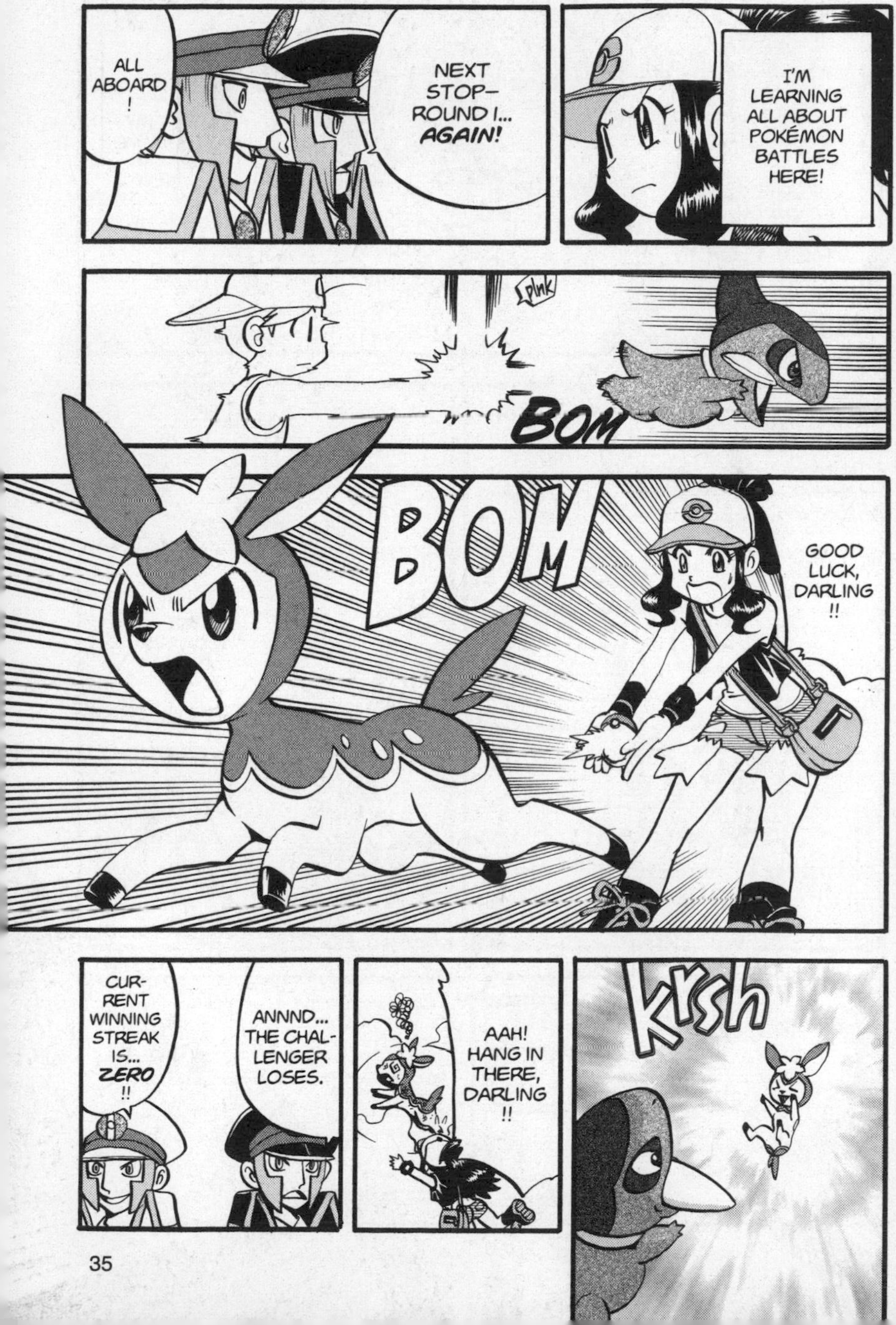
I'M LEARNING ALL ABOUT POKÉMON BATTLES HERE!
NEXT STOP— ROUND I... AGAIN!
ALL ABOARD!
plink
BOM
GOOD LUCK, DARLING!!
BOM
krsh
AAH! HANG IN THERE, DARLING!!
ANNND... THE CHALLENGER LOSES.
CUR-RENT WINNING STREAK IS... ZERO!!

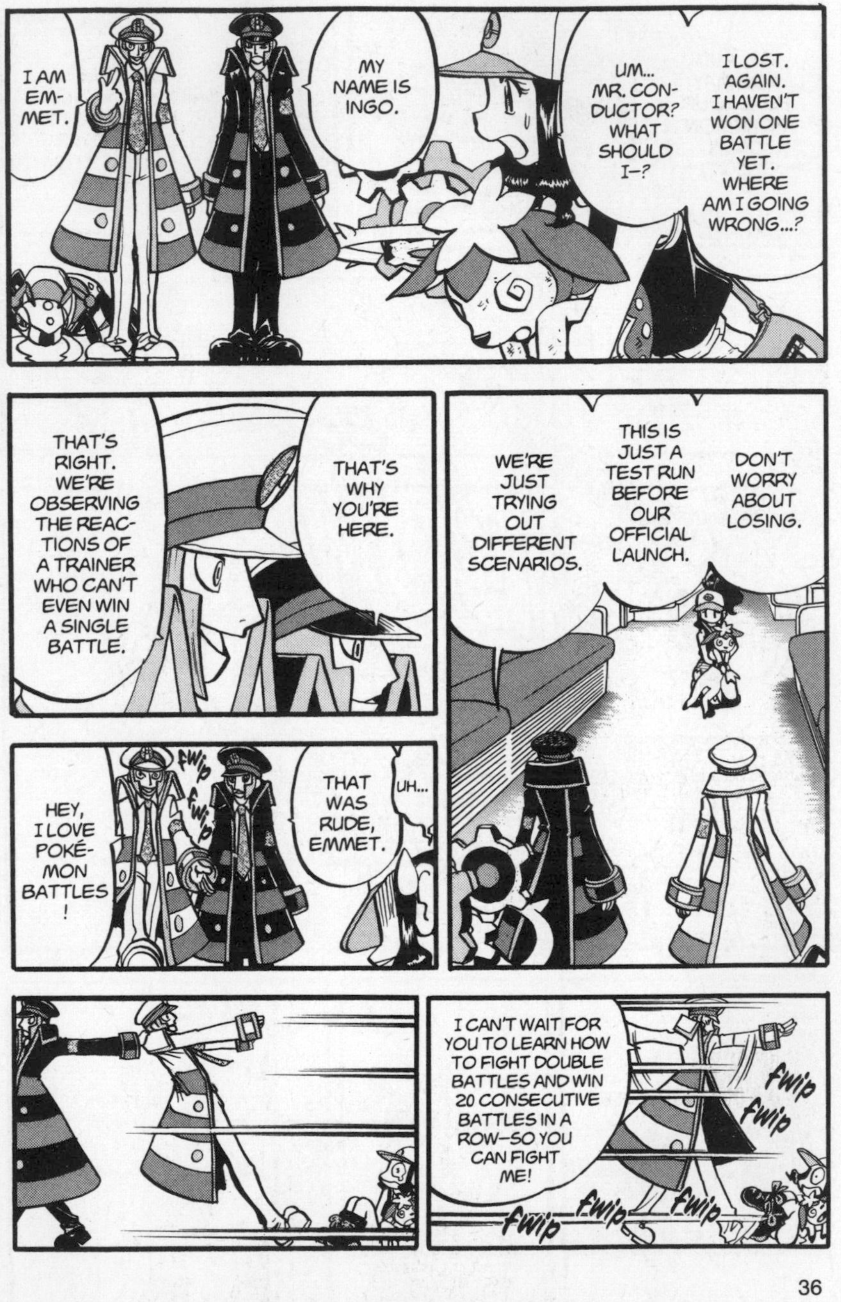

I LOST. AGAIN. I HAVEN'T WON ONE BATTLE YET. WHERE AM I GOING WRONG...?
UM... MR. CONDUCTOR? WHAT SHOULD I–?
MY NAME IS INGO.
I AM EMMET.
DON'T WORRY ABOUT LOSING.
THIS IS JUST A TEST RUN BEFORE OUR OFFICIAL LAUNCH.
WE'RE JUST TRYING OUT DIFFERENT SCENARIOS.
THAT'S WHY YOU'RE HERE.
THAT'S RIGHT. WE'RE OBSERVING THE REACTIONS OF A TRAINER WHO CAN'T EVEN WIN A SINGLE BATTLE.
UH...
THAT WAS RUDE, EMMET.
fwip fwip
HEY, I LOVE POKÉMON BATTLES!
fwip fwip
I CAN'T WAIT FOR YOU TO LEARN HOW TO FIGHT DOUBLE BATTLES AND WIN 20 CONSECUTIVE BATTLES IN A ROW–SO YOU CAN FIGHT ME!
fwip fwip fwip

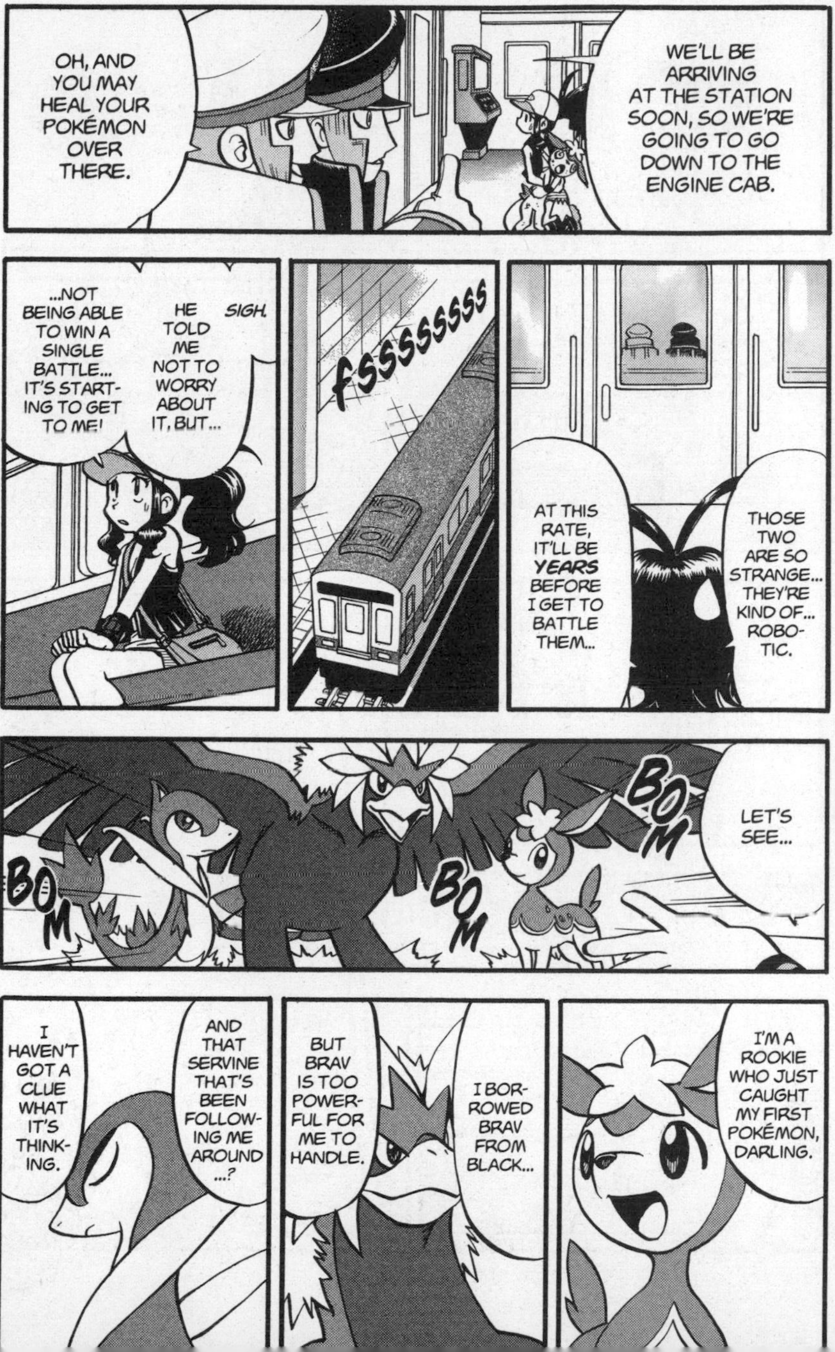
WE'LL BE ARRIVING AT THE STATION SOON, SO WE'RE GOING TO GO DOWN TO THE ENGINE CAB.
OH, AND YOU MAY HEAL YOUR POKÉMON OVER THERE.
THOSE TWO ARE SO STRANGE... THEY'RE KIND OF... ROBOTIC.
AT THIS RATE, IT'LL BE *YEARS* BEFORE I GET TO BATTLE THEM...
fSSSSSSSS
SIGH.
HE TOLD ME NOT TO WORRY ABOUT IT, BUT...
...NOT BEING ABLE TO WIN A SINGLE BATTLE... IT'S STARTING TO GET TO ME!
LET'S SEE...
BOM
BOM
BOM
I'M A ROOKIE WHO JUST CAUGHT MY FIRST POKÉMON, DARLING.
I BORROWED BRAV FROM BLACK...
BUT BRAV IS TOO POWERFUL FOR ME TO HANDLE.
AND THAT SERVINE THAT'S BEEN FOLLOWING ME AROUND...?
I HAVEN'T GOT A CLUE WHAT IT'S THINKING.

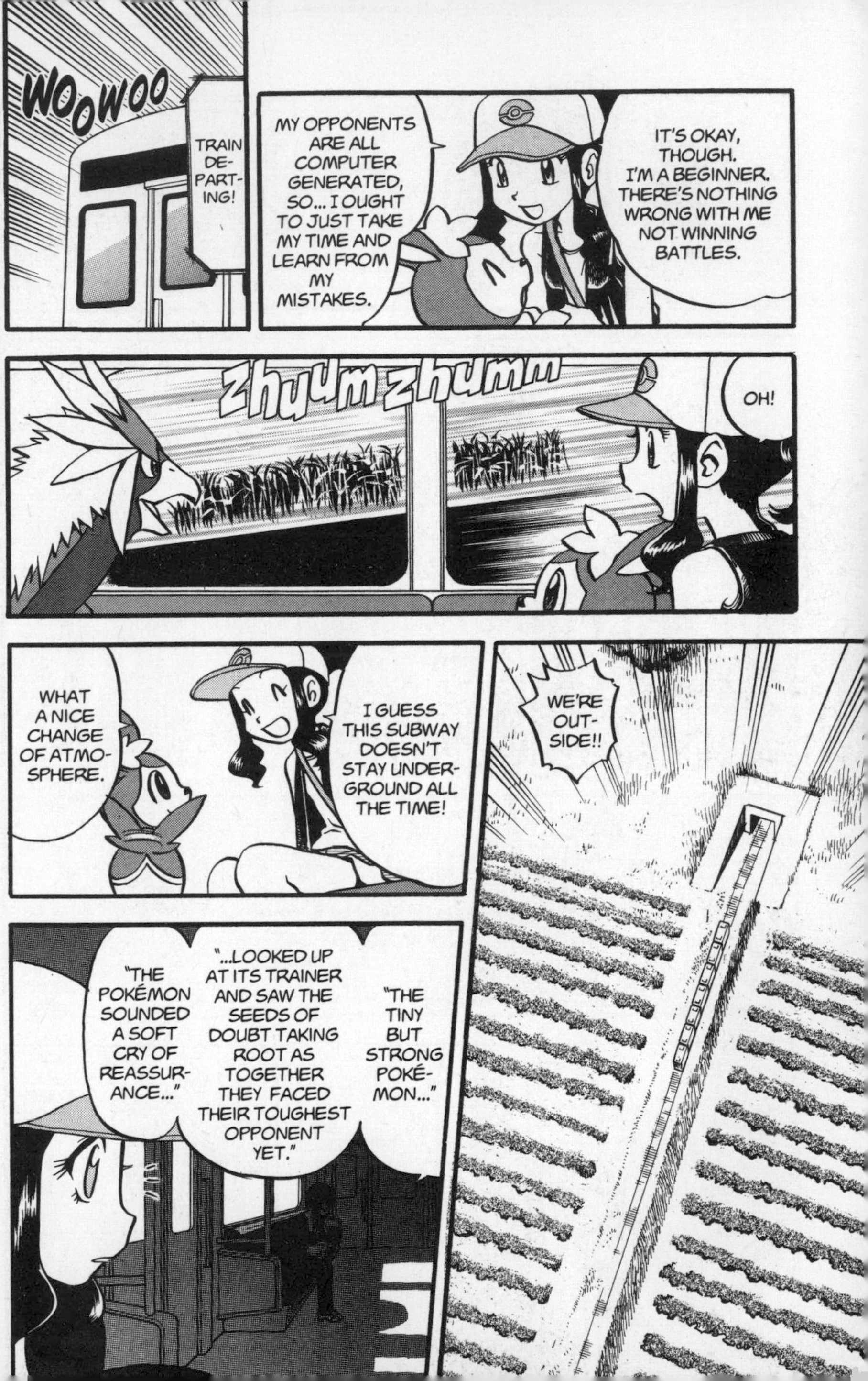
IT'S OKAY, THOUGH. I'M A BEGINNER. THERE'S NOTHING WRONG WITH ME NOT WINNING BATTLES.
MY OPPONENTS ARE ALL COMPUTER GENERATED, SO... I OUGHT TO JUST TAKE MY TIME AND LEARN FROM MY MISTAKES.
WOOWOO
TRAIN DE-PART-ING!
OH!
ZHUUM ZHUMM
WE'RE OUT-SIDE!!
I GUESS THIS SUBWAY DOESN'T STAY UNDER-GROUND ALL THE TIME!
WHAT A NICE CHANGE OF ATMO-SPHERE.
"THE TINY BUT STRONG POKÉ-MON..."
"...LOOKED UP AT ITS TRAINER AND SAW THE SEEDS OF DOUBT TAKING ROOT AS TOGETHER THEY FACED THEIR TOUGHEST OPPONENT YET."
"THE POKÉMON SOUNDED A SOFT CRY OF REASSUR-ANCE..."

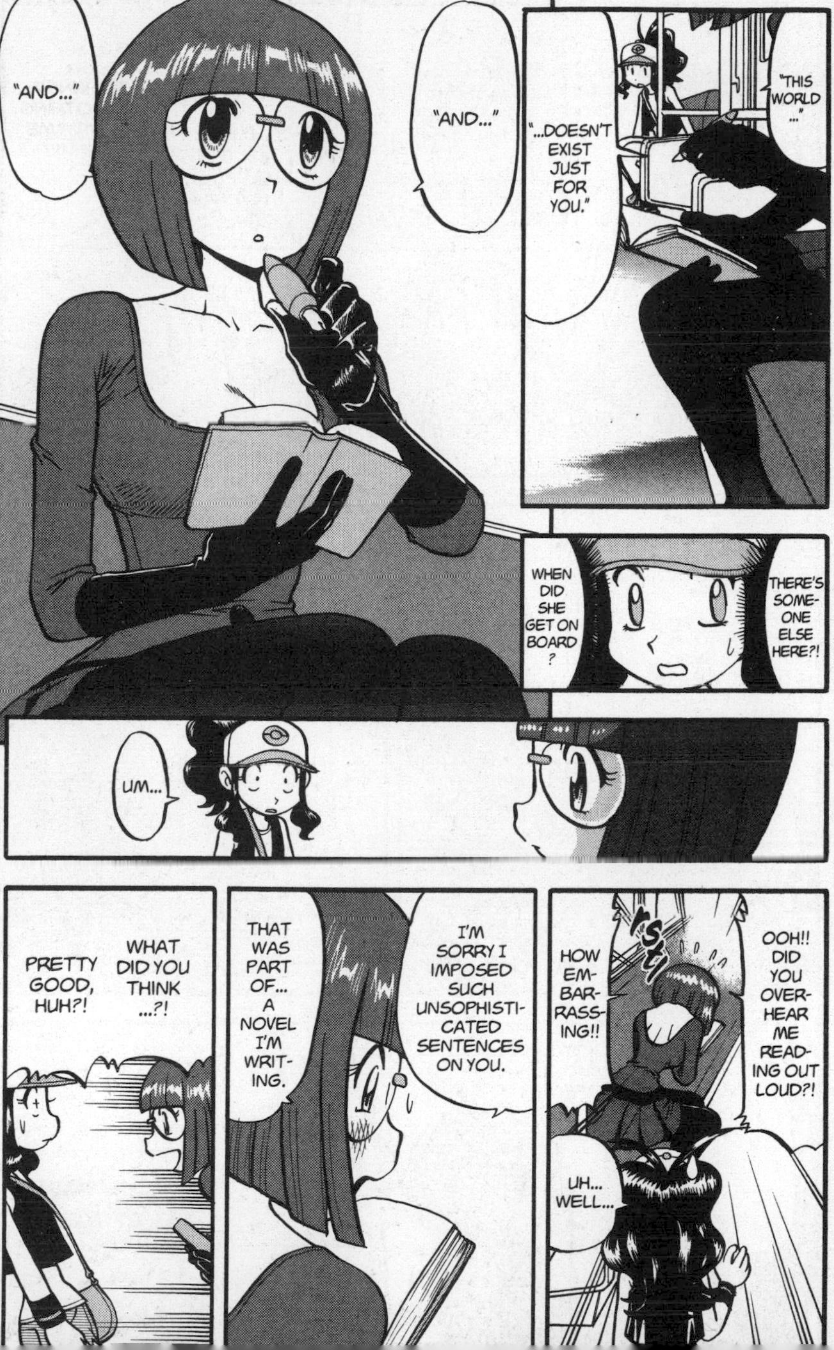
"THIS WORLD ..."
"...DOESN'T EXIST JUST FOR YOU."
THERE'S SOME-ONE ELSE HERE?!
WHEN DID SHE GET ON BOARD ?
"AND..."
"AND..."
UM...
rstl
OOH!! DID YOU OVER-HEAR ME READ-ING OUT LOUD?!
HOW EM-BAR-RASS-ING!!
UH... WELL...
I'M SORRY I IMPOSED SUCH UNSOPHISTI-CATED SENTENCES ON YOU.
THAT WAS PART OF... A NOVEL I'M WRIT-ING.
WHAT DID YOU THINK ...?!
PRETTY GOOD, HUH?!

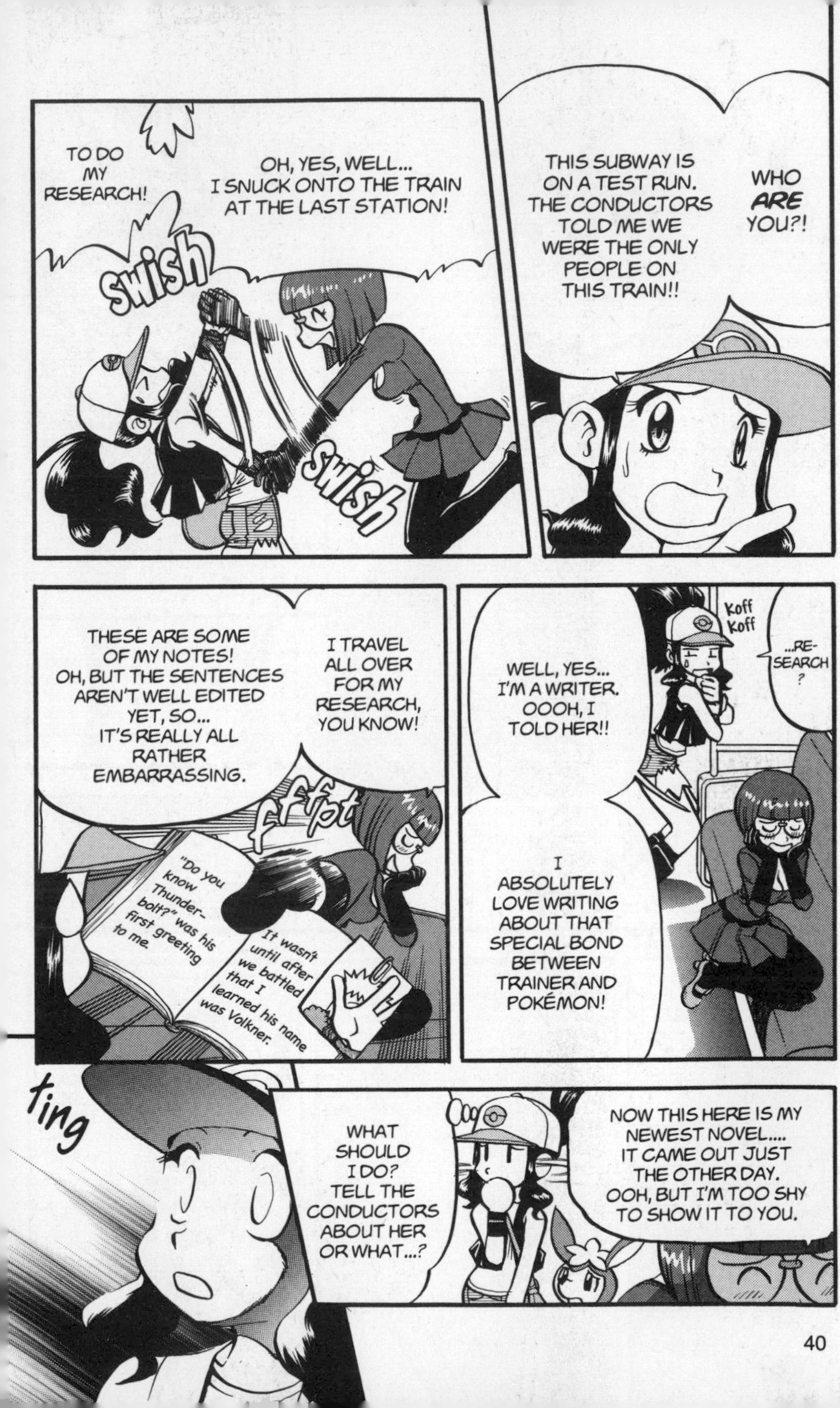
WHO ARE YOU?!
THIS SUBWAY IS ON A TEST RUN. THE CONDUCTORS TOLD ME WE WERE THE ONLY PEOPLE ON THIS TRAIN!!
OH, YES, WELL... I SNUCK ONTO THE TRAIN AT THE LAST STATION!
TO DO MY RESEARCH!
swish
swish
...RE-SEARCH?
Koff Koff
WELL, YES... I'M A WRITER. OOOH, I TOLD HER!!
I ABSOLUTELY LOVE WRITING ABOUT THAT SPECIAL BOND BETWEEN TRAINER AND POKÉMON!
I TRAVEL ALL OVER FOR MY RESEARCH, YOU KNOW!
THESE ARE SOME OF MY NOTES! OH, BUT THE SENTENCES AREN'T WELL EDITED YET, SO... IT'S REALLY ALL RATHER EMBARRASSING.
ffpt
"Do you know Thunder-bolt?" was his first greeting to me.
It wasn't until after we battled that I learned his name was Volkner.
NOW THIS HERE IS MY NEWEST NOVEL.... IT CAME OUT JUST THE OTHER DAY. OOH, BUT I'M TOO SHY TO SHOW IT TO YOU.
WHAT SHOULD I DO? TELL THE CONDUCTORS ABOUT HER OR WHAT...?
ting

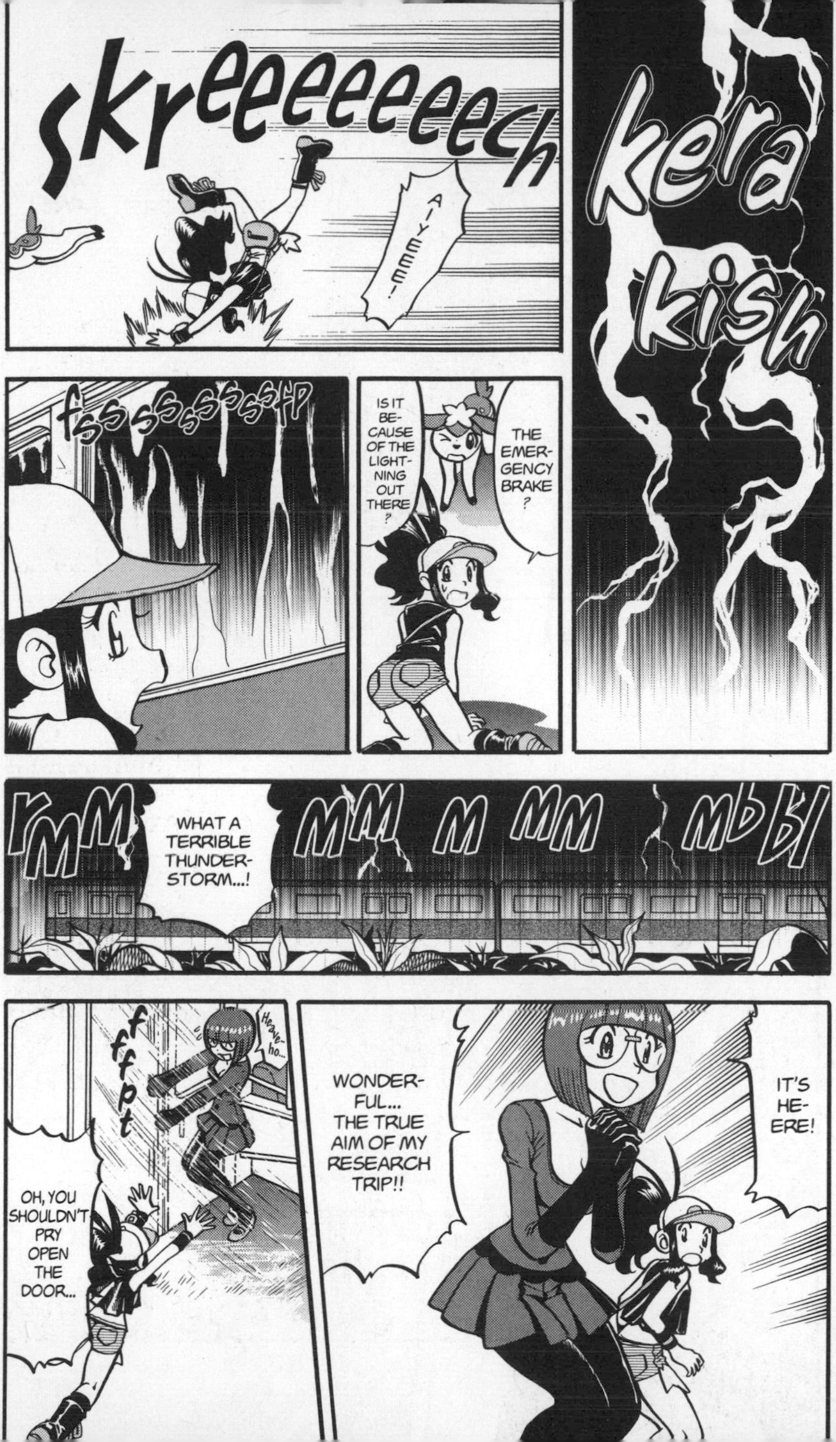
kera kish
skyeeeeeeeech
AIYEEE!
THE EMERGENCY BRAKE?
IS IT BECAUSE OF THE LIGHTNING OUT THERE?
fssssssssstp
rMM MM M MM mbbl
WHAT A TERRIBLE THUNDERSTORM...!
IT'S HE-ERE!
WONDERFUL... THE TRUE AIM OF MY RESEARCH TRIP!!
Heave-ho...
ffffpt
OH, YOU SHOULDN'T PRY OPEN THE DOOR...

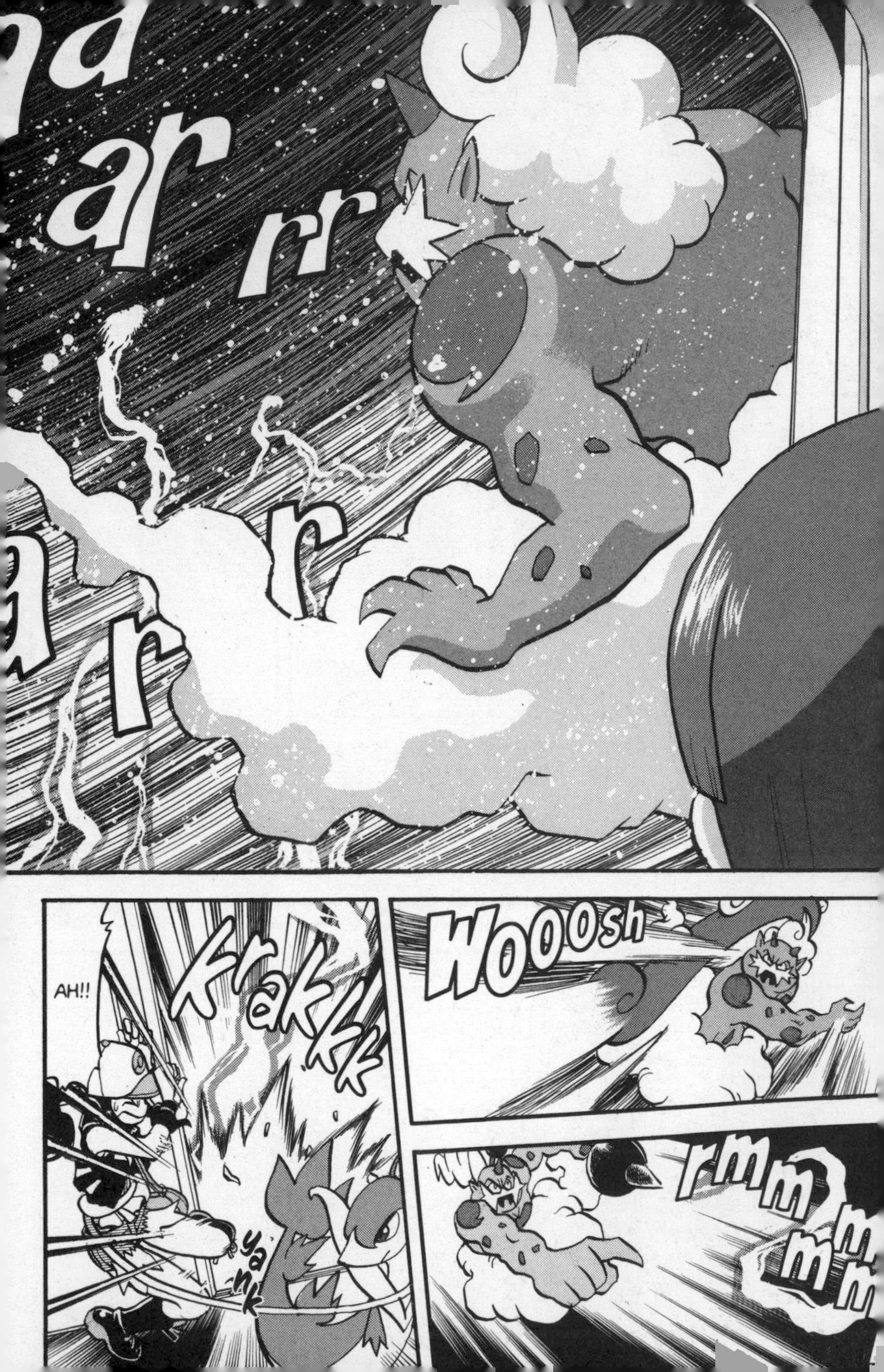

ar
rr
r
r
WOOOsh
rmmmmmm
AH!!
Krakkk
yank

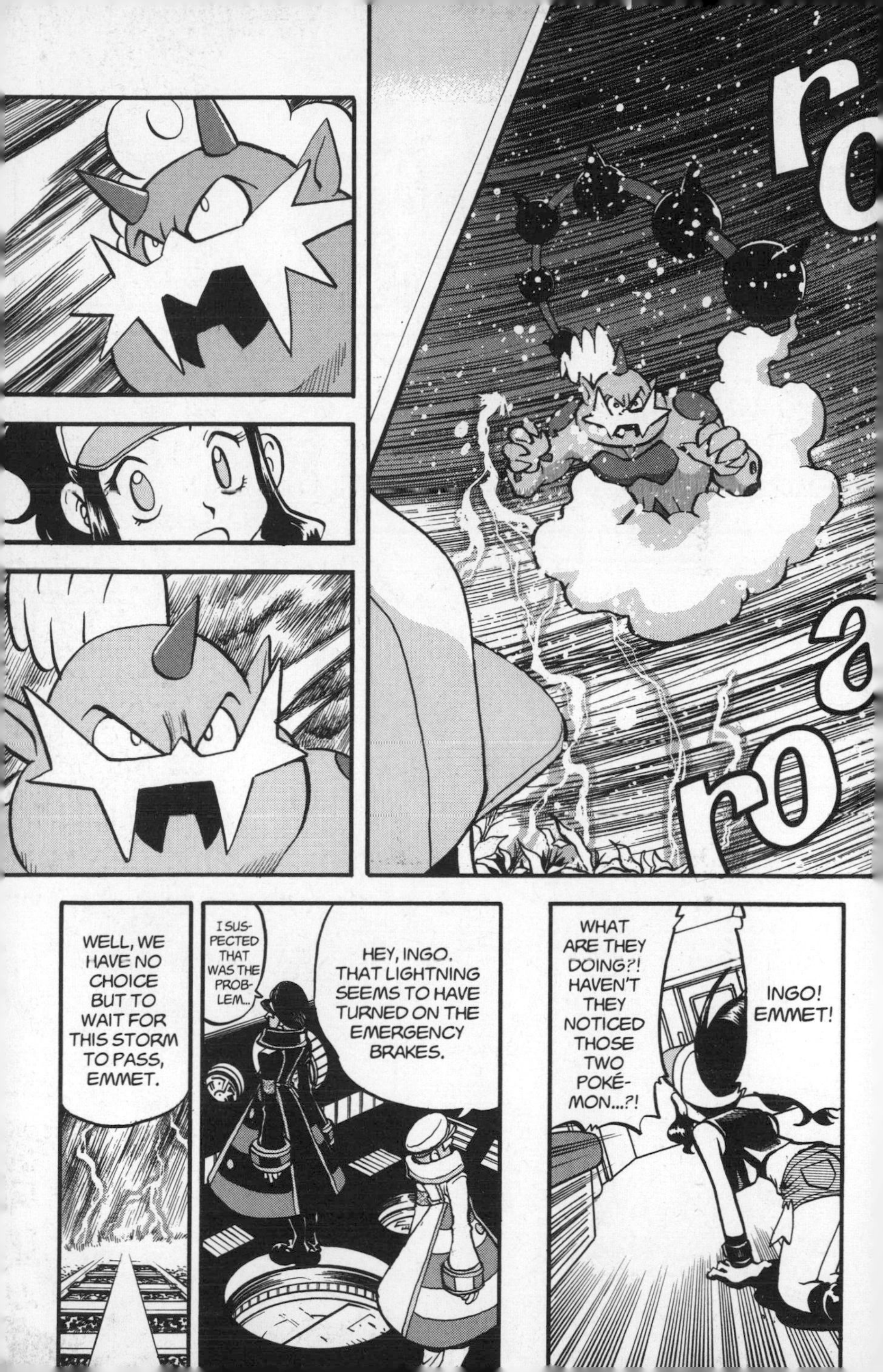
INGO! EMMET!
WHAT ARE THEY DOING?! HAVEN'T THEY NOTICED THOSE TWO POKÉMON...?!
HEY, INGO. THAT LIGHTNING SEEMS TO HAVE TURNED ON THE EMERGENCY BRAKES.
I SUSPECTED THAT WAS THE PROBLEM...
WELL, WE HAVE NO CHOICE BUT TO WAIT FOR THIS STORM TO PASS, EMMET.

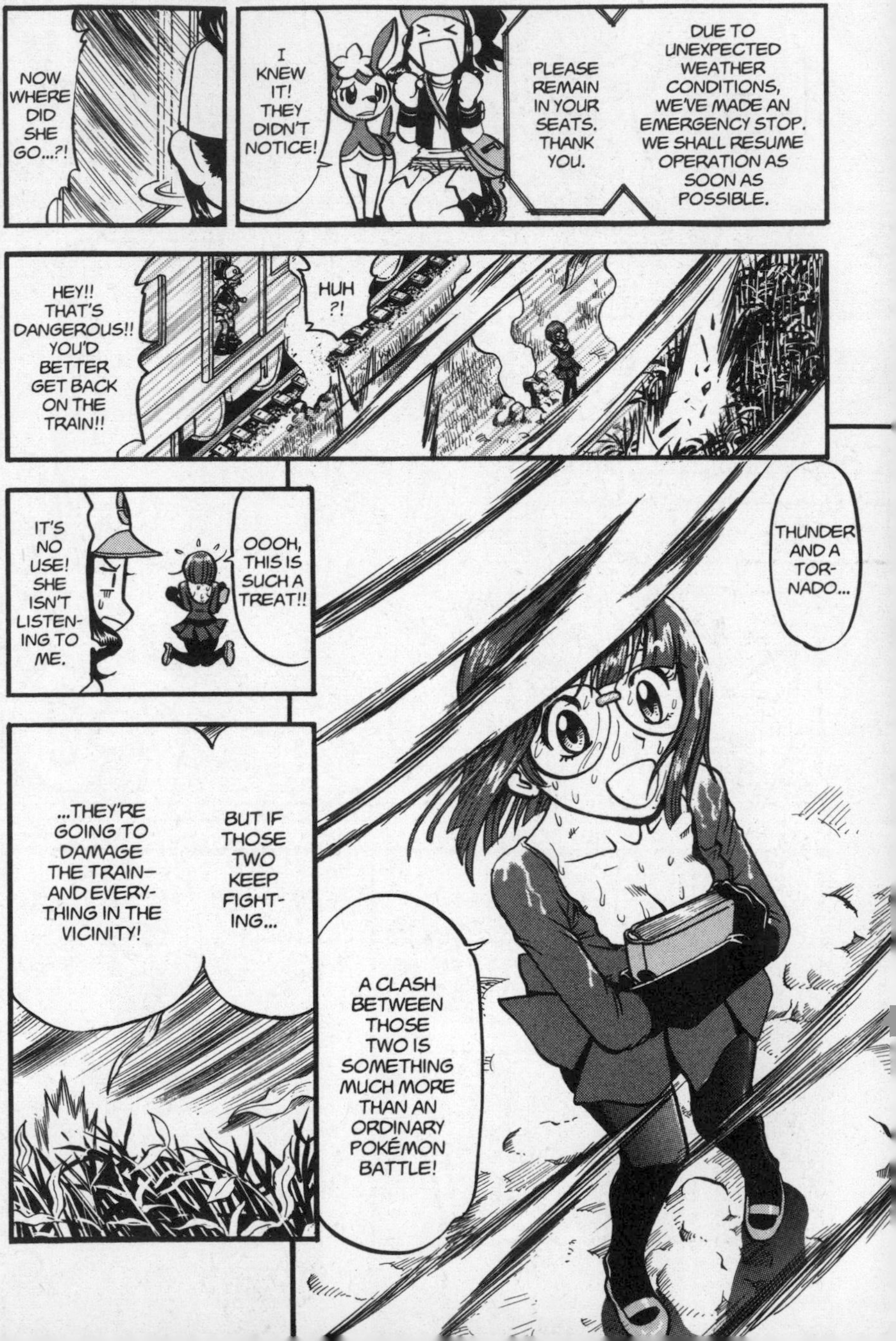
DUE TO UNEXPECTED WEATHER CONDITIONS, WE'VE MADE AN EMERGENCY STOP. WE SHALL RESUME OPERATION AS SOON AS POSSIBLE.
PLEASE REMAIN IN YOUR SEATS. THANK YOU.
I KNEW IT! THEY DIDN'T NOTICE!
NOW WHERE DID SHE GO...?!
HUH ?!
HEY!! THAT'S DANGEROUS!! YOU'D BETTER GET BACK ON THE TRAIN!!
THUNDER AND A TOR-NADO...
A CLASH BETWEEN THOSE TWO IS SOMETHING MUCH MORE THAN AN ORDINARY POKÉMON BATTLE!
OOOH, THIS IS SUCH A TREAT!!
IT'S NO USE! SHE ISN'T LISTEN-ING TO ME.
BUT IF THOSE TWO KEEP FIGHT-ING...
...THEY'RE GOING TO DAMAGE THE TRAIN— AND EVERY-THING IN THE VICINITY!

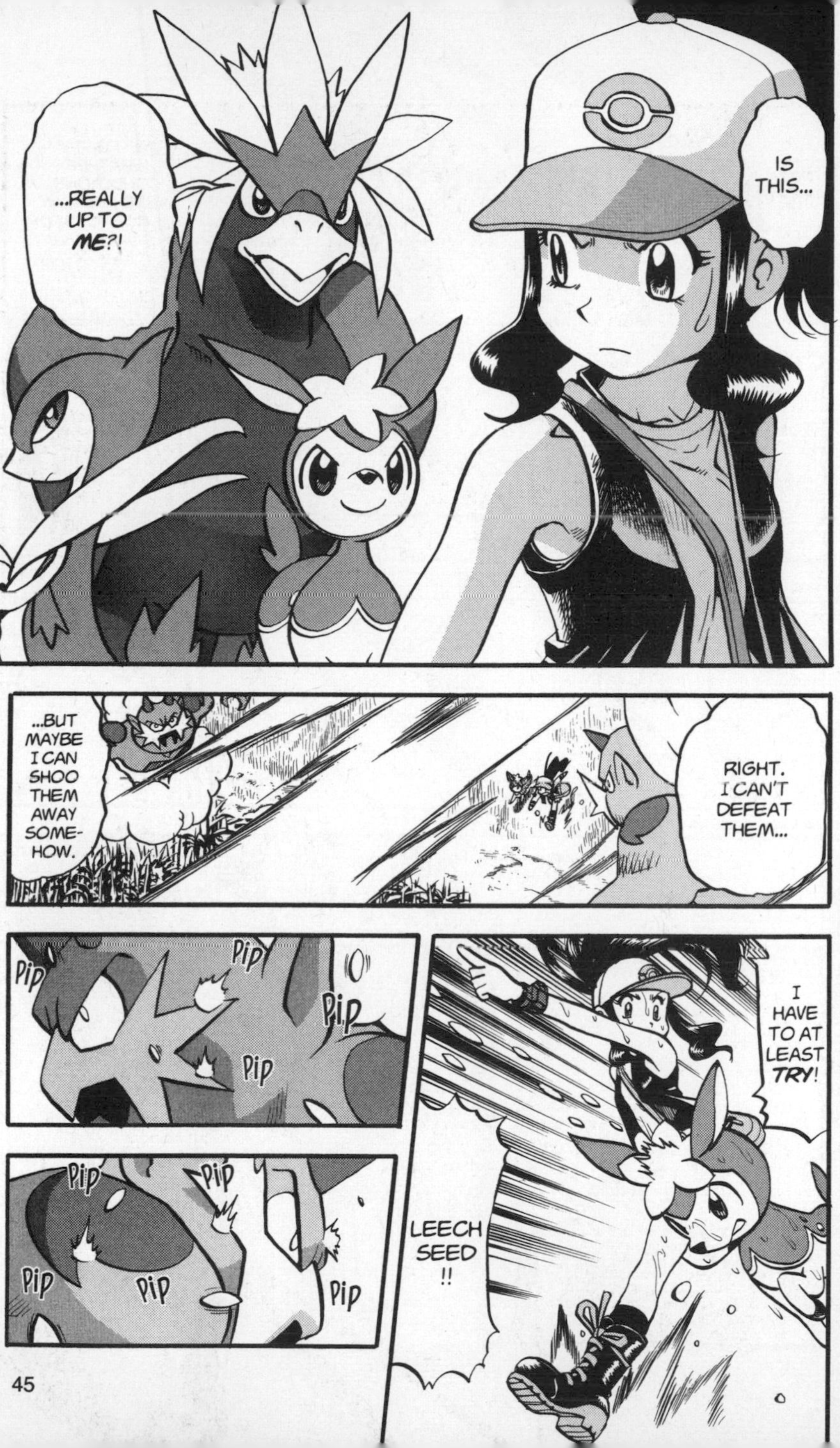
IS THIS...
...REALLY UP TO *ME*?!
RIGHT. I CAN'T DEFEAT THEM...
...BUT MAYBE I CAN SHOO THEM AWAY SOME-HOW.
I HAVE TO AT LEAST *TRY*!
LEECH SEED !!
Pip
Pip
Pip
Pip
Pip
Pip
Pip
Pip
Pip

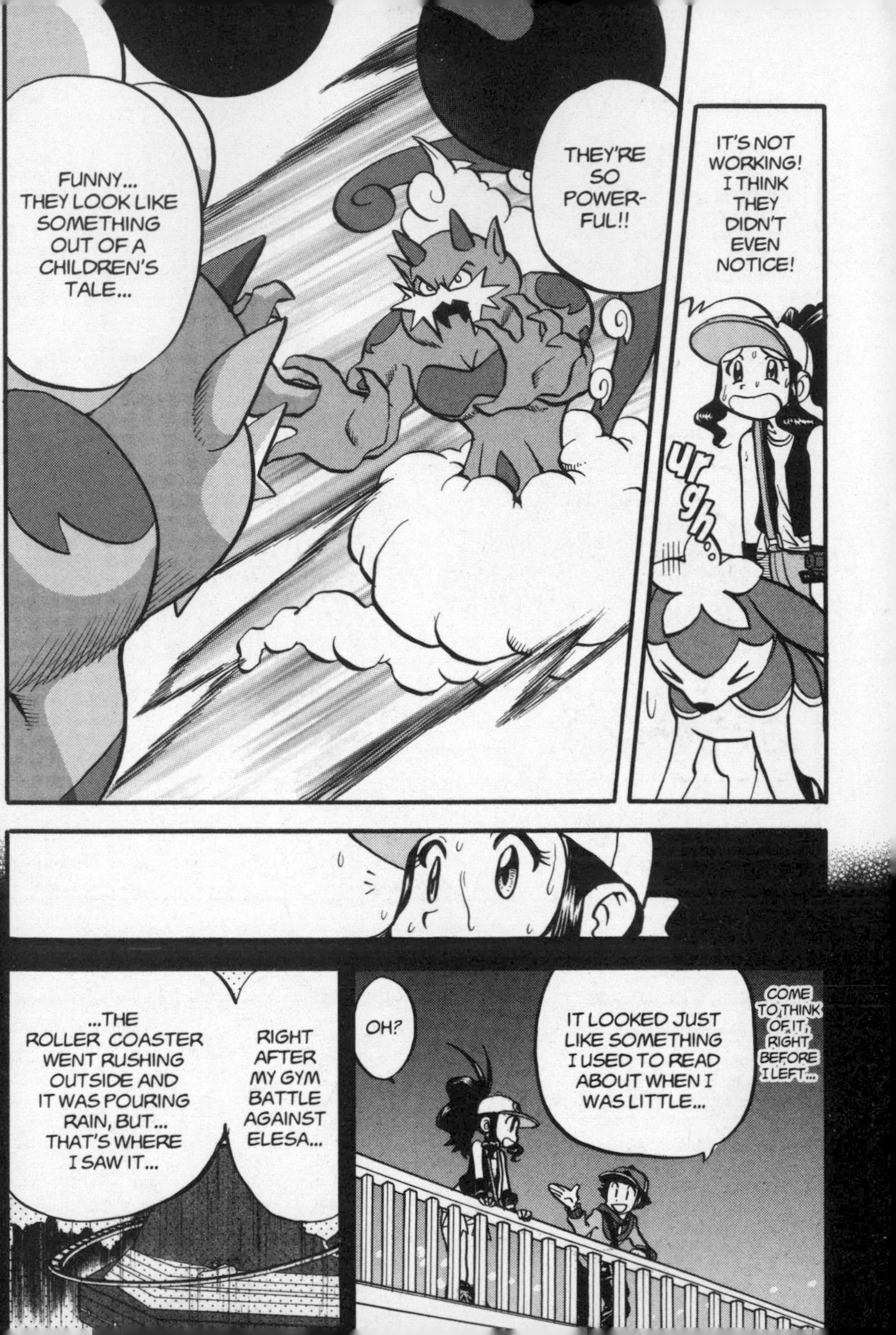
IT'S NOT WORKING! I THINK THEY DIDN'T EVEN NOTICE!
urgh..
THEY'RE SO POWER-FUL!!
FUNNY... THEY LOOK LIKE SOMETHING OUT OF A CHILDREN'S TALE...
COME TO THINK OF IT, RIGHT BEFORE I LEFT...
IT LOOKED JUST LIKE SOMETHING I USED TO READ ABOUT WHEN I WAS LITTLE...
OH?
RIGHT AFTER MY GYM BATTLE AGAINST ELESA...
...THE ROLLER COASTER WENT RUSHING OUTSIDE AND IT WAS POURING RAIN, BUT... THAT'S WHERE I SAW IT...

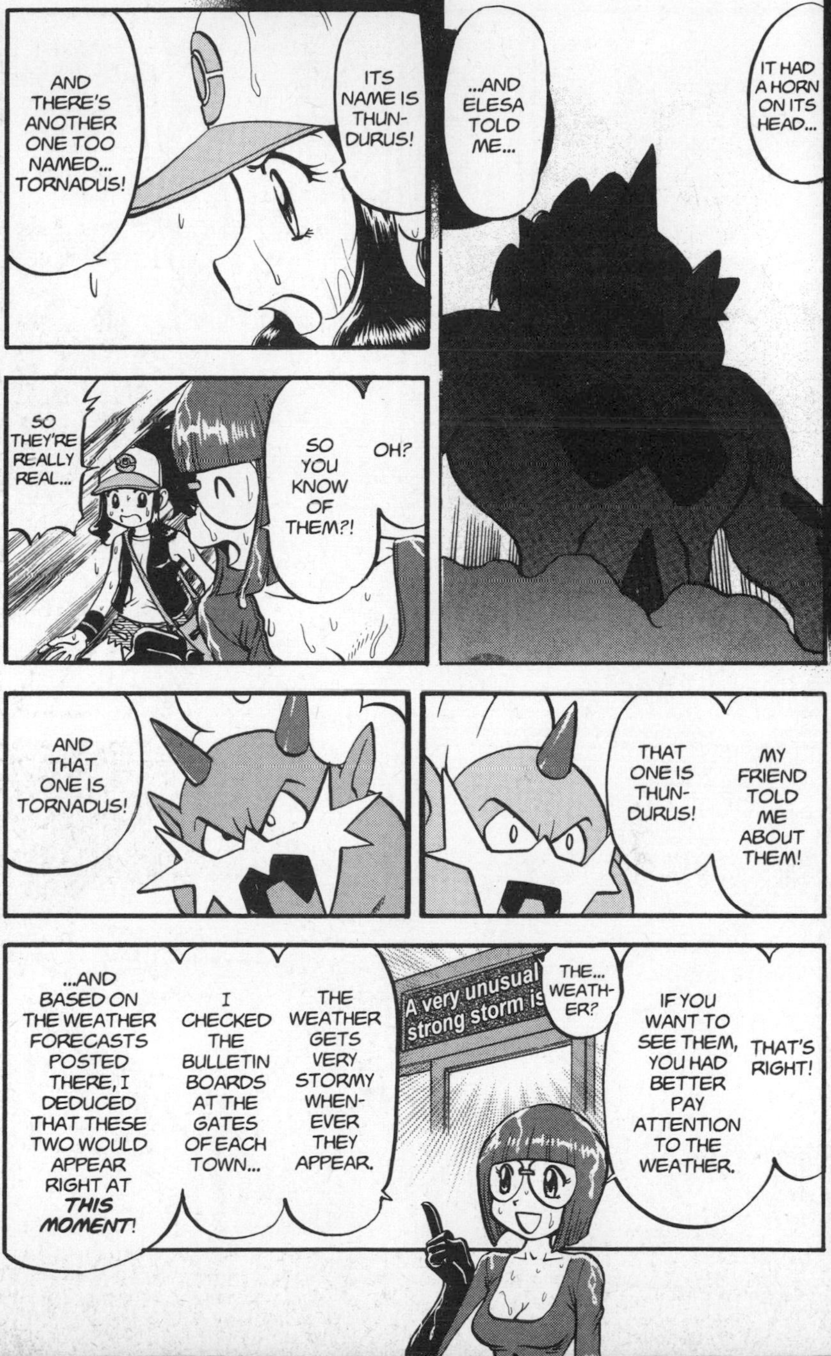
IT HAD A HORN ON ITS HEAD...
...AND ELESA TOLD ME...
ITS NAME IS THUN-DURUS!
AND THERE'S ANOTHER ONE TOO NAMED... TORNADUS!
OH?
SO YOU KNOW OF THEM?!
SO THEY'RE REALLY REAL...
MY FRIEND TOLD ME ABOUT THEM!
THAT ONE IS THUN-DURUS!
AND THAT ONE IS TORNADUS!
THAT'S RIGHT!
IF YOU WANT TO SEE THEM, YOU HAD BETTER PAY ATTENTION TO THE WEATHER.
THE... WEATH-ER?
A very unusual strong storm is
THE WEATHER GETS VERY STORMY WHEN-EVER THEY APPEAR.
I CHECKED THE BULLETIN BOARDS AT THE GATES OF EACH TOWN...
...AND BASED ON THE WEATHER FORECASTS POSTED THERE, I DEDUCED THAT THESE TWO WOULD APPEAR RIGHT AT *THIS MOMENT*!

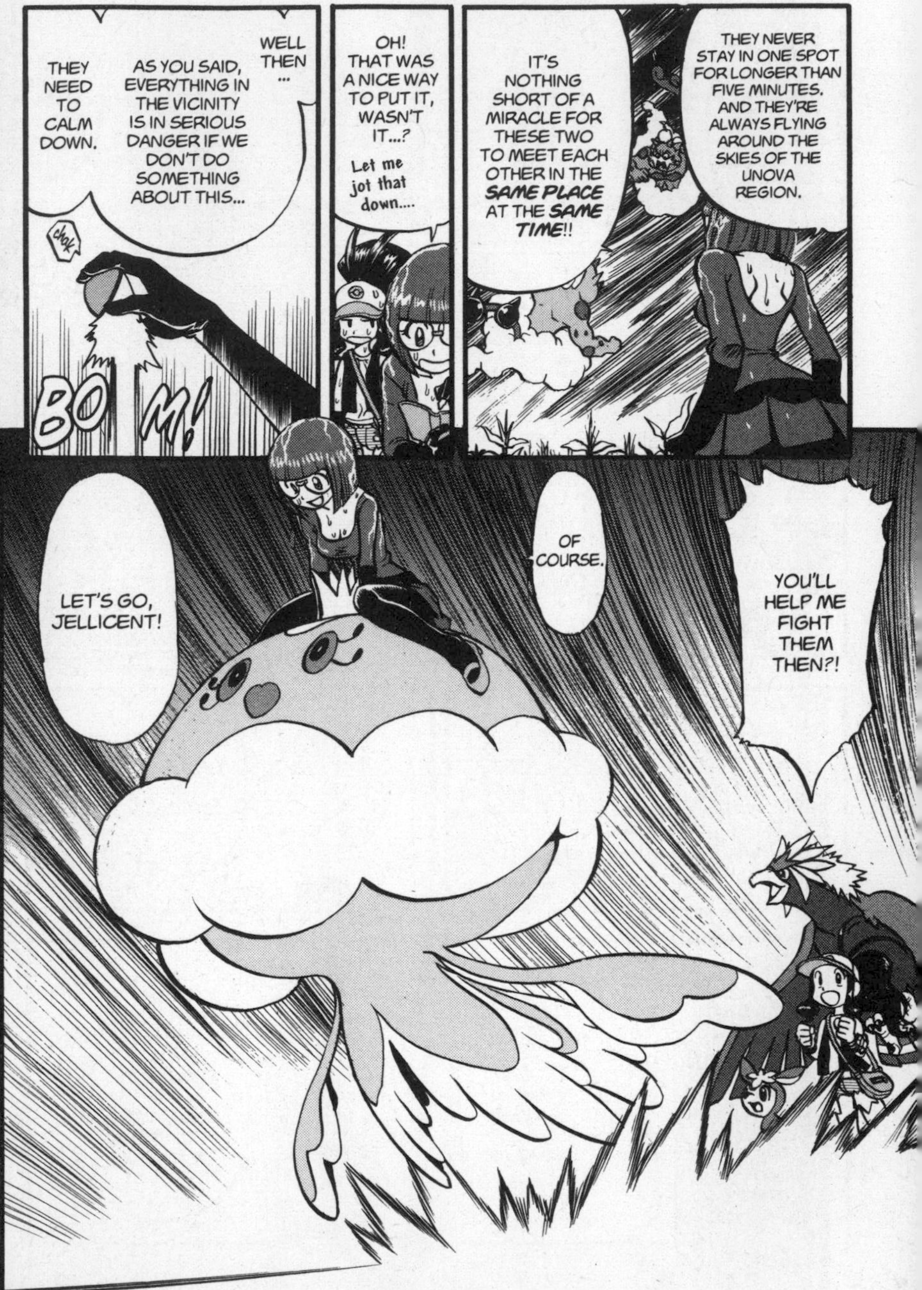

THEY NEVER STAY IN ONE SPOT FOR LONGER THAN FIVE MINUTES. AND THEY'RE ALWAYS FLYING AROUND THE SKIES OF THE UNOVA REGION.
IT'S NOTHING SHORT OF A MIRACLE FOR THESE TWO TO MEET EACH OTHER IN THE SAME PLACE AT THE SAME TIME!!
OH! THAT WAS A NICE WAY TO PUT IT, WASN'T IT...?
Let me jot that down....
WELL THEN ...
AS YOU SAID, EVERYTHING IN THE VICINITY IS IN SERIOUS DANGER IF WE DON'T DO SOMETHING ABOUT THIS...
THEY NEED TO CALM DOWN.
chok
BO M!
YOU'LL HELP ME FIGHT THEM THEN?!
OF COURSE.
LET'S GO, JELLICENT!

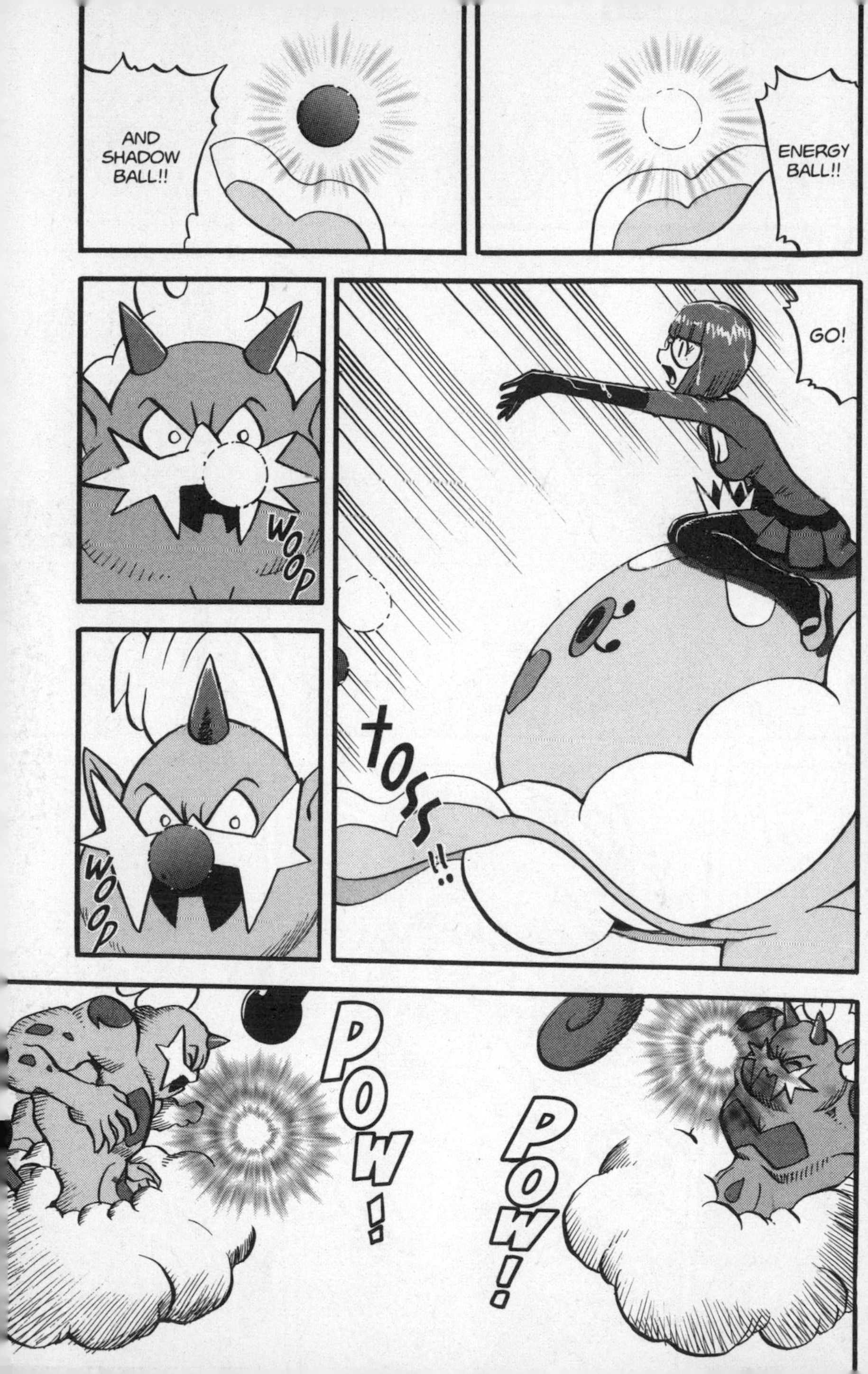
ENERGY BALL!!
AND SHADOW BALL!!
GO!
TOSS!!
WOOP
WOOP
POW!!
POW!!

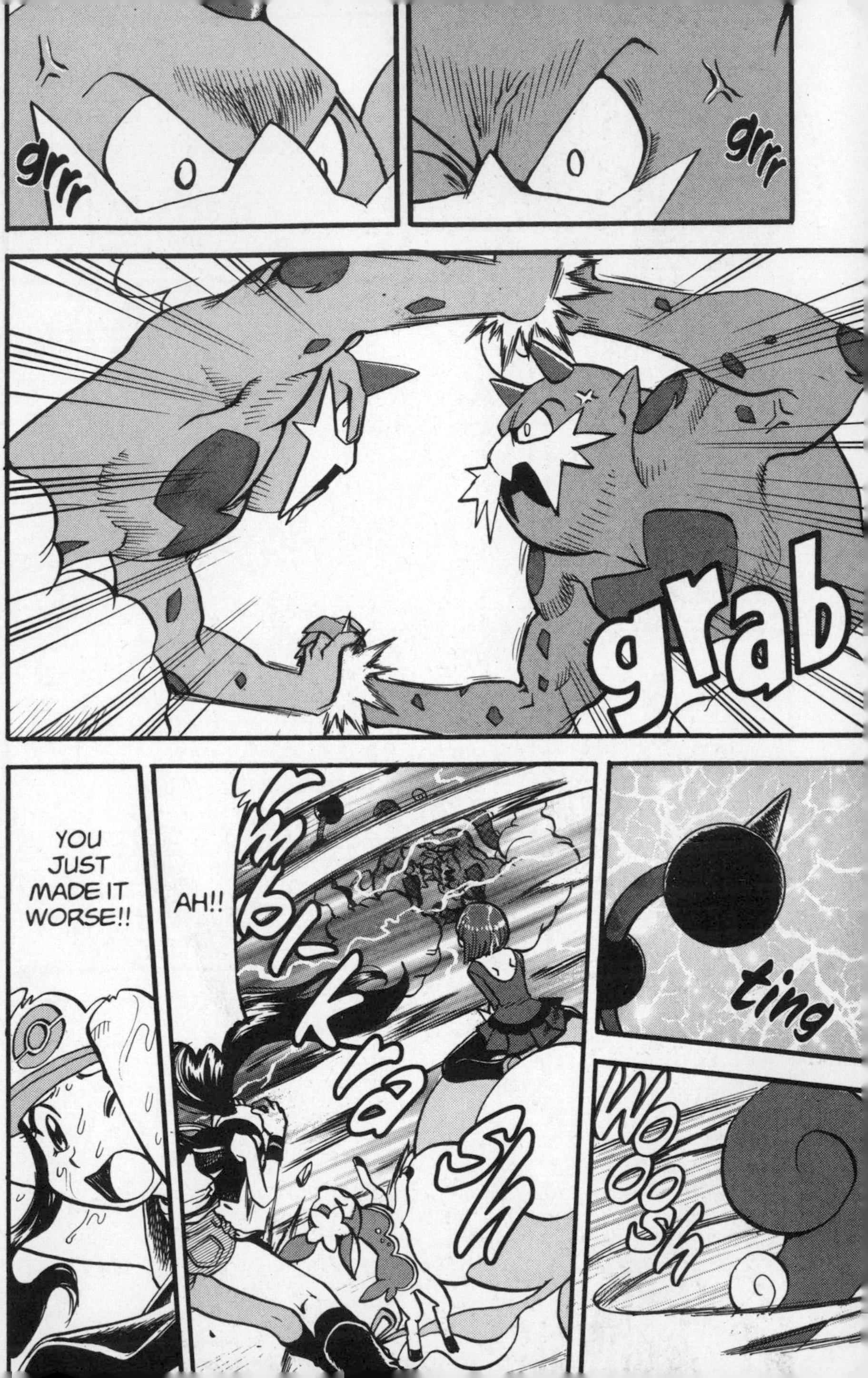
grrr
grrr
grab
ting
whoosh
AH!!
krash
YOU JUST MADE IT WORSE!!

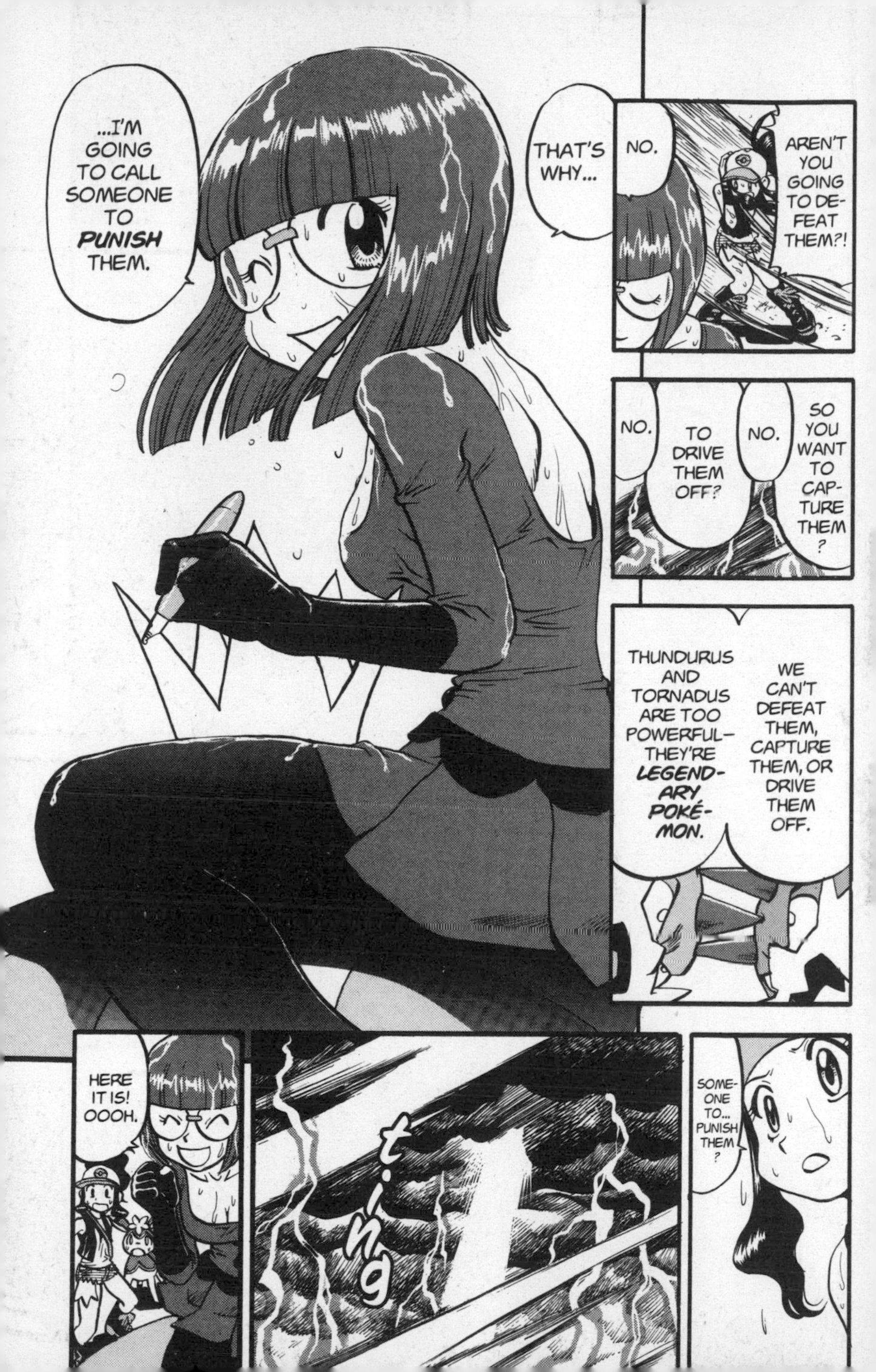
AREN'T YOU GOING TO DEFEAT THEM?!
NO.
THAT'S WHY...
SO YOU WANT TO CAPTURE THEM?
NO.
TO DRIVE THEM OFF?
NO.
WE CAN'T DEFEAT THEM, CAPTURE THEM, OR DRIVE THEM OFF.
THUNDURUS AND TORNADUS ARE TOO POWERFUL–THEY'RE LEGENDARY POKÉMON.
...I'M GOING TO CALL SOMEONE TO PUNISH THEM.
SOMEONE TO... PUNISH THEM?
ting
HERE IT IS! OOOH.

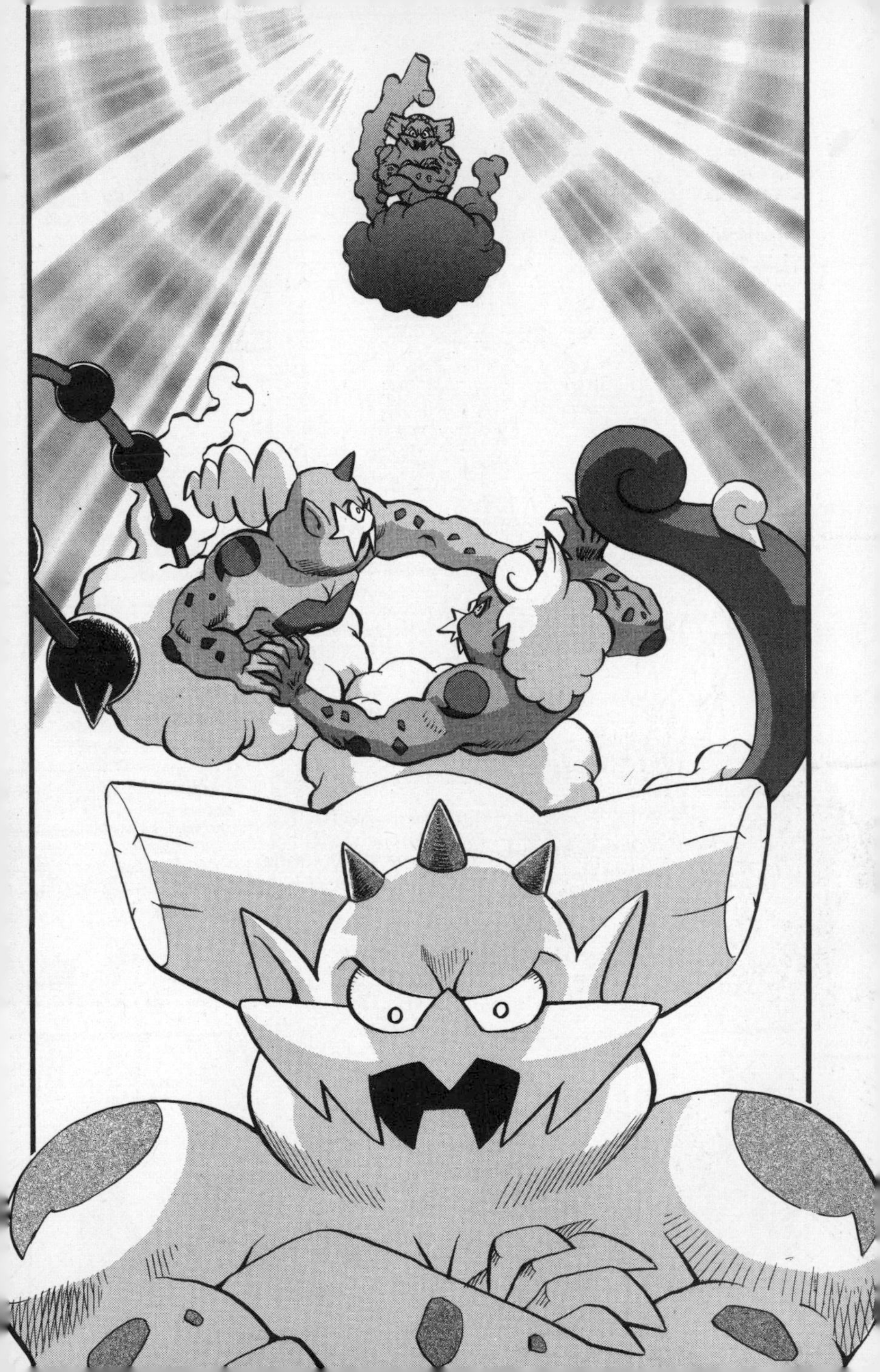

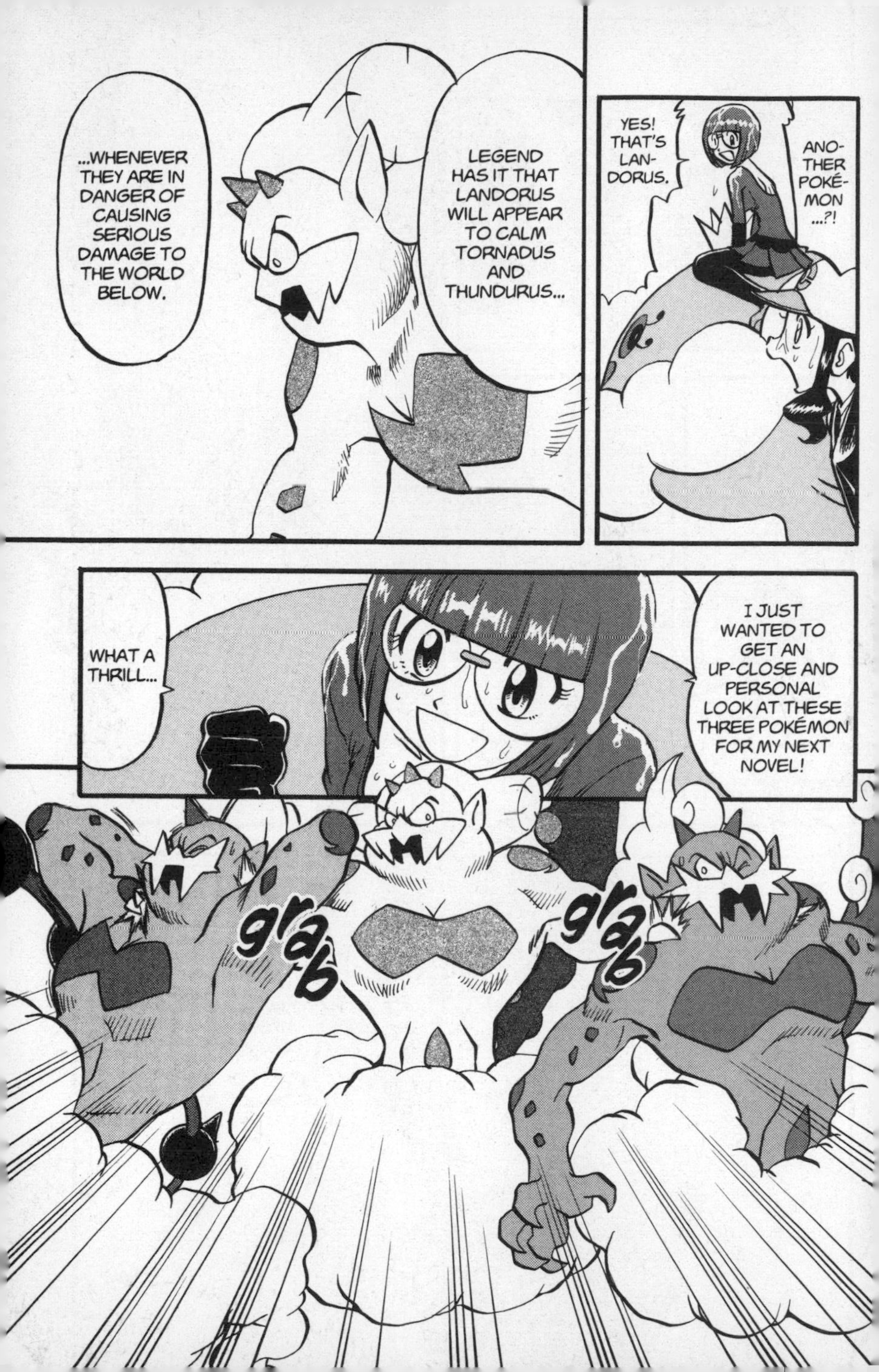
ANOTHER POKÉMON ...?!
YES! THAT'S LANDORUS.
LEGEND HAS IT THAT LANDORUS WILL APPEAR TO CALM TORNADUS AND THUNDURUS...
...WHENEVER THEY ARE IN DANGER OF CAUSING SERIOUS DAMAGE TO THE WORLD BELOW.
I JUST WANTED TO GET AN UP-CLOSE AND PERSONAL LOOK AT THESE THREE POKÉMON FOR MY NEXT NOVEL!
WHAT A THRILL...
grab
grab

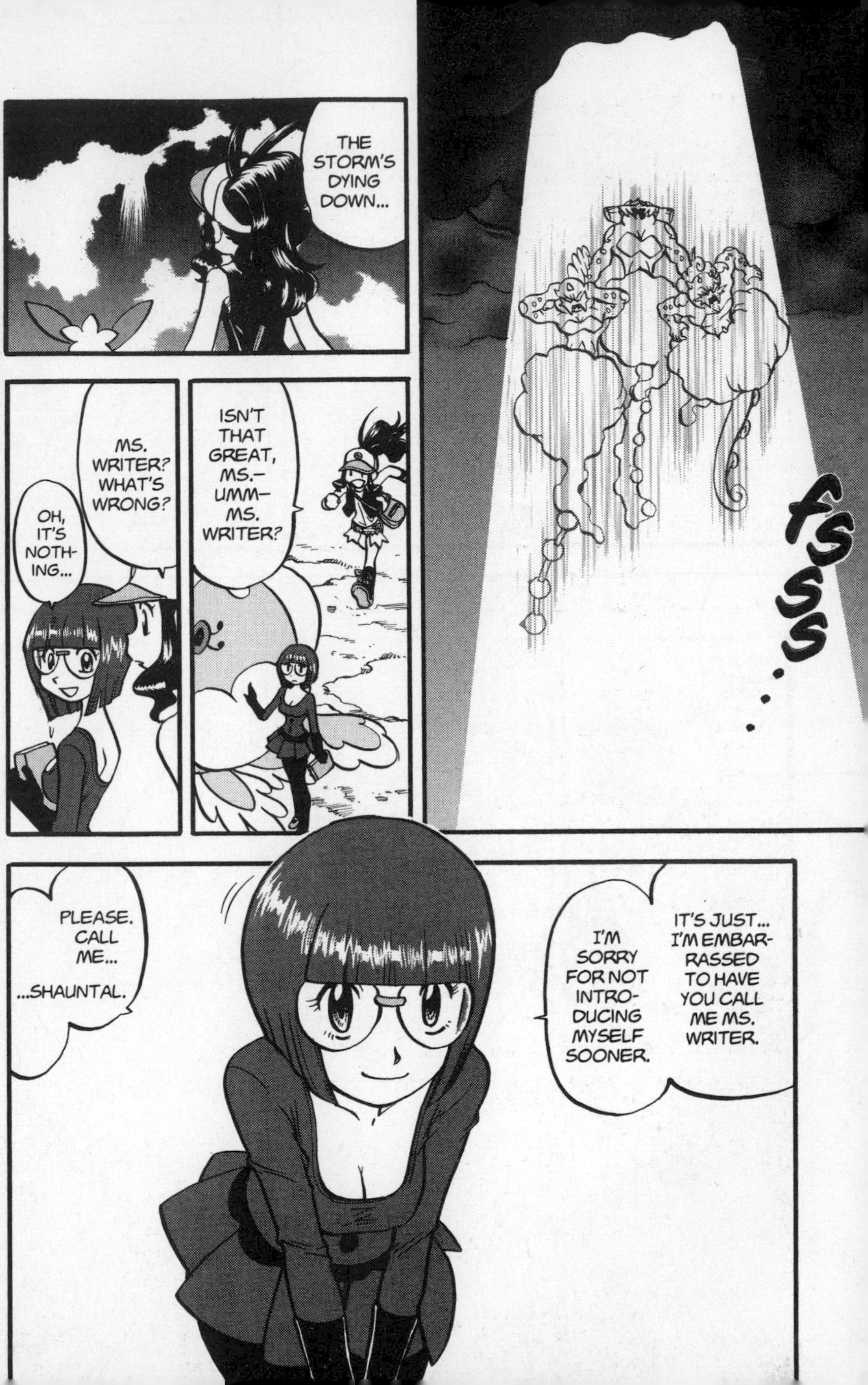
FSSS...
THE STORM'S DYING DOWN...
ISN'T THAT GREAT, MS.— UMM— MS. WRITER?
MS. WRITER? WHAT'S WRONG?
OH, IT'S NOTHING...
IT'S JUST... I'M EMBARRASSED TO HAVE YOU CALL ME MS. WRITER.
I'M SORRY FOR NOT INTRODUCING MYSELF SOONER.
PLEASE. CALL ME...
...SHAUNTAL.

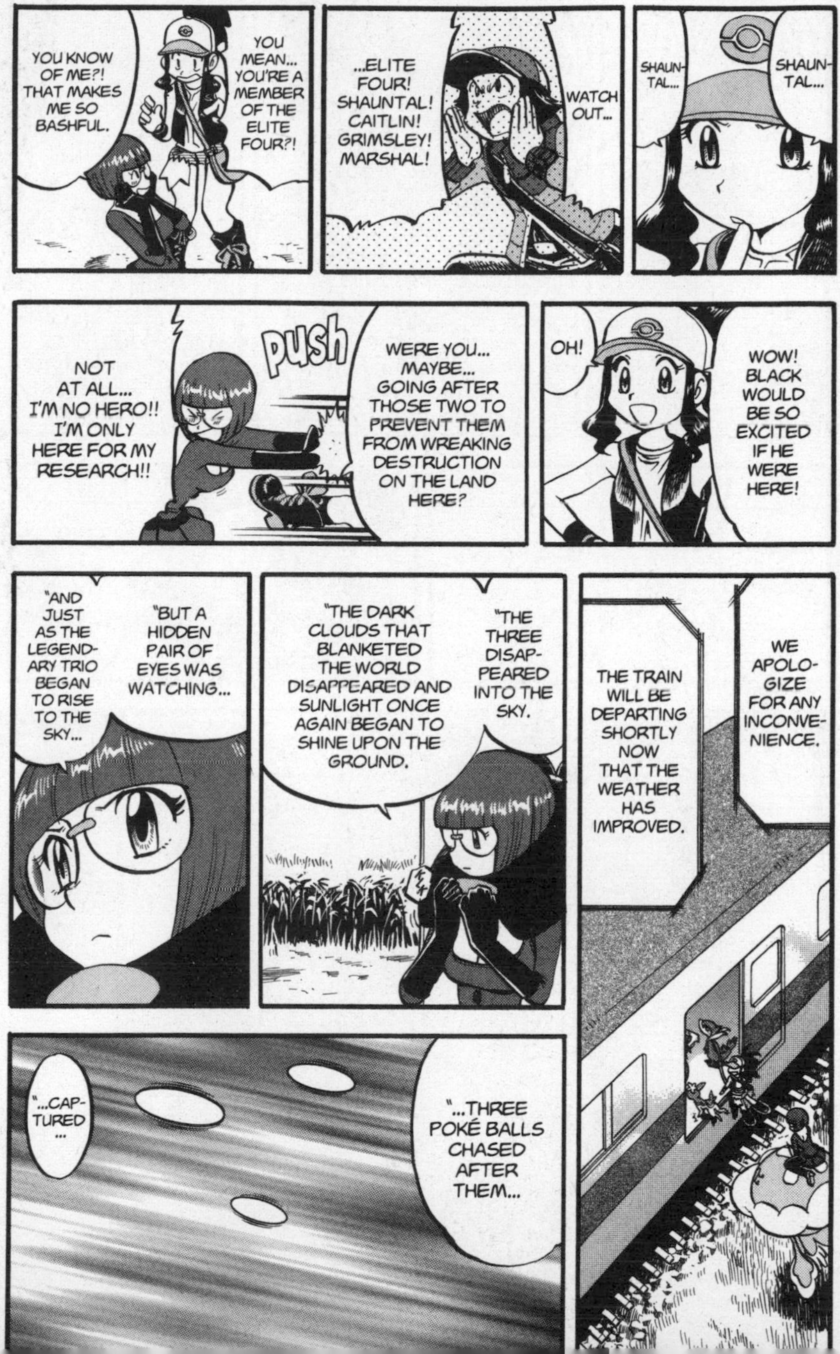
SHAUN-TAL...
SHAUN-TAL...
WATCH OUT...
...ELITE FOUR! SHAUNTAL! CAITLIN! GRIMSLEY! MARSHAL!
YOU MEAN... YOU'RE A MEMBER OF THE ELITE FOUR?!
YOU KNOW OF ME?! THAT MAKES ME SO BASHFUL.
WOW! BLACK WOULD BE SO EXCITED IF HE WERE HERE!
OH!
WERE YOU... MAYBE... GOING AFTER THOSE TWO TO PREVENT THEM FROM WREAKING DESTRUCTION ON THE LAND HERE?
push
NOT AT ALL... I'M NO HERO!! I'M ONLY HERE FOR MY RESEARCH!!
WE APOLO-GIZE FOR ANY INCONVE-NIENCE.
THE TRAIN WILL BE DEPARTING SHORTLY NOW THAT THE WEATHER HAS IMPROVED.
"THE THREE DISAP-PEARED INTO THE SKY.
"THE DARK CLOUDS THAT BLANKETED THE WORLD DISAPPEARED AND SUNLIGHT ONCE AGAIN BEGAN TO SHINE UPON THE GROUND.
"AND JUST AS THE LEGEND-ARY TRIO BEGAN TO RISE TO THE SKY...
"BUT A HIDDEN PAIR OF EYES WAS WATCHING...
"...THREE POKÉ BALLS CHASED AFTER THEM...
"...CAP-TURED...

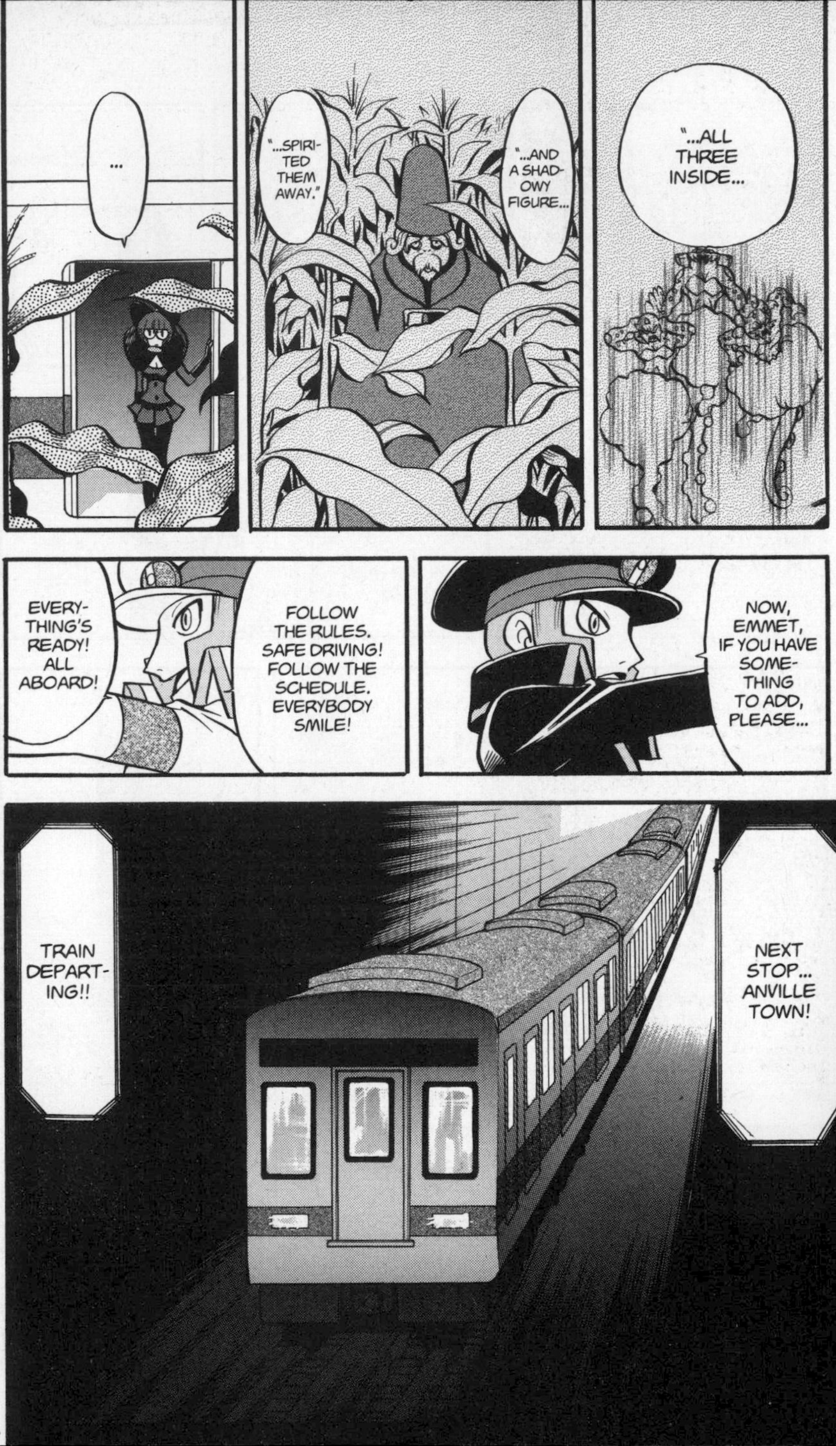
"...ALL THREE INSIDE...
"...AND A SHADOWY FIGURE...
"...SPIRITED THEM AWAY."
...
NOW, EMMET, IF YOU HAVE SOMETHING TO ADD, PLEASE...
FOLLOW THE RULES. SAFE DRIVING! FOLLOW THE SCHEDULE. EVERYBODY SMILE!
EVERYTHING'S READY! ALL ABOARD!
NEXT STOP... ANVILLE TOWN!
TRAIN DEPARTING!!

ADVENTURE MAP

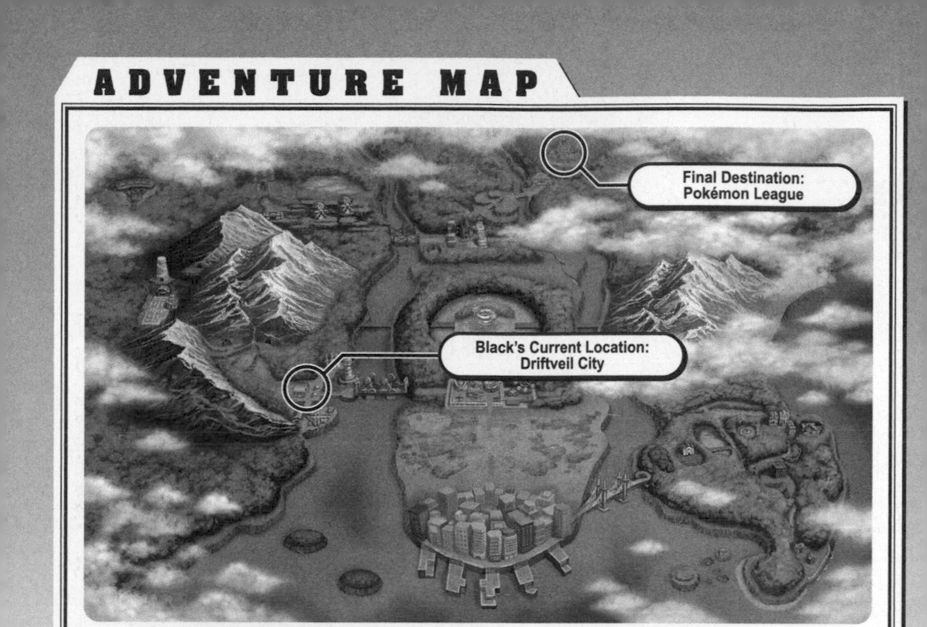

Final Destination:
Pokémon League
Black's Current Location:
Driftveil City

BLACK

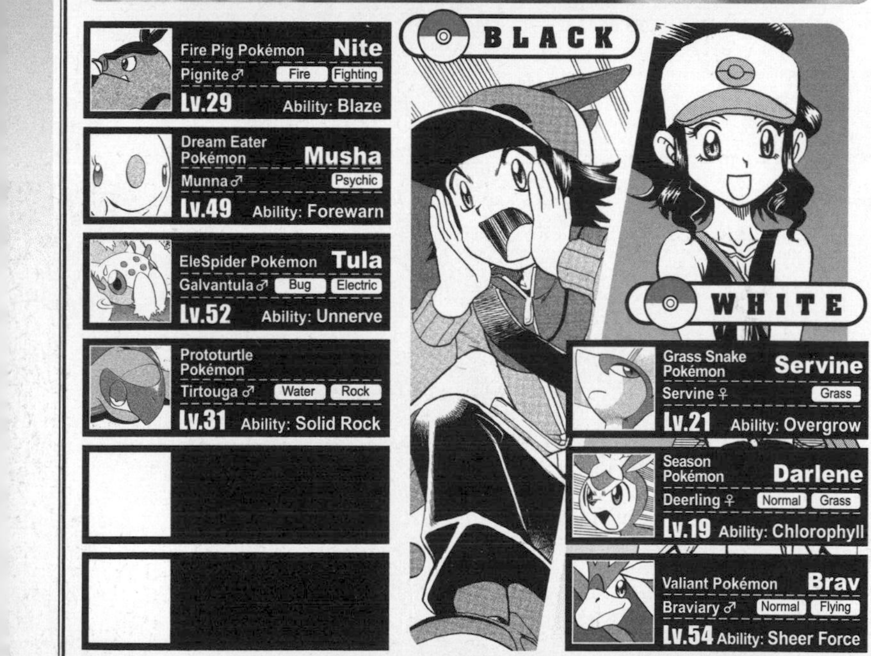

Nite
Fire Pig Pokémon
Pignite ♂ | Fire | Fighting
Lv.29 Ability: Blaze

Musha
Dream Eater Pokémon
Munna ♂ | Psychic
Lv.49 Ability: Forewarn

Tula
EleSpider Pokémon
Galvantula ♂ | Bug | Electric
Lv.52 Ability: Unnerve

Tirtouga
Prototurtle Pokémon
Tirtouga ♂ | Water | Rock
Lv.31 Ability: Solid Rock

WHITE

Servine
Grass Snake Pokémon
Servine ♀ | Grass
Lv.21 Ability: Overgrow

Darlene
Season Pokémon
Deerling ♀ | Normal | Grass
Lv.19 Ability: Chlorophyll

Brav
Valiant Pokémon
Braviary ♂ | Normal | Flying
Lv.54 Ability: Sheer Force

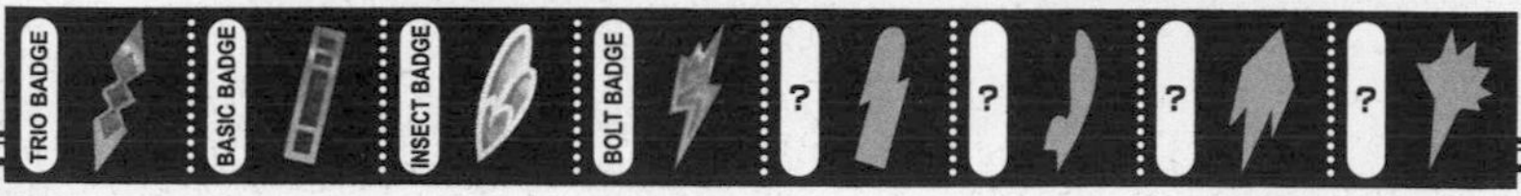

TRIO BADGE
BASIC BADGE
INSECT BADGE
BOLT BADGE
?
?
?
?

Pokémon™ Adventures Black & White

VANILLITE

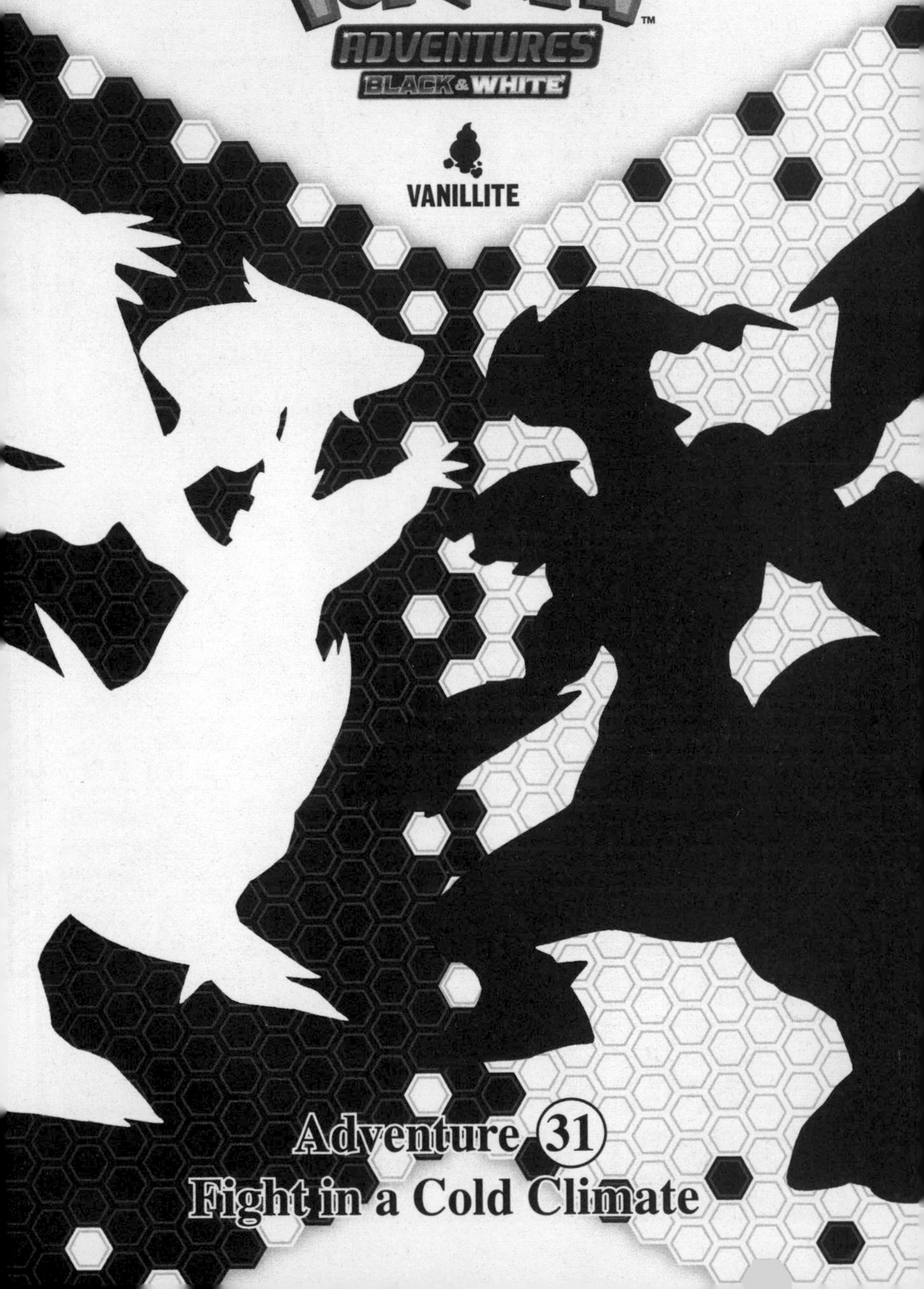

Adventure 31
Fight in a Cold Climate

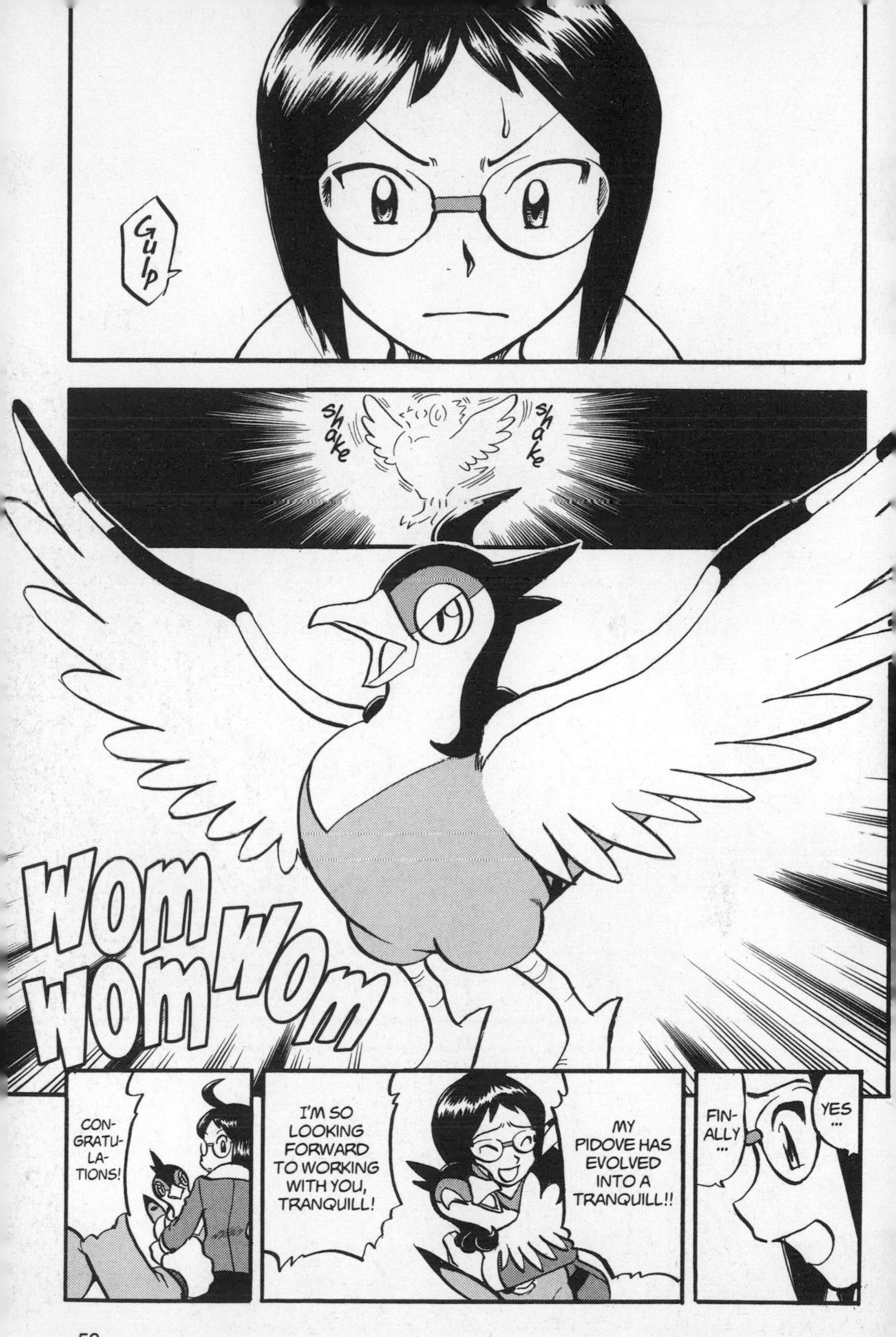
Gulp
shake
shake
WOM WOM WOM WOM
YES ...
FIN-ALLY ...
MY PIDOVE HAS EVOLVED INTO A TRANQUILL!!
I'M SO LOOKING FORWARD TO WORKING WITH YOU, TRANQUILL!
CON-GRATU-LA-TIONS!

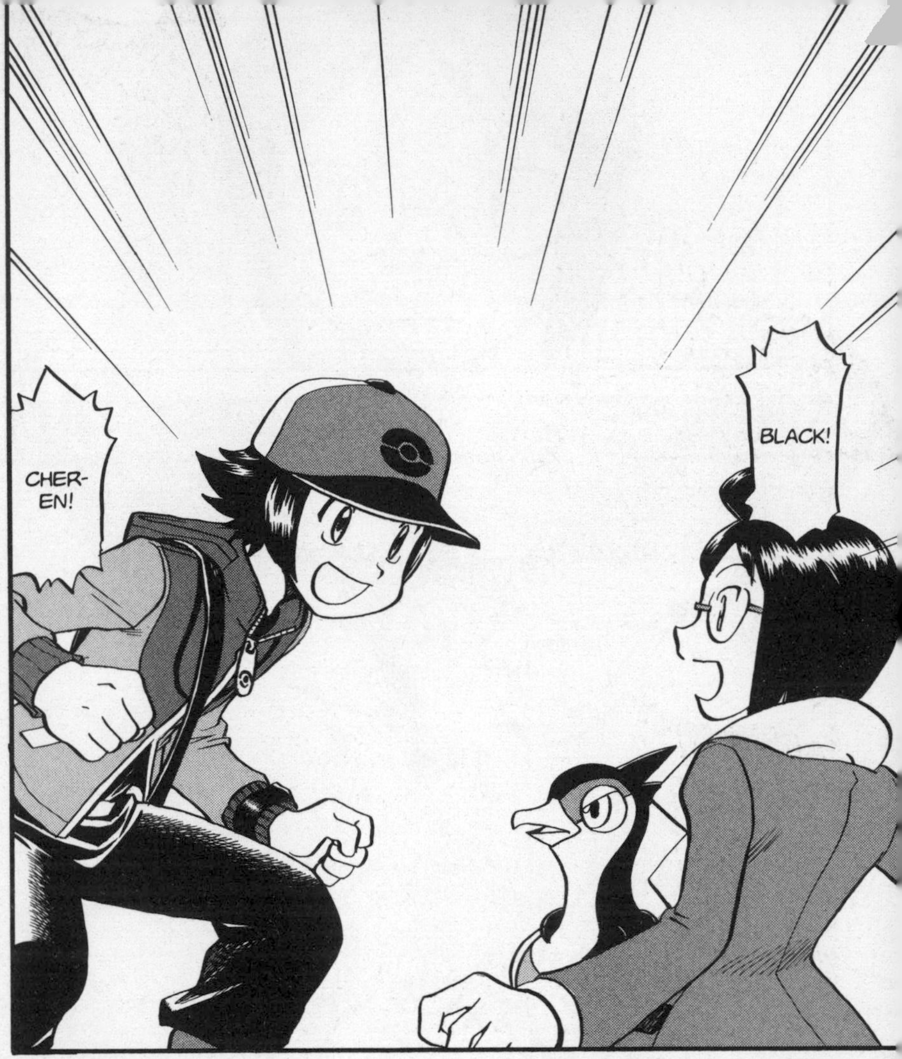
BLACK!
CHER-EN!

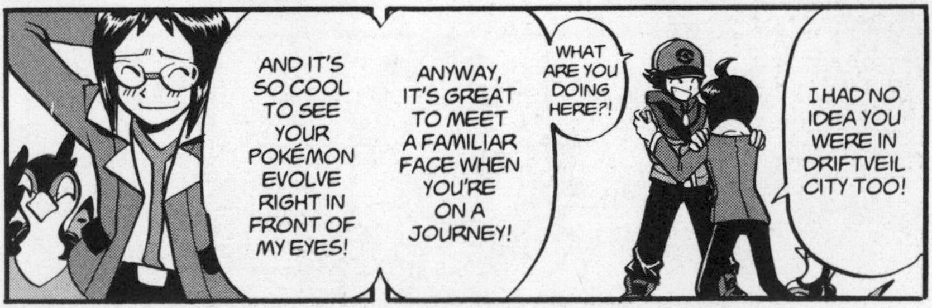
I HAD NO IDEA YOU WERE IN DRIFTVEIL CITY TOO!
WHAT ARE YOU DOING HERE?!
ANYWAY, IT'S GREAT TO MEET A FAMILIAR FACE WHEN YOU'RE ON A JOURNEY!
AND IT'S SO COOL TO SEE YOUR POKÉMON EVOLVE RIGHT IN FRONT OF MY EYES!

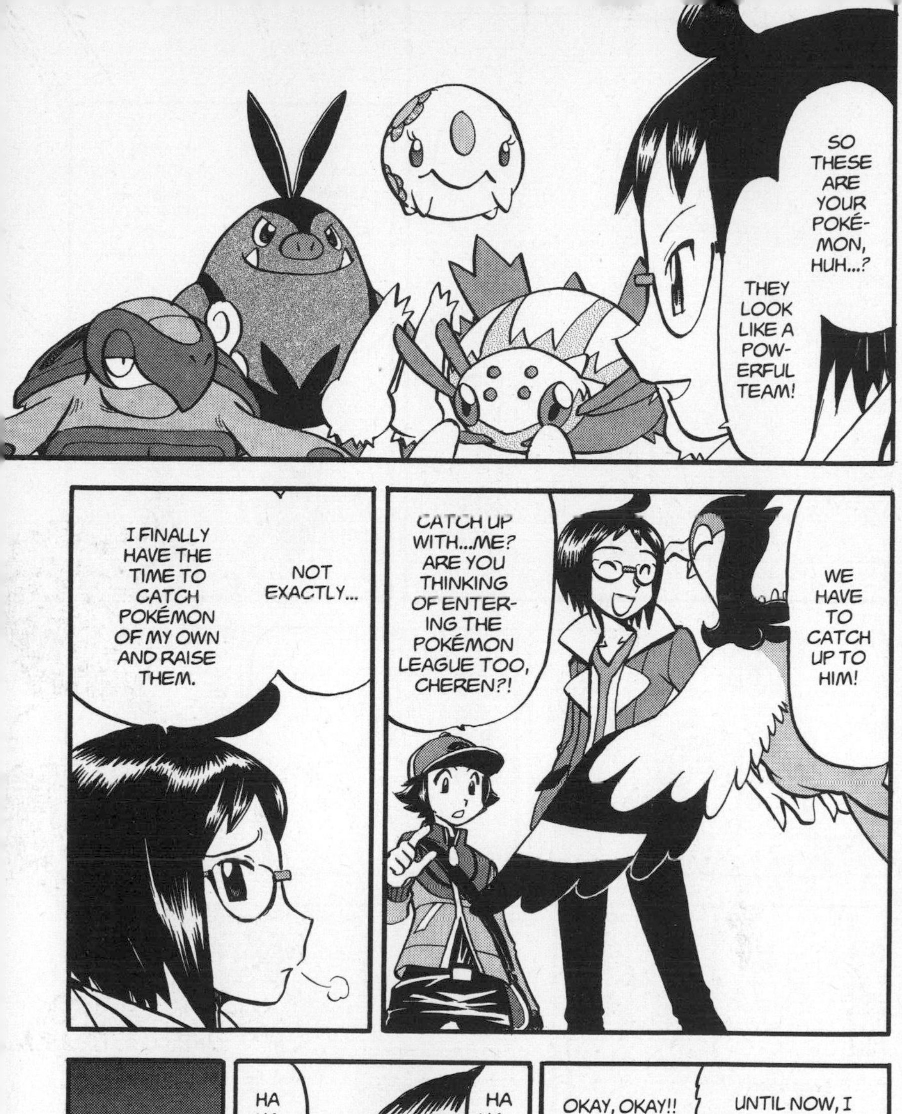

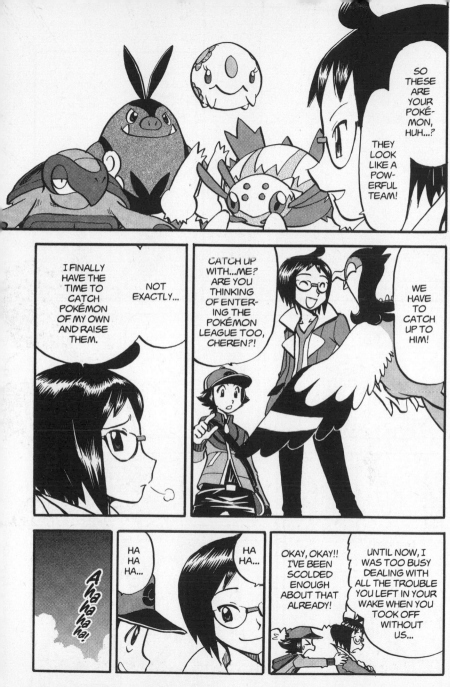

SO THESE ARE YOUR POKÉMON, HUH...?
THEY LOOK LIKE A POWERFUL TEAM!
WE HAVE TO CATCH UP TO HIM!
CATCH UP WITH...ME? ARE YOU THINKING OF ENTERING THE POKÉMON LEAGUE TOO, CHEREN?!
NOT EXACTLY...
I FINALLY HAVE THE TIME TO CATCH POKÉMON OF MY OWN AND RAISE THEM.
UNTIL NOW, I WAS TOO BUSY DEALING WITH ALL THE TROUBLE YOU LEFT IN YOUR WAKE WHEN YOU TOOK OFF WITHOUT US...
OKAY, OKAY!! I'VE BEEN SCOLDED ENOUGH ABOUT THAT ALREADY!
HA HA...
HA HA HA...
A ha ha ha ha!

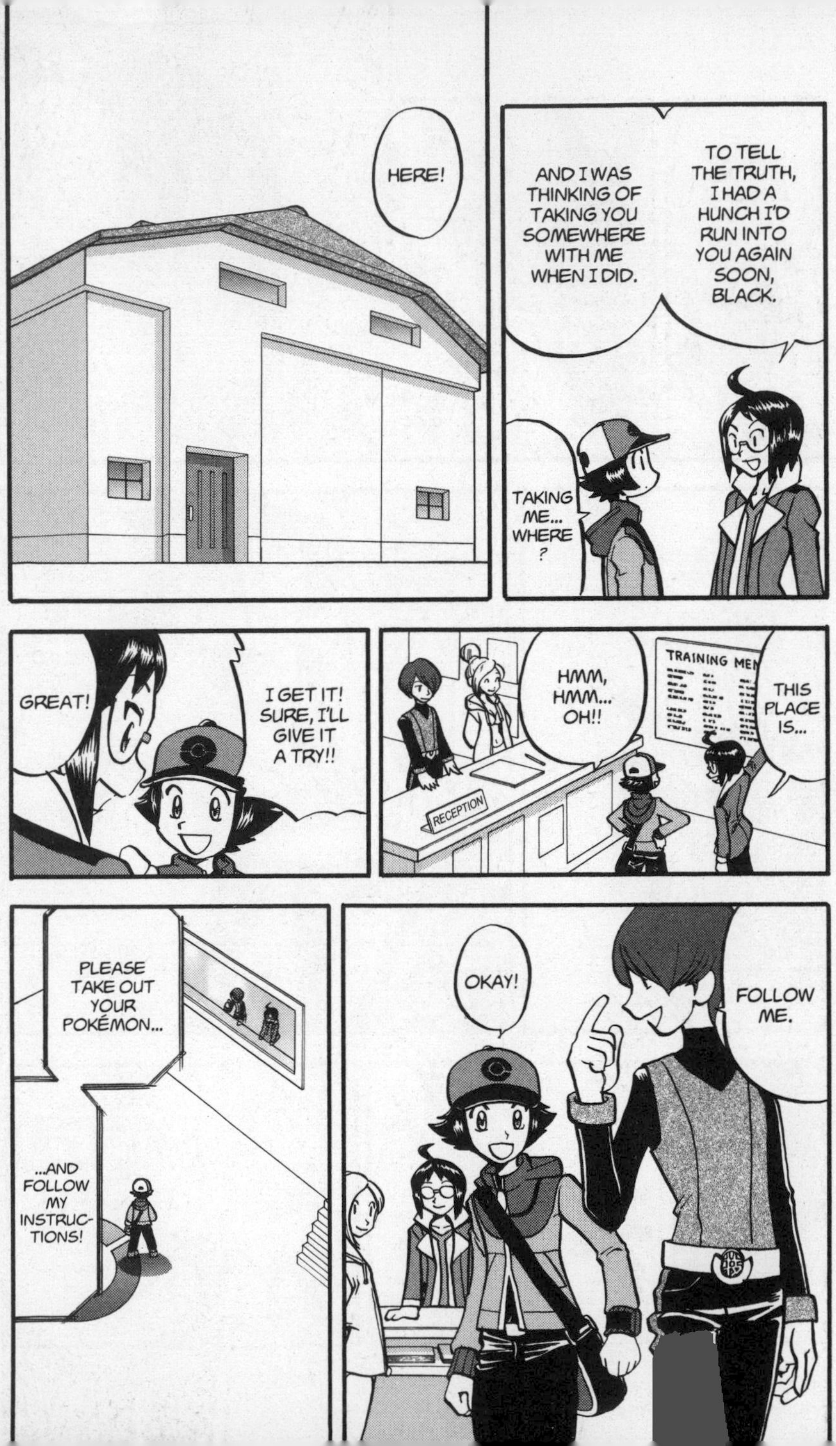
TO TELL THE TRUTH, I HAD A HUNCH I'D RUN INTO YOU AGAIN SOON, BLACK.
AND I WAS THINKING OF TAKING YOU SOMEWHERE WITH ME WHEN I DID.
TAKING ME... WHERE?
HERE!
THIS PLACE IS...
TRAINING MEN
HMM, HMM... OH!!
RECEPTION
I GET IT! SURE, I'LL GIVE IT A TRY!!
GREAT!
FOLLOW ME.
OKAY!
PLEASE TAKE OUT YOUR POKÉMON...
...AND FOLLOW MY INSTRUCTIONS!

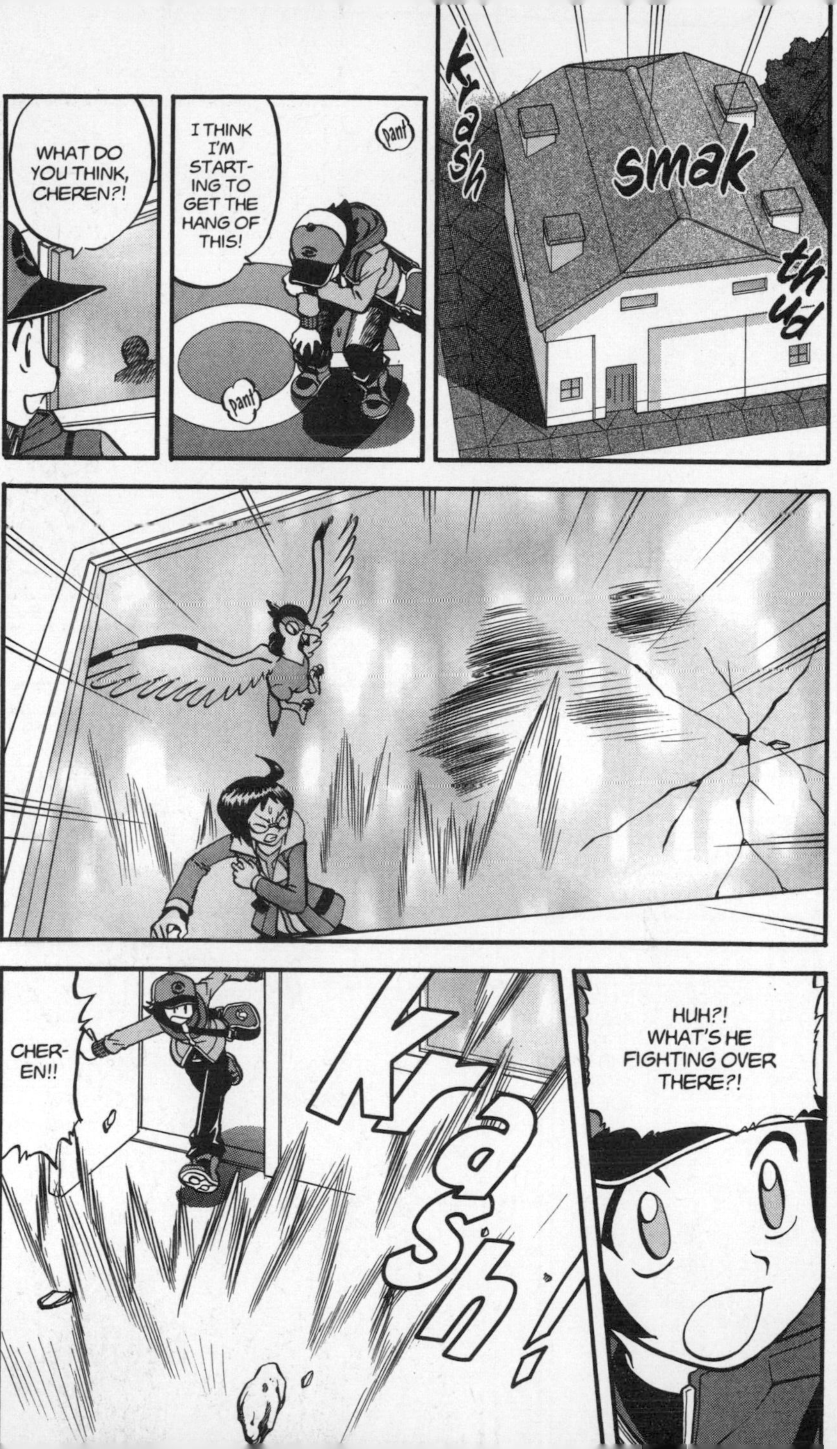
krash
smak
thud
pant
I THINK I'M STARTING TO GET THE HANG OF THIS!
pant
WHAT DO YOU THINK, CHEREN?!
HUH?! WHAT'S HE FIGHTING OVER THERE?!
Krash!
CHER-EN!!

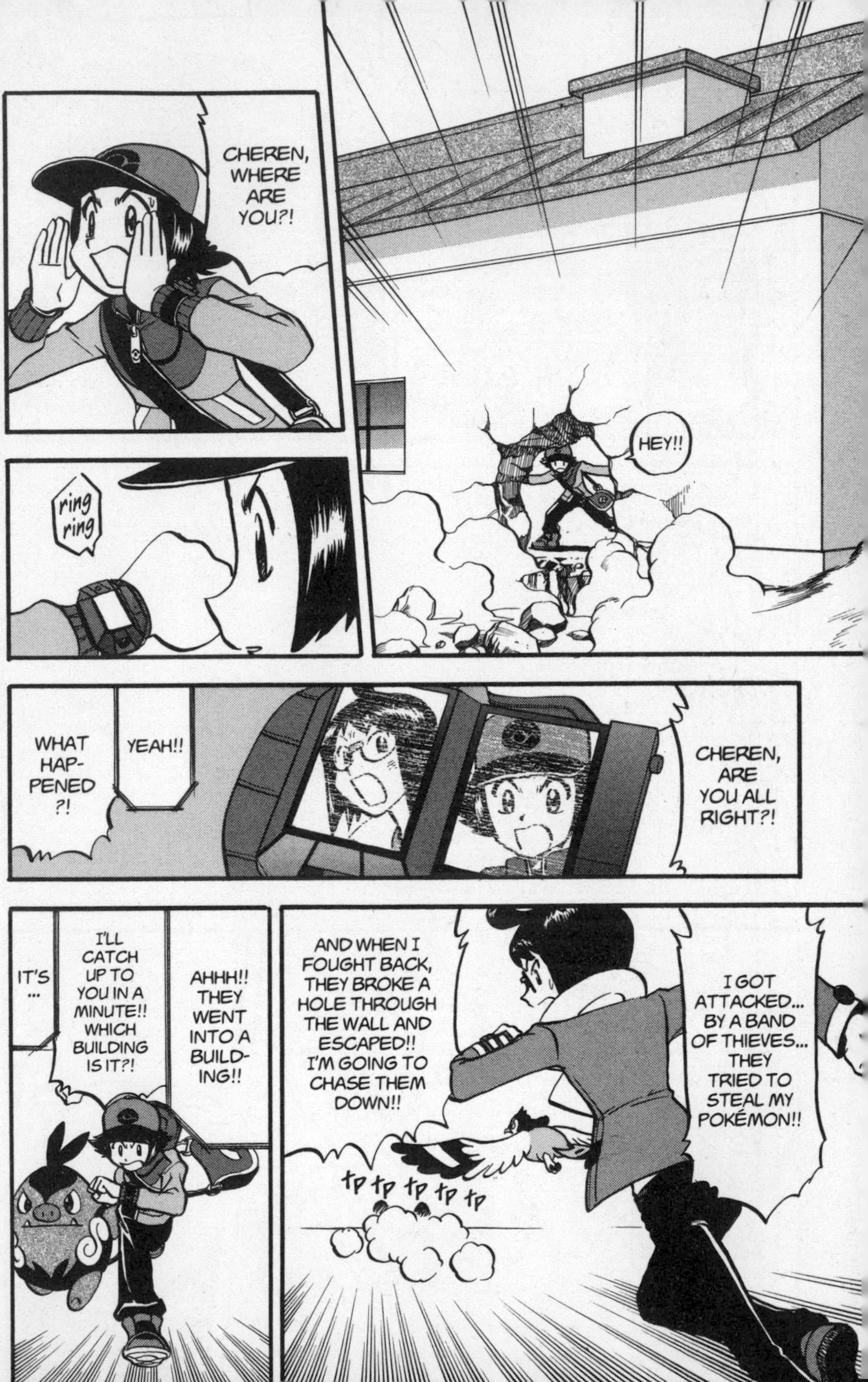
HEY!!
CHEREN, WHERE ARE YOU?!
ring ring
CHEREN, ARE YOU ALL RIGHT?!
YEAH!!
WHAT HAP-PENED?!
I GOT ATTACKED... BY A BAND OF THIEVES... THEY TRIED TO STEAL MY POKÉMON!!
AND WHEN I FOUGHT BACK, THEY BROKE A HOLE THROUGH THE WALL AND ESCAPED!! I'M GOING TO CHASE THEM DOWN!!
tp tp tp tp tp
AHHH!! THEY WENT INTO A BUILD-ING!!
I'LL CATCH UP TO YOU IN A MINUTE!! WHICH BUILDING IS IT?!
IT'S ...

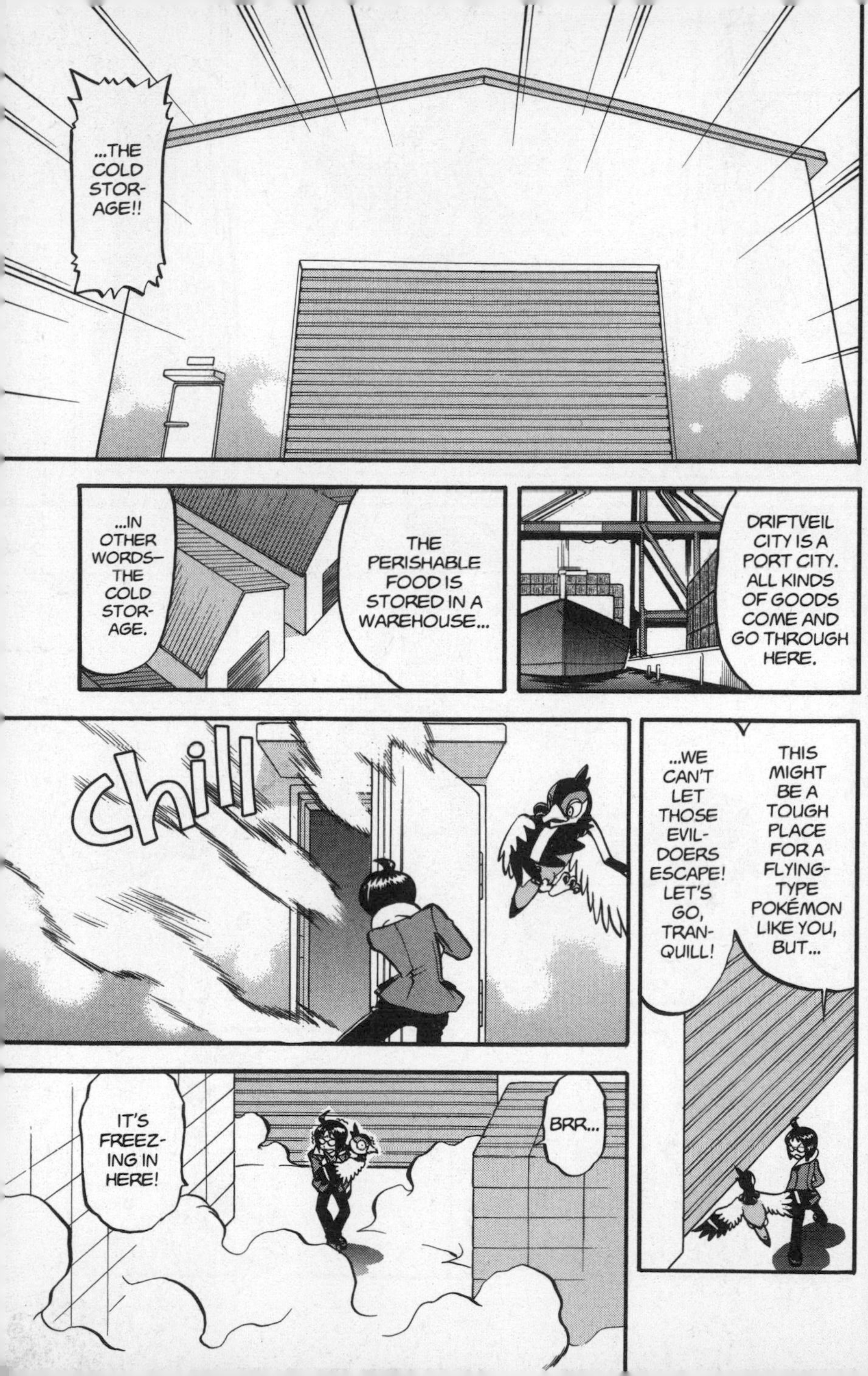
...THE COLD STORAGE!!
DRIFTVEIL CITY IS A PORT CITY. ALL KINDS OF GOODS COME AND GO THROUGH HERE.
THE PERISHABLE FOOD IS STORED IN A WAREHOUSE...
...IN OTHER WORDS—THE COLD STORAGE.
THIS MIGHT BE A TOUGH PLACE FOR A FLYING-TYPE POKÉMON LIKE YOU, BUT...
...WE CAN'T LET THOSE EVILDOERS ESCAPE! LET'S GO, TRANQUILL!
Chill
BRR...
IT'S FREEZING IN HERE!

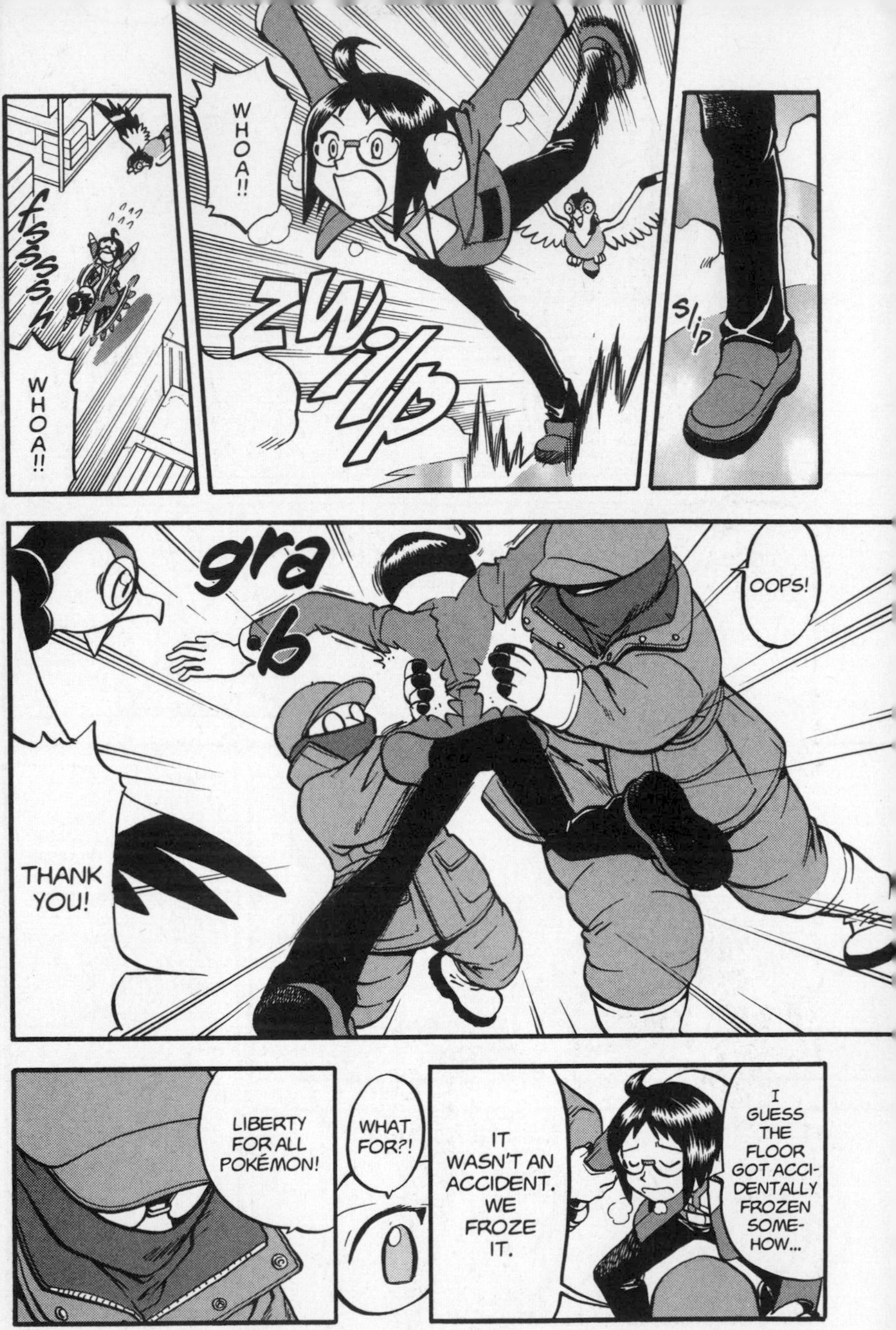
slip
WHOA!!
zwip
fsssh
WHOA!!
OOPS!
grab
THANK YOU!
I GUESS THE FLOOR GOT ACCIDENTALLY FROZEN SOMEHOW...
IT WASN'T AN ACCIDENT. WE FROZE IT.
WHAT FOR?!
LIBERTY FOR ALL POKÉMON!

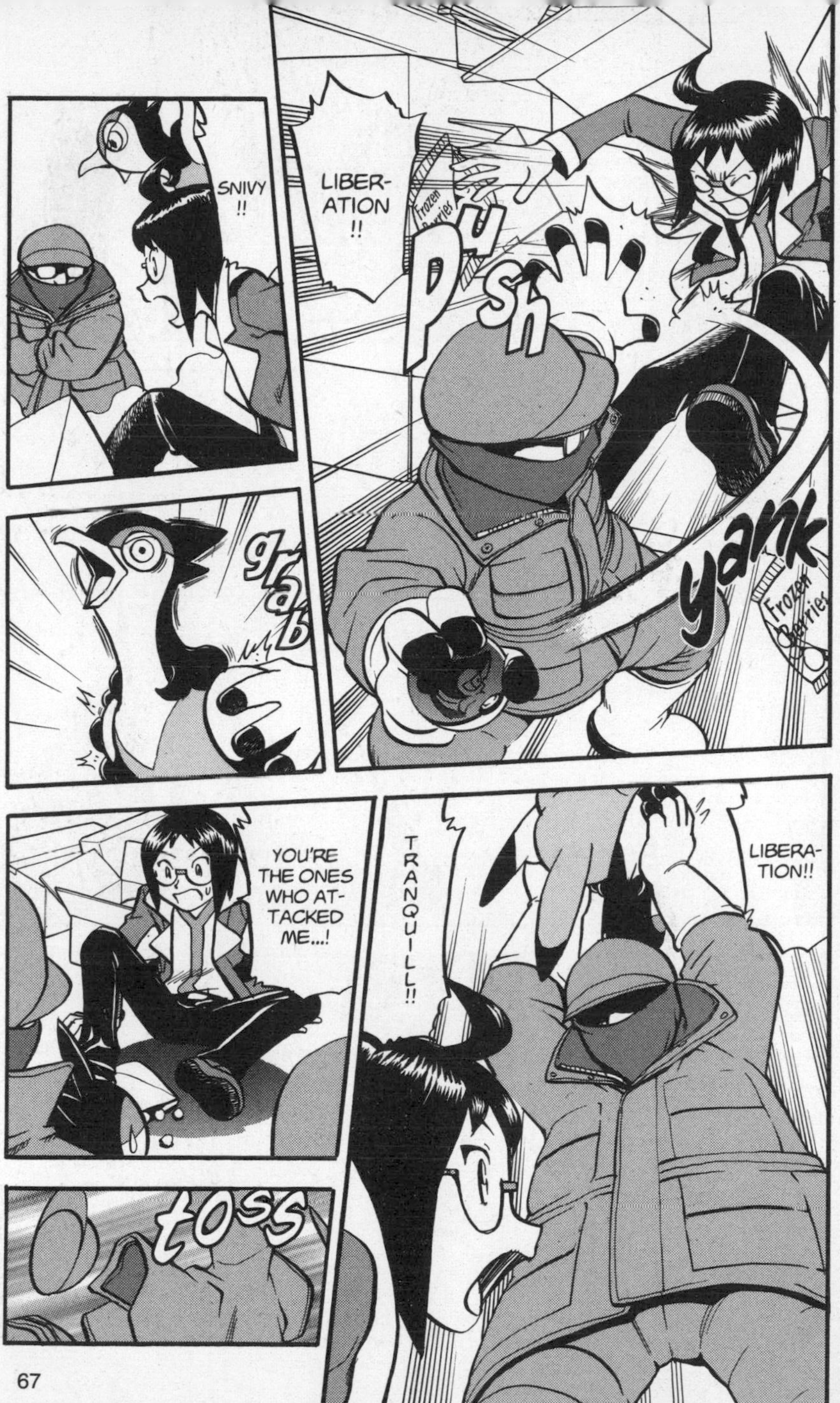
LIBER-
ATION
!!
Frozen Berries
push
yank
Frozen Berries
SNIVY
!!
grab
LIBERA-
TION!!
TRANQUILL!!
YOU'RE
THE ONES
WHO AT-
TACKED
ME...!
toss

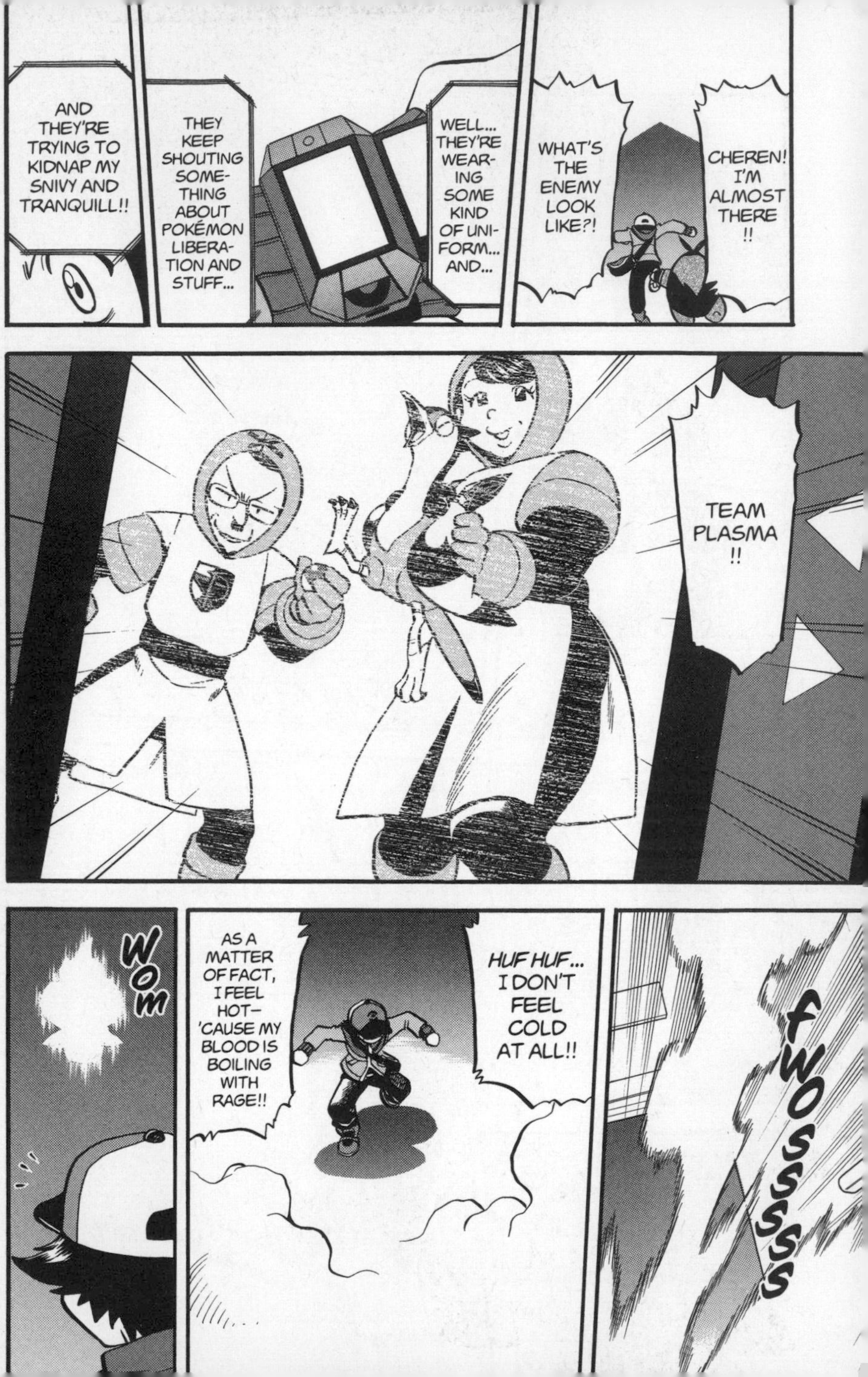
CHEREN! I'M ALMOST THERE !!
WHAT'S THE ENEMY LOOK LIKE?!
WELL... THEY'RE WEAR-ING SOME KIND OF UNI-FORM... AND...
THEY KEEP SHOUTING SOME-THING ABOUT POKÉMON LIBERA-TION AND STUFF...
AND THEY'RE TRYING TO KIDNAP MY SNIVY AND TRANQUILL!!
TEAM PLASMA !!
FWOSSSSS
HUF HUF... I DON'T FEEL COLD AT ALL!!
AS A MATTER OF FACT, I FEEL HOT—'CAUSE MY BLOOD IS BOILING WITH RAGE!!
WOM

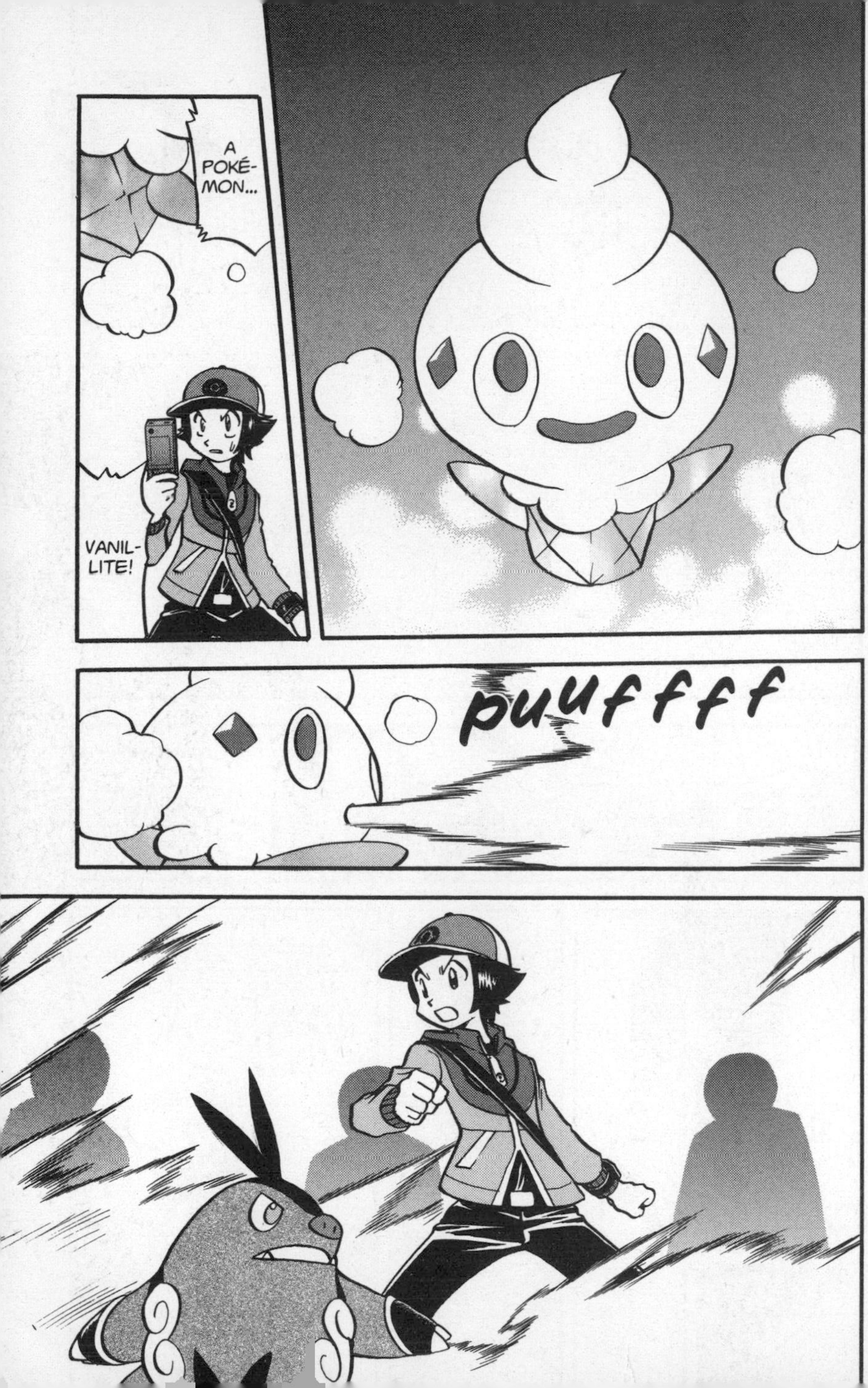
A POKÉ-MON...
VANIL-LITE!
puuffff

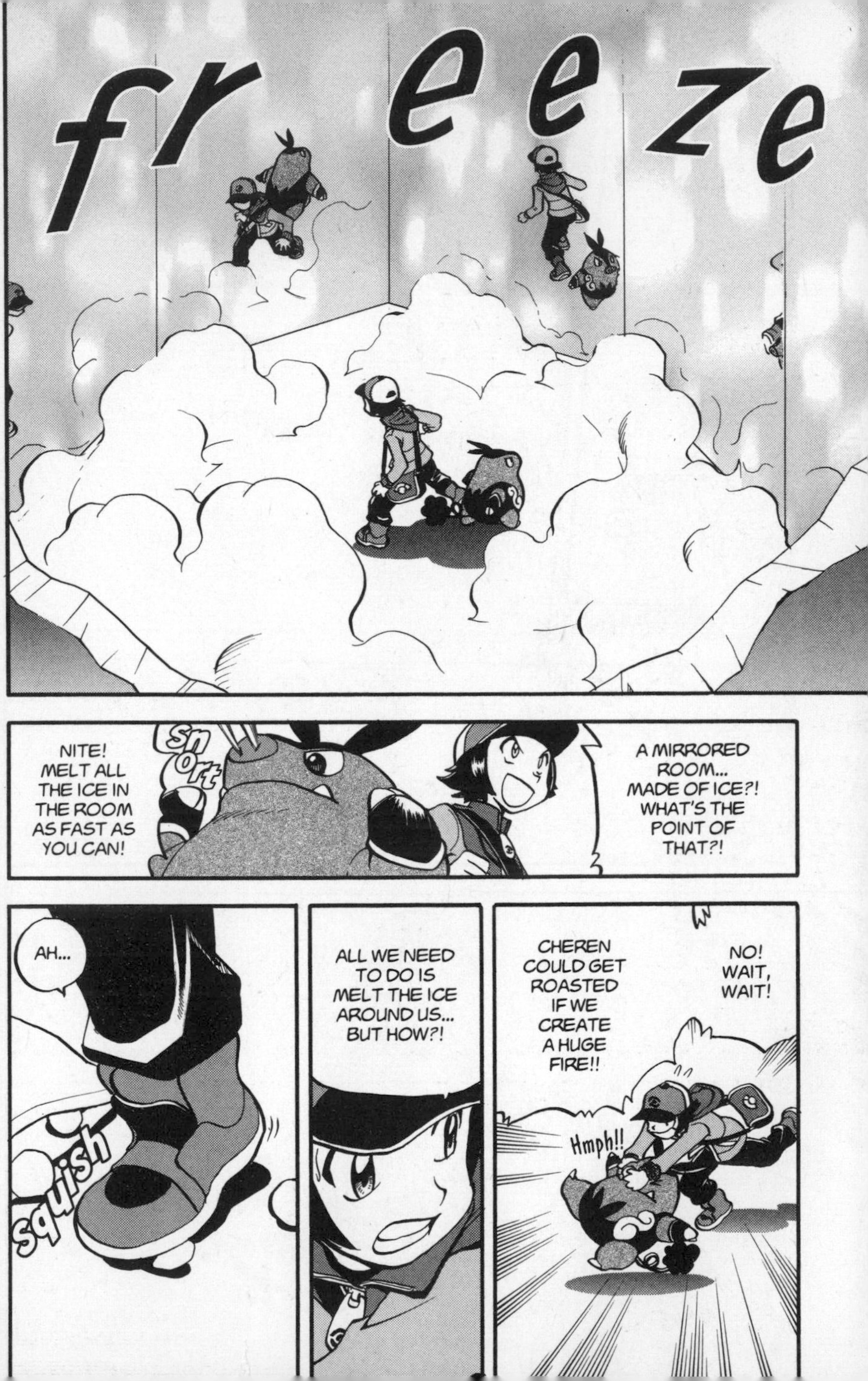
freeze
A MIRRORED ROOM... MADE OF ICE?! WHAT'S THE POINT OF THAT?!
snort
NITE! MELT ALL THE ICE IN THE ROOM AS FAST AS YOU CAN!
NO! WAIT, WAIT!
CHEREN COULD GET ROASTED IF WE CREATE A HUGE FIRE!!
Hmph!!
ALL WE NEED TO DO IS MELT THE ICE AROUND US... BUT HOW?!
AH...
squish

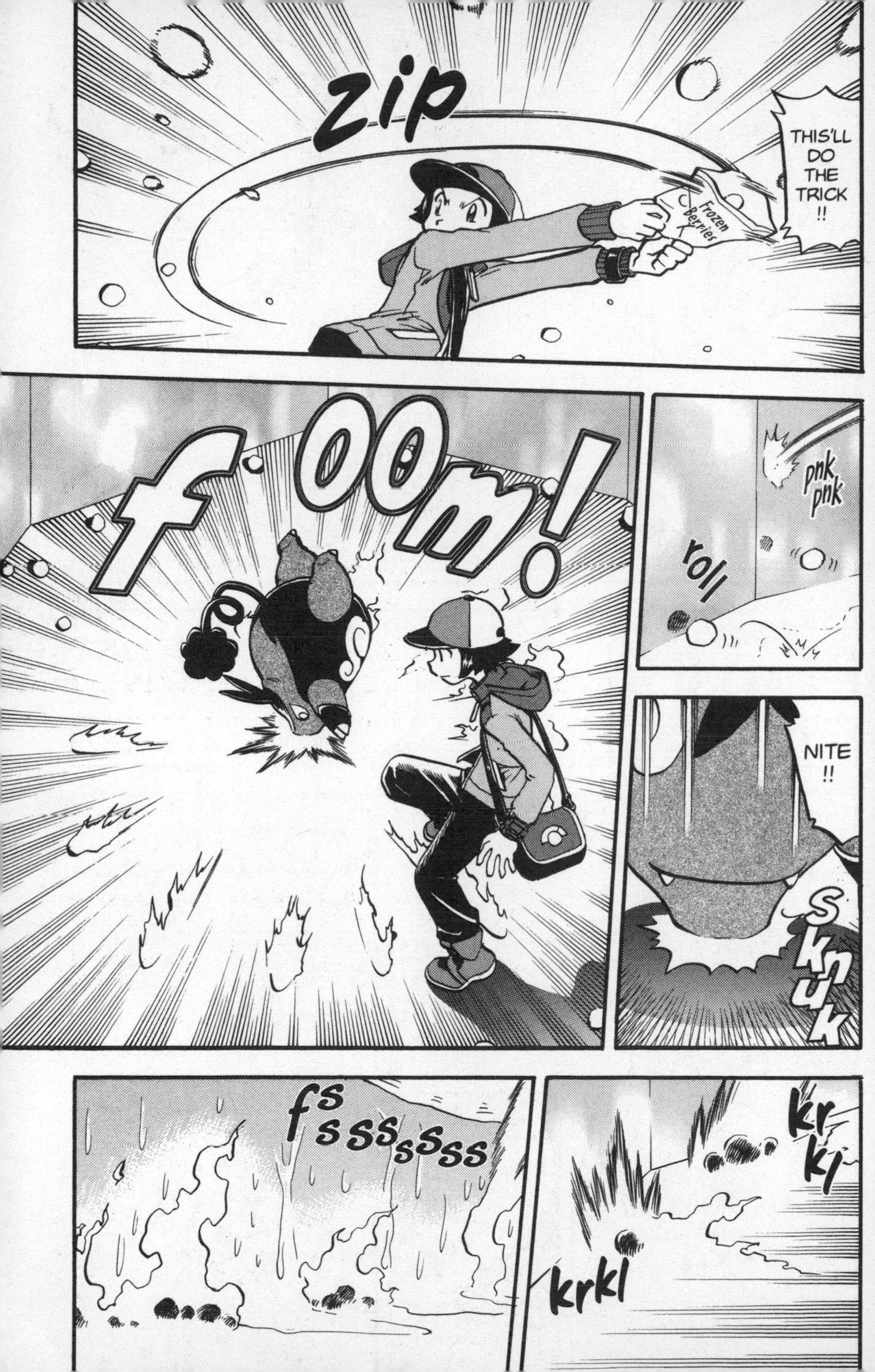
THIS'LL DO THE TRICK!!
zip
Frozen Berries
pnk pnk
roll
NITE!!
sknuk
fOOm!
krkl
krkl
fssssssss

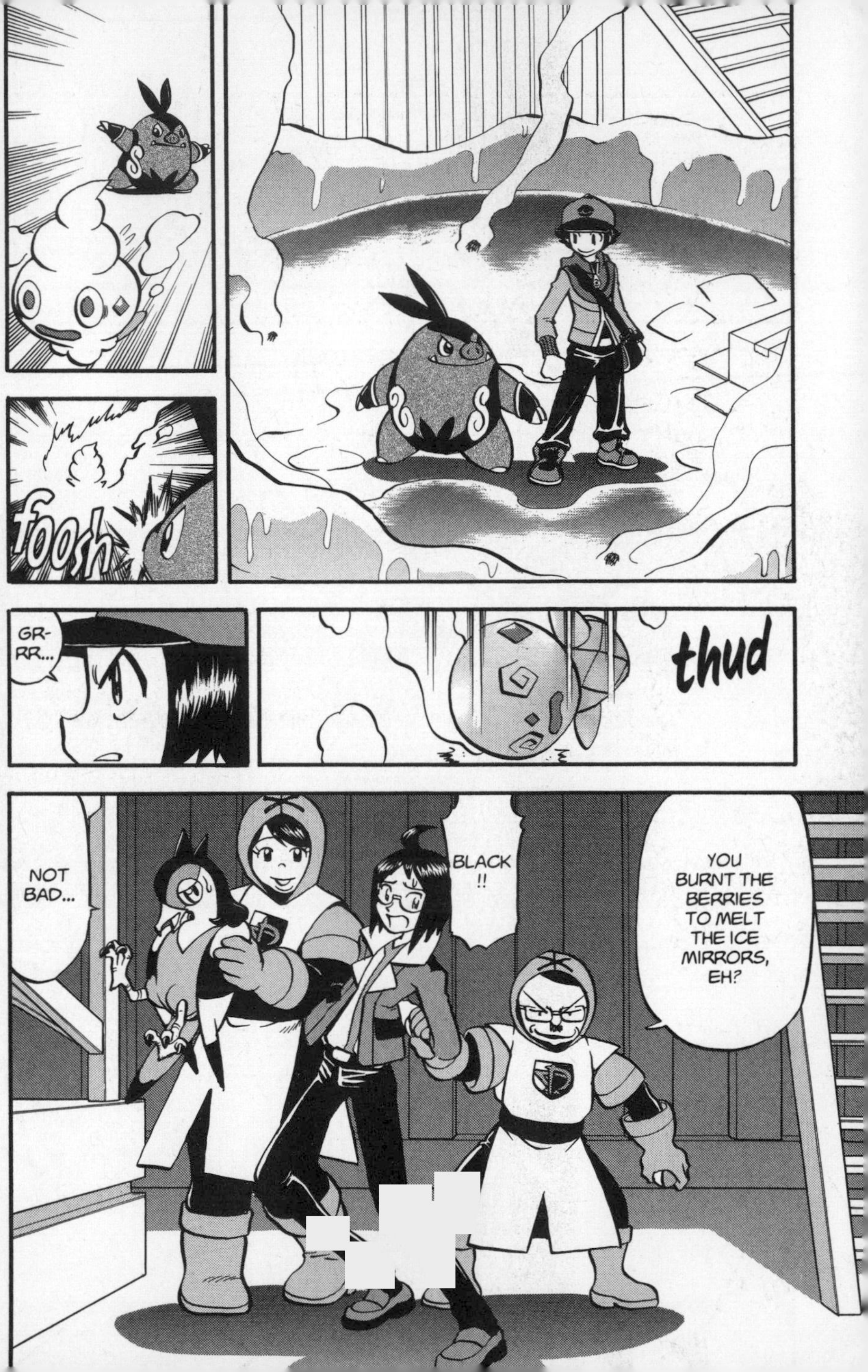
foosh
thud
GR-RR...
YOU BURNT THE BERRIES TO MELT THE ICE MIRRORS, EH?
BLACK !!
NOT BAD...

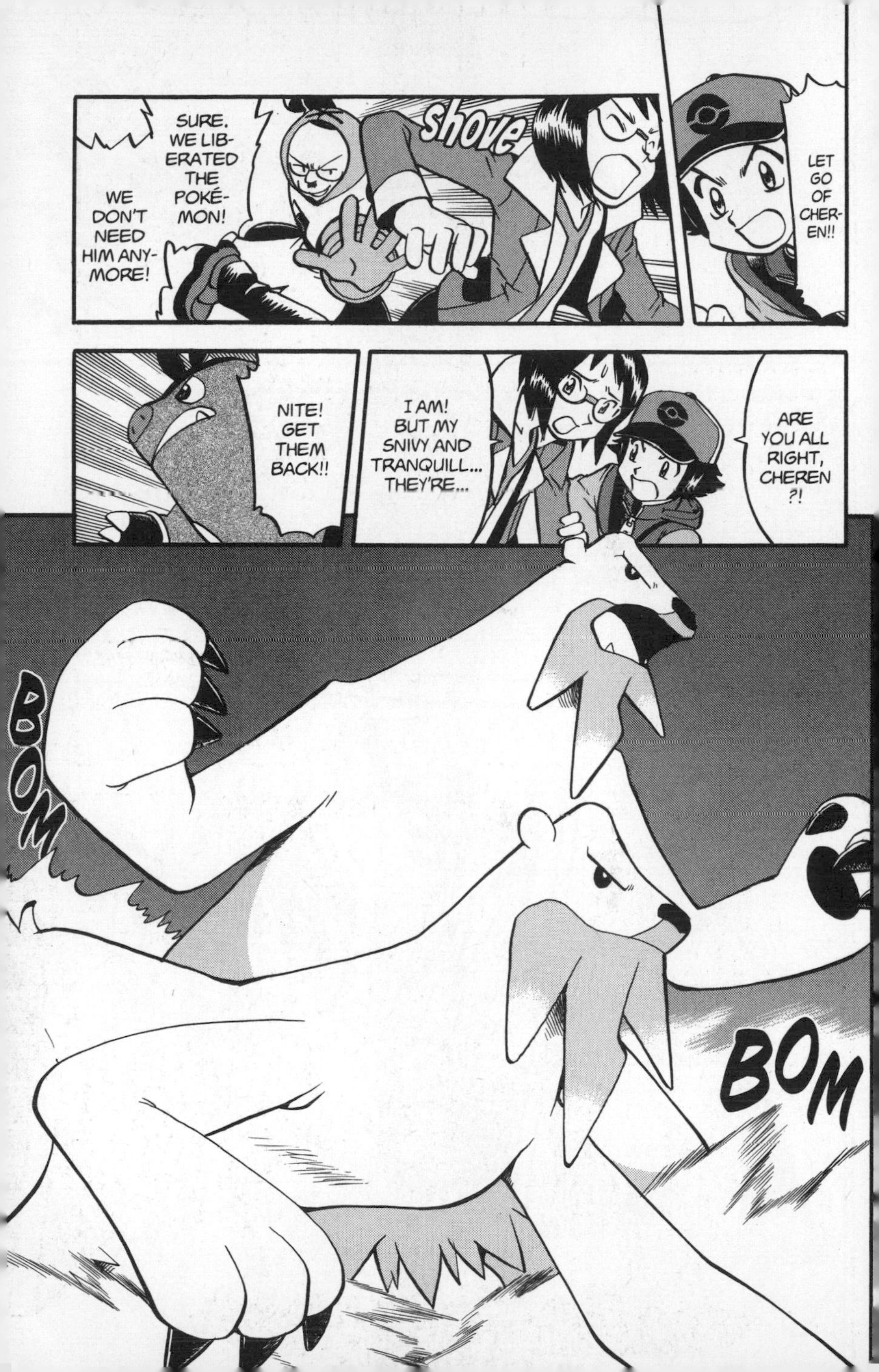
LET GO OF CHEREN!!
SHOVE
SURE. WE LIBERATED THE POKÉMON!
WE DON'T NEED HIM ANYMORE!
ARE YOU ALL RIGHT, CHEREN?!
I AM! BUT MY SNIVY AND TRANQUILL... THEY'RE...
NITE! GET THEM BACK!!
BOM
BOM

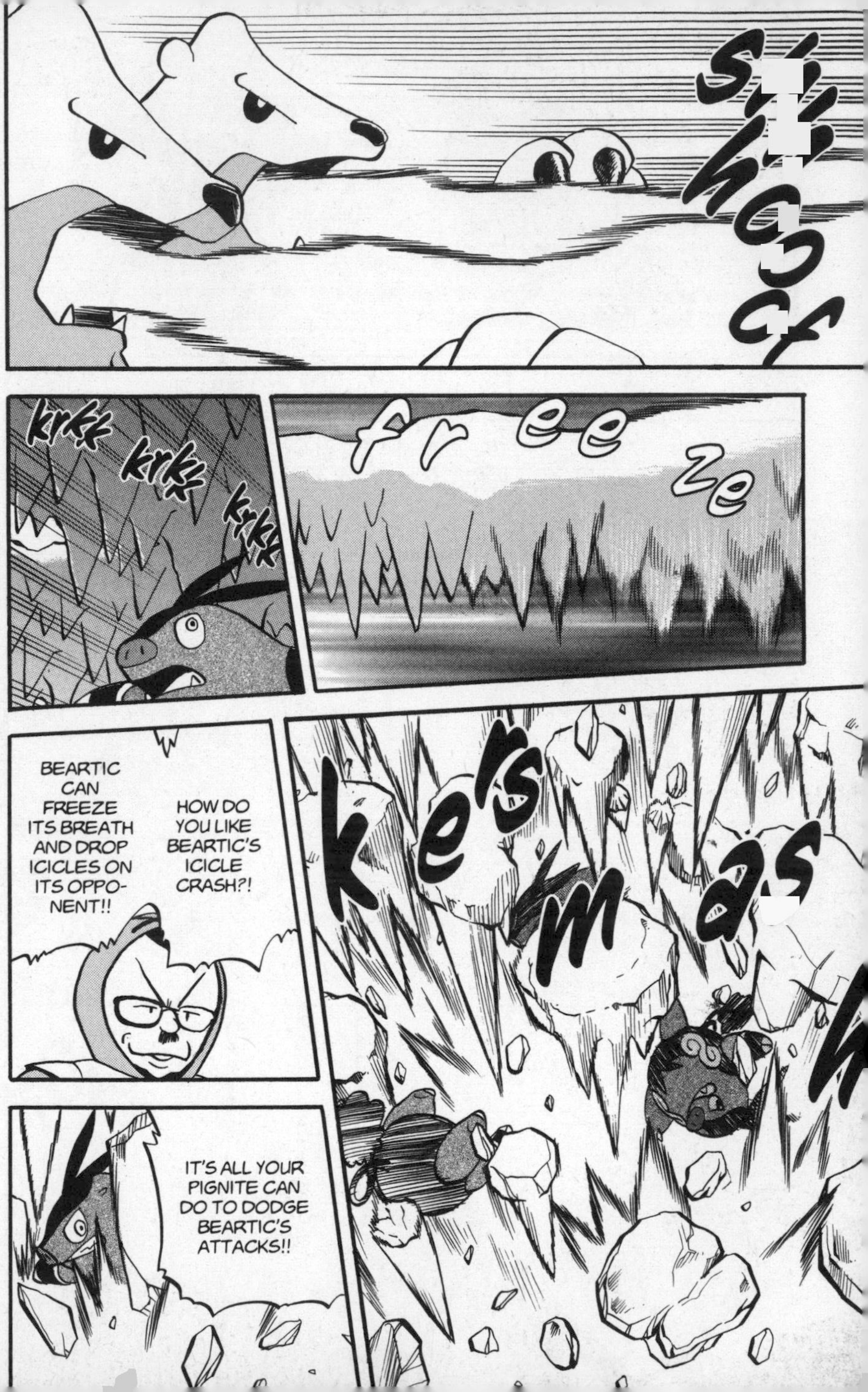
freeze
krkk
krkk
krkk
HOW DO YOU LIKE BEARTIC'S ICICLE CRASH?!
BEARTIC CAN FREEZE ITS BREATH AND DROP ICICLES ON ITS OPPONENT!!
IT'S ALL YOUR PIGNITE CAN DO TO DODGE BEARTIC'S ATTACKS!!

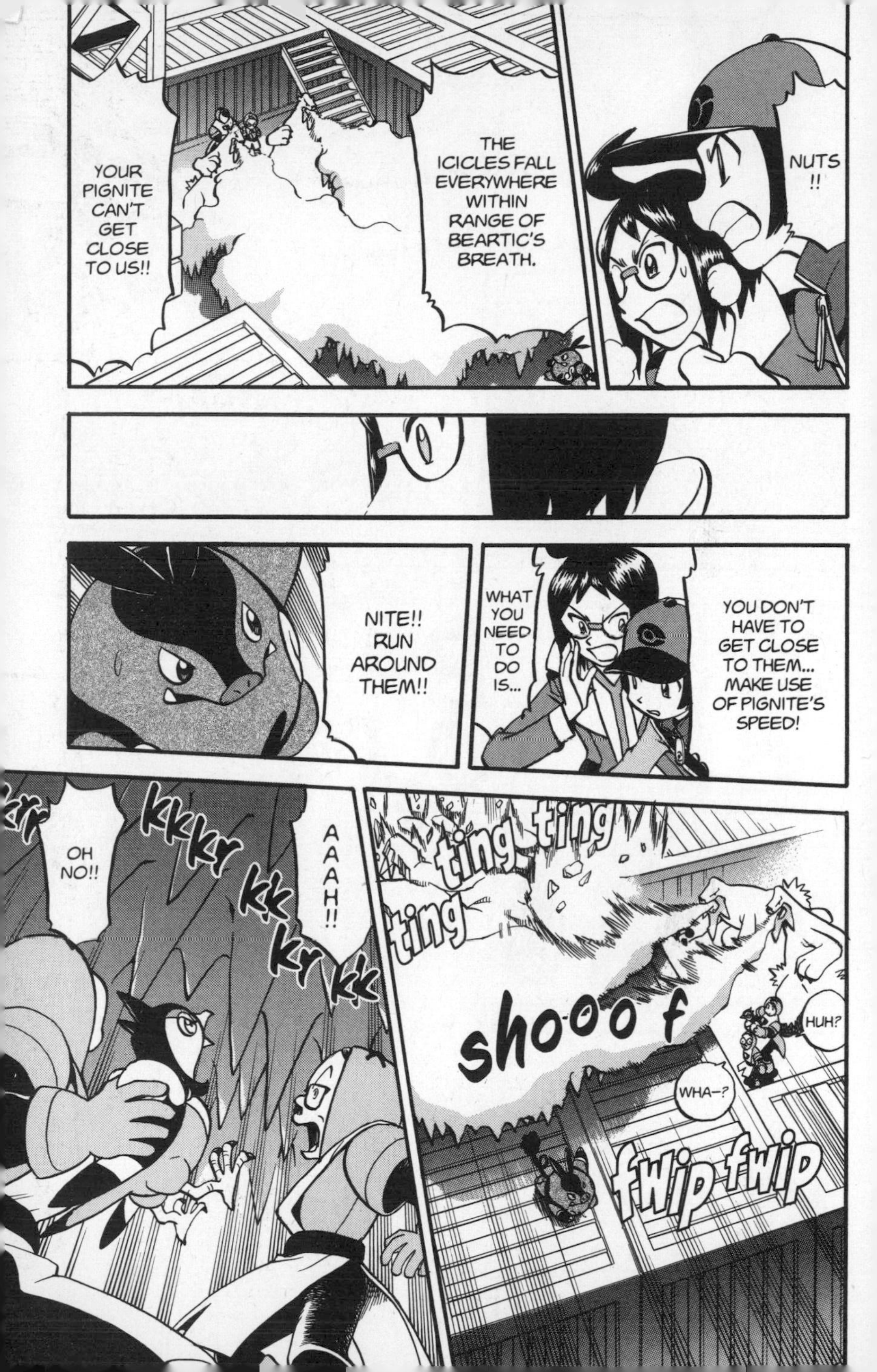
NUTS !!
THE ICICLES FALL EVERYWHERE WITHIN RANGE OF BEARTIC'S BREATH.
YOUR PIGNITE CAN'T GET CLOSE TO US!!
YOU DON'T HAVE TO GET CLOSE TO THEM... MAKE USE OF PIGNITE'S SPEED!
WHAT YOU NEED TO DO IS...
NITE!! RUN AROUND THEM!!
ting ting
ting
HUH?
shoooof
WHA-?
fwip fwip
AAAAH!!
kkkr
kk
kr
kk
OH NO!!

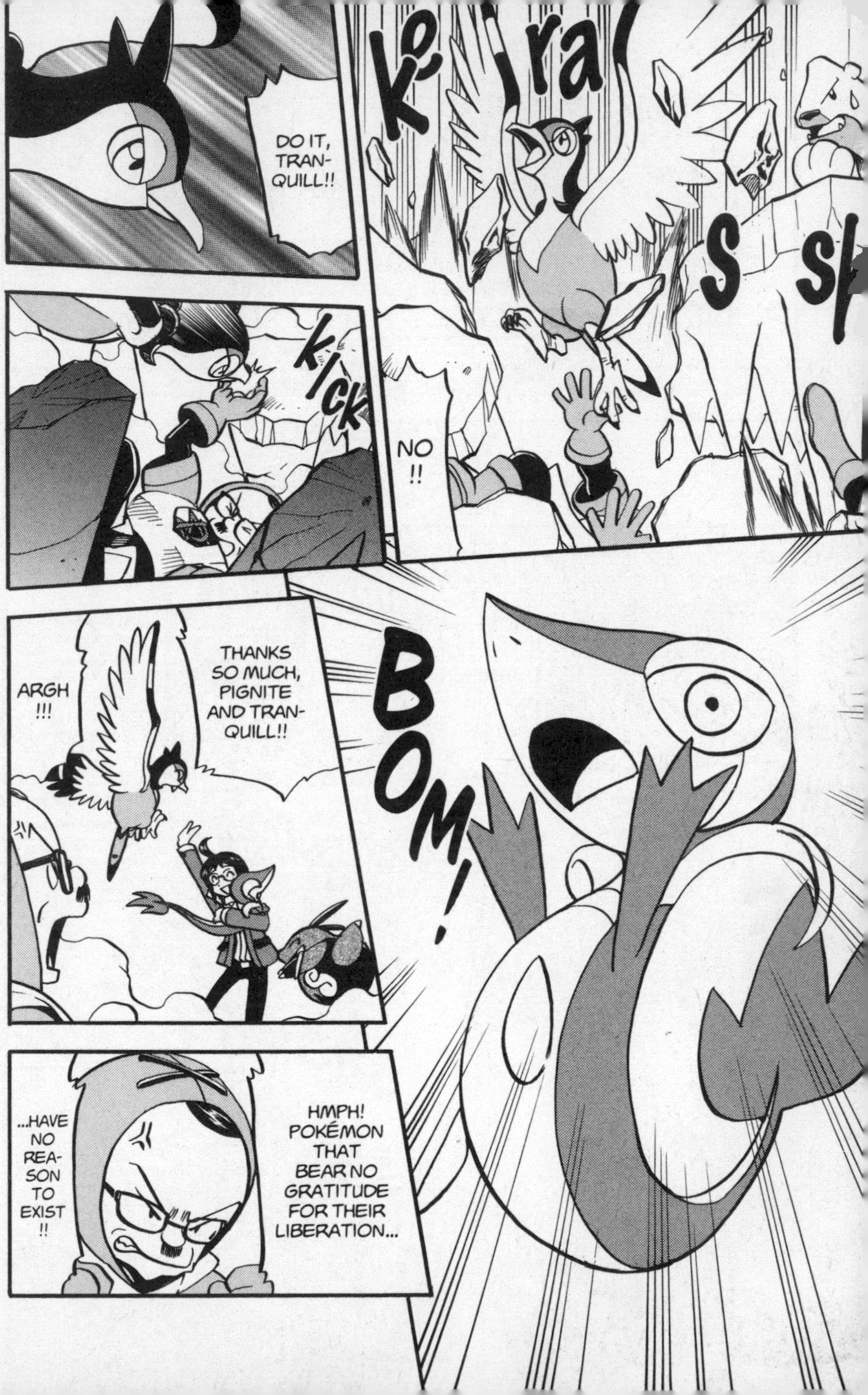

ke
ra
S sh
NO !!
DO IT, TRAN-QUILL!!
KICK
BOOM!
THANKS SO MUCH, PIGNITE AND TRAN-QUILL!!
ARGH !!!
HMPH! POKÉMON THAT BEAR NO GRATITUDE FOR THEIR LIBERATION...
...HAVE NO REA-SON TO EXIST !!

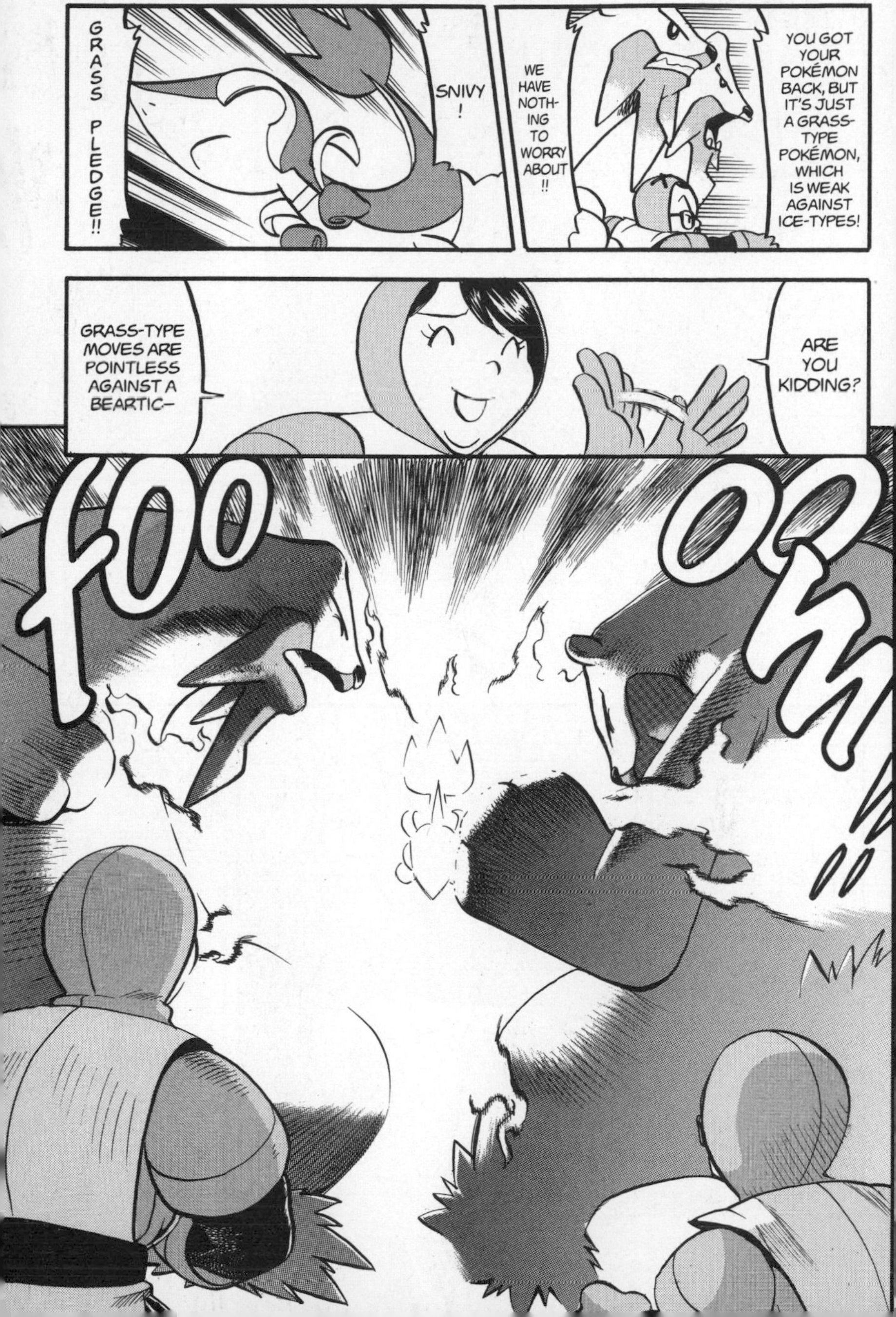
YOU GOT YOUR POKÉMON BACK, BUT IT'S JUST A GRASS-TYPE POKÉMON, WHICH IS WEAK AGAINST ICE-TYPES!
WE HAVE NOTHING TO WORRY ABOUT!!
SNIVY!
GRASS PLEDGE!!
ARE YOU KIDDING?
GRASS-TYPE MOVES ARE POINTLESS AGAINST A BEARTIC—
FOOOOM!!

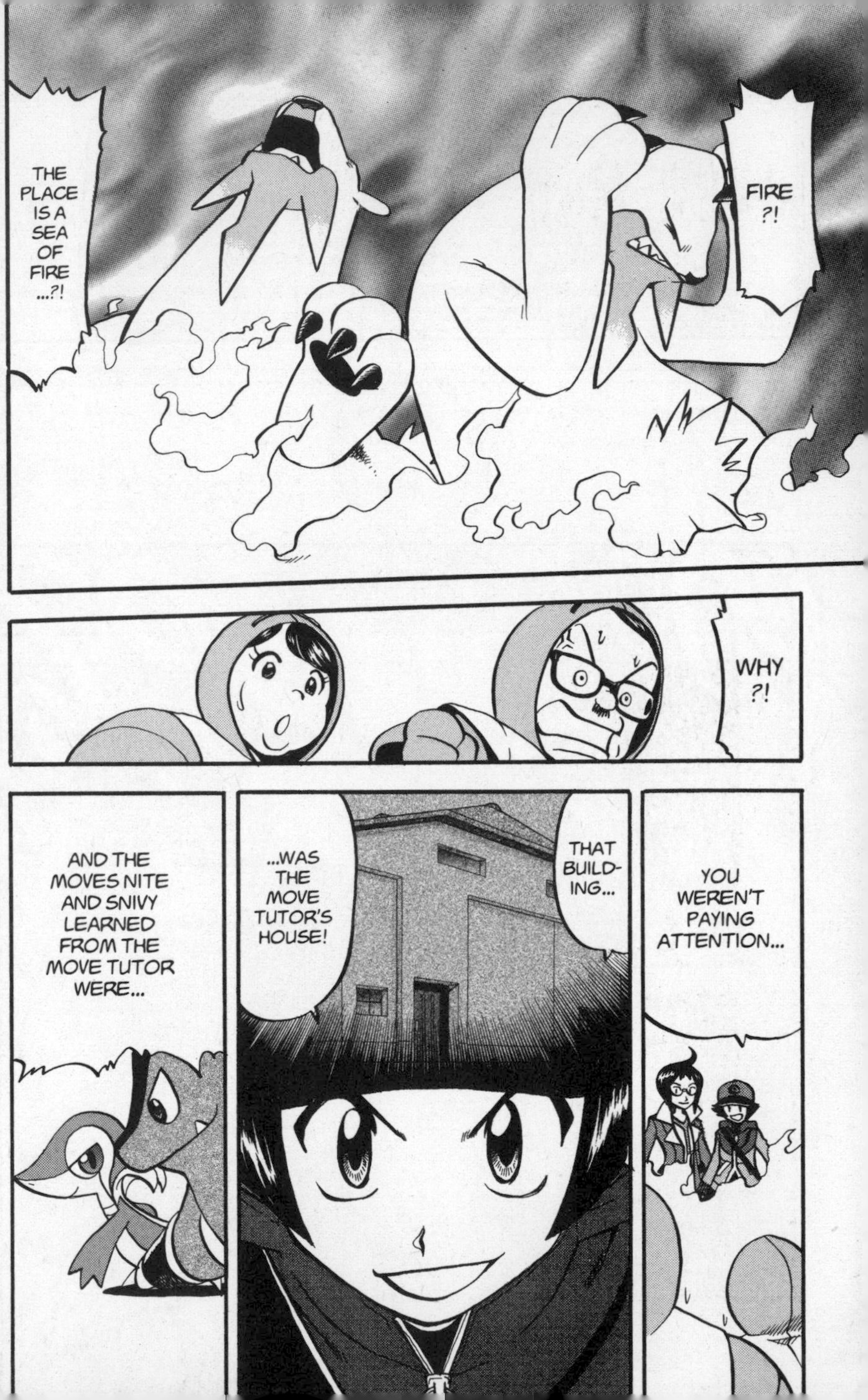
FIRE ?!
THE PLACE IS A SEA OF FIRE ...?!
WHY ?!
YOU WEREN'T PAYING ATTENTION...
THAT BUILD-ING...
...WAS THE MOVE TUTOR'S HOUSE!
AND THE MOVES NITE AND SNIVY LEARNED FROM THE MOVE TUTOR WERE...

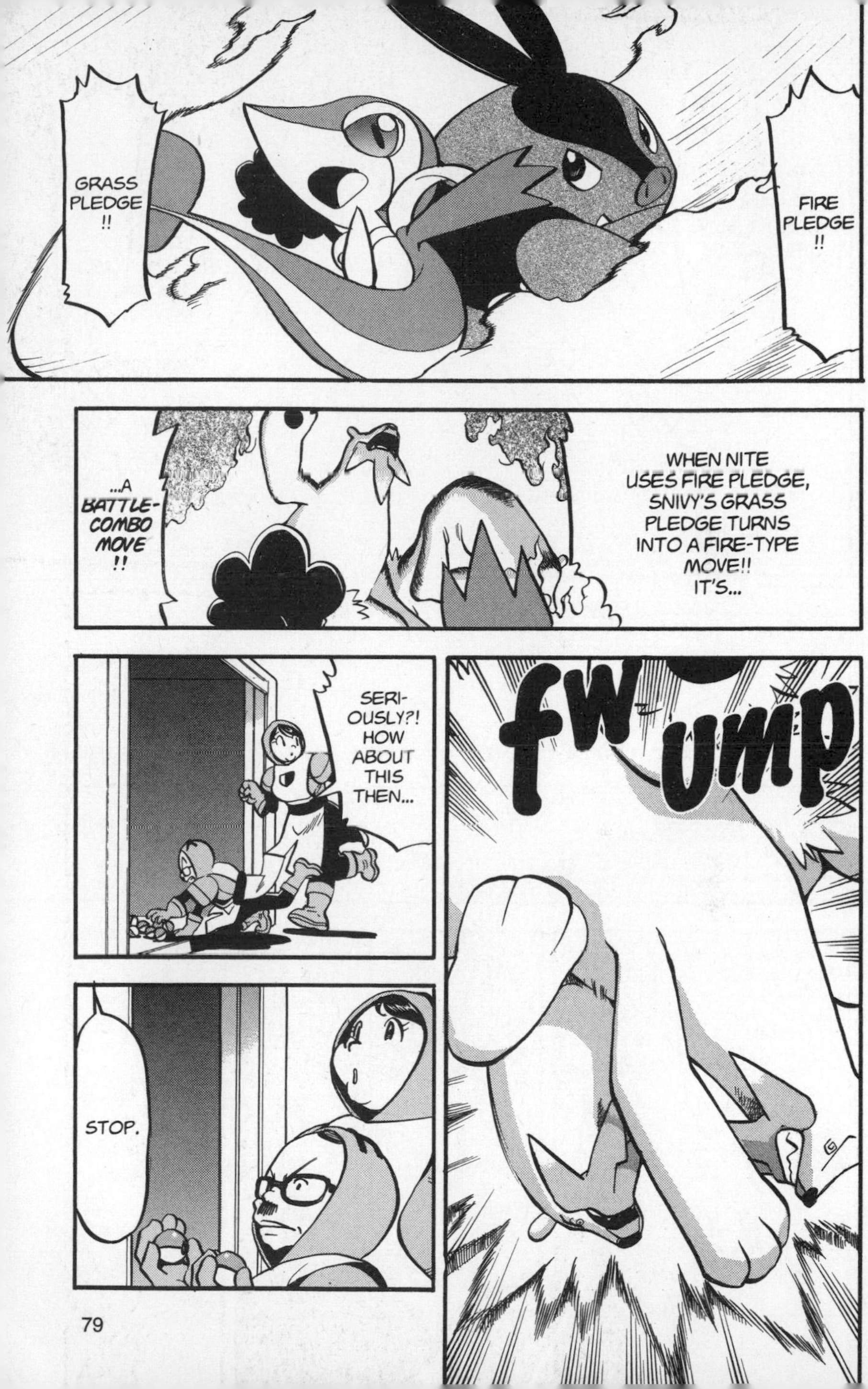
FIRE PLEDGE !!
GRASS PLEDGE !!
WHEN NITE USES FIRE PLEDGE, SNIVY'S GRASS PLEDGE TURNS INTO A FIRE-TYPE MOVE!! IT'S...
...A BATTLE-COMBO MOVE !!
FWUMP
SERI-OUSLY?! HOW ABOUT THIS THEN...
STOP.

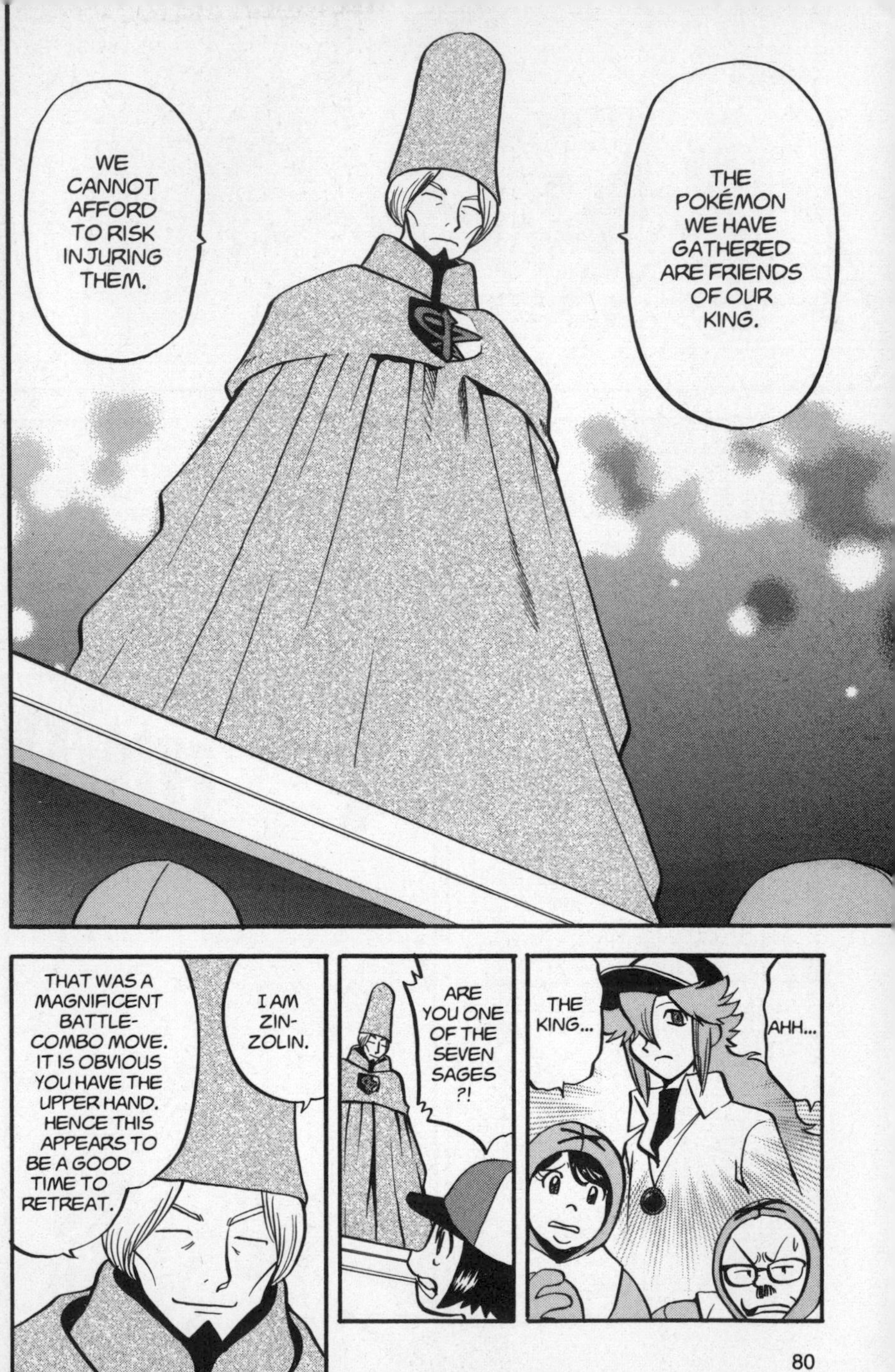
THE POKÉMON WE HAVE GATHERED ARE FRIENDS OF OUR KING.
WE CANNOT AFFORD TO RISK INJURING THEM.
AHH...
THE KING...
ARE YOU ONE OF THE SEVEN SAGES ?!
I AM ZIN-ZOLIN.
THAT WAS A MAGNIFICENT BATTLE-COMBO MOVE. IT IS OBVIOUS YOU HAVE THE UPPER HAND. HENCE THIS APPEARS TO BE A GOOD TIME TO RETREAT.

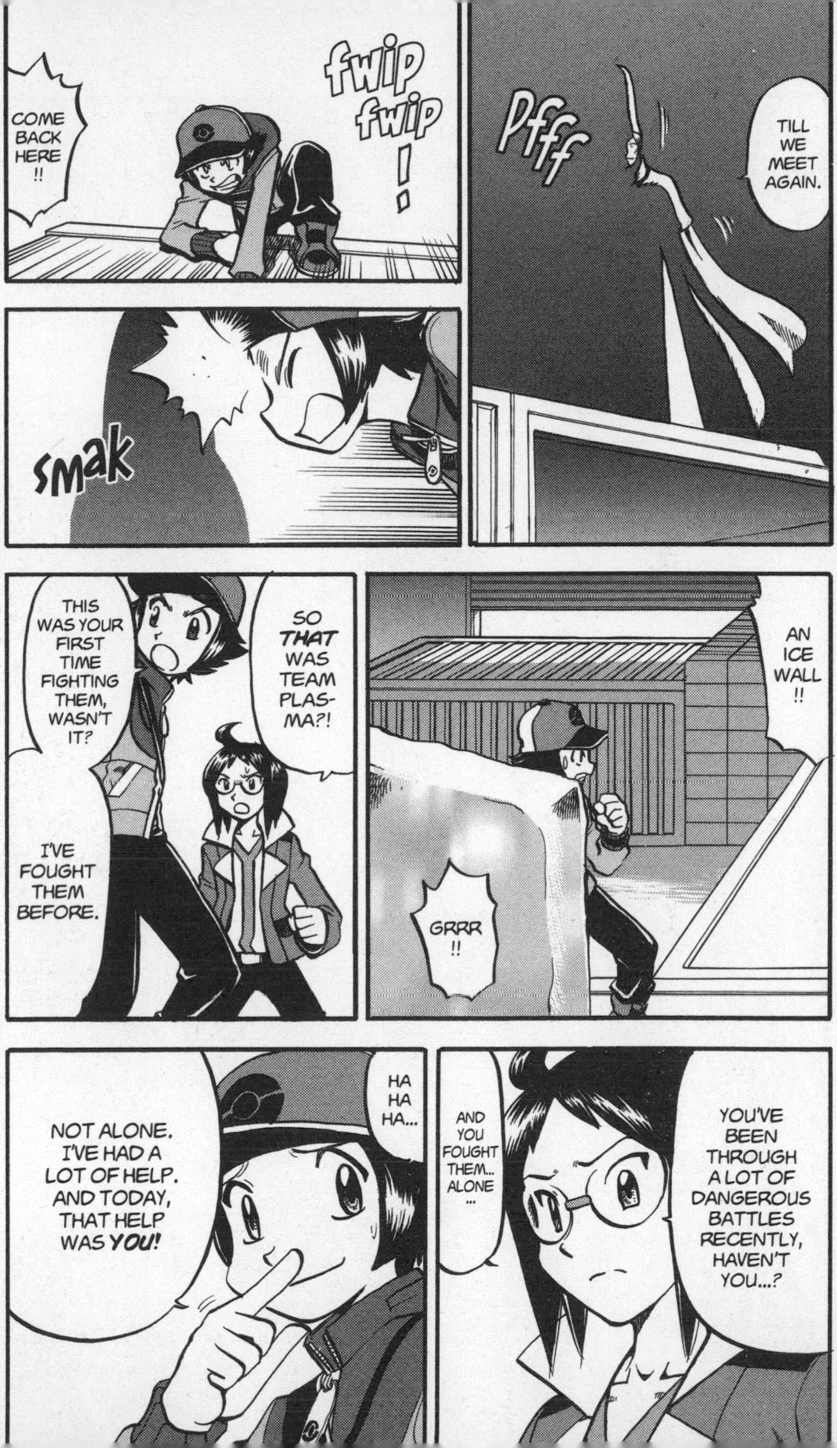
Pfff
TILL WE MEET AGAIN.
fwip fwip!
COME BACK HERE!!
SMAK
AN ICE WALL!!
GRRR!!
SO THAT WAS TEAM PLASMA?!
THIS WAS YOUR FIRST TIME FIGHTING THEM, WASN'T IT?
I'VE FOUGHT THEM BEFORE.
YOU'VE BEEN THROUGH A LOT OF DANGEROUS BATTLES RECENTLY, HAVEN'T YOU...?
AND YOU FOUGHT THEM... ALONE...
HA HA HA...
NOT ALONE. I'VE HAD A LOT OF HELP. AND TODAY, THAT HELP WAS YOU!

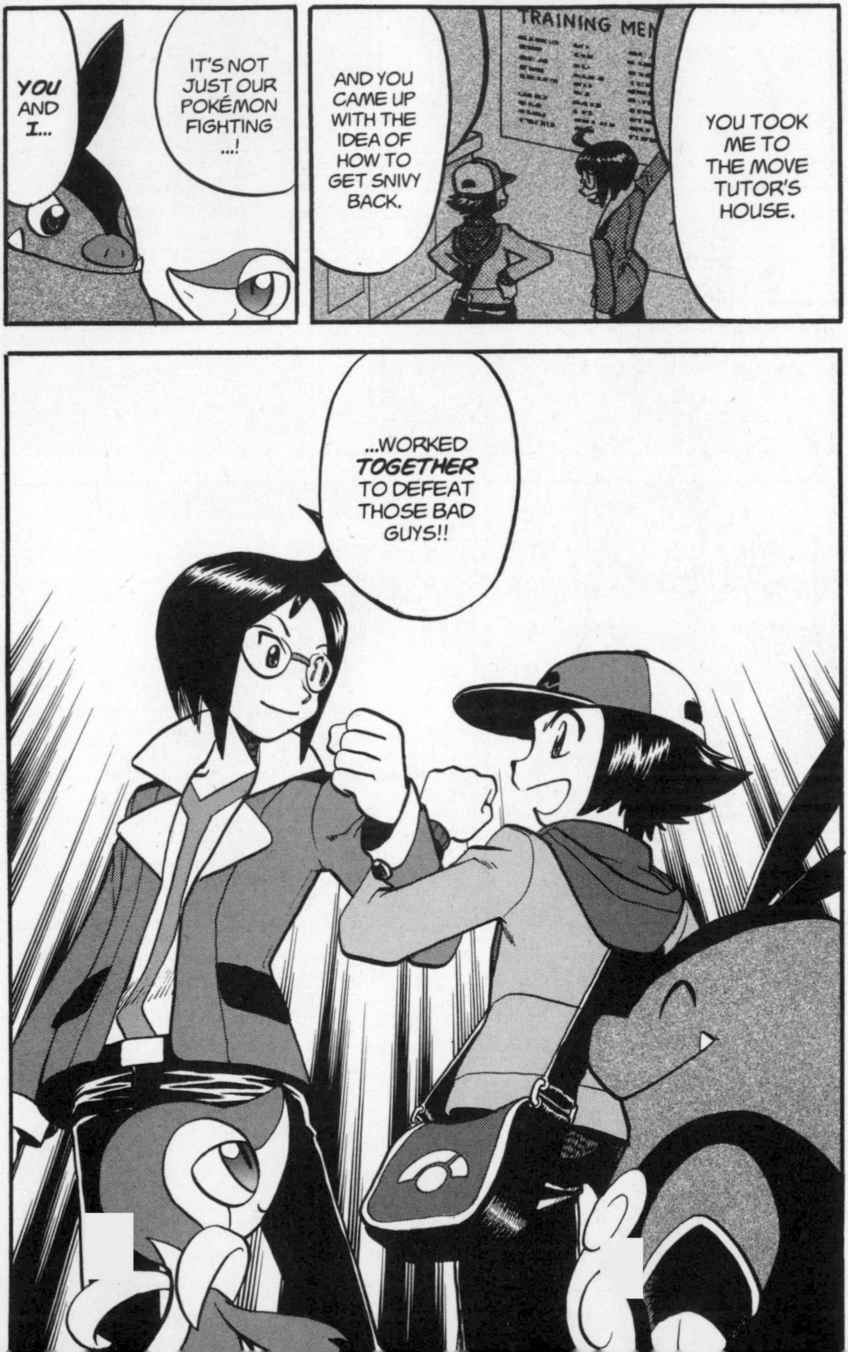
YOU TOOK ME TO THE MOVE TUTOR'S HOUSE.
TRAINING MEN
AND YOU CAME UP WITH THE IDEA OF HOW TO GET SNIVY BACK.
IT'S NOT JUST OUR POKÉMON FIGHTING ...!
YOU AND I...
...WORKED ***TOGETHER*** TO DEFEAT THOSE BAD GUYS!!

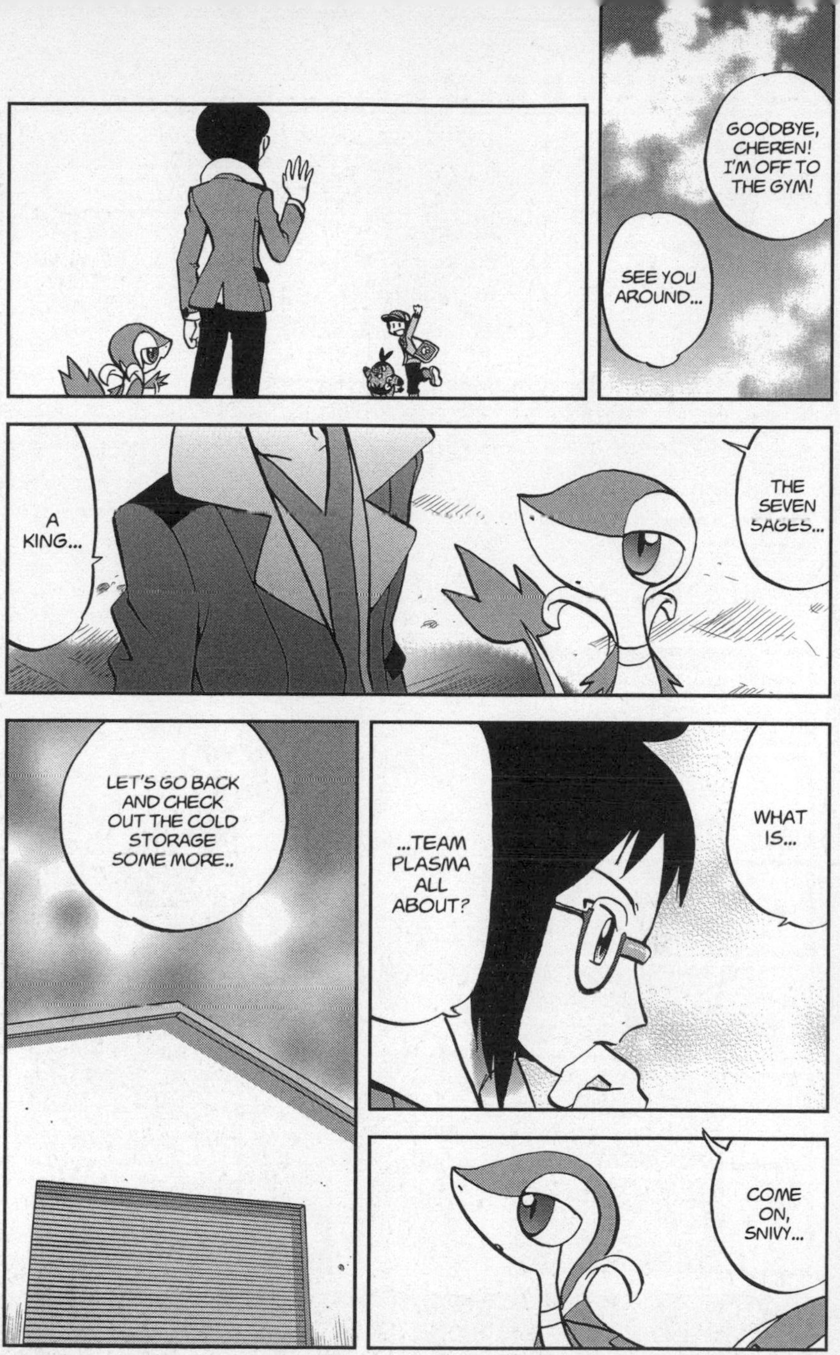
GOODBYE, CHEREN! I'M OFF TO THE GYM!
SEE YOU AROUND...
THE SEVEN SAGES...
A KING...
WHAT IS...
...TEAM PLASMA ALL ABOUT?
COME ON, SNIVY...
LET'S GO BACK AND CHECK OUT THE COLD STORAGE SOME MORE..

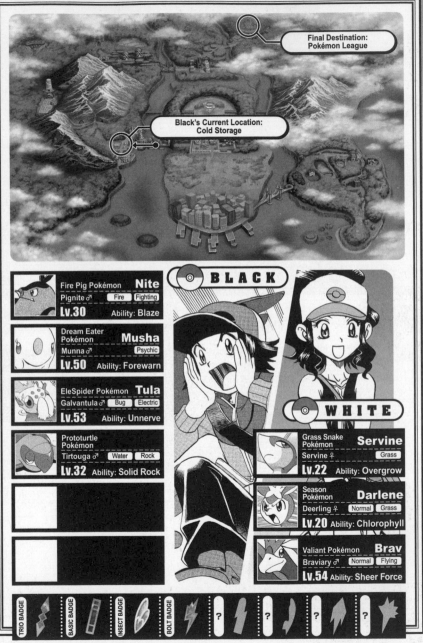

ADVENTURE MAP

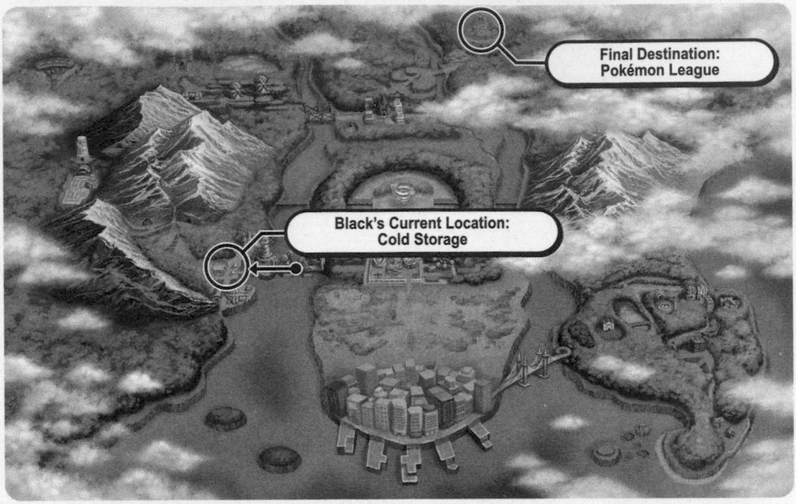
Final Destination: Pokémon League
Black's Current Location: Cold Storage

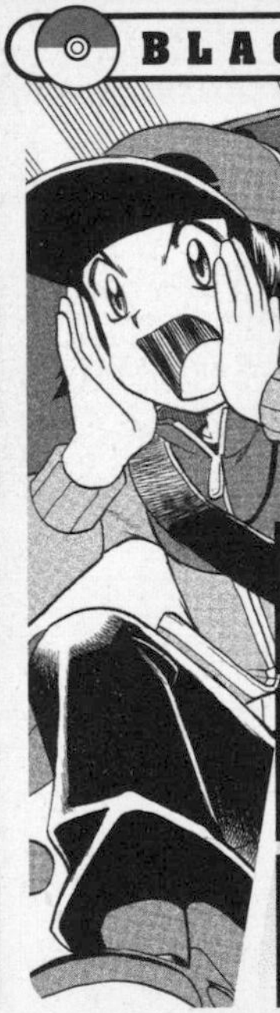
BLACK

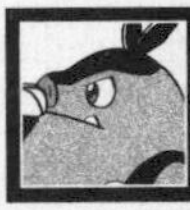

Nite
Fire Pig Pokémon
Pignite ♂ Fire Fighting
Lv.30 Ability: Blaze

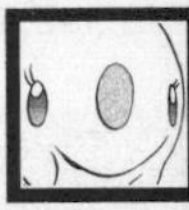

Musha
Dream Eater Pokémon
Munna ♂ Psychic
Lv.50 Ability: Forewarn

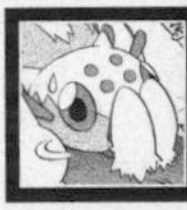

Tula
EleSpider Pokémon
Galvantula ♂ Bug Electric
Lv.53 Ability: Unnerve

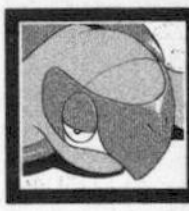

Prototurtle Pokémon
Tirtouga ♂ Water Rock
Lv.32 Ability: Solid Rock

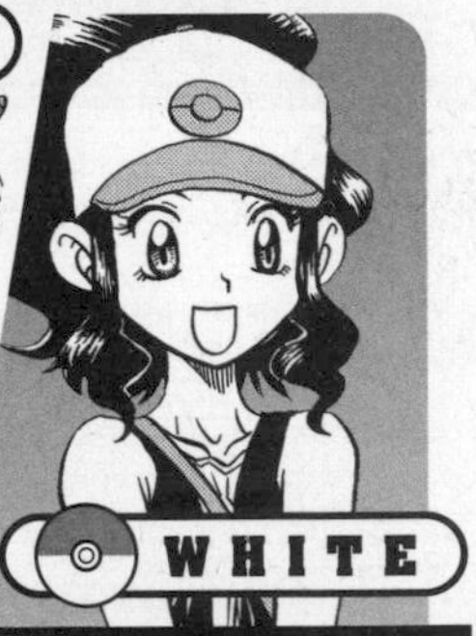
WHITE

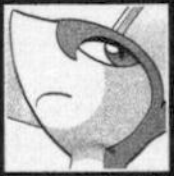

Servine
Grass Snake Pokémon
Servine ♀ Grass
Lv.22 Ability: Overgrow

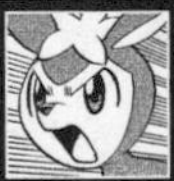

Darlene
Season Pokémon
Deerling ♀ Normal Grass
Lv.20 Ability: Chlorophyll

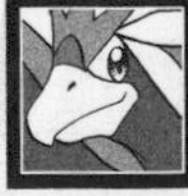

Brav
Valiant Pokémon
Braviary ♂ Normal Flying
Lv.54 Ability: Sheer Force

TRIO BADGE · BASIC BADGE · INSECT BADGE · BOLT BADGE · ? · ? · ? · ?

POKéMON ADVENTURES BLACK & WHITE

EXCADRILL

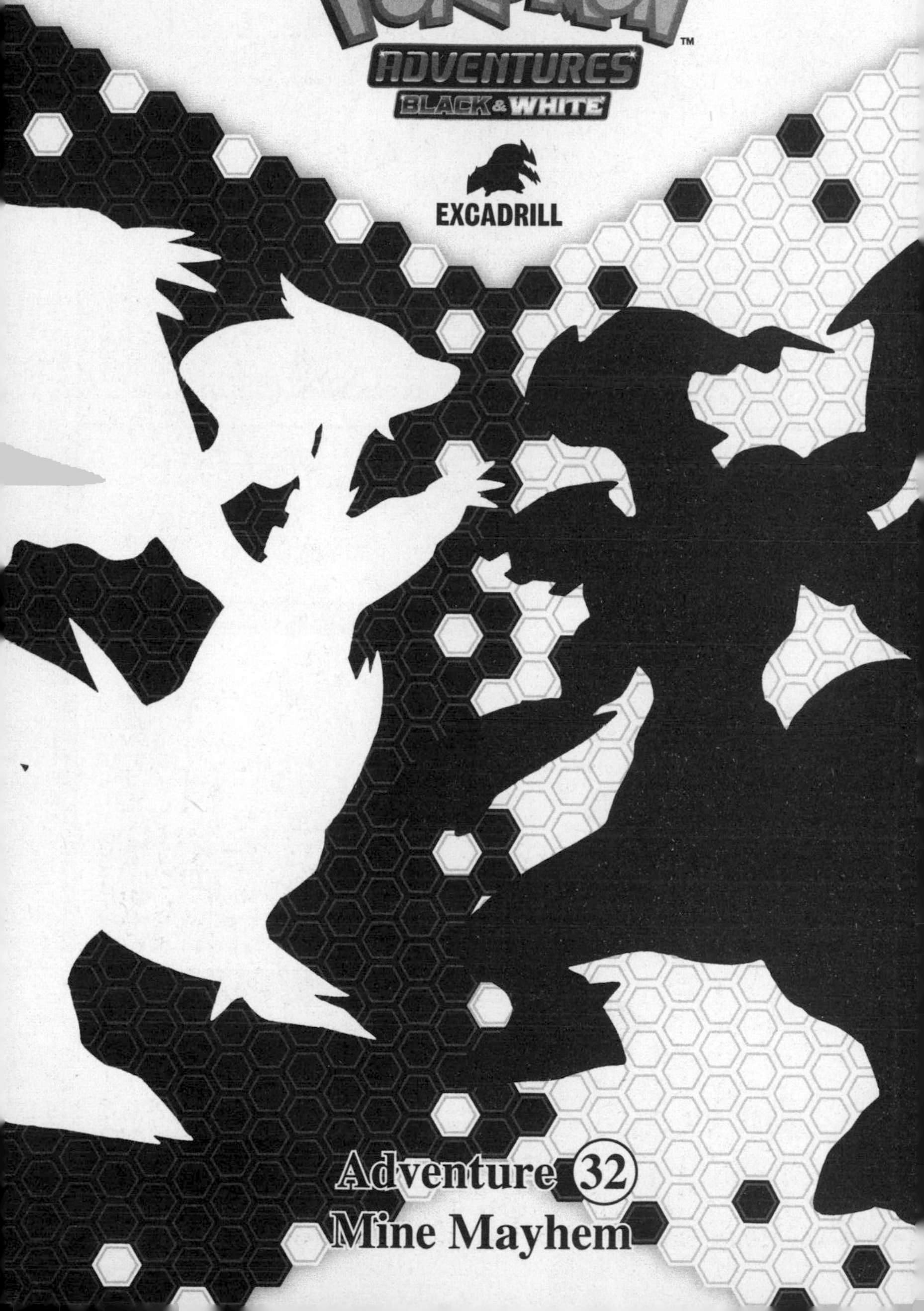

Adventure 32
Mine Mayhem

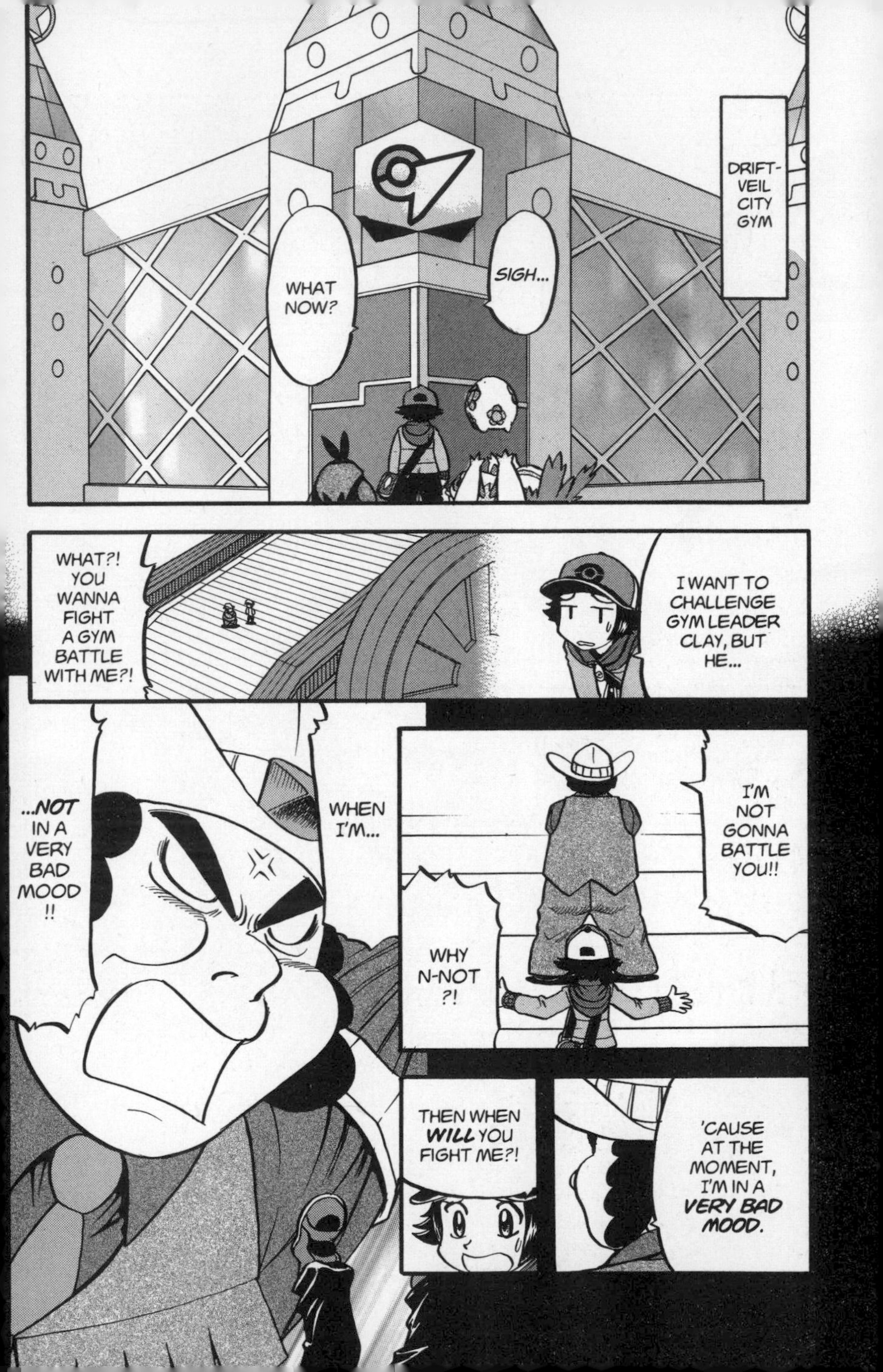
DRIFT-VEIL CITY GYM
SIGH...
WHAT NOW?
I WANT TO CHALLENGE GYM LEADER CLAY, BUT HE...
WHAT?! YOU WANNA FIGHT A GYM BATTLE WITH ME?!
I'M NOT GONNA BATTLE YOU!!
WHY N-NOT ?!
'CAUSE AT THE MOMENT, I'M IN A *VERY BAD MOOD*.
THEN WHEN *WILL* YOU FIGHT ME?!
WHEN I'M...
...*NOT* IN A VERY BAD MOOD !!

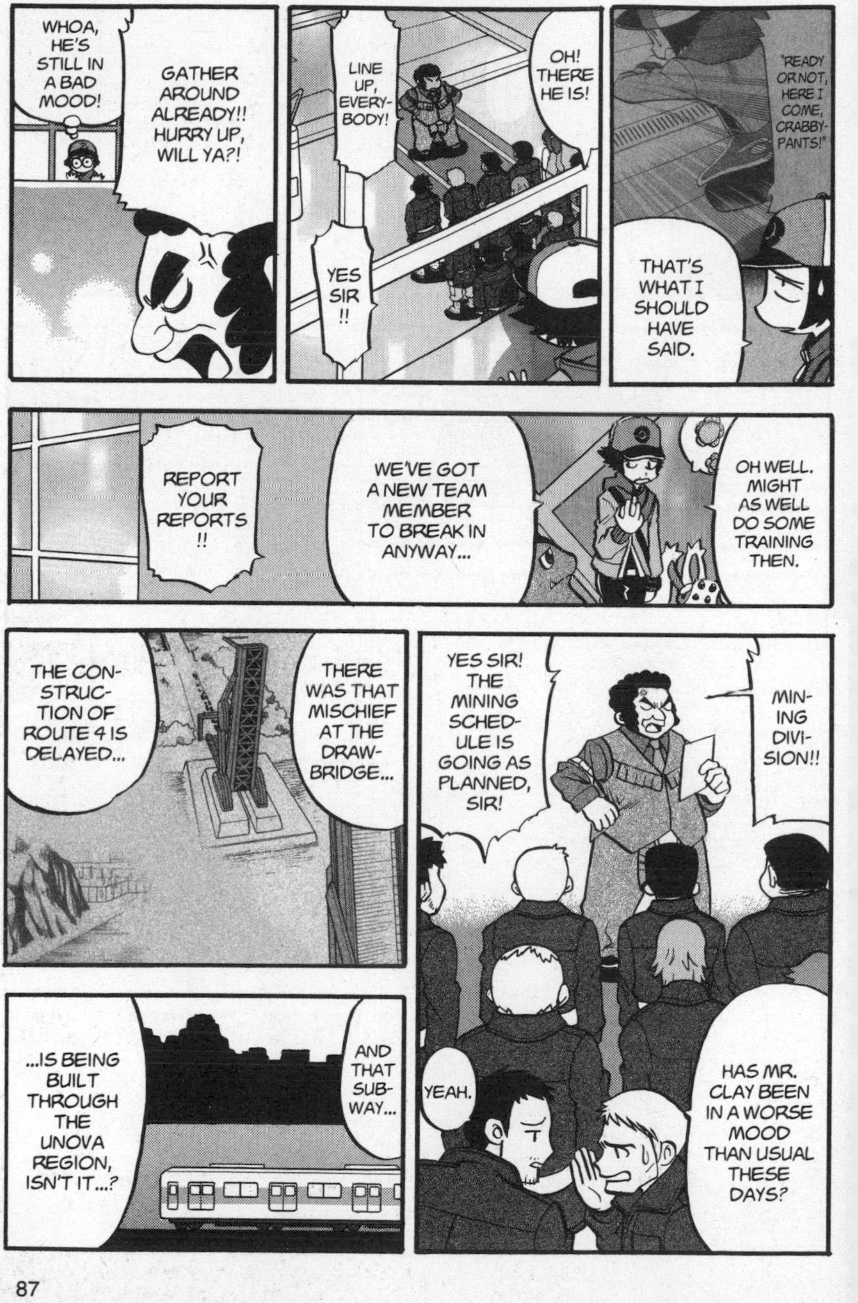
"READY OR NOT, HERE I COME, CRABBY-PANTS!"
THAT'S WHAT I SHOULD HAVE SAID.
OH! THERE HE IS!
LINE UP, EVERYBODY!
YES SIR!!
GATHER AROUND ALREADY!! HURRY UP, WILL YA?!
WHOA, HE'S STILL IN A BAD MOOD!
OH WELL. MIGHT AS WELL DO SOME TRAINING THEN.
WE'VE GOT A NEW TEAM MEMBER TO BREAK IN ANYWAY...
REPORT YOUR REPORTS!!
MINING DIVISION!!
YES SIR! THE MINING SCHEDULE IS GOING AS PLANNED, SIR!
HAS MR. CLAY BEEN IN A WORSE MOOD THAN USUAL THESE DAYS?
YEAH.
THERE WAS THAT MISCHIEF AT THE DRAWBRIDGE...
THE CONSTRUCTION OF ROUTE 4 IS DELAYED...
AND THAT SUBWAY...
...IS BEING BUILT THROUGH THE UNOVA REGION, ISN'T IT...?

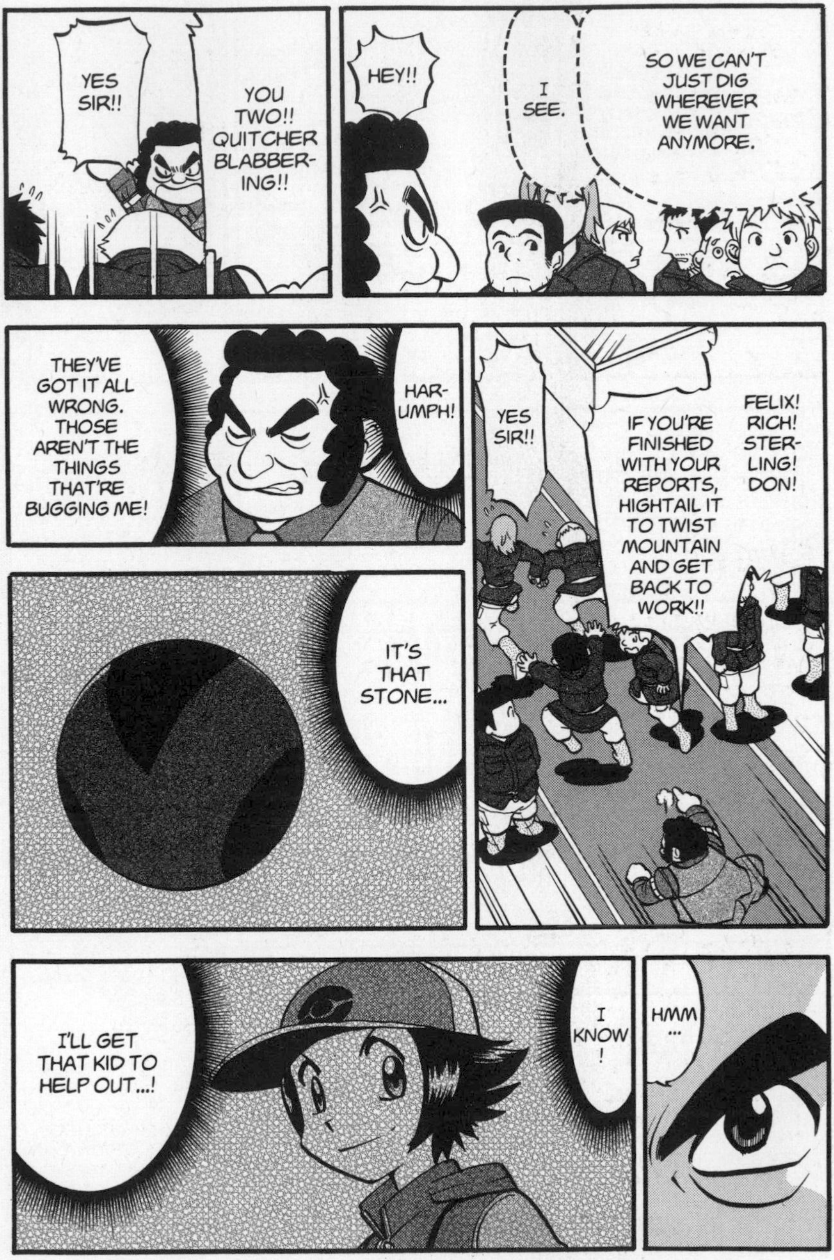
SO WE CAN'T JUST DIG WHEREVER WE WANT ANYMORE.
I SEE.
HEY!!
YOU TWO!! QUITCHER BLABBER-ING!!
YES SIR!!
FELIX! RICH! STER-LING! DON!
IF YOU'RE FINISHED WITH YOUR REPORTS, HIGHTAIL IT TO TWIST MOUNTAIN AND GET BACK TO WORK!!
YES SIR!!
HAR-UMPH!
THEY'VE GOT IT ALL WRONG. THOSE AREN'T THE THINGS THAT'RE BUGGING ME!
IT'S THAT STONE...
HMM ...
I KNOW !
I'LL GET THAT KID TO HELP OUT...!

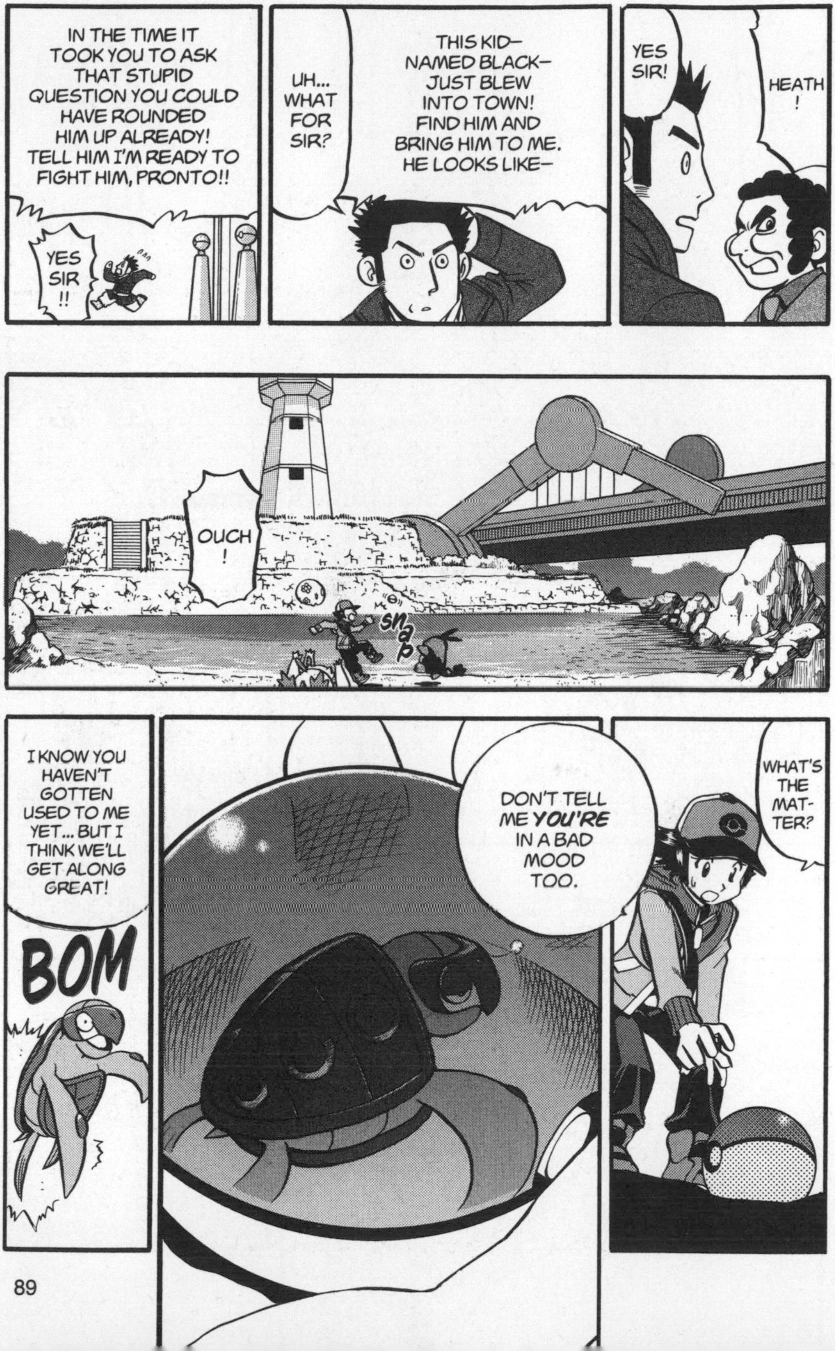
HEATH!
YES SIR!
THIS KID— NAMED BLACK— JUST BLEW INTO TOWN! FIND HIM AND BRING HIM TO ME. HE LOOKS LIKE—
UH... WHAT FOR SIR?
IN THE TIME IT TOOK YOU TO ASK THAT STUPID QUESTION YOU COULD HAVE ROUNDED HIM UP ALREADY! TELL HIM I'M READY TO FIGHT HIM, PRONTO!!
YES SIR!!
OUCH!
SNAP
WHAT'S THE MAT-TER?
DON'T TELL ME ***YOU'RE*** IN A BAD MOOD TOO.
I KNOW YOU HAVEN'T GOTTEN USED TO ME YET... BUT I THINK WE'LL GET ALONG GREAT!
BOM

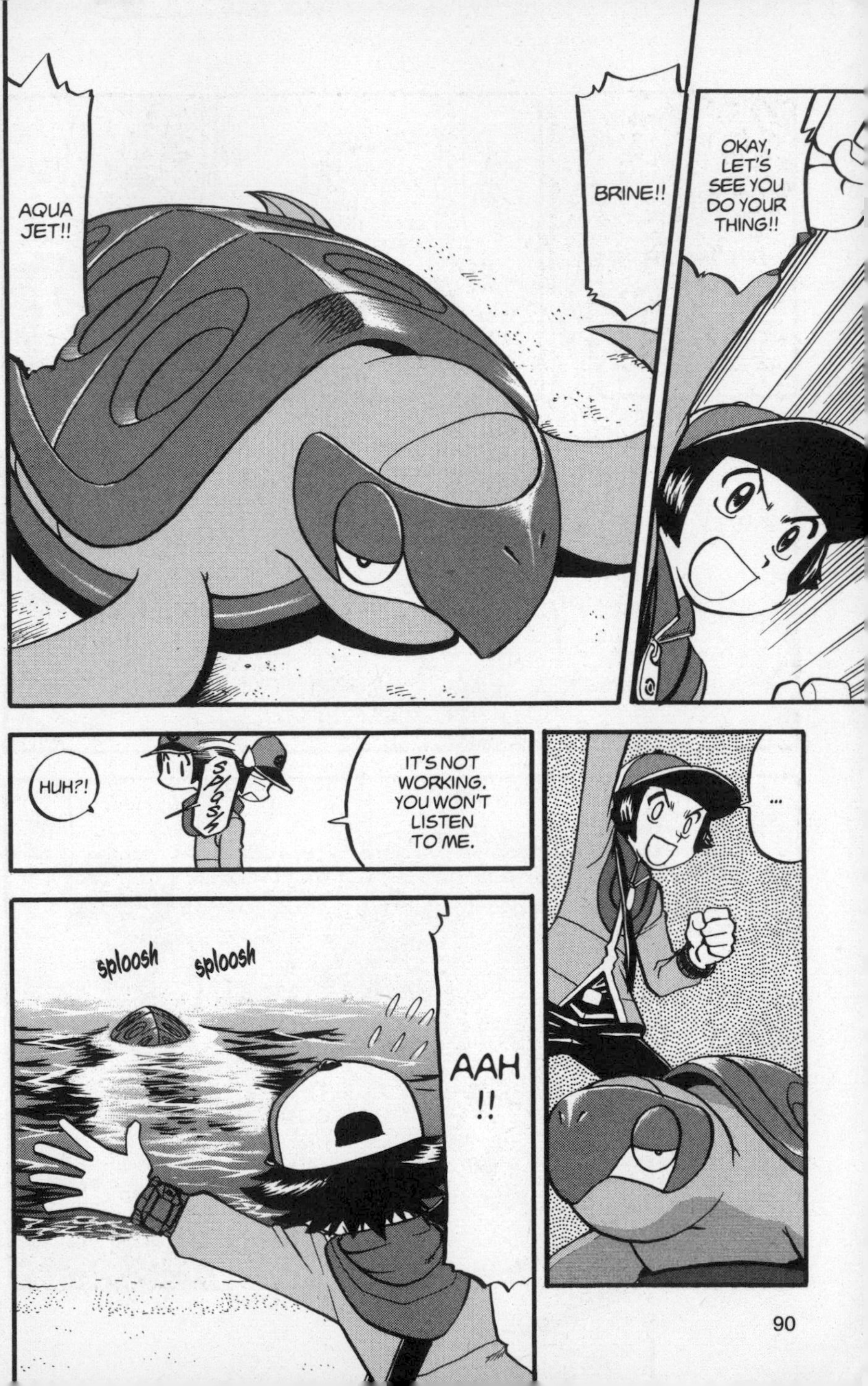
OKAY, LET'S SEE YOU DO YOUR THING!!
BRINE!!
AQUA JET!!
...
IT'S NOT WORKING. YOU WON'T LISTEN TO ME.
SPLOOSH
HUH?!
sploosh sploosh
AAH!!

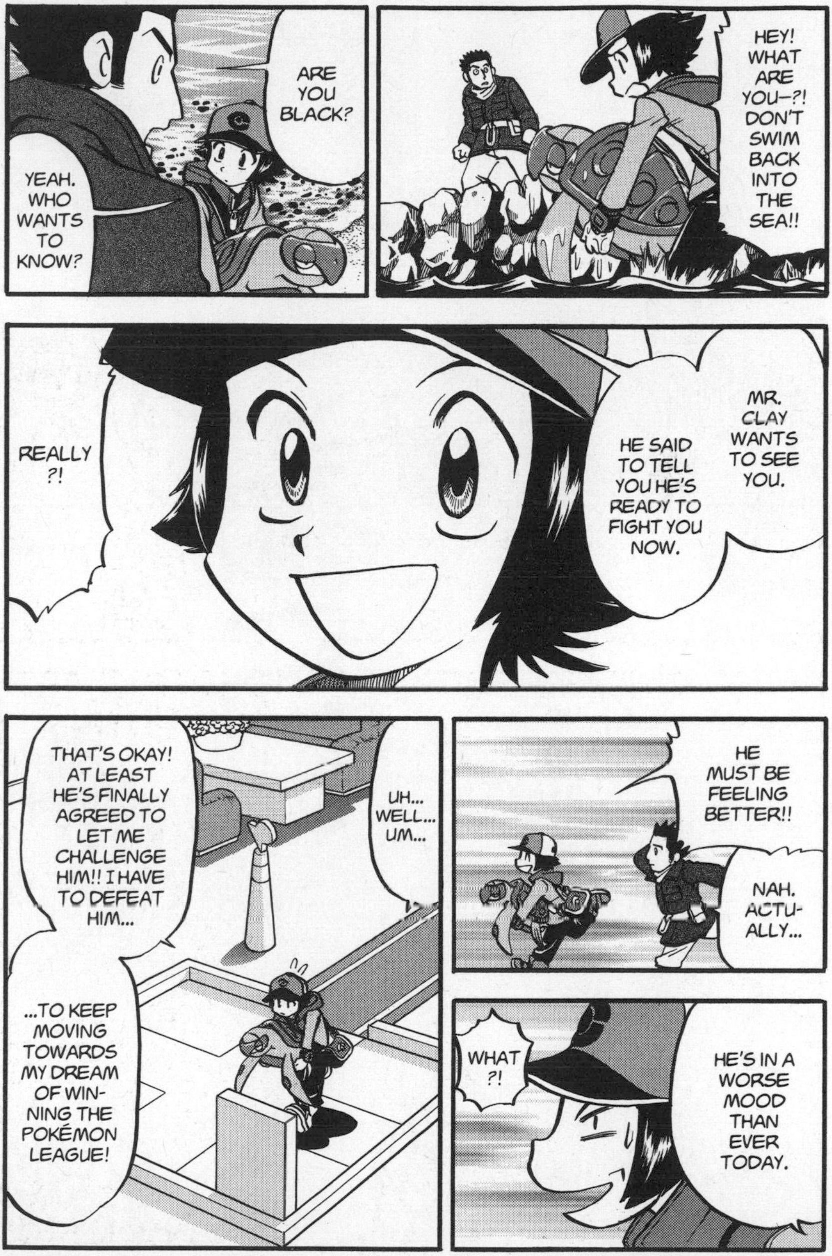
HEY! WHAT ARE YOU–?! DON'T SWIM BACK INTO THE SEA!!
ARE YOU BLACK?
YEAH. WHO WANTS TO KNOW?
MR. CLAY WANTS TO SEE YOU.
HE SAID TO TELL YOU HE'S READY TO FIGHT YOU NOW.
REALLY ?!
HE MUST BE FEELING BETTER!!
NAH. ACTU-ALLY...
HE'S IN A WORSE MOOD THAN EVER TODAY.
WHAT ?!
UH... WELL... UM...
THAT'S OKAY! AT LEAST HE'S FINALLY AGREED TO LET ME CHALLENGE HIM!! I HAVE TO DEFEAT HIM...
...TO KEEP MOVING TOWARDS MY DREAM OF WIN-NING THE POKÉMON LEAGUE!

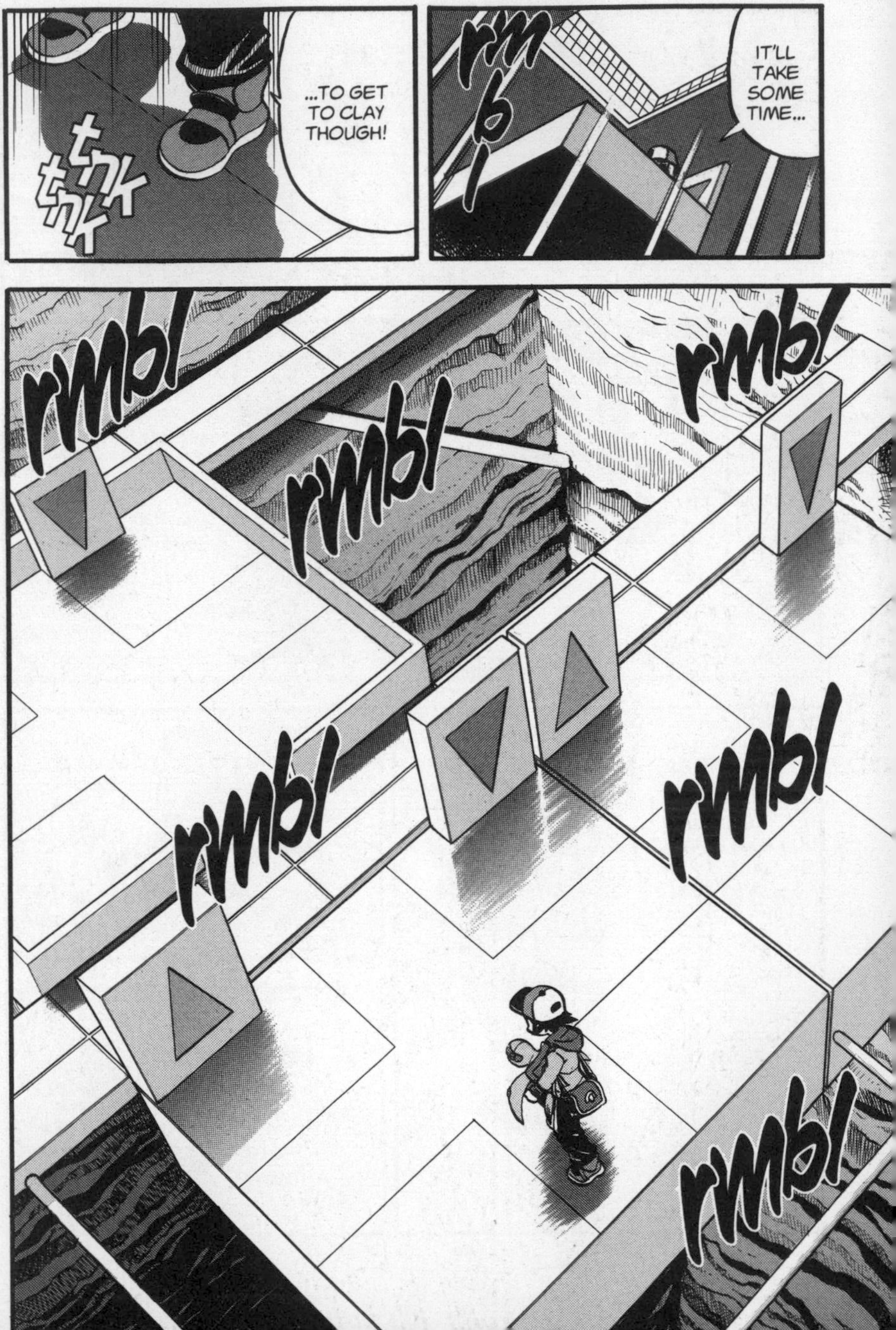
IT'LL TAKE SOME TIME...
...TO GET TO CLAY THOUGH!
rmb!
rmb!
rmb!
rmb!
rmb!
rmb!
rmb!

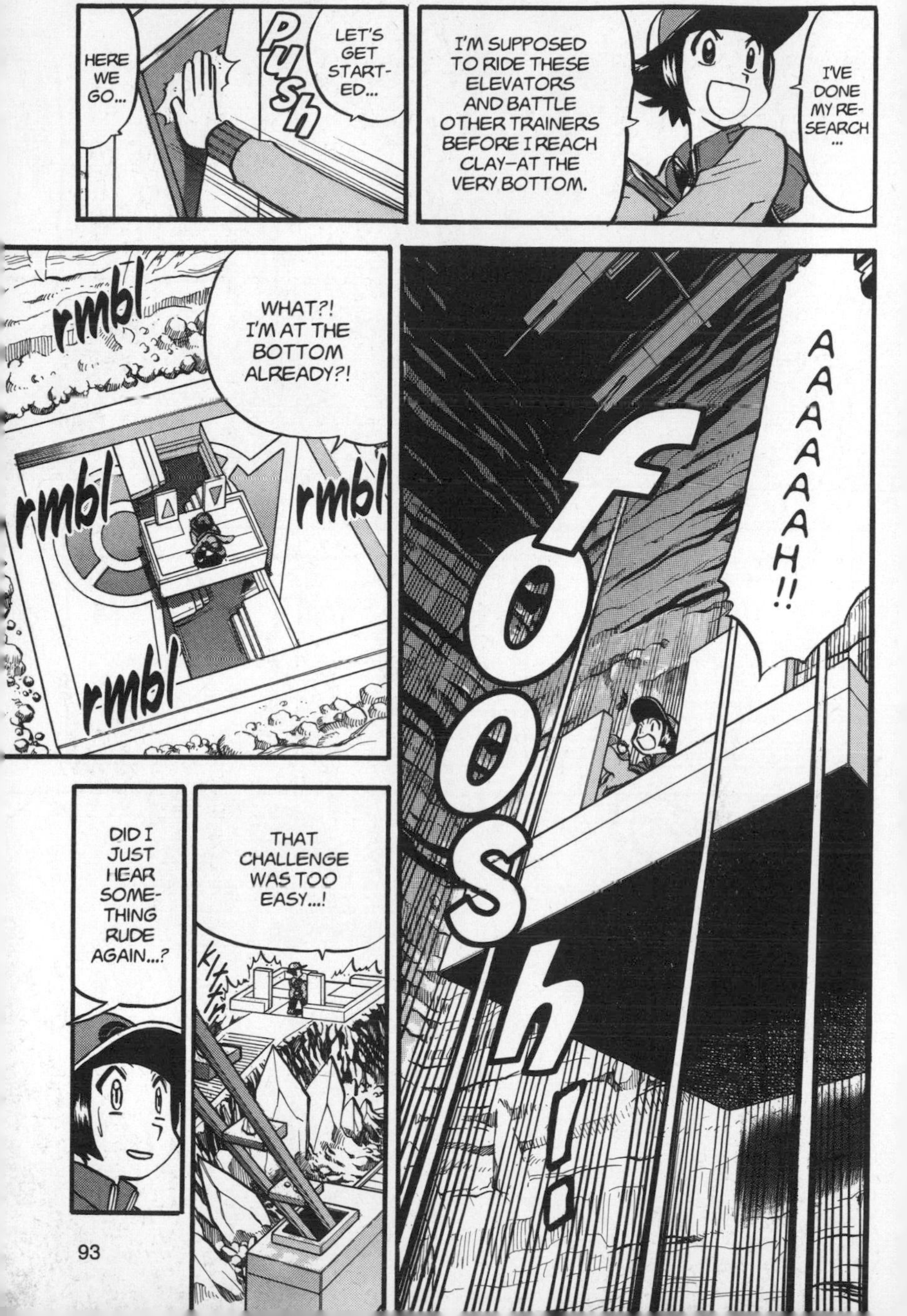
I'VE DONE MY RE-SEARCH...
I'M SUPPOSED TO RIDE THESE ELEVATORS AND BATTLE OTHER TRAINERS BEFORE I REACH CLAY—AT THE VERY BOTTOM.
LET'S GET START-ED...
Push
HERE WE GO...
AAAAAAAH!!
foosh!
WHAT?! I'M AT THE BOTTOM ALREADY?!
rmbl
rmbl
rmbl
rmbl
THAT CHALLENGE WAS TOO EASY...!
DID I JUST HEAR SOME-THING RUDE AGAIN...?

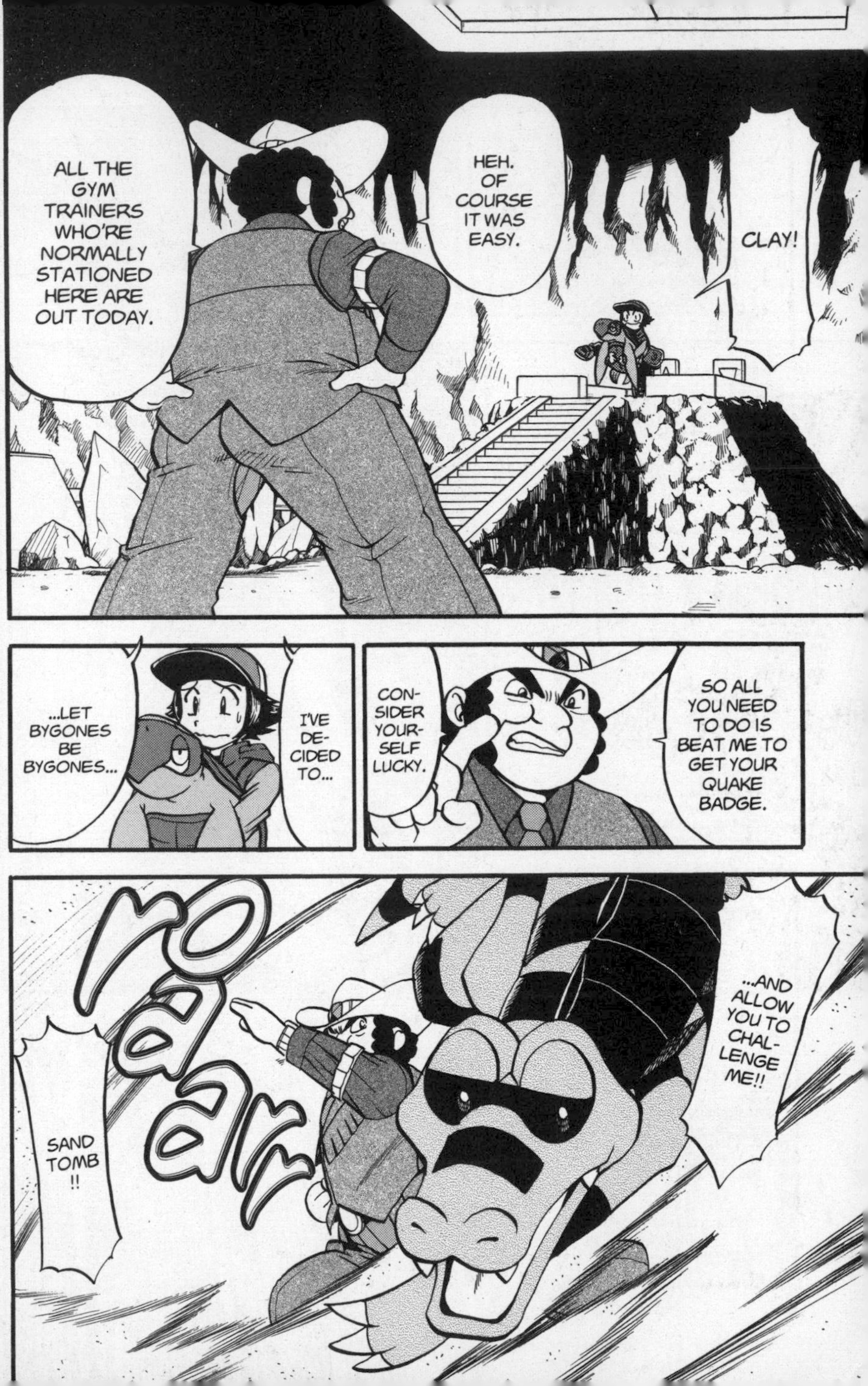
CLAY!
HEH. OF COURSE IT WAS EASY.
ALL THE GYM TRAINERS WHO'RE NORMALLY STATIONED HERE ARE OUT TODAY.
SO ALL YOU NEED TO DO IS BEAT ME TO GET YOUR QUAKE BADGE.
CONSIDER YOURSELF LUCKY.
I'VE DECIDED TO...
...LET BYGONES BE BYGONES...
...AND ALLOW YOU TO CHALLENGE ME!!
roaar
SAND TOMB!!

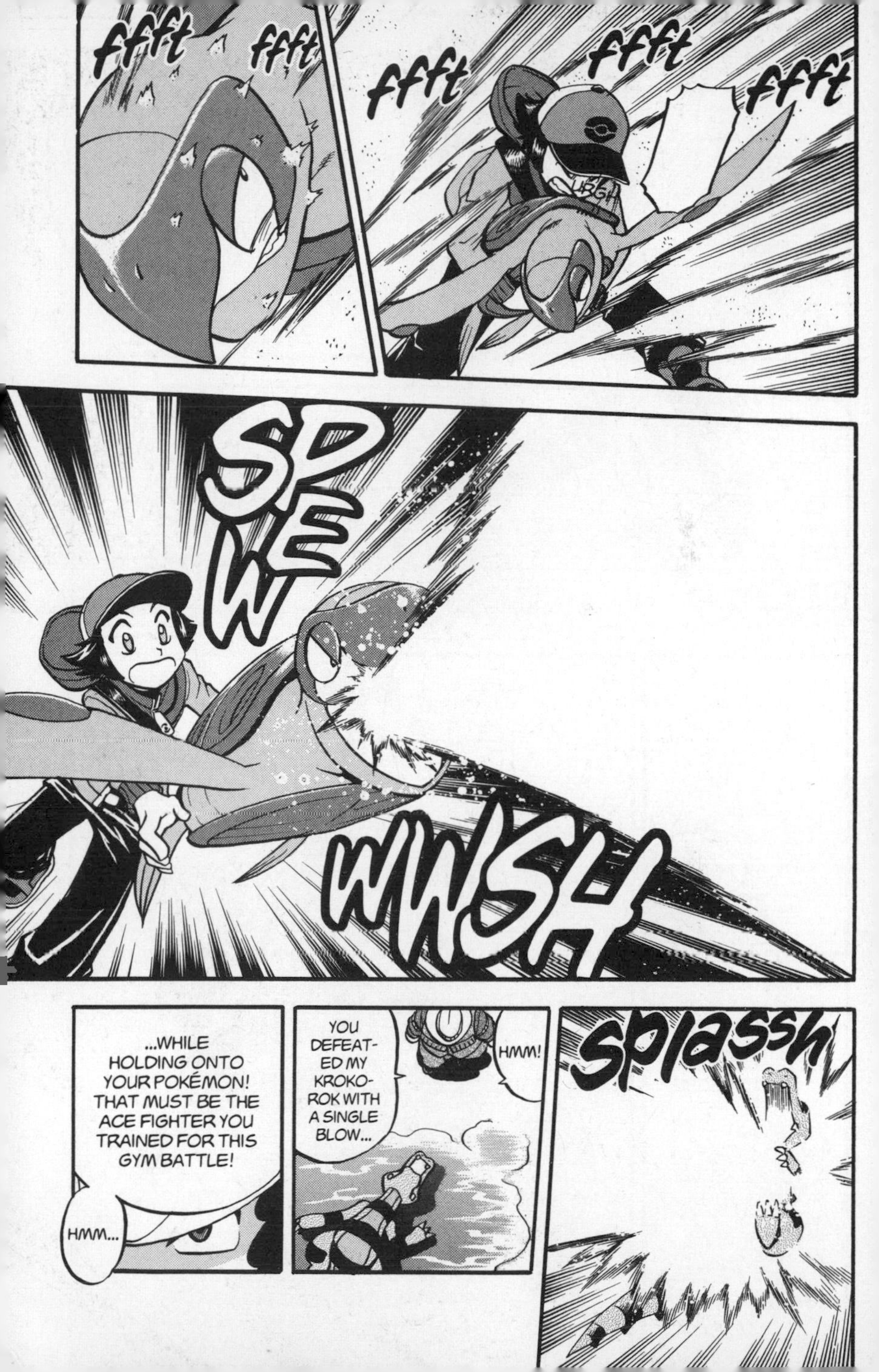
ffft
ffft
URGH
ffft
ffft
SPEW
WWSH
splassh
HMM!
YOU DEFEATED MY KROKOROK WITH A SINGLE BLOW...
...WHILE HOLDING ONTO YOUR POKÉMON! THAT MUST BE THE ACE FIGHTER YOU TRAINED FOR THIS GYM BATTLE!
HMM...

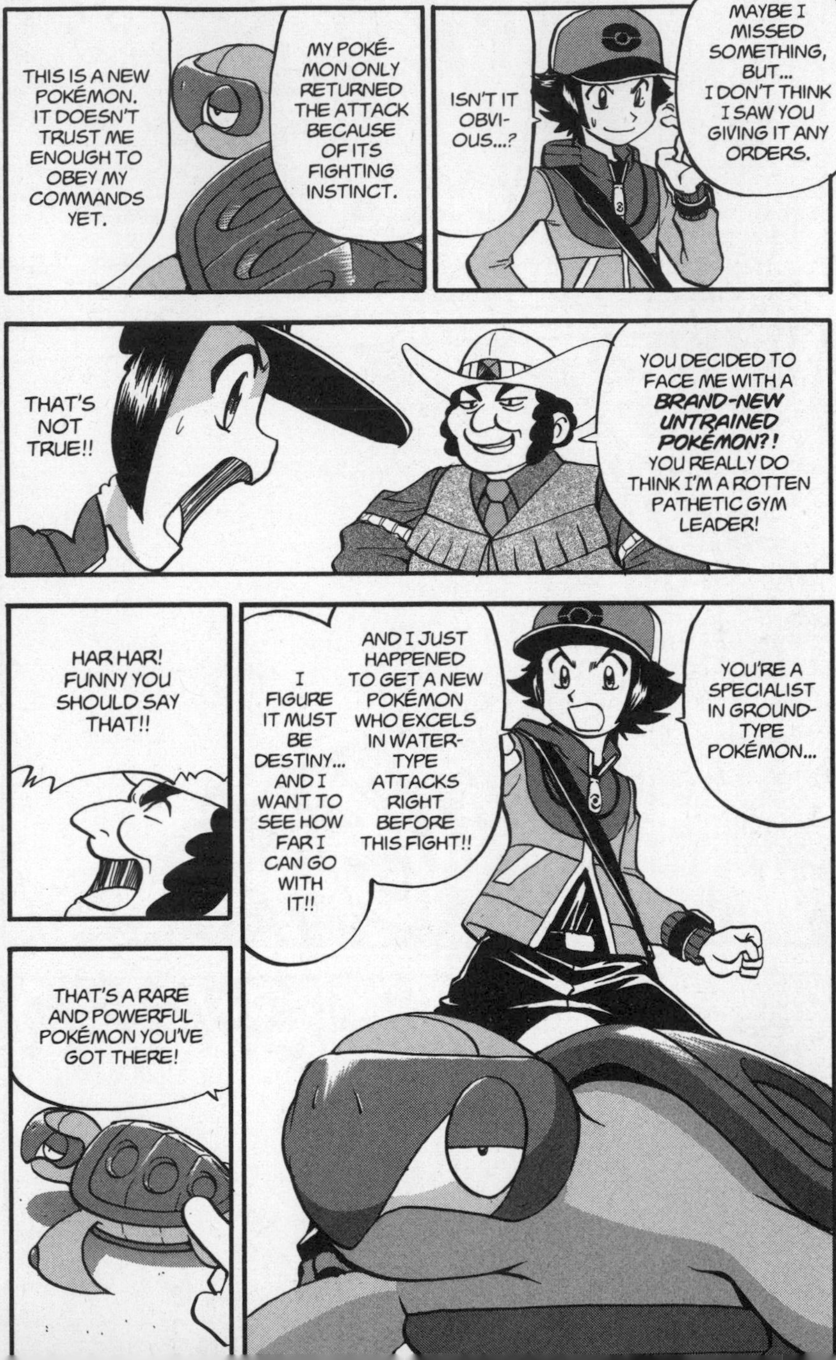
MAYBE I MISSED SOMETHING, BUT... I DON'T THINK I SAW YOU GIVING IT ANY ORDERS.
ISN'T IT OBVIOUS...?
MY POKÉMON ONLY RETURNED THE ATTACK BECAUSE OF ITS FIGHTING INSTINCT.
THIS IS A NEW POKÉMON. IT DOESN'T TRUST ME ENOUGH TO OBEY MY COMMANDS YET.
YOU DECIDED TO FACE ME WITH A ***BRAND-NEW UNTRAINED POKÉMON?!*** YOU REALLY DO THINK I'M A ROTTEN PATHETIC GYM LEADER!
THAT'S NOT TRUE!!
YOU'RE A SPECIALIST IN GROUND-TYPE POKÉMON...
AND I JUST HAPPENED TO GET A NEW POKÉMON WHO EXCELS IN WATER-TYPE ATTACKS RIGHT BEFORE THIS FIGHT!!
I FIGURE IT MUST BE DESTINY... AND I WANT TO SEE HOW FAR I CAN GO WITH IT!!
HAR HAR! FUNNY YOU SHOULD SAY THAT!!
THAT'S A RARE AND POWERFUL POKÉMON YOU'VE GOT THERE!

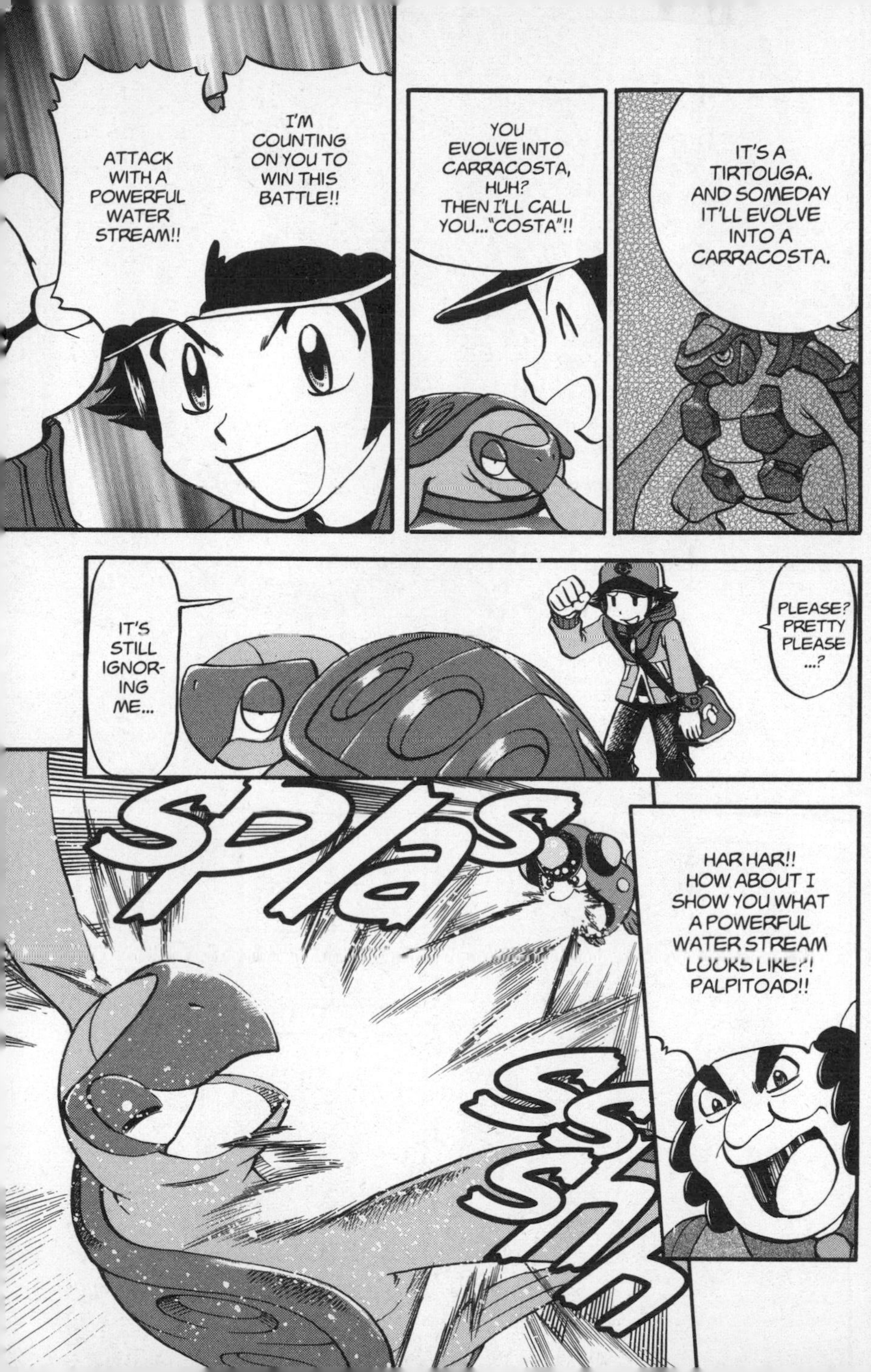
IT'S A TIRTOUGA. AND SOMEDAY IT'LL EVOLVE INTO A CARRACOSTA.
YOU EVOLVE INTO CARRACOSTA, HUH? THEN I'LL CALL YOU..."COSTA"!!
I'M COUNTING ON YOU TO WIN THIS BATTLE!!
ATTACK WITH A POWERFUL WATER STREAM!!
PLEASE? PRETTY PLEASE ...?
IT'S STILL IGNOR-ING ME...
HAR HAR!! HOW ABOUT I SHOW YOU WHAT A POWERFUL WATER STREAM LOOKS LIKE?! PALPITOAD!!
splas
sssh

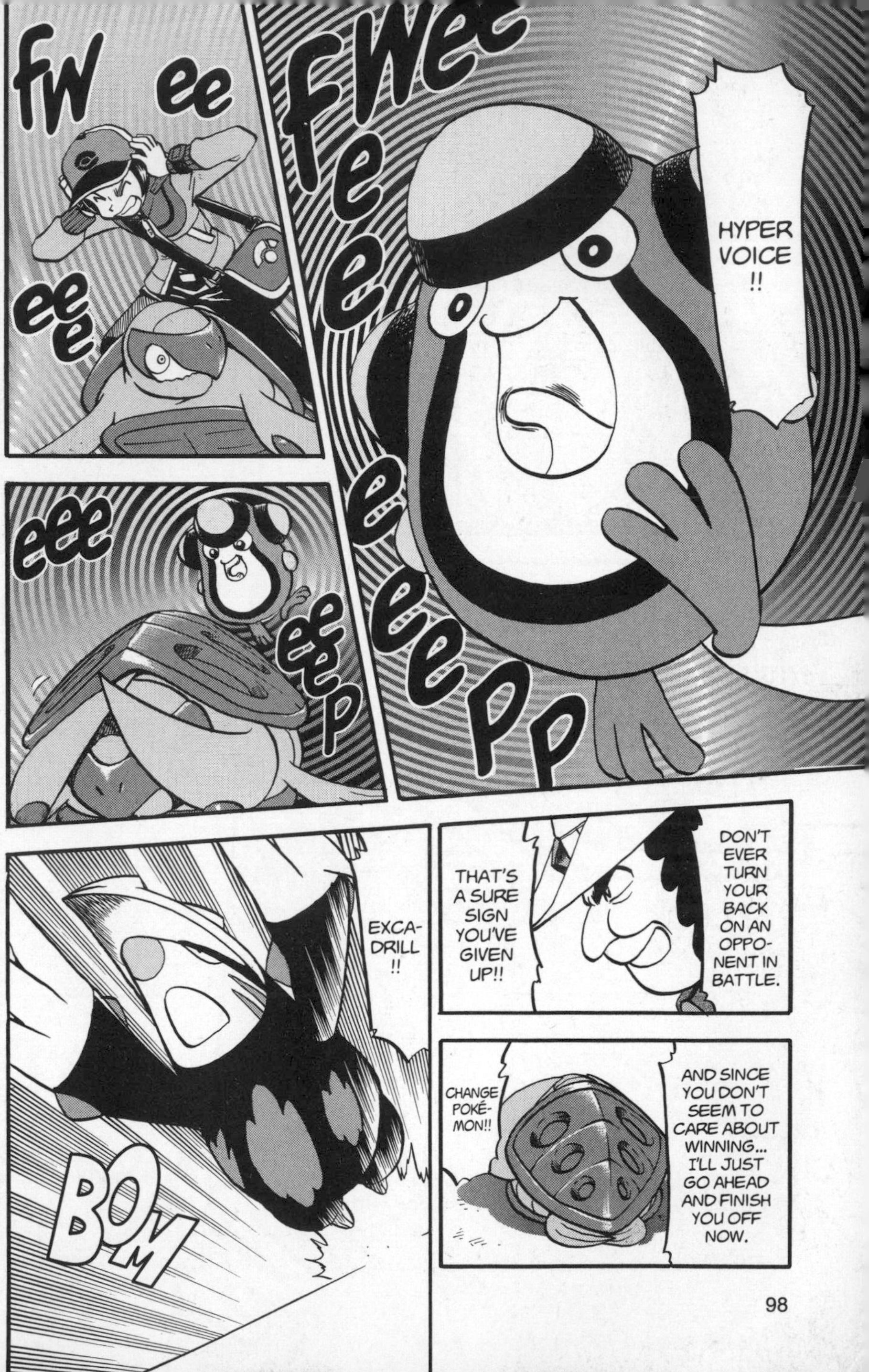
HYPER VOICE !!
FWEEEEEEEEP
FWEEEEE
EEEEEEEP
DON'T EVER TURN YOUR BACK ON AN OPPONENT IN BATTLE.
THAT'S A SURE SIGN YOU'VE GIVEN UP!!
AND SINCE YOU DON'T SEEM TO CARE ABOUT WINNING... I'LL JUST GO AHEAD AND FINISH YOU OFF NOW.
CHANGE POKÉMON!!
EXCA-DRILL !!
BOOM

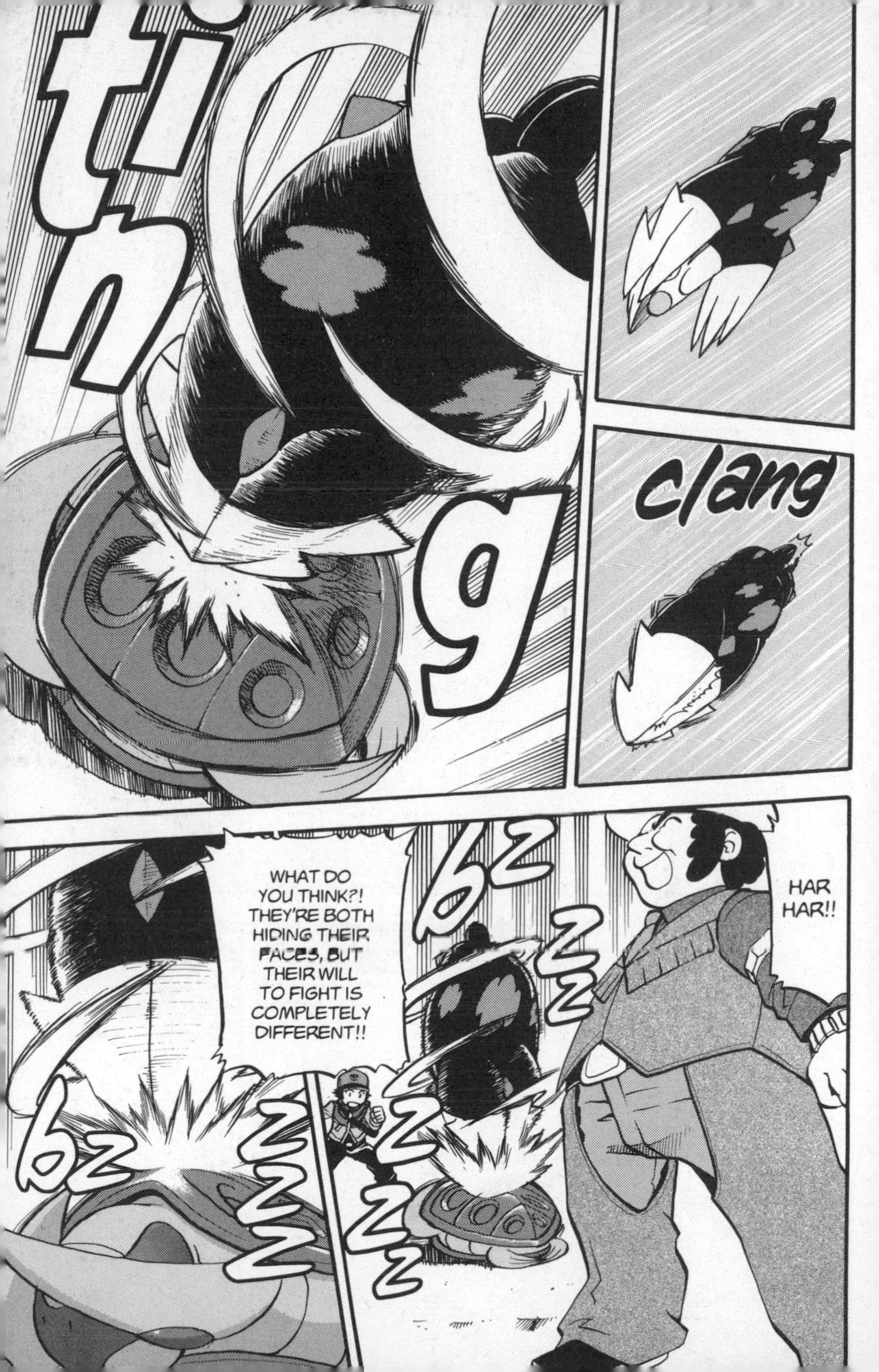
clang
ting
HAR HAR!!
bzzz
WHAT DO YOU THINK?! THEY'RE BOTH HIDING THEIR FACES, BUT THEIR WILL TO FIGHT IS COMPLETELY DIFFERENT!!
bzzzz

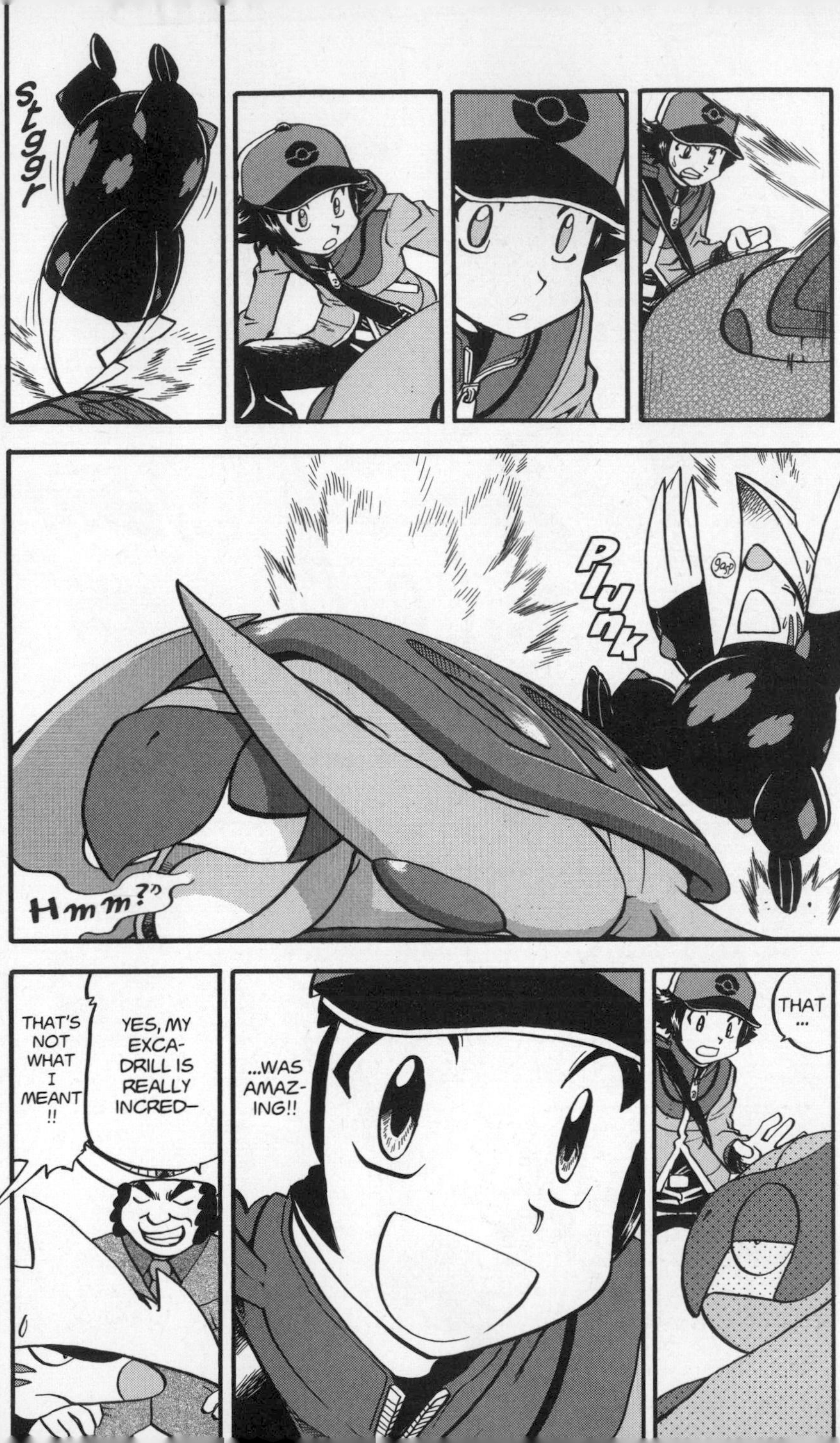
Stggr
Plunk
gasp
gasp
Hmm?
THAT ...
...WAS AMAZING!!
YES, MY EXCADRILL IS REALLY INCRED—
THAT'S NOT WHAT I MEANT!!

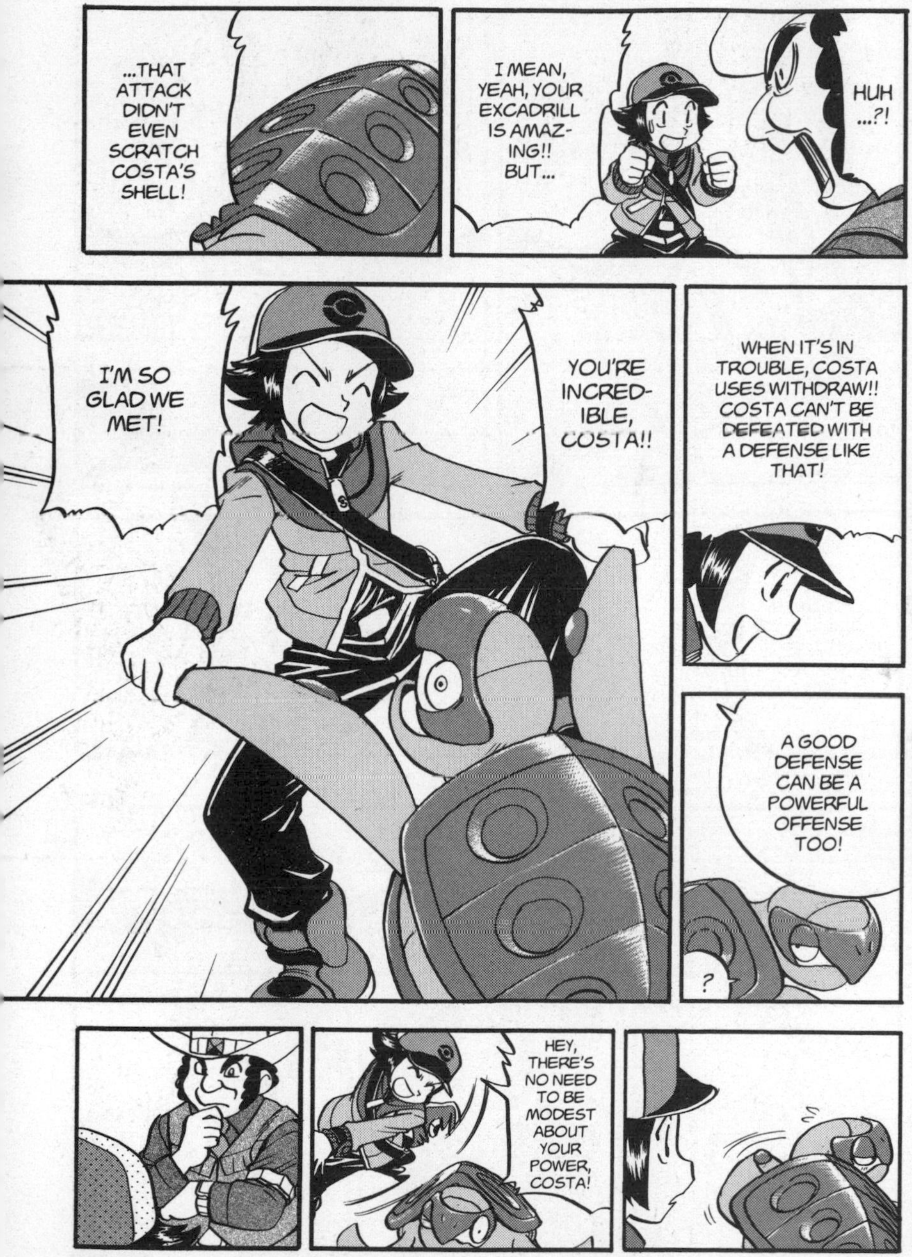
HUH ...?!
I MEAN, YEAH, YOUR EXCADRILL IS AMAZING!! BUT...
...THAT ATTACK DIDN'T EVEN SCRATCH COSTA'S SHELL!
WHEN IT'S IN TROUBLE, COSTA USES WITHDRAW!! COSTA CAN'T BE DEFEATED WITH A DEFENSE LIKE THAT!
A GOOD DEFENSE CAN BE A POWERFUL OFFENSE TOO!
?
YOU'RE INCREDIBLE, COSTA!!
I'M SO GLAD WE MET!
HEY, THERE'S NO NEED TO BE MODEST ABOUT YOUR POWER, COSTA!

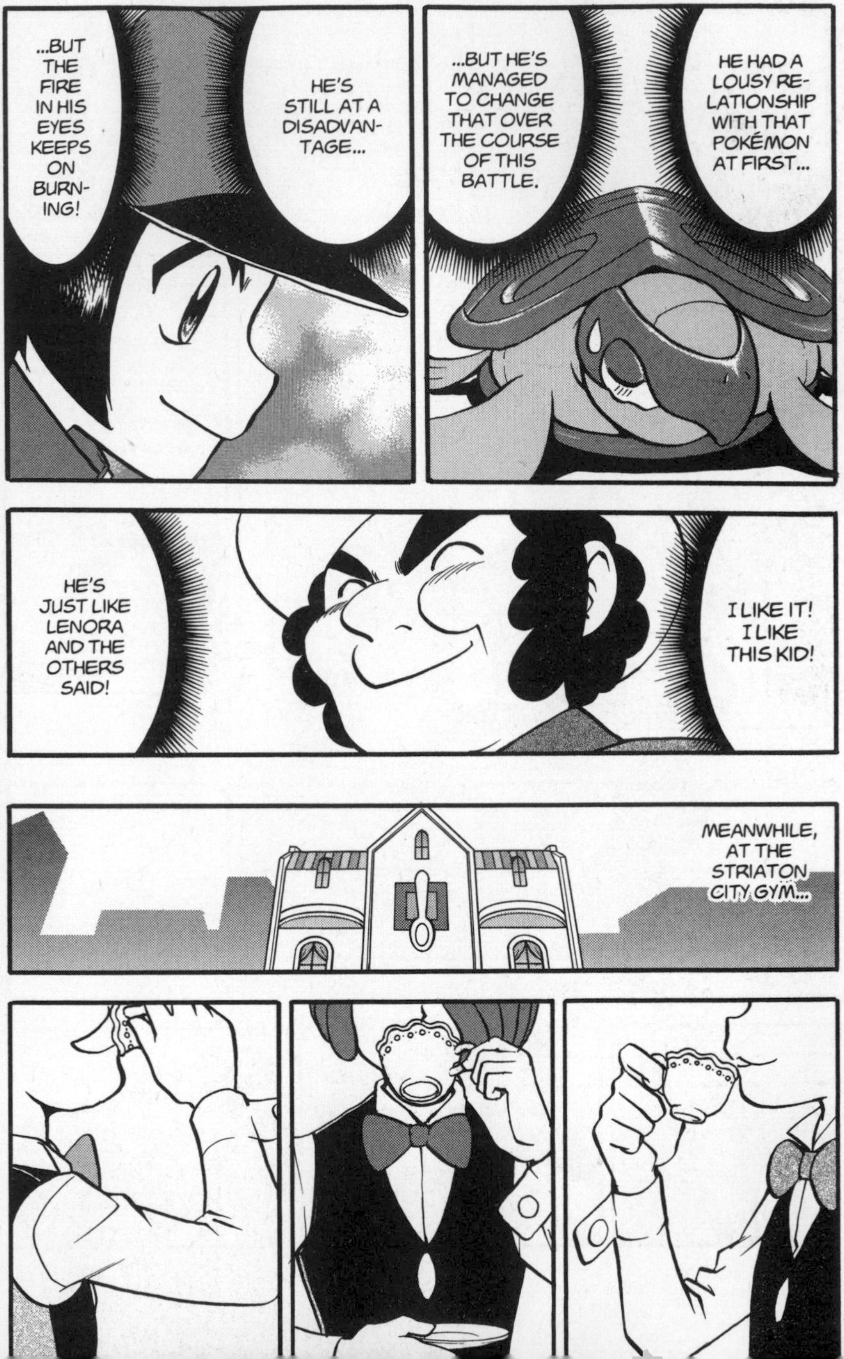
HE HAD A LOUSY RE-LATIONSHIP WITH THAT POKÉMON AT FIRST...
...BUT HE'S MANAGED TO CHANGE THAT OVER THE COURSE OF THIS BATTLE.
HE'S STILL AT A DISADVAN-TAGE...
...BUT THE FIRE IN HIS EYES KEEPS ON BURN-ING!
I LIKE IT! I LIKE THIS KID!
HE'S JUST LIKE LENORA AND THE OTHERS SAID!
MEANWHILE, AT THE STRIATON CITY GYM...

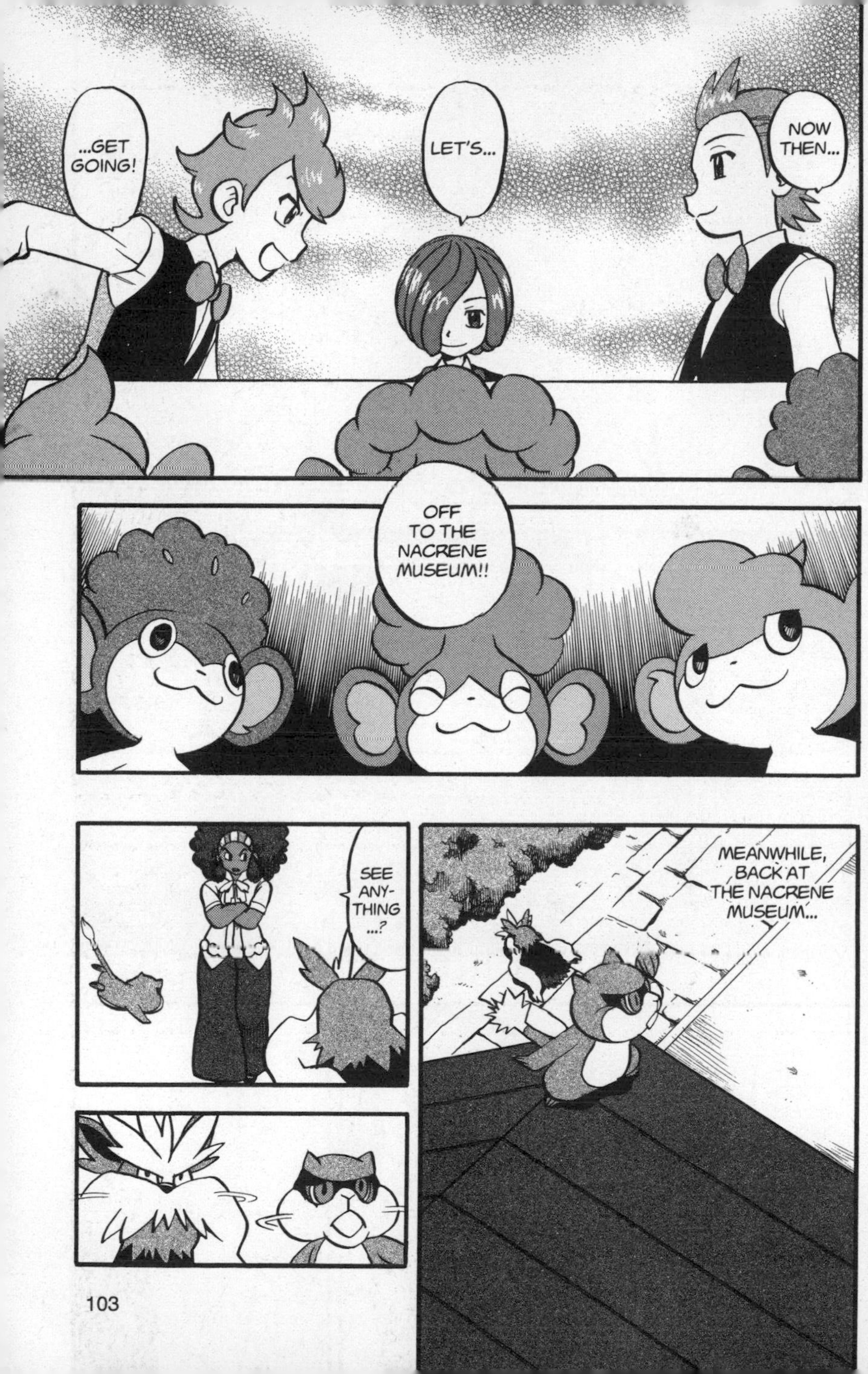
NOW THEN...
LET'S...
...GET GOING!
OFF TO THE NACRENE MUSEUM!!
MEANWHILE, BACK AT THE NACRENE MUSEUM...
SEE ANYTHING...?

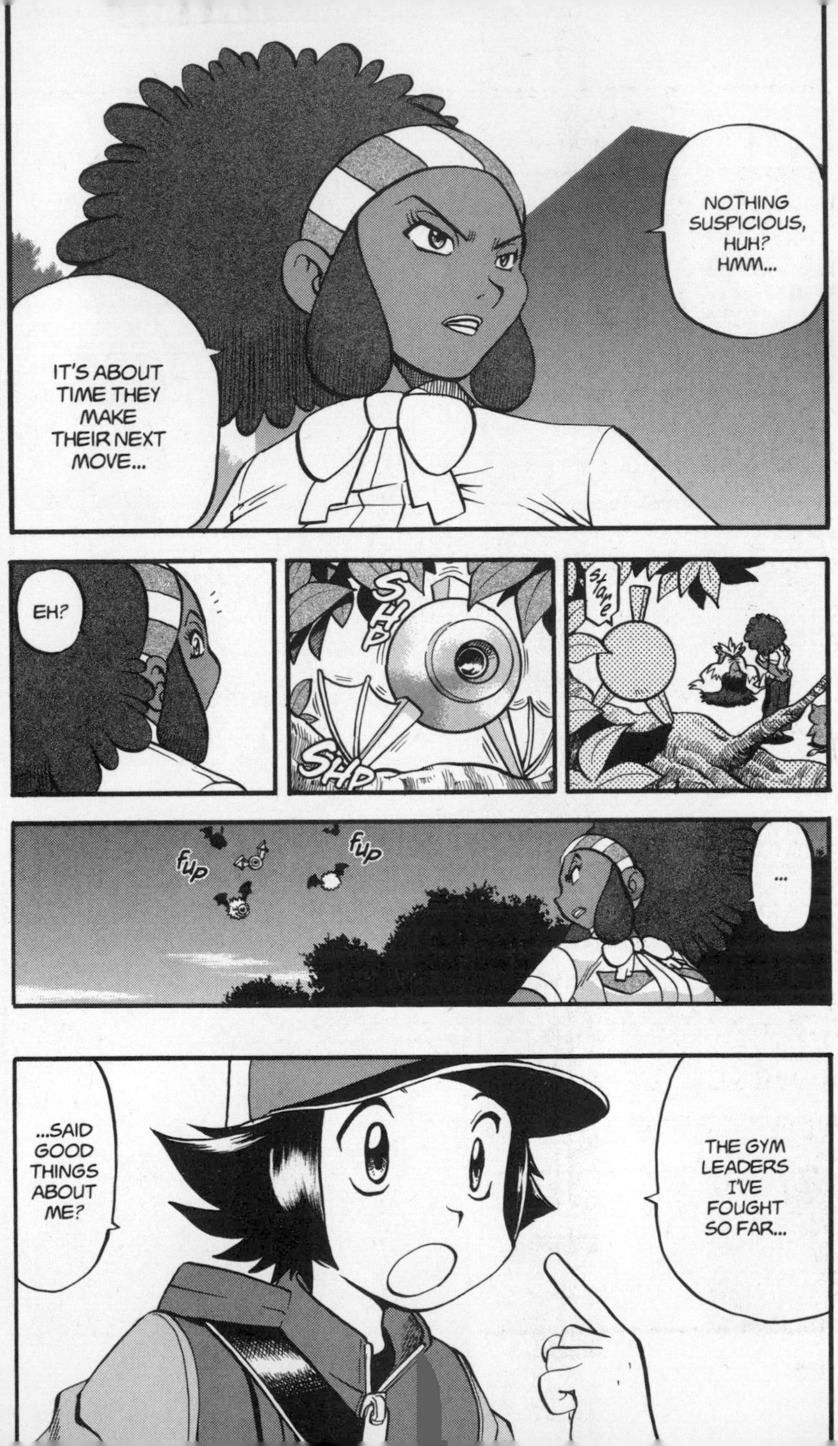
NOTHING SUSPICIOUS, HUH? HMM...
IT'S ABOUT TIME THEY MAKE THEIR NEXT MOVE...
stare
SHP
SHP
EH?
...
fup
fup
THE GYM LEADERS I'VE FOUGHT SO FAR...
...SAID GOOD THINGS ABOUT ME?

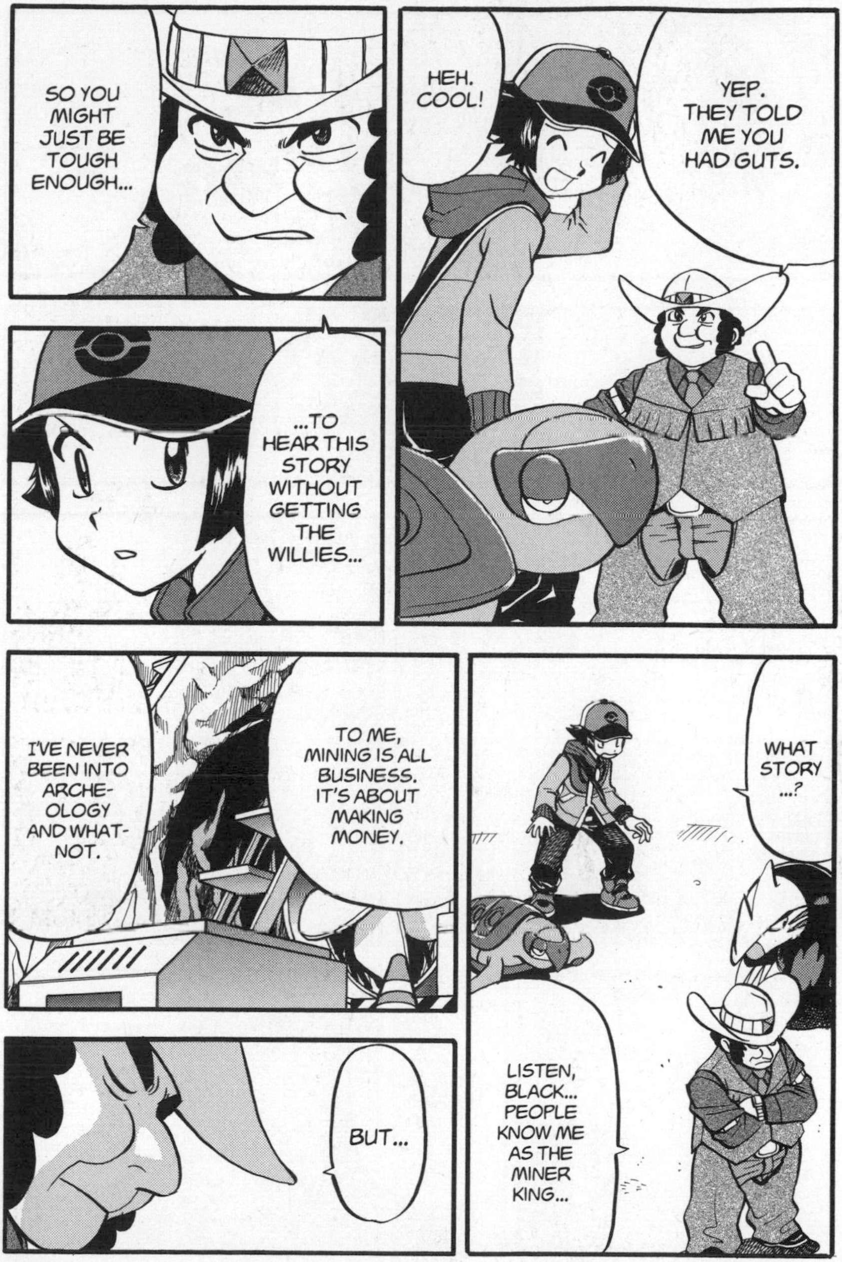
YEP. THEY TOLD ME YOU HAD GUTS.
HEH. COOL!
SO YOU MIGHT JUST BE TOUGH ENOUGH...
...TO HEAR THIS STORY WITHOUT GETTING THE WILLIES...
WHAT STORY ...?
LISTEN, BLACK... PEOPLE KNOW ME AS THE MINER KING...
TO ME, MINING IS ALL BUSINESS. IT'S ABOUT MAKING MONEY.
I'VE NEVER BEEN INTO ARCHE- OLOGY AND WHAT- NOT.
BUT...

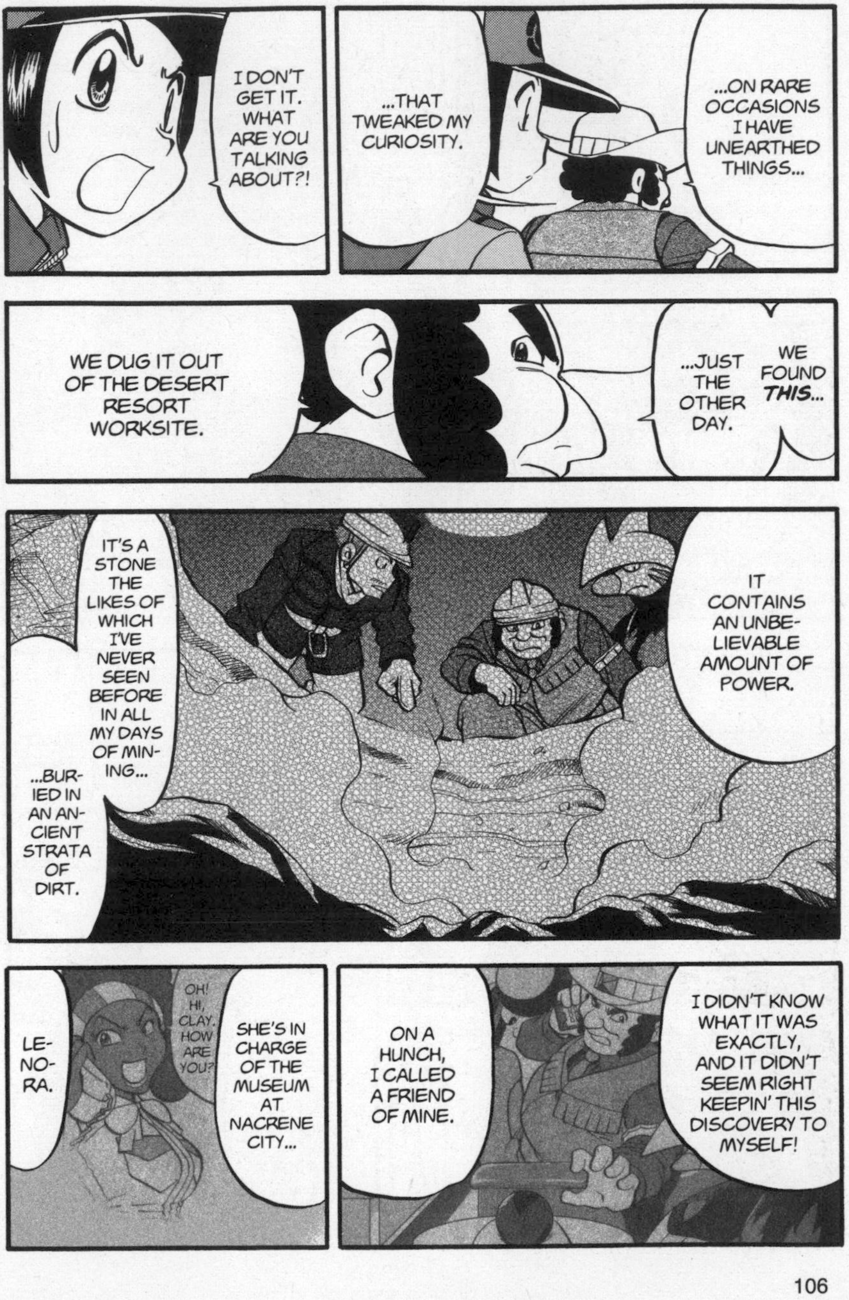
...ON RARE OCCASIONS I HAVE UNEARTHED THINGS...
...THAT TWEAKED MY CURIOSITY.
I DON'T GET IT. WHAT ARE YOU TALKING ABOUT?!
WE FOUND *THIS*...
...JUST THE OTHER DAY.
WE DUG IT OUT OF THE DESERT RESORT WORKSITE.
IT CONTAINS AN UNBELIEVABLE AMOUNT OF POWER.
IT'S A STONE THE LIKES OF WHICH I'VE NEVER SEEN BEFORE IN ALL MY DAYS OF MINING...
...BURIED IN AN ANCIENT STRATA OF DIRT.
I DIDN'T KNOW WHAT IT WAS EXACTLY, AND IT DIDN'T SEEM RIGHT KEEPIN' THIS DISCOVERY TO MYSELF!
ON A HUNCH, I CALLED A FRIEND OF MINE.
SHE'S IN CHARGE OF THE MUSEUM AT NACRENE CITY...
OH! HI, CLAY. HOW ARE YOU?
LENORA.

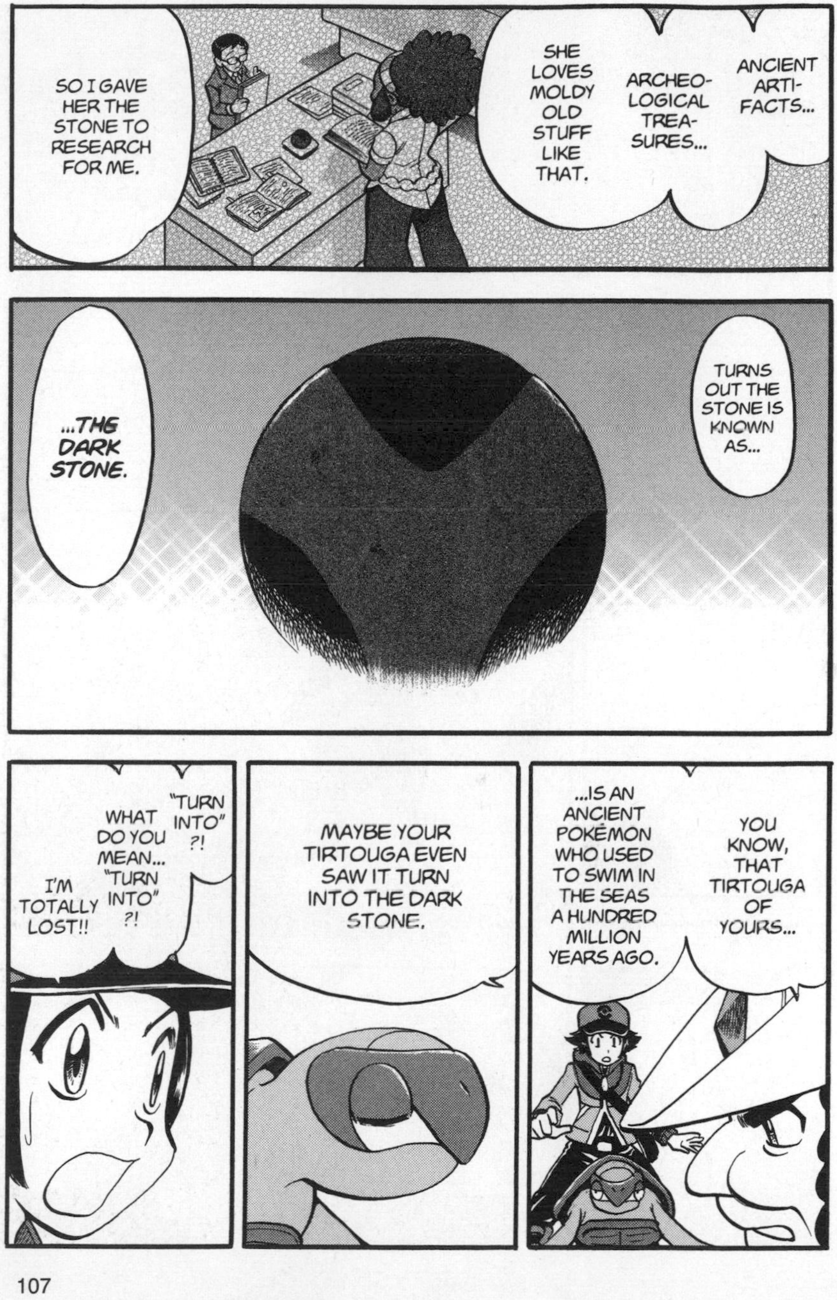
ANCIENT ARTIFACTS...
ARCHEOLOGICAL TREASURES...
SHE LOVES MOLDY OLD STUFF LIKE THAT.
SO I GAVE HER THE STONE TO RESEARCH FOR ME.
TURNS OUT THE STONE IS KNOWN AS...
...THE DARK STONE.
YOU KNOW, THAT TIRTOUGA OF YOURS...
...IS AN ANCIENT POKÉMON WHO USED TO SWIM IN THE SEAS A HUNDRED MILLION YEARS AGO.
MAYBE YOUR TIRTOUGA EVEN SAW IT TURN INTO THE DARK STONE.
"TURN INTO"?!
WHAT DO YOU MEAN... "TURN INTO"?!
I'M TOTALLY LOST!!

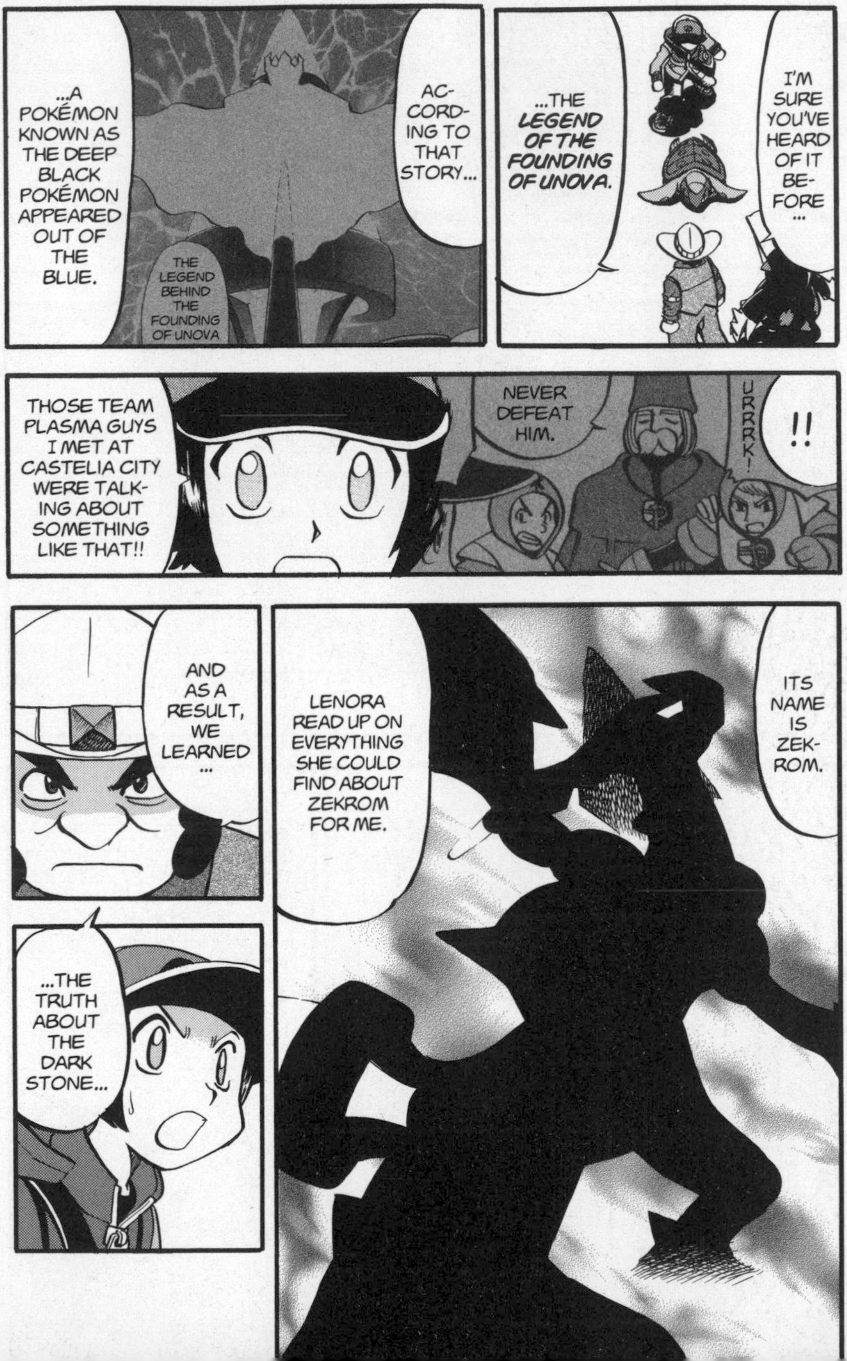
I'M SURE YOU'VE HEARD OF IT BEFORE...
...THE LEGEND OF THE FOUNDING OF UNOVA.
ACCORDING TO THAT STORY...
...A POKÉMON KNOWN AS THE DEEP BLACK POKÉMON APPEARED OUT OF THE BLUE.
THE LEGEND BEHIND THE FOUNDING OF UNOVA
!!
URRRK!
NEVER DEFEAT HIM.
THOSE TEAM PLASMA GUYS I MET AT CASTELIA CITY WERE TALKING ABOUT SOMETHING LIKE THAT!!
ITS NAME IS ZEKROM.
LENORA READ UP ON EVERYTHING SHE COULD FIND ABOUT ZEKROM FOR ME.
AND AS A RESULT, WE LEARNED...
...THE TRUTH ABOUT THE DARK STONE...

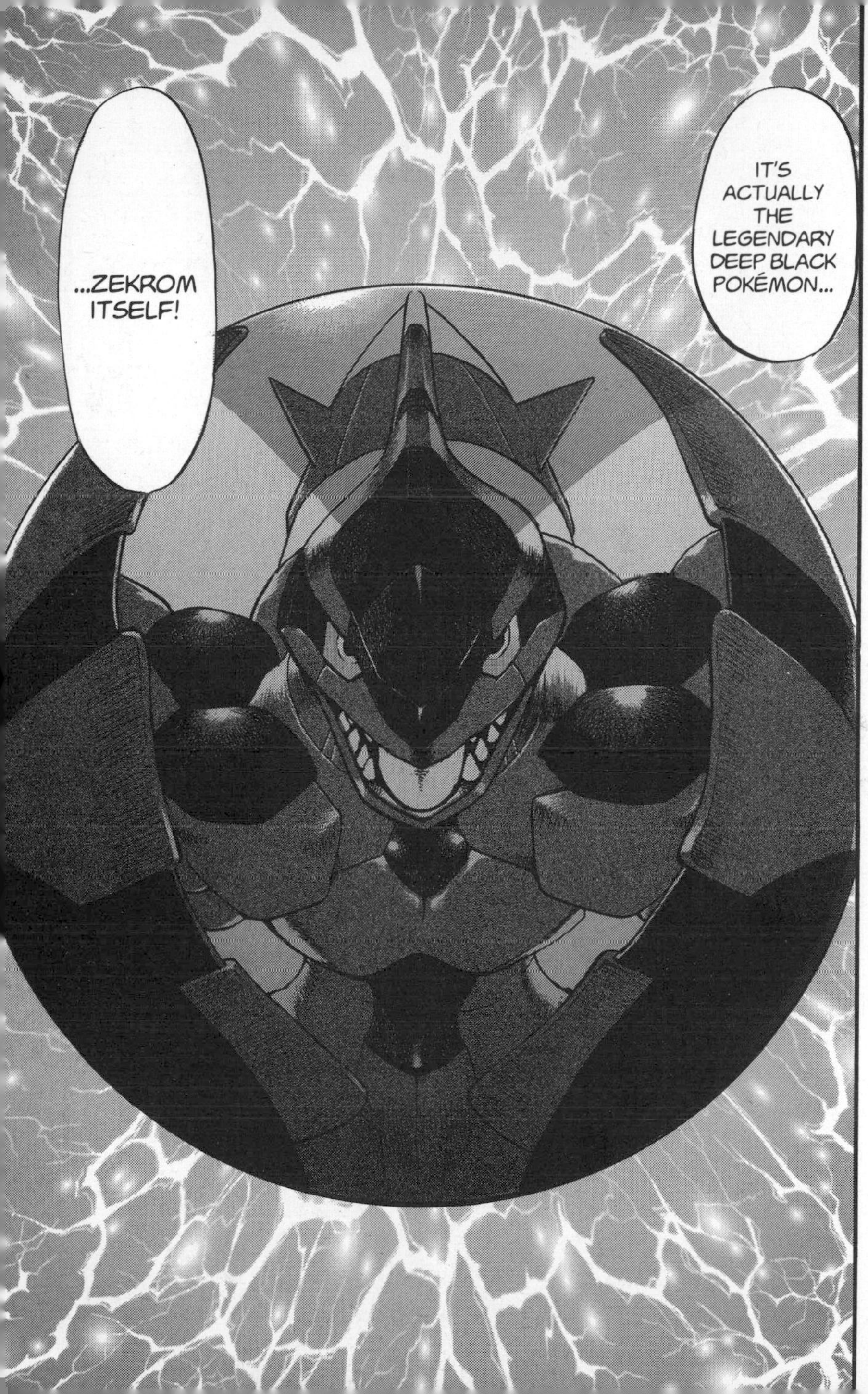
IT'S ACTUALLY THE LEGENDARY DEEP BLACK POKÉMON...
...ZEKROM ITSELF!

ADVENTURE MAP

Final Destination:
Pokémon League

Black's Current Location:
Driftveil City Gym

BLACK

Fire Pig Pokémon	**Nite**	
Pignite ♂	Fire	Fighting
Lv.31	Ability: Blaze	

Dream Eater Pokémon	**Musha**	
Munna ♂	Psychic	
Lv.51	Ability: Forewarn	

EleSpider Pokémon	**Tula**	
Galvantula ♂	Bug	Electric
Lv.54	Ability: Unnerve	

Prototurtle Pokémon	**Costa**	
Tirtouga ♂	Water	Rock
Lv.33	Ability: Solid Rock	

WHITE

Grass Snake Pokémon	**Servine**	
Servine ♀	Grass	
Lv.23	Ability: Overgrow	

Season Pokémon	**Darlene**	
Deerling ♀	Normal	Grass
Lv.21	Ability: Chlorophyll	

Valiant Pokémon	**Brav**	
Braviary ♂	Normal	Flying
Lv.54	Ability: Sheer Force	

TRIO BADGE · BASIC BADGE · INSECT BADGE · BOLT BADGE · ? · ? · ? · ?

Pokémon™ Adventures Black & White

KROKOROK

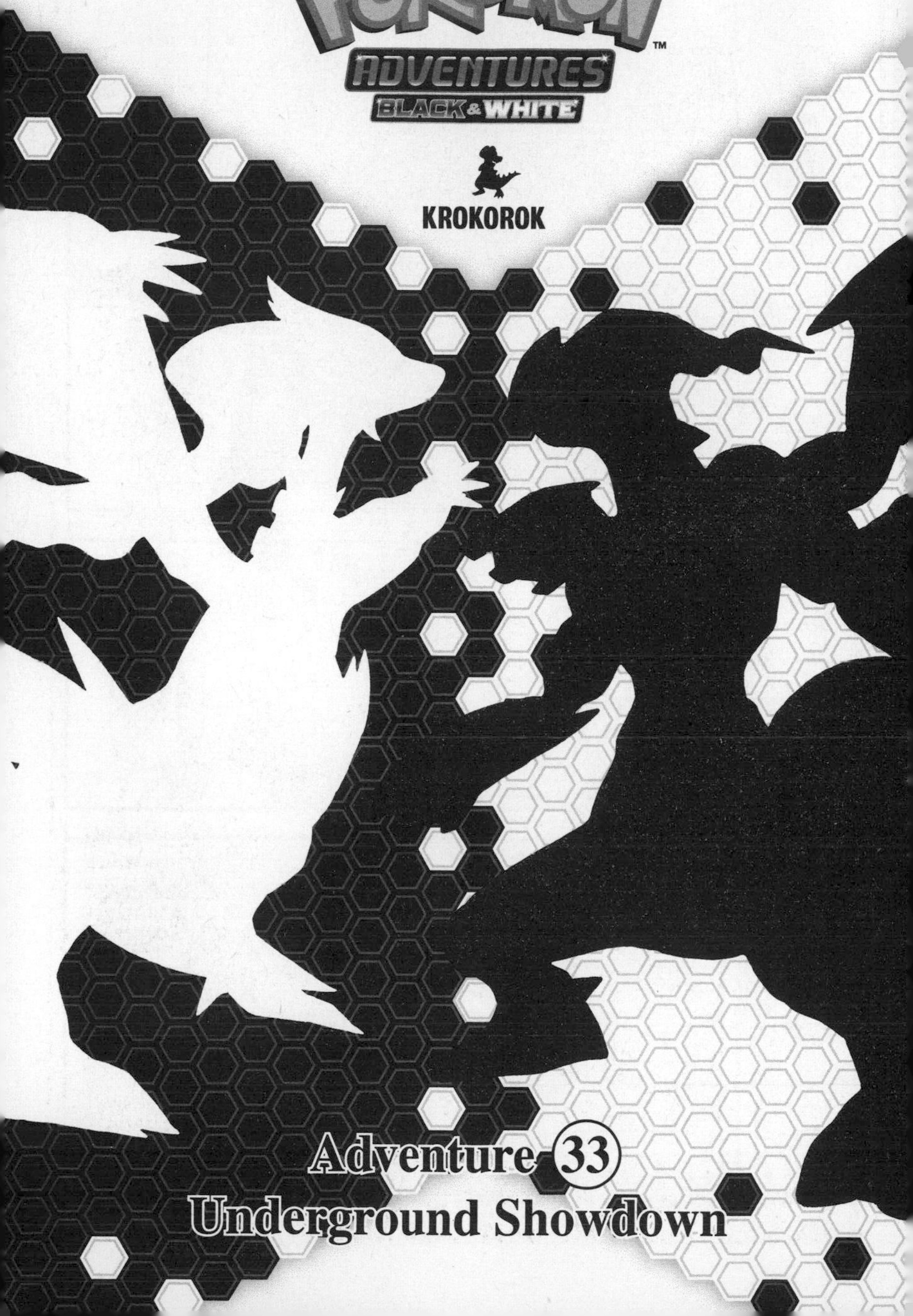

Adventure 33
Underground Showdown

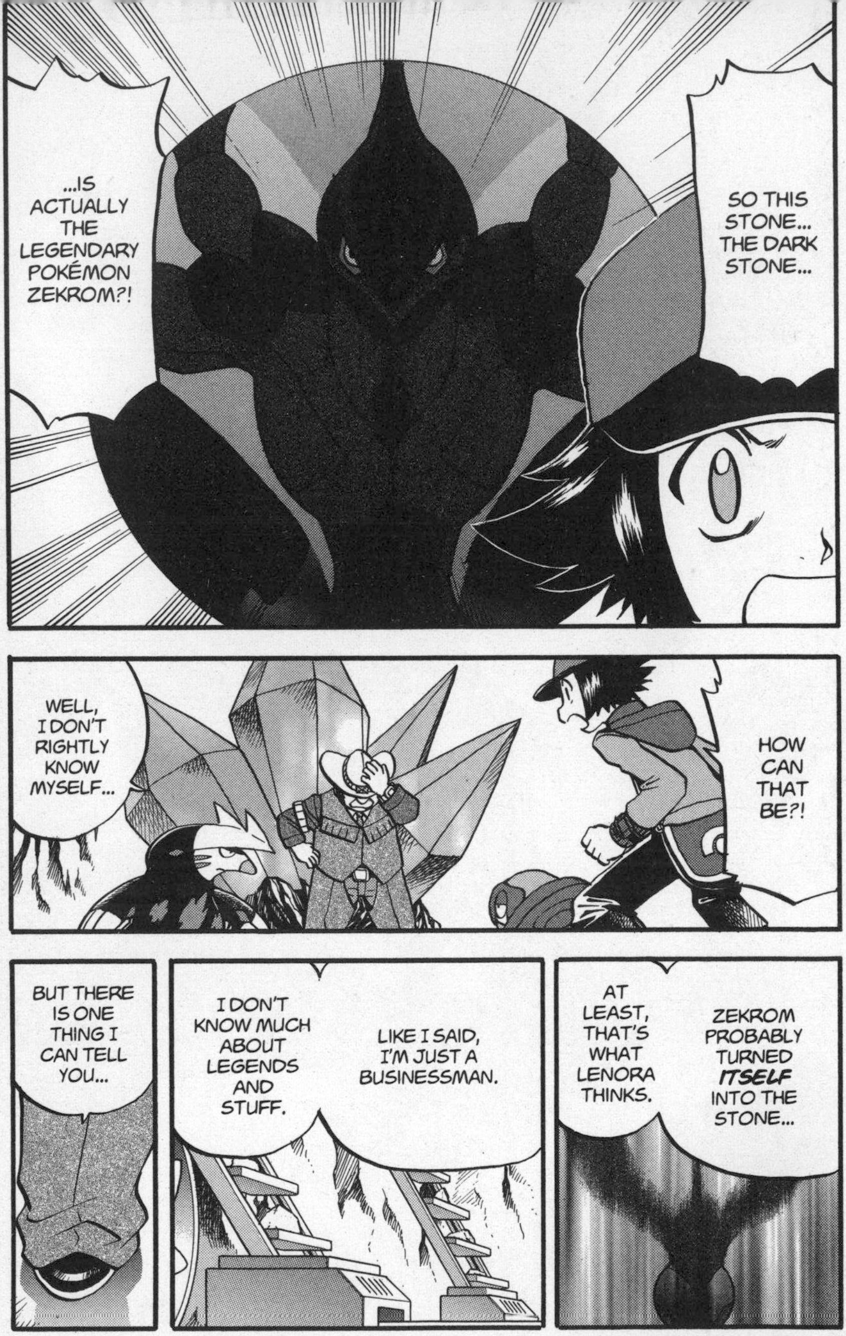
SO THIS STONE... THE DARK STONE...
...IS ACTUALLY THE LEGENDARY POKÉMON ZEKROM?!
HOW CAN THAT BE?!
WELL, I DON'T RIGHTLY KNOW MYSELF...
ZEKROM PROBABLY TURNED *ITSELF* INTO THE STONE...
AT LEAST, THAT'S WHAT LENORA THINKS.
LIKE I SAID, I'M JUST A BUSINESSMAN.
I DON'T KNOW MUCH ABOUT LEGENDS AND STUFF.
BUT THERE IS ONE THING I CAN TELL YOU...

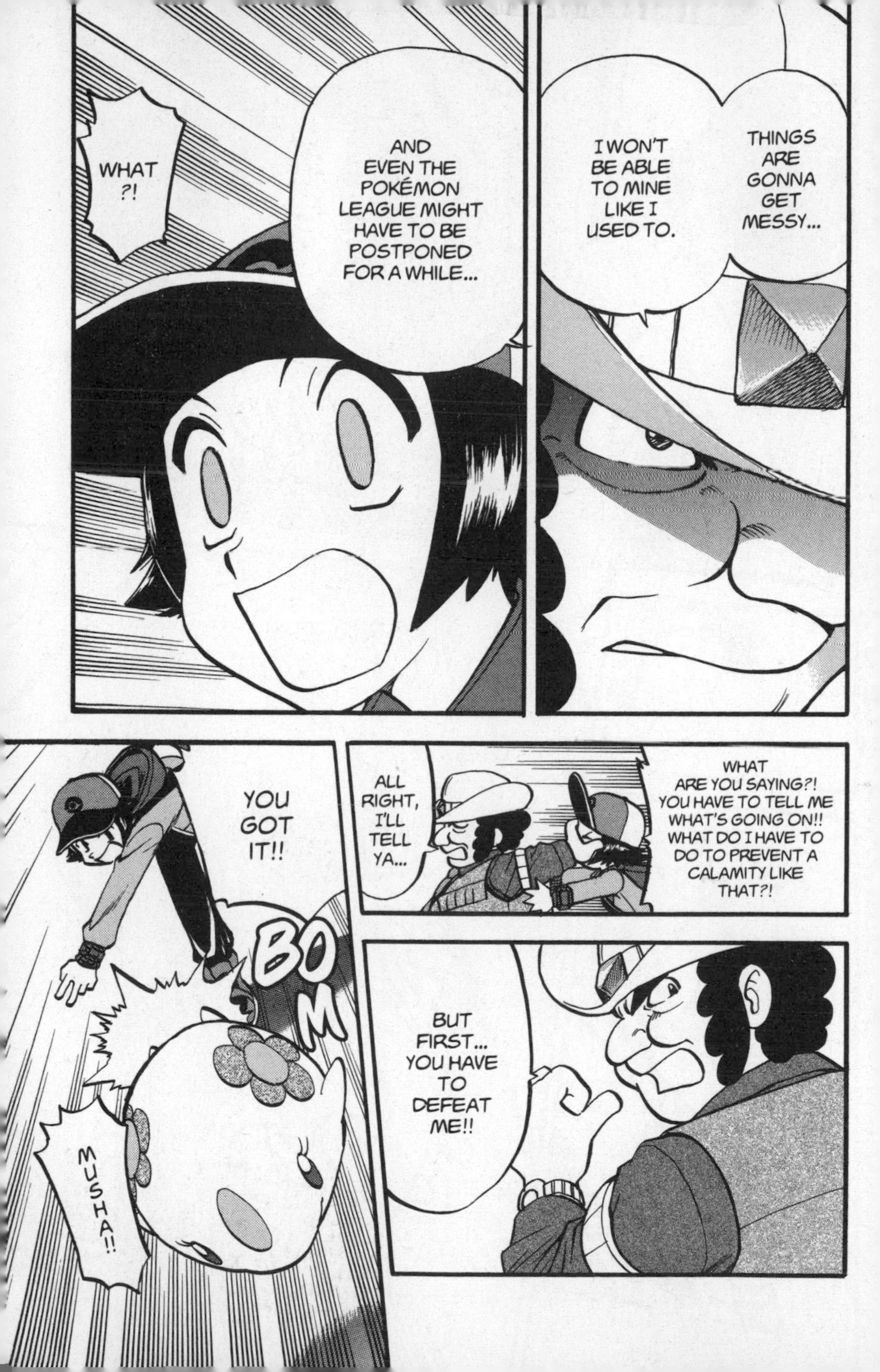
THINGS ARE GONNA GET MESSY...
I WON'T BE ABLE TO MINE LIKE I USED TO.
AND EVEN THE POKÉMON LEAGUE MIGHT HAVE TO BE POSTPONED FOR A WHILE...
WHAT?!
WHAT ARE YOU SAYING?! YOU HAVE TO TELL ME WHAT'S GOING ON!! WHAT DO I HAVE TO DO TO PREVENT A CALAMITY LIKE THAT?!
ALL RIGHT, I'LL TELL YA...
BUT FIRST... YOU HAVE TO DEFEAT ME!!
YOU GOT IT!!
BOOM
MUSHA!!

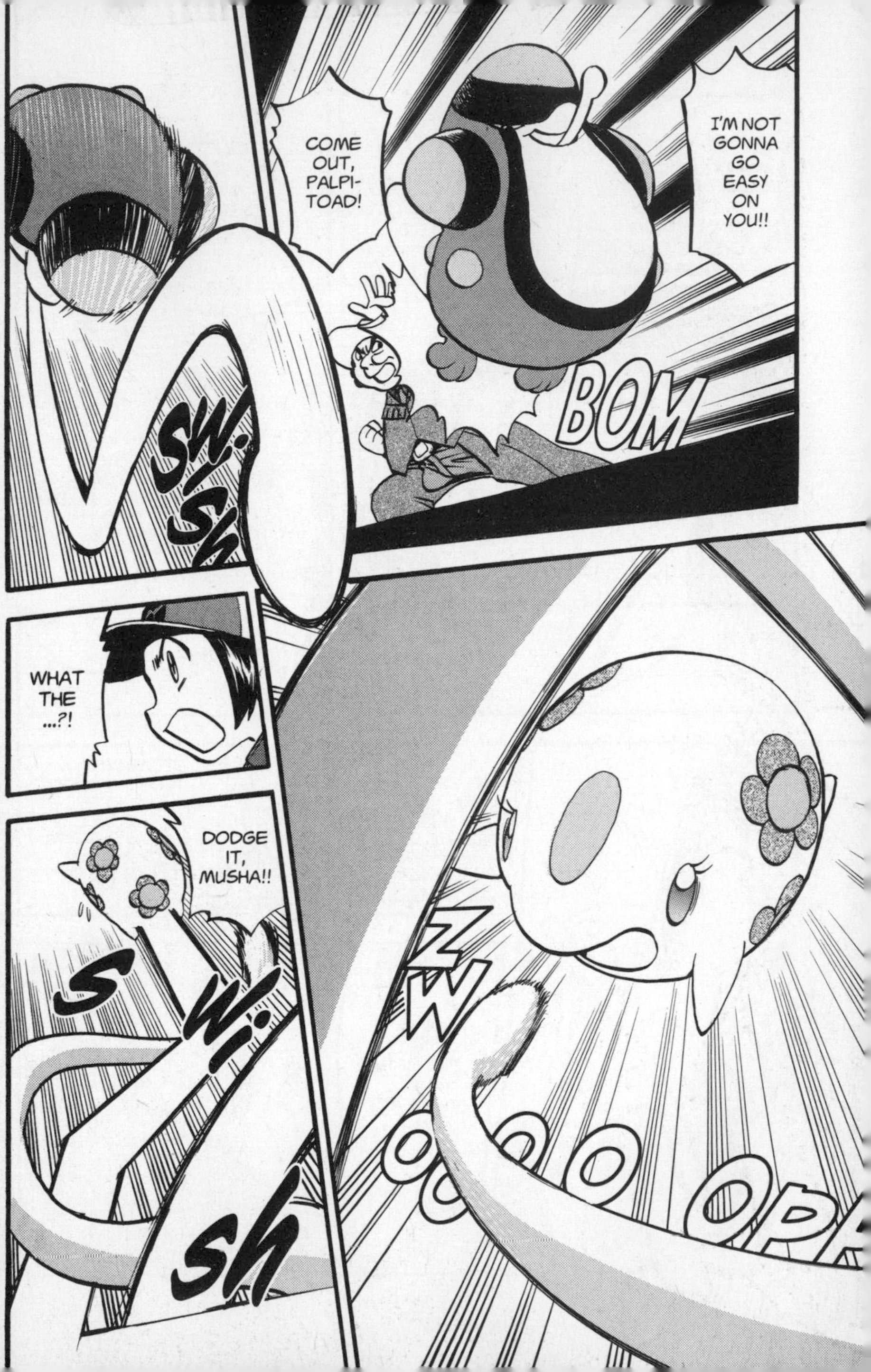
I'M NOT GONNA GO EASY ON YOU!!
COME OUT, PALPITOAD!
BOM
SWISH
ZWOOOOOOP
WHAT THE ...?!
DODGE IT, MUSHA!!
SWISH

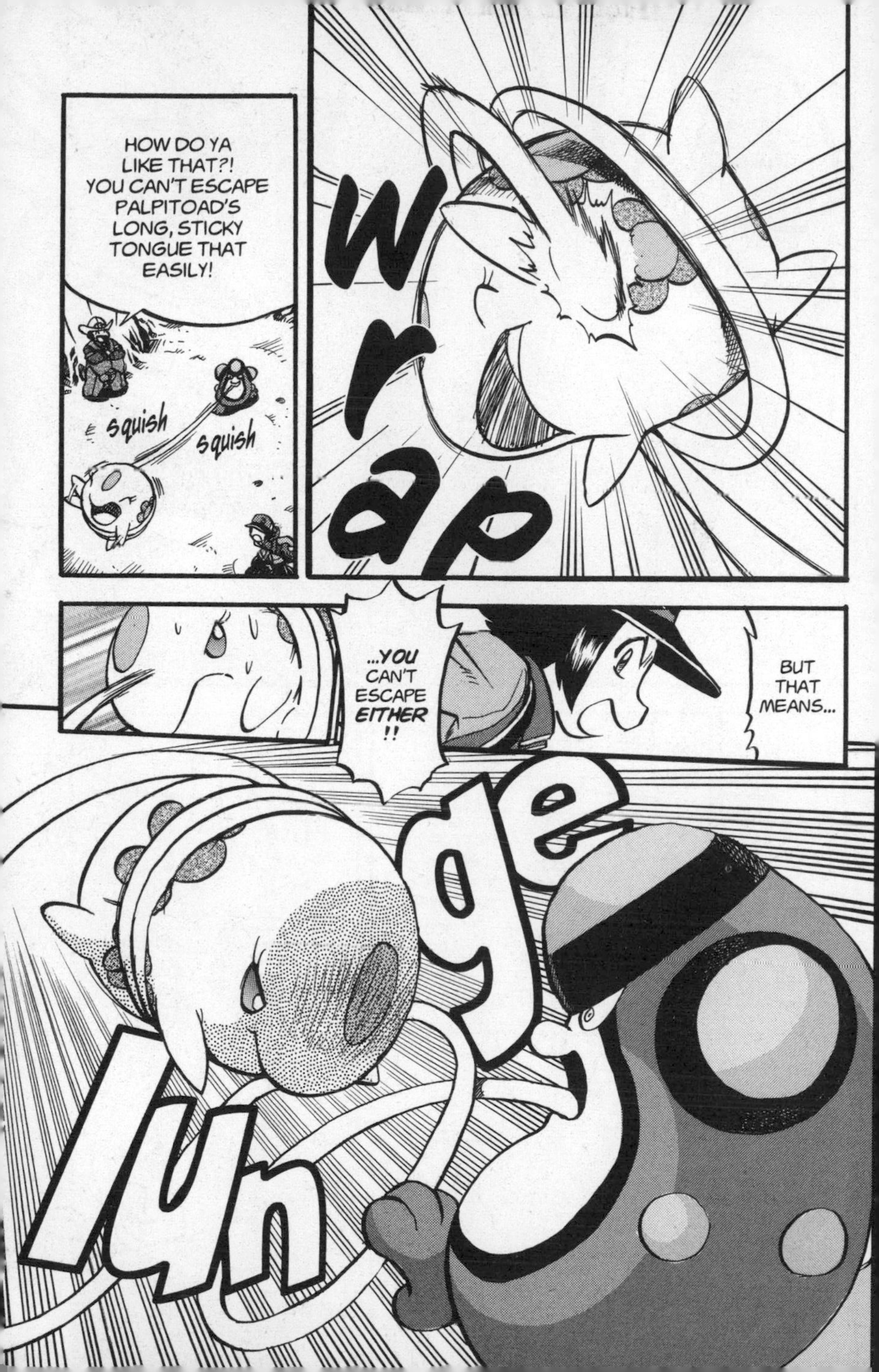

wrap
HOW DO YA LIKE THAT?! YOU CAN'T ESCAPE PALPITOAD'S LONG, STICKY TONGUE THAT EASILY!
squish
squish
BUT THAT MEANS...
...YOU CAN'T ESCAPE EITHER!!
lunge

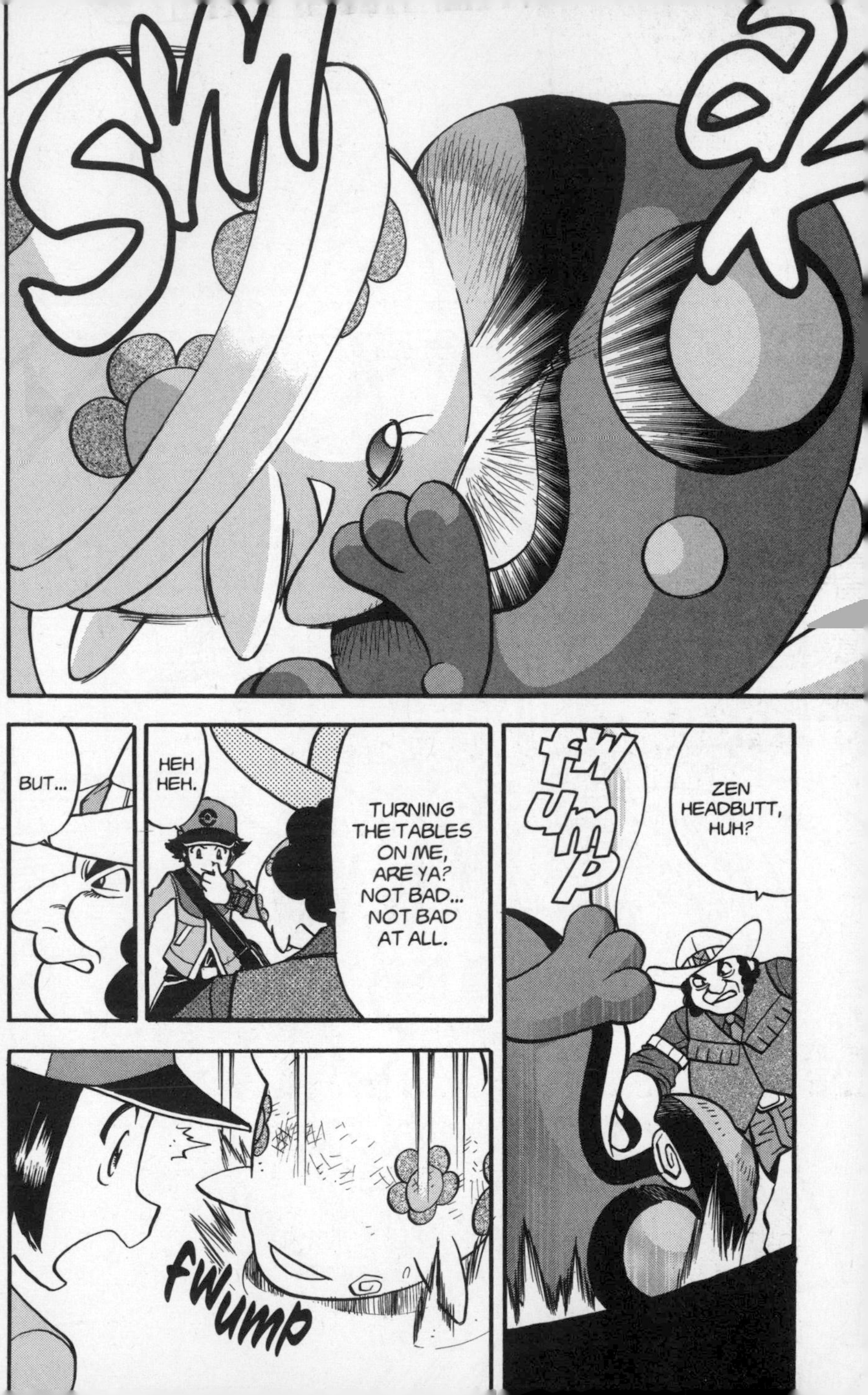
fWUMP
ZEN HEADBUTT, HUH?
TURNING THE TABLES ON ME, ARE YA? NOT BAD... NOT BAD AT ALL.
HEH HEH.
BUT...
fWUMP

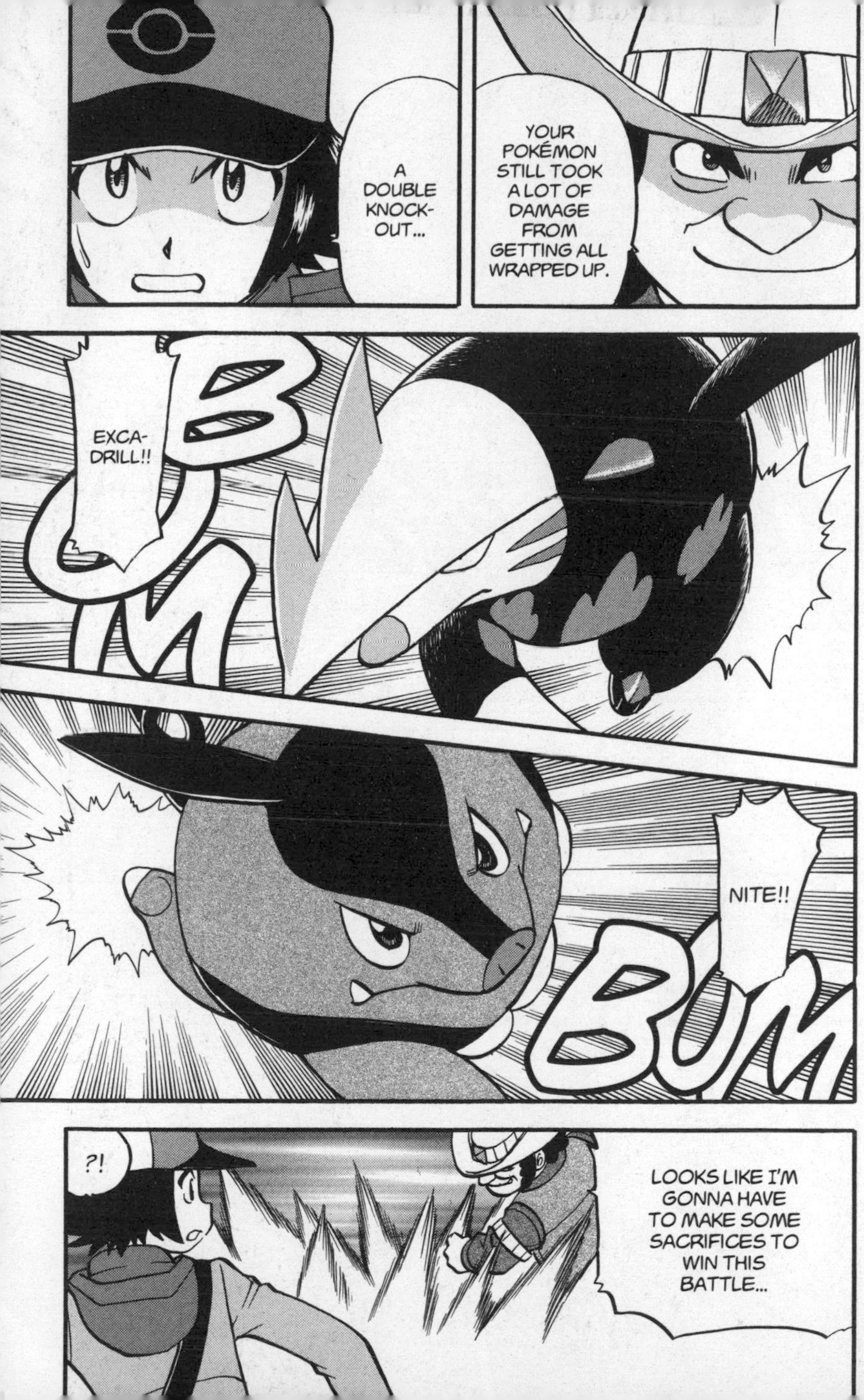
YOUR POKÉMON STILL TOOK A LOT OF DAMAGE FROM GETTING ALL WRAPPED UP.
A DOUBLE KNOCK-OUT...
EXCA-DRILL!!
NITE!!
BUM
LOOKS LIKE I'M GONNA HAVE TO MAKE SOME SACRIFICES TO WIN THIS BATTLE...
?!

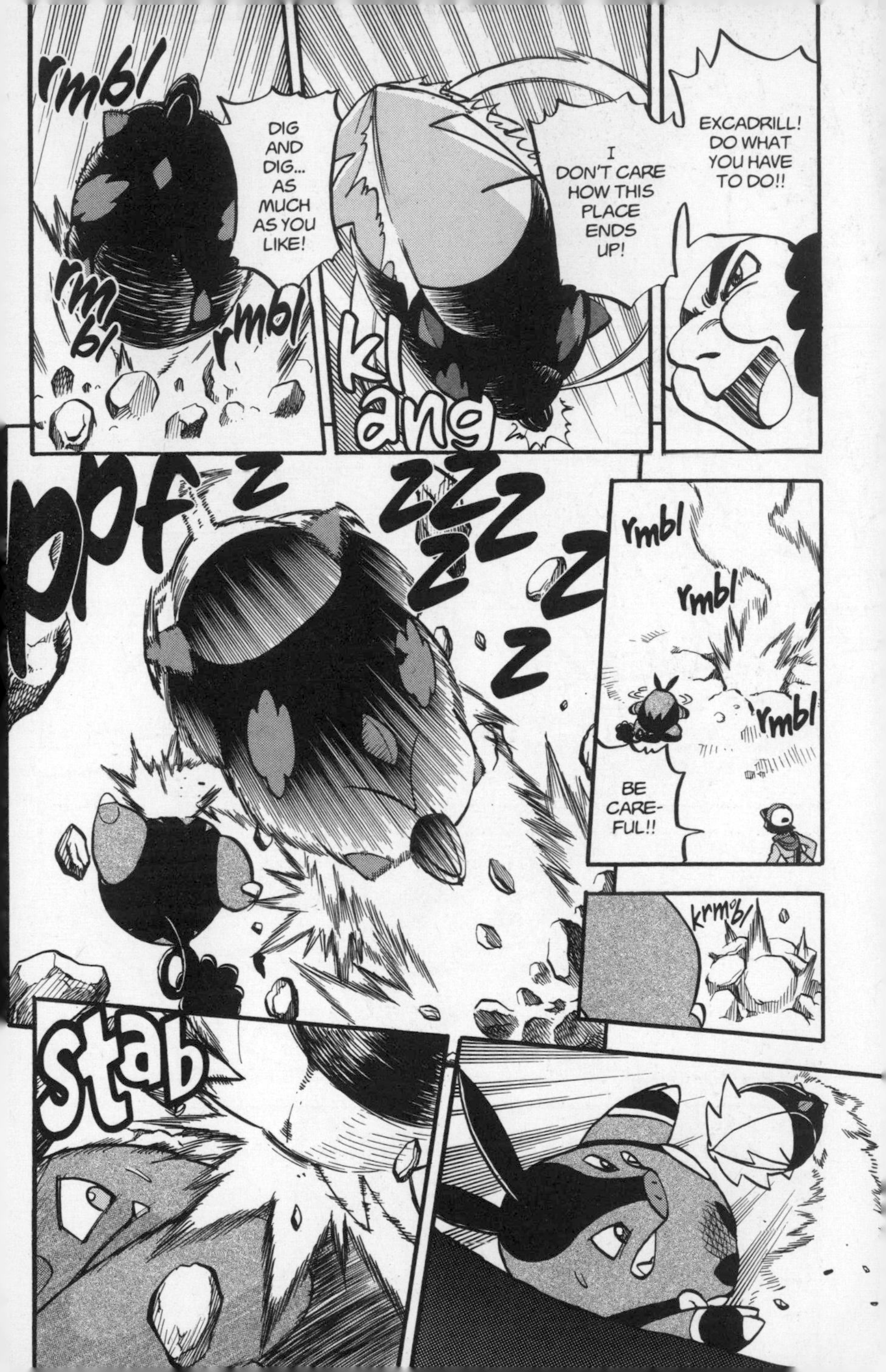
EXCADRILL! DO WHAT YOU HAVE TO DO!!
I DON'T CARE HOW THIS PLACE ENDS UP!
klang
rmbl
DIG AND DIG... AS MUCH AS YOU LIKE!
rmbl
rmbl
rmbl
rmbl
rmbl
BE CAREFUL!!
krmbl
ppf
Z
ZZZ
Z
Z
Z
stab

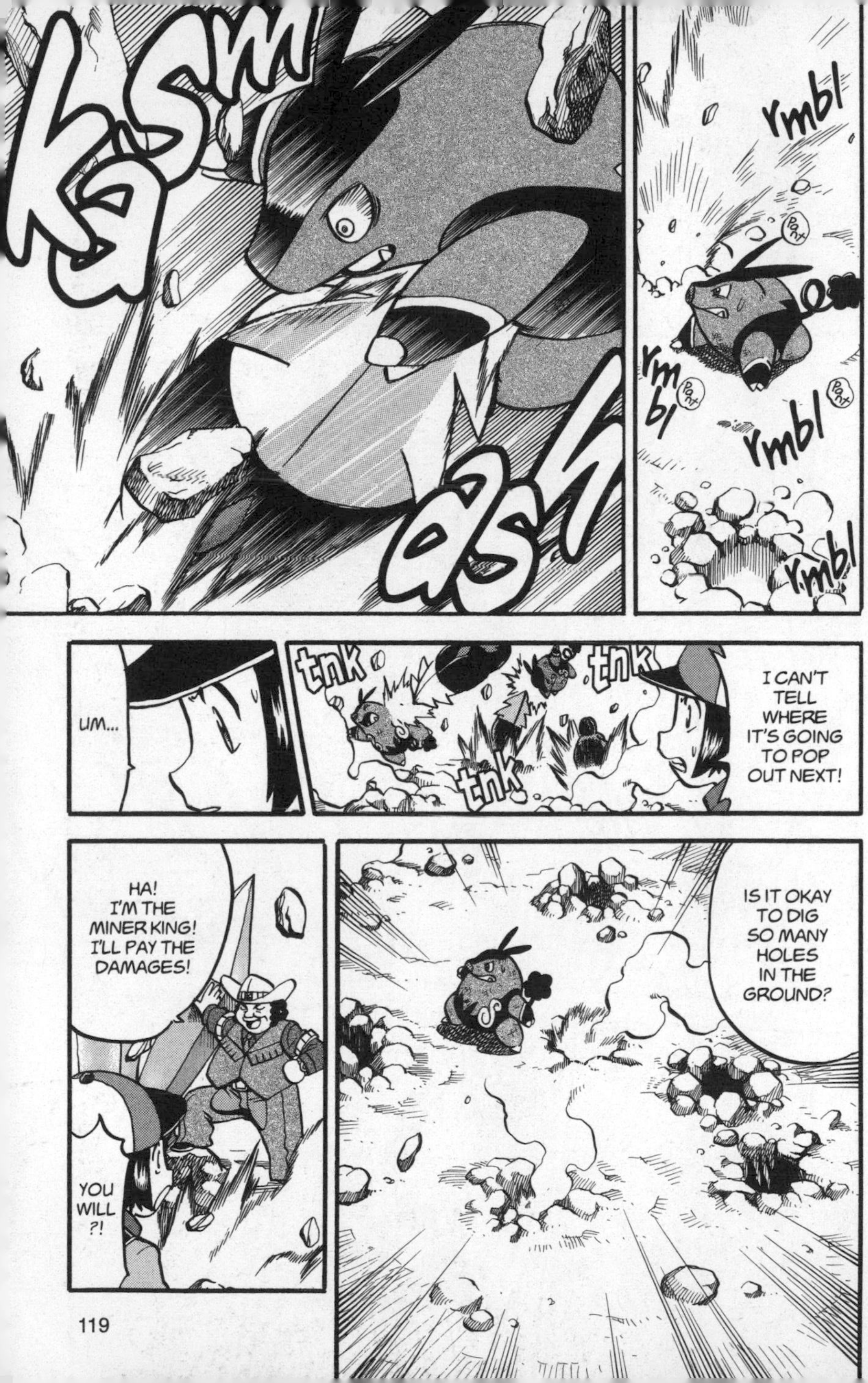
Rmbl
Pant
Rmbl
Pant
Rmbl
Pant
Rmbl
Rmbl
kaSmash
I CAN'T TELL WHERE IT'S GOING TO POP OUT NEXT!
tnk
tnk
tnk
UM...
IS IT OKAY TO DIG SO MANY HOLES IN THE GROUND?
HA! I'M THE MINER KING! I'LL PAY THE DAMAGES!
YOU WILL ?!

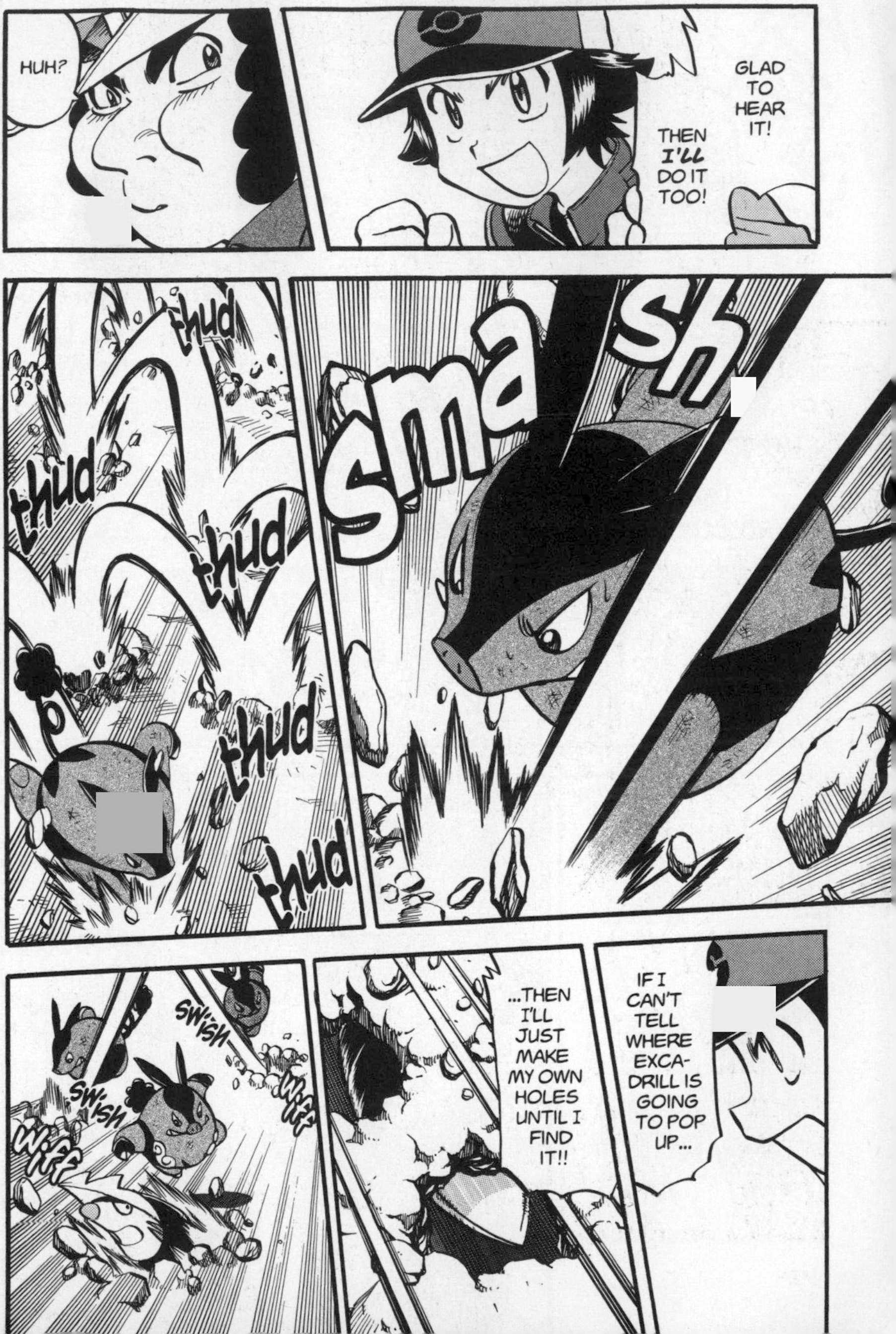
GLAD TO HEAR IT!
THEN I'LL DO IT TOO!
HUH?
smash
thud
thud
thud
thud
thud
IF I CAN'T TELL WHERE EXCA-DRILL IS GOING TO POP UP...
...THEN I'LL JUST MAKE MY OWN HOLES UNTIL I FIND IT!!
SWISH
WIFF
SWISH
WIFF

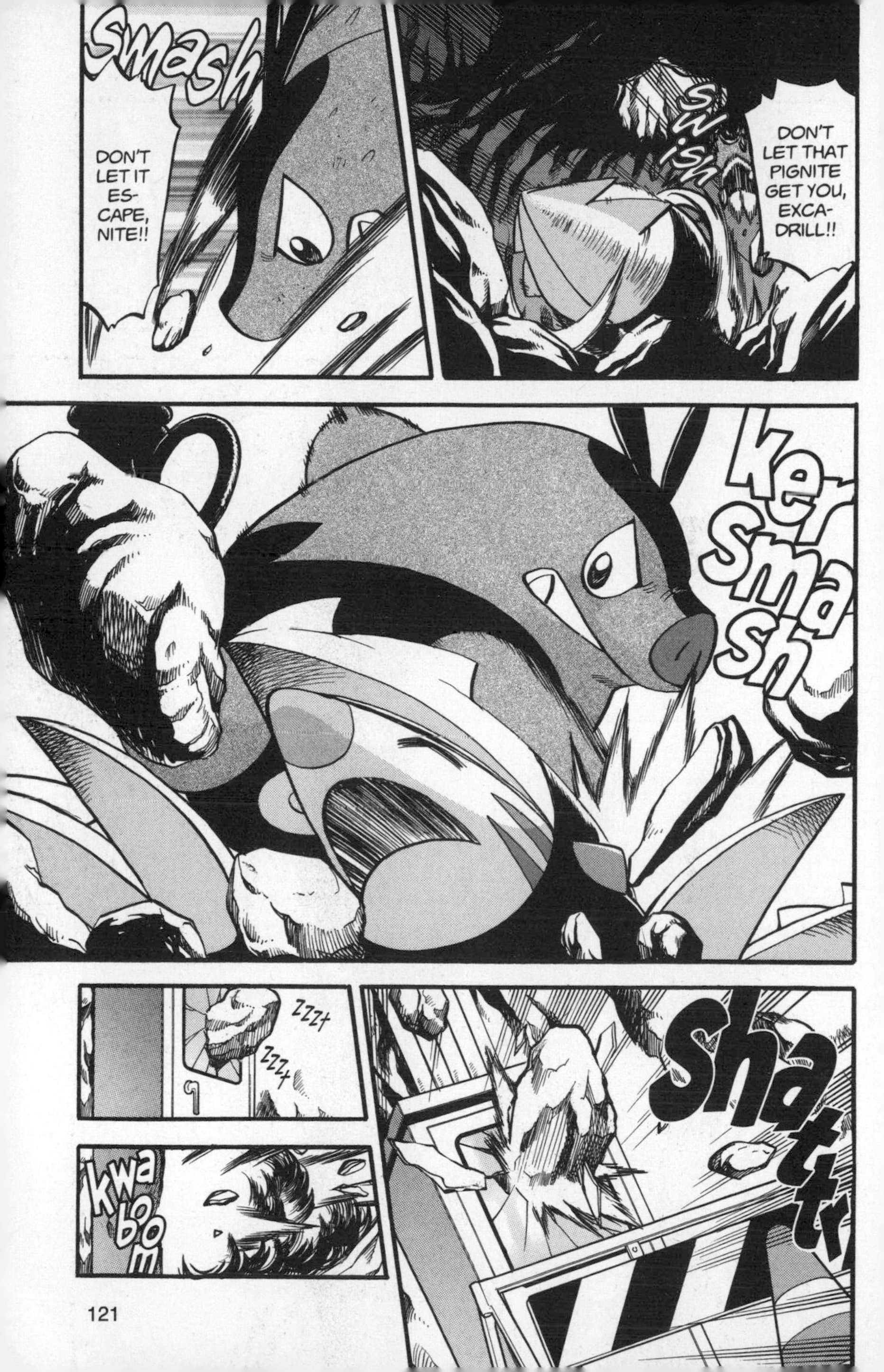
swish
DON'T LET THAT PIGNITE GET YOU, EXCA-DRILL!!
smash
DON'T LET IT ES-CAPE, NITE!!
ker-smash
shattr
zzzt
zzzt
kwaboom

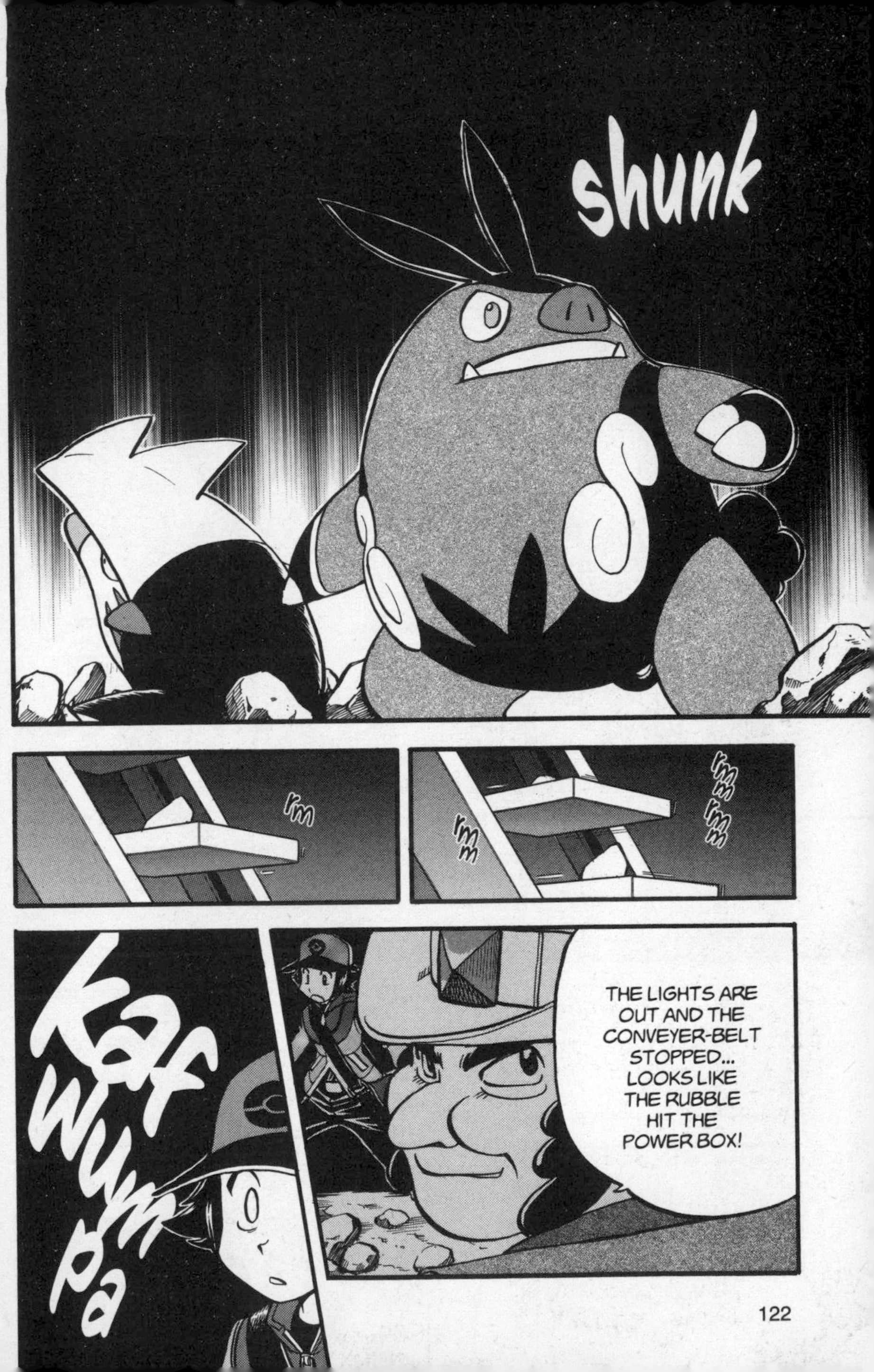
shunk
rmm rmm
rmm
rm
THE LIGHTS ARE OUT AND THE CONVEYER-BELT STOPPED... LOOKS LIKE THE RUBBLE HIT THE POWER BOX!
kaf wumpa

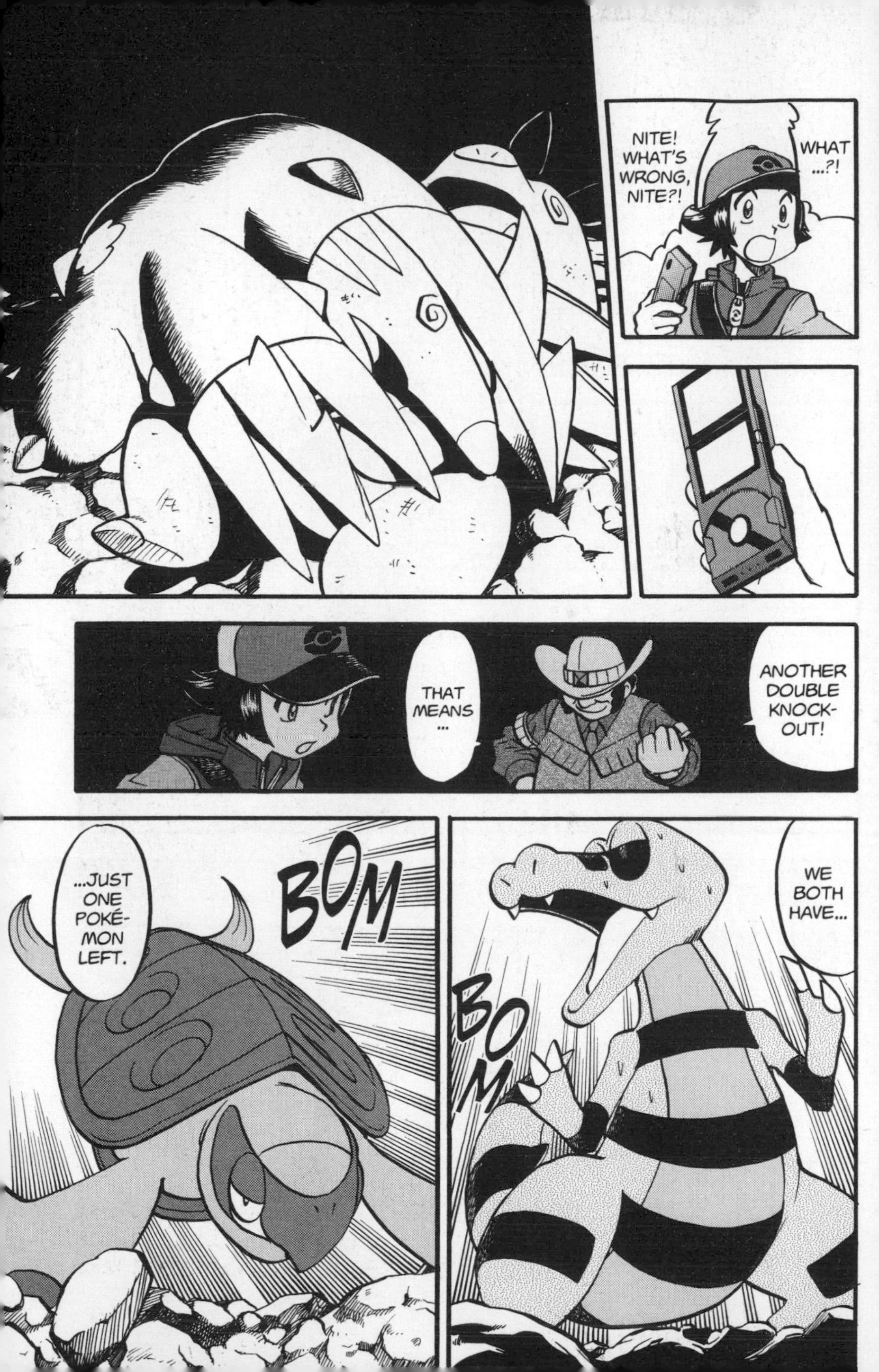
WHAT ...?!
NITE! WHAT'S WRONG, NITE?!
ANOTHER DOUBLE KNOCK-OUT!
THAT MEANS ...
WE BOTH HAVE...
BOM BOM
BOM
...JUST ONE POKÉMON LEFT.

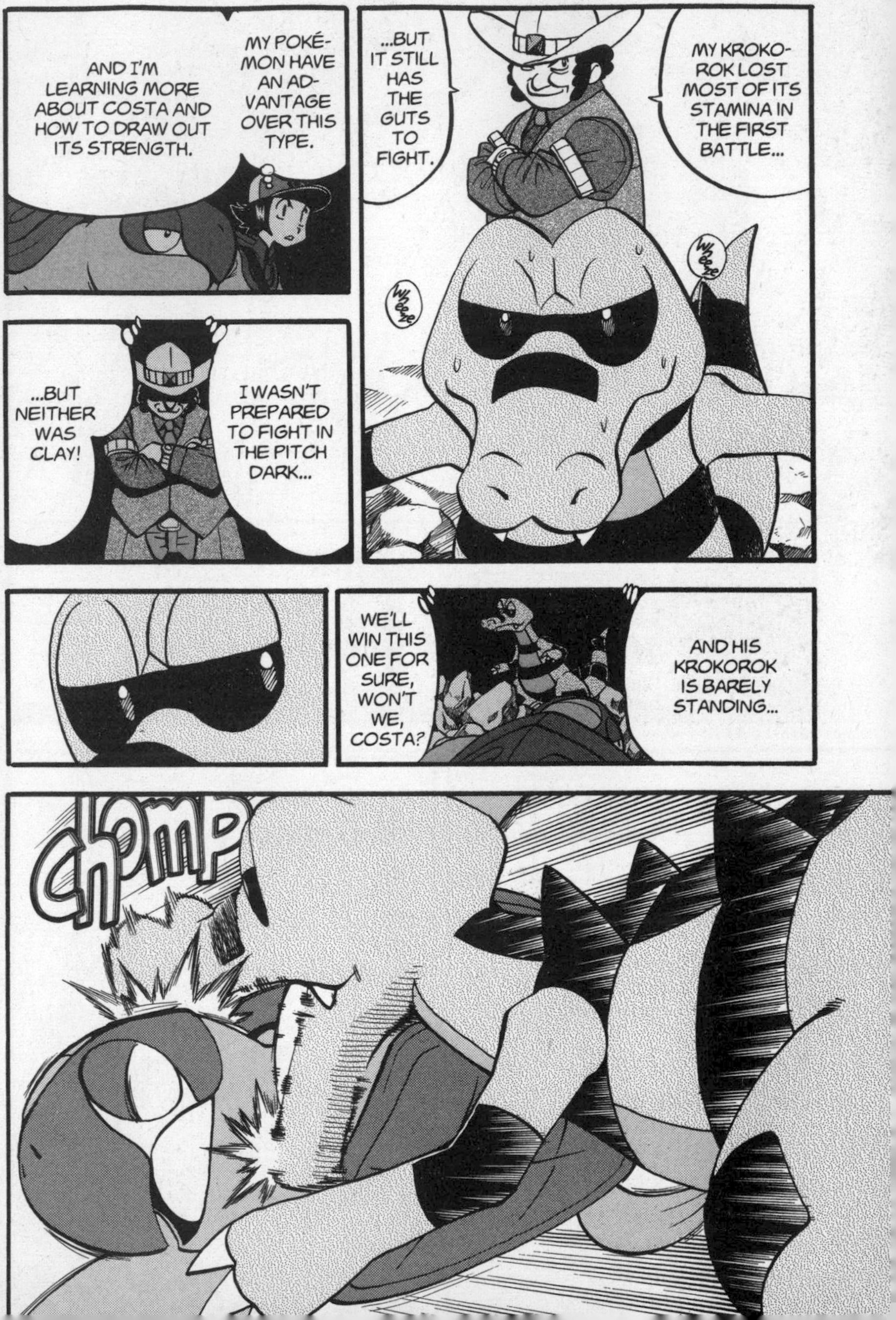
MY KROKOROK LOST MOST OF ITS STAMINA IN THE FIRST BATTLE...
...BUT IT STILL HAS THE GUTS TO FIGHT.
wheeze
wheeze
MY POKÉMON HAVE AN ADVANTAGE OVER THIS TYPE.
AND I'M LEARNING MORE ABOUT COSTA AND HOW TO DRAW OUT ITS STRENGTH.
I WASN'T PREPARED TO FIGHT IN THE PITCH DARK...
...BUT NEITHER WAS CLAY!
AND HIS KROKOROK IS BARELY STANDING...
WE'LL WIN THIS ONE FOR SURE, WON'T WE, COSTA?
CHOMP

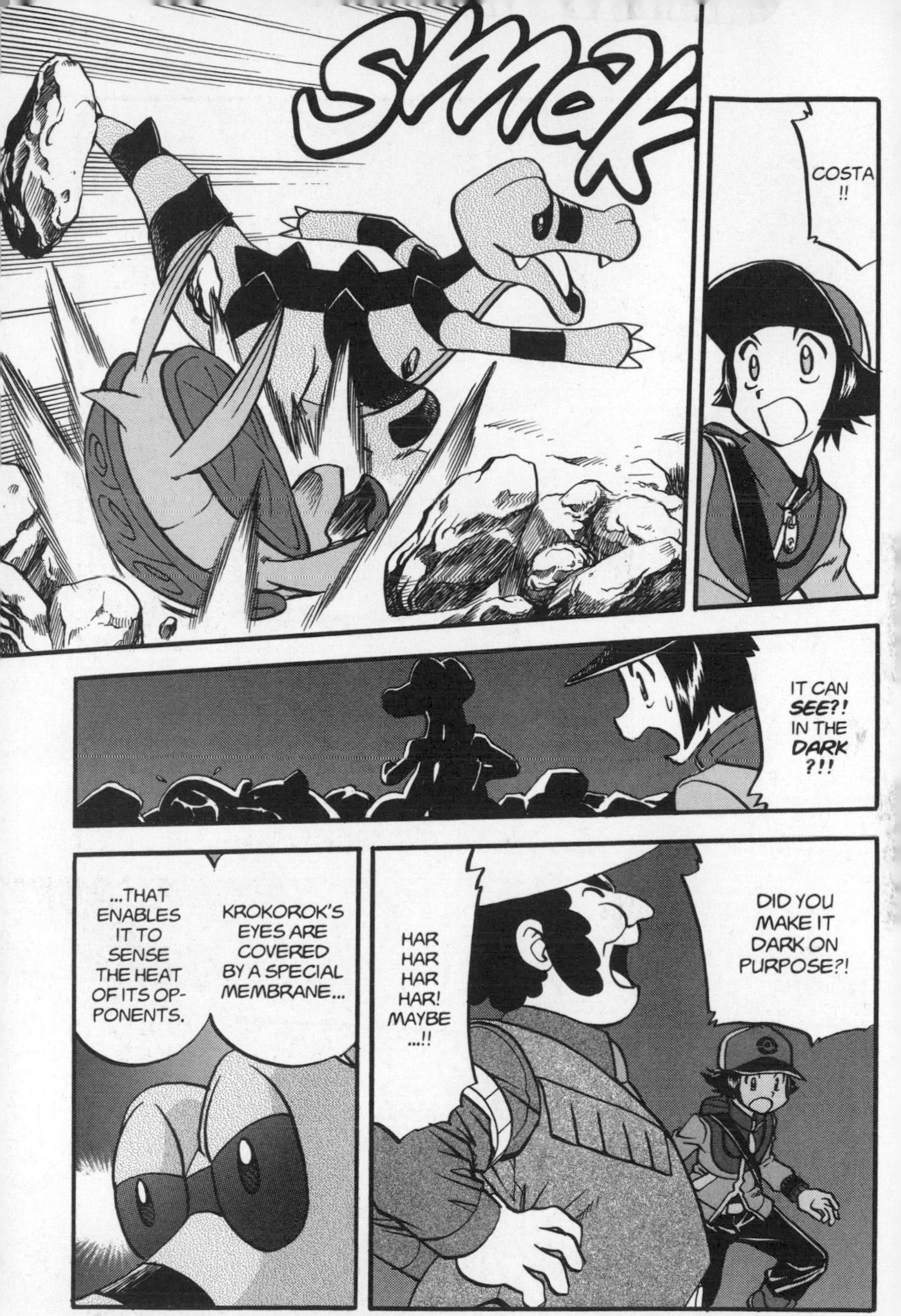
COSTA !!
SMAK
IT CAN SEE?! IN THE DARK ?!!
DID YOU MAKE IT DARK ON PURPOSE?!
HAR HAR HAR HAR! MAYBE ...!!
KROKOROK'S EYES ARE COVERED BY A SPECIAL MEMBRANE...
...THAT ENABLES IT TO SENSE THE HEAT OF ITS OP-PONENTS.

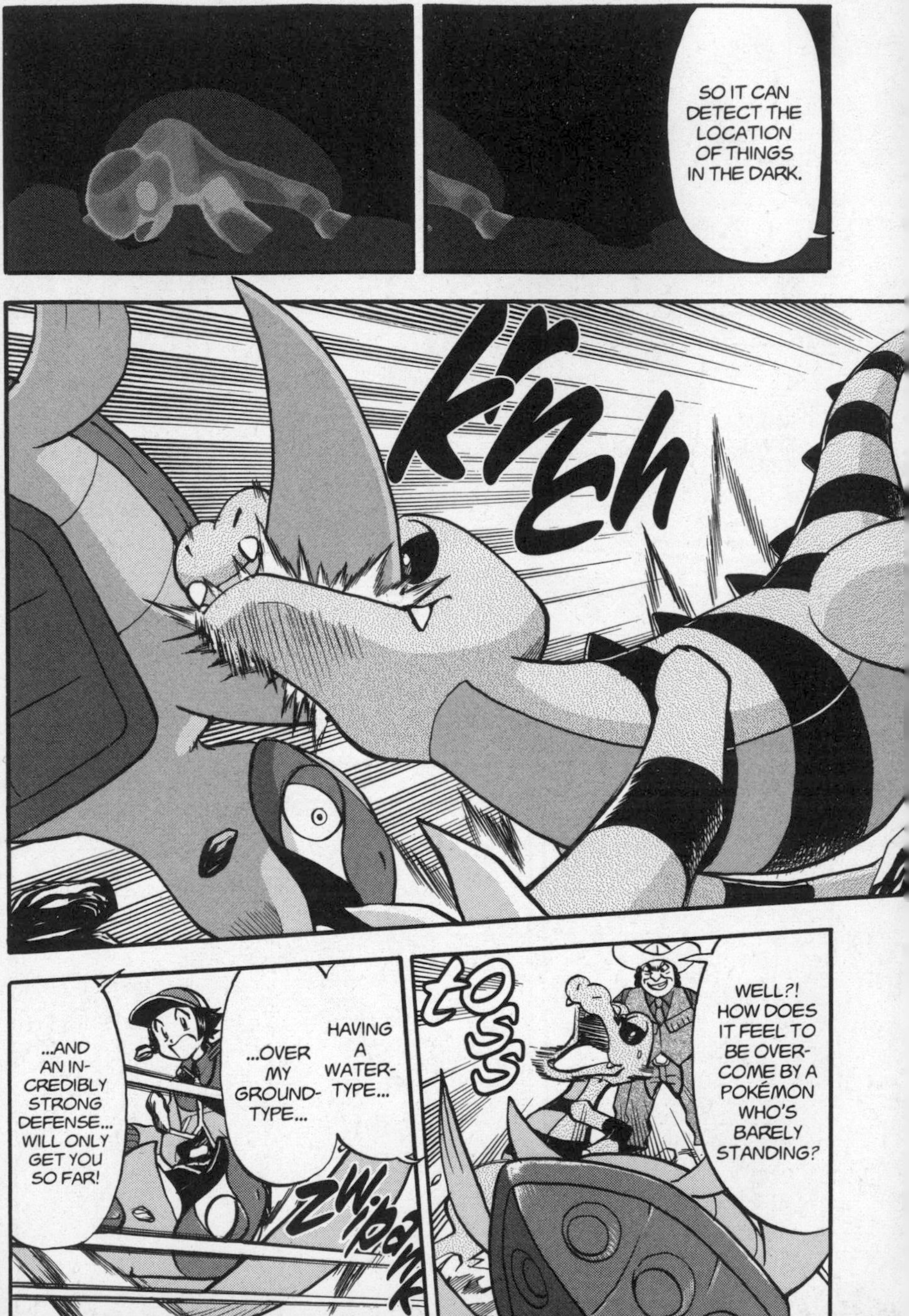
SO IT CAN DETECT THE LOCATION OF THINGS IN THE DARK.
krnch
WELL?! HOW DOES IT FEEL TO BE OVER-COME BY A POKÉMON WHO'S BARELY STANDING?
toss
HAVING A WATER-TYPE...
...OVER MY GROUND-TYPE...
...AND AN IN-CREDIBLY STRONG DEFENSE... WILL ONLY GET YOU SO FAR!
zwipank

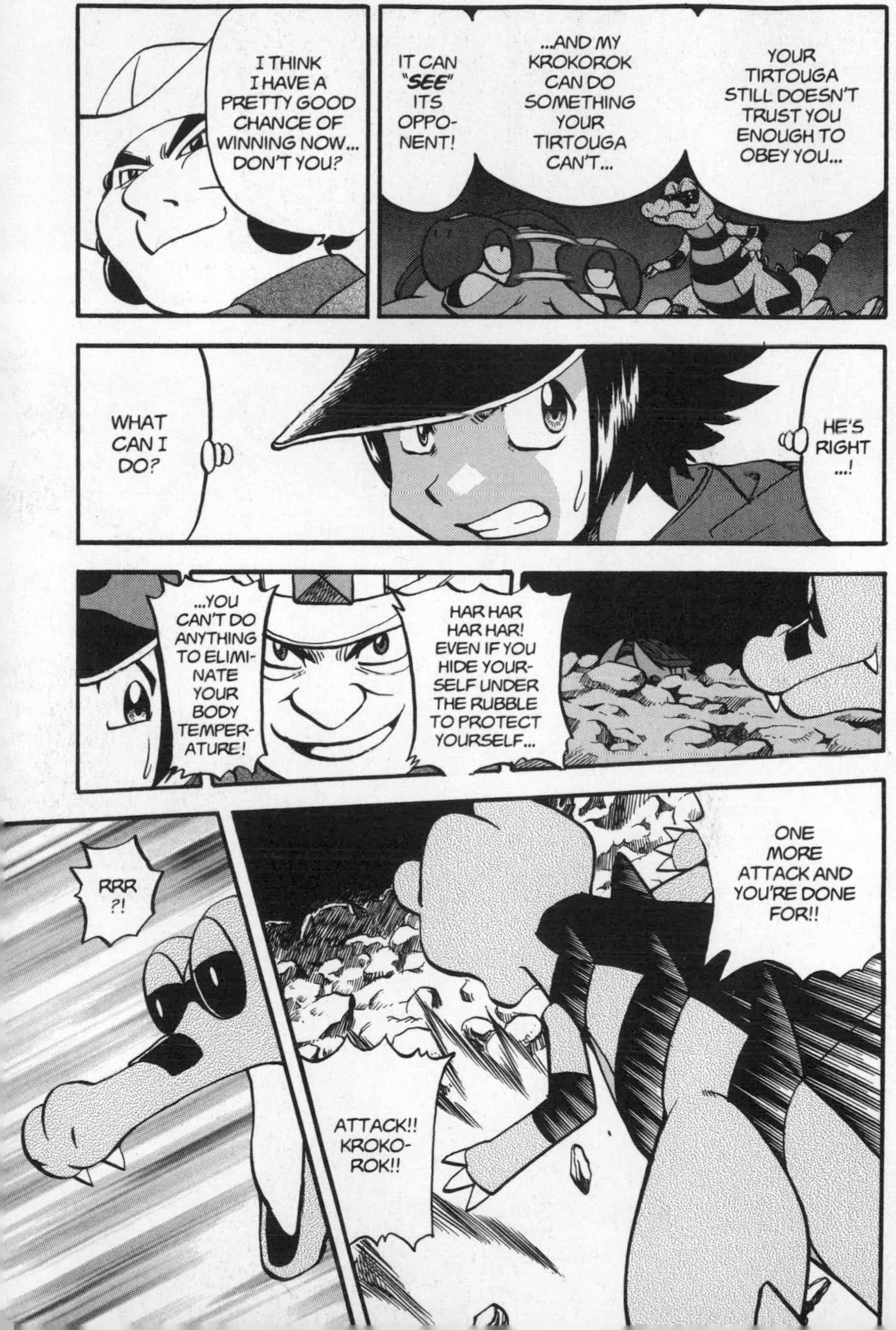
YOUR TIRTOUGA STILL DOESN'T TRUST YOU ENOUGH TO OBEY YOU...
...AND MY KROKOROK CAN DO SOMETHING YOUR TIRTOUGA CAN'T...
IT CAN "SEE" ITS OPPONENT!
I THINK I HAVE A PRETTY GOOD CHANCE OF WINNING NOW... DON'T YOU?
HE'S RIGHT ...!
WHAT CAN I DO?
HAR HAR HAR HAR! EVEN IF YOU HIDE YOURSELF UNDER THE RUBBLE TO PROTECT YOURSELF...
...YOU CAN'T DO ANYTHING TO ELIMINATE YOUR BODY TEMPERATURE!
ONE MORE ATTACK AND YOU'RE DONE FOR!!
ATTACK!! KROKOROK!!
RRR ?!

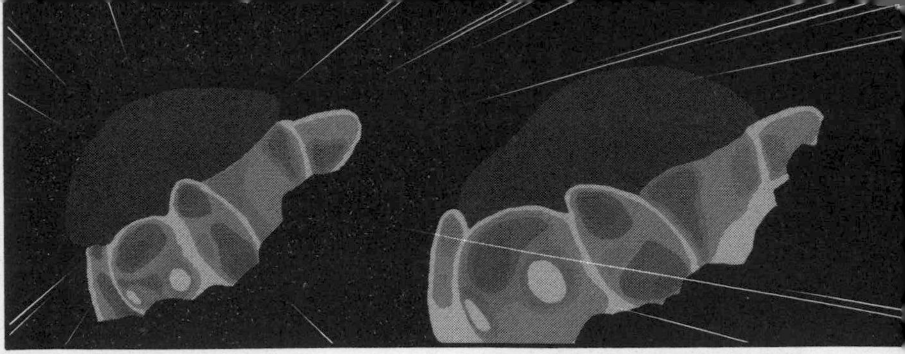
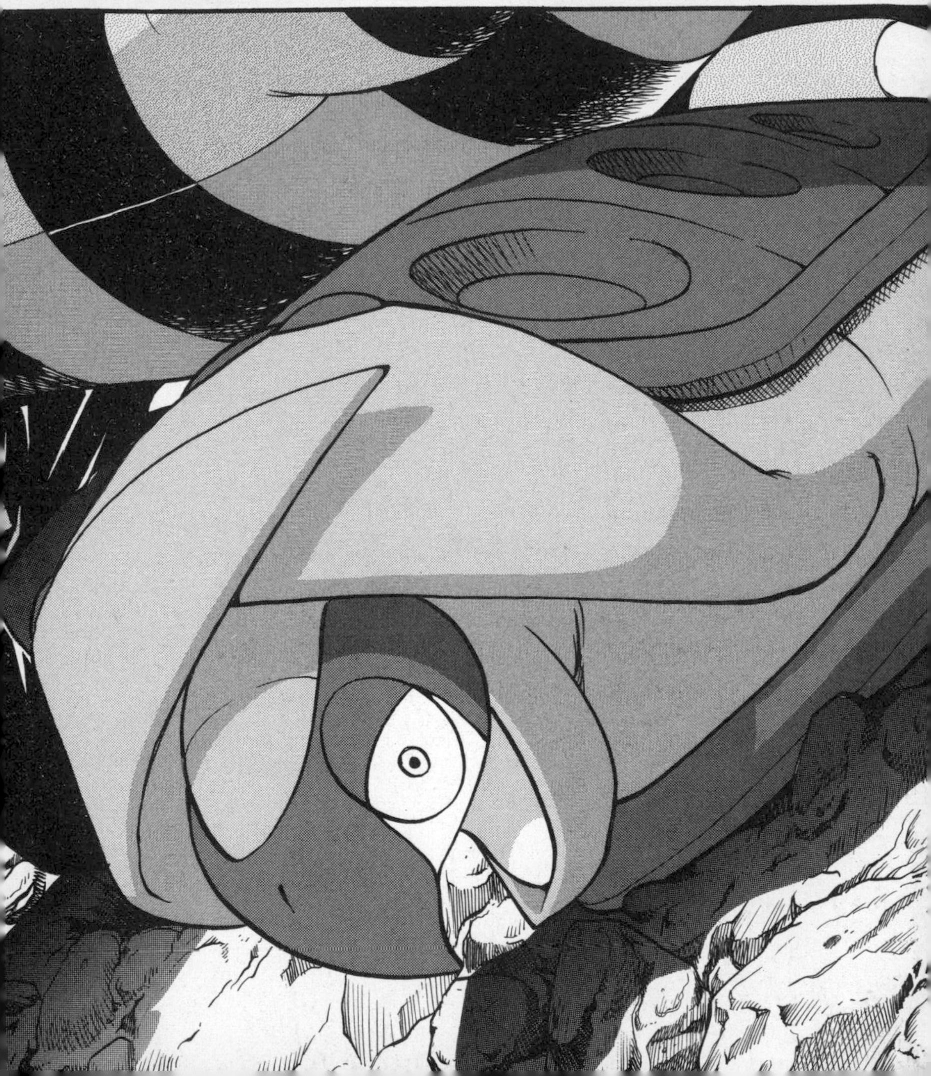

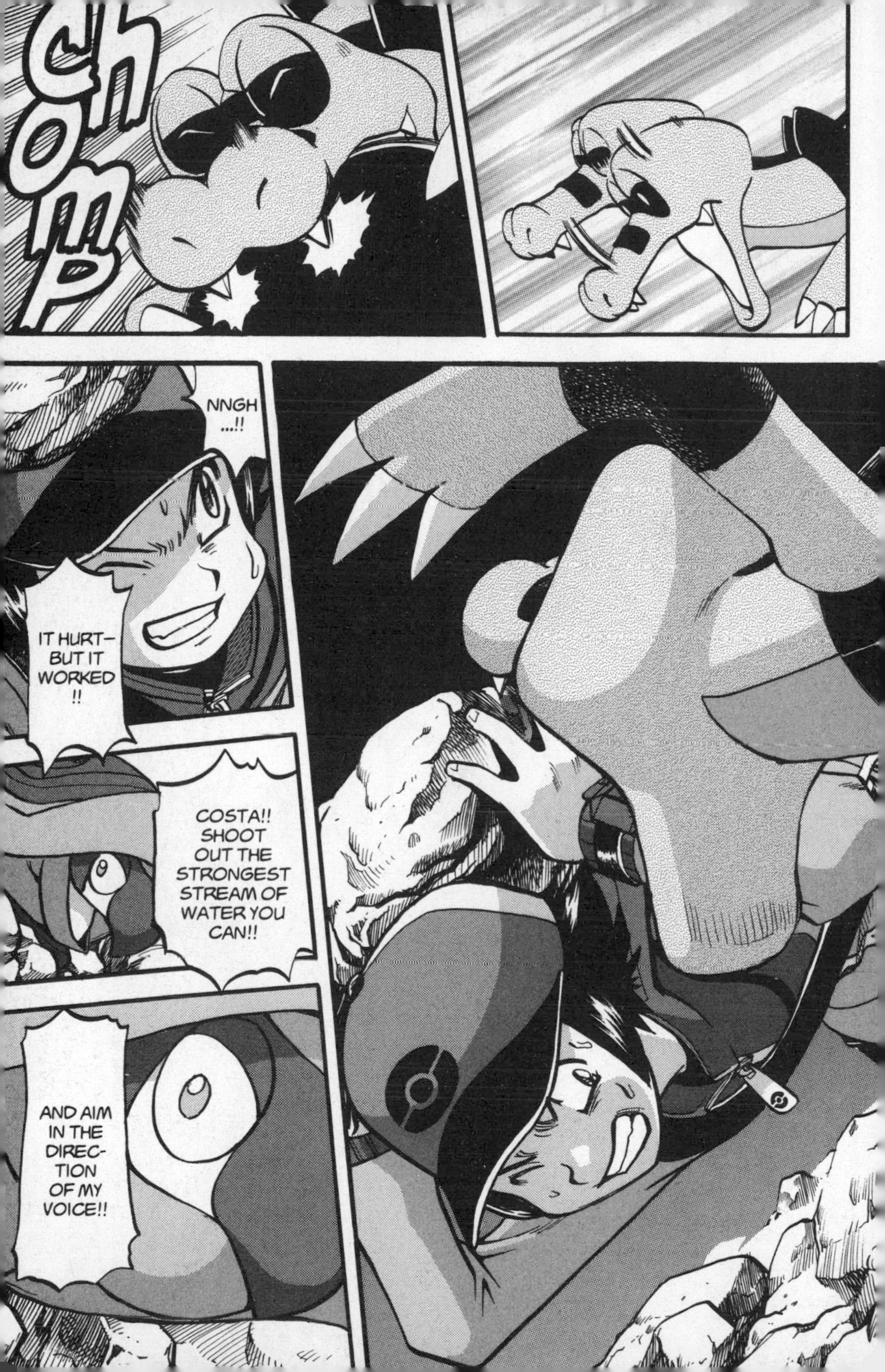
CHOMP
NNGH ...!!
IT HURT—BUT IT WORKED!!
COSTA!! SHOOT OUT THE STRONGEST STREAM OF WATER YOU CAN!!
AND AIM IN THE DIRECTION OF MY VOICE!!

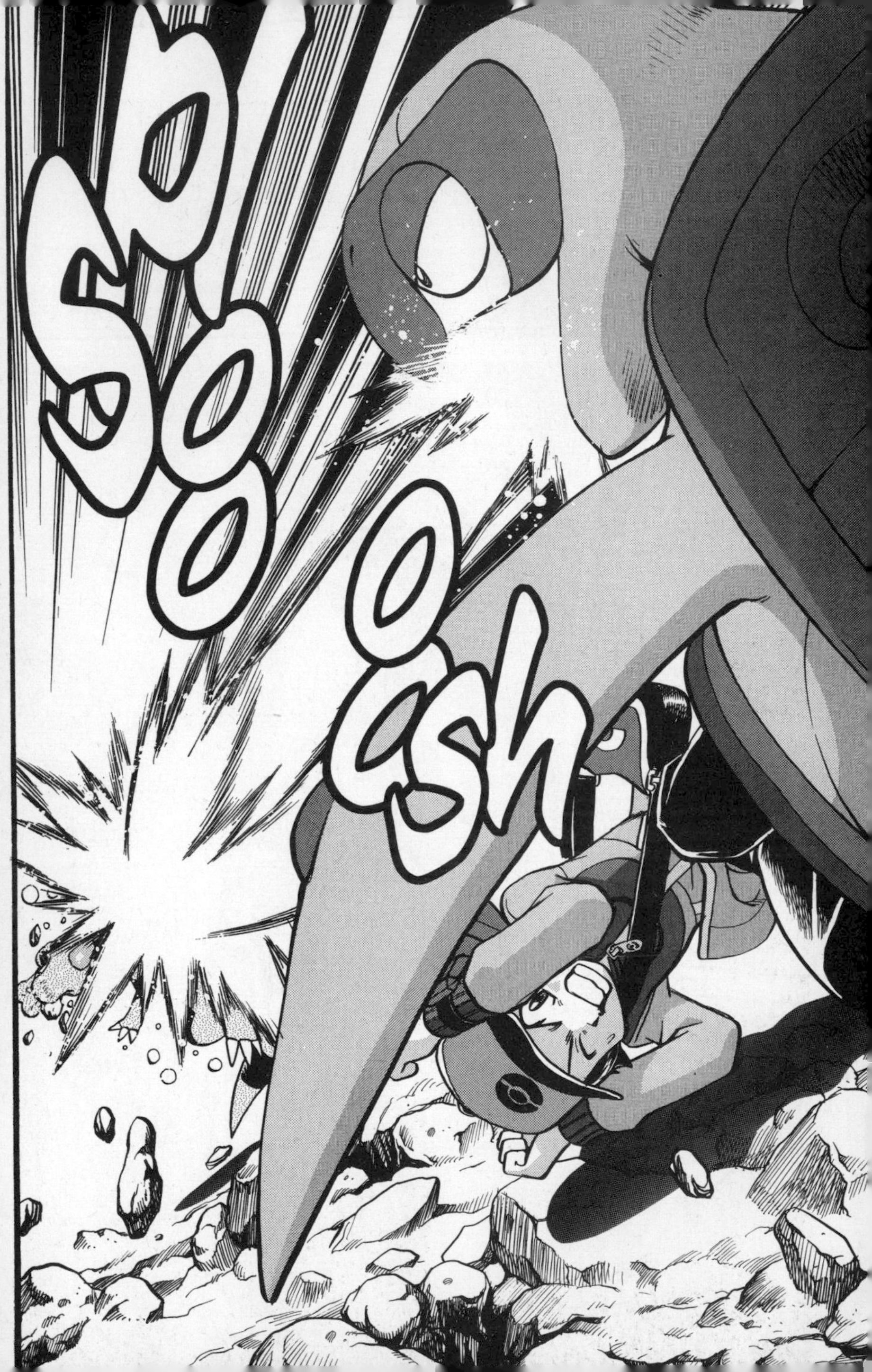
Sgooosh

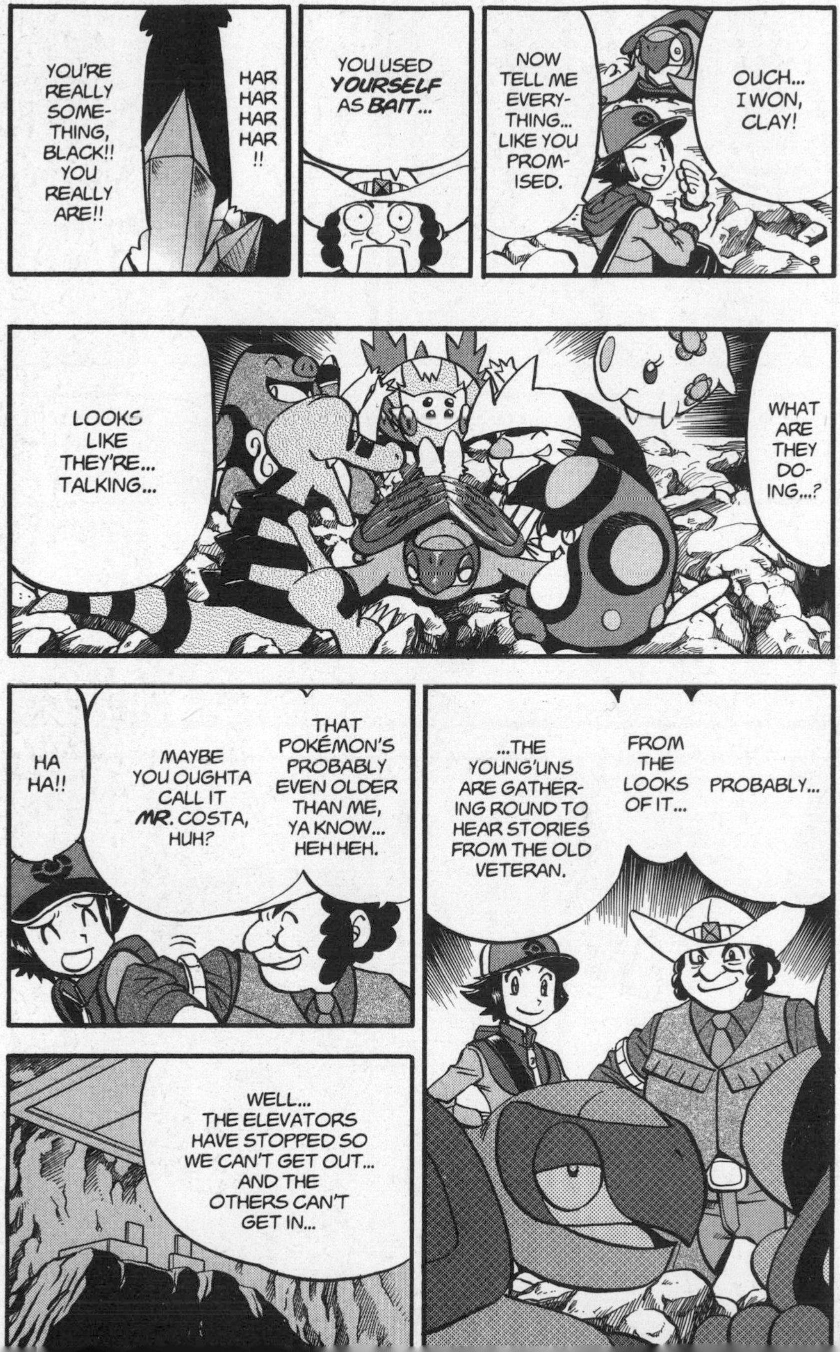
OUCH... I WON, CLAY!
NOW TELL ME EVERYTHING... LIKE YOU PROMISED.
YOU USED **YOURSELF** AS **BAIT**...
HAR HAR HAR HAR!!
YOU'RE REALLY SOMETHING, BLACK!! YOU REALLY ARE!!
WHAT ARE THEY DOING...?
LOOKS LIKE THEY'RE... TALKING...
PROBABLY...
FROM THE LOOKS OF IT...
...THE YOUNG'UNS ARE GATHERING ROUND TO HEAR STORIES FROM THE OLD VETERAN.
THAT POKÉMON'S PROBABLY EVEN OLDER THAN ME, YA KNOW... HEH HEH.
MAYBE YOU OUGHTA CALL IT **MR.** COSTA, HUH?
HA HA!!
WELL... THE ELEVATORS HAVE STOPPED SO WE CAN'T GET OUT... AND THE OTHERS CAN'T GET IN...

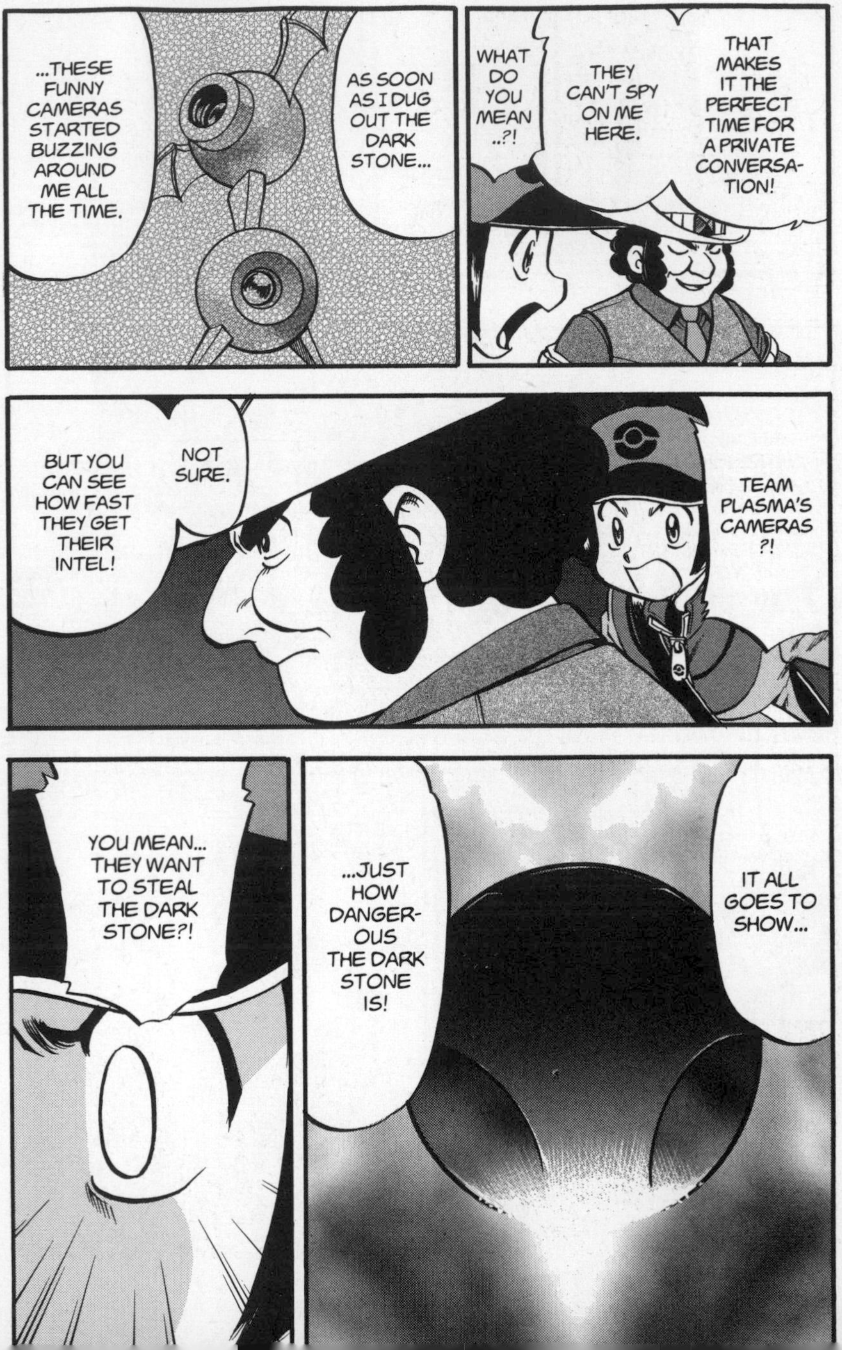
THAT MAKES IT THE PERFECT TIME FOR A PRIVATE CONVERSA-TION!
THEY CAN'T SPY ON ME HERE.
WHAT DO YOU MEAN ..?!
AS SOON AS I DUG OUT THE DARK STONE...
...THESE FUNNY CAMERAS STARTED BUZZING AROUND ME ALL THE TIME.
TEAM PLASMA'S CAMERAS ?!
NOT SURE.
BUT YOU CAN SEE HOW FAST THEY GET THEIR INTEL!
IT ALL GOES TO SHOW...
...JUST HOW DANGER-OUS THE DARK STONE IS!
YOU MEAN... THEY WANT TO STEAL THE DARK STONE?!

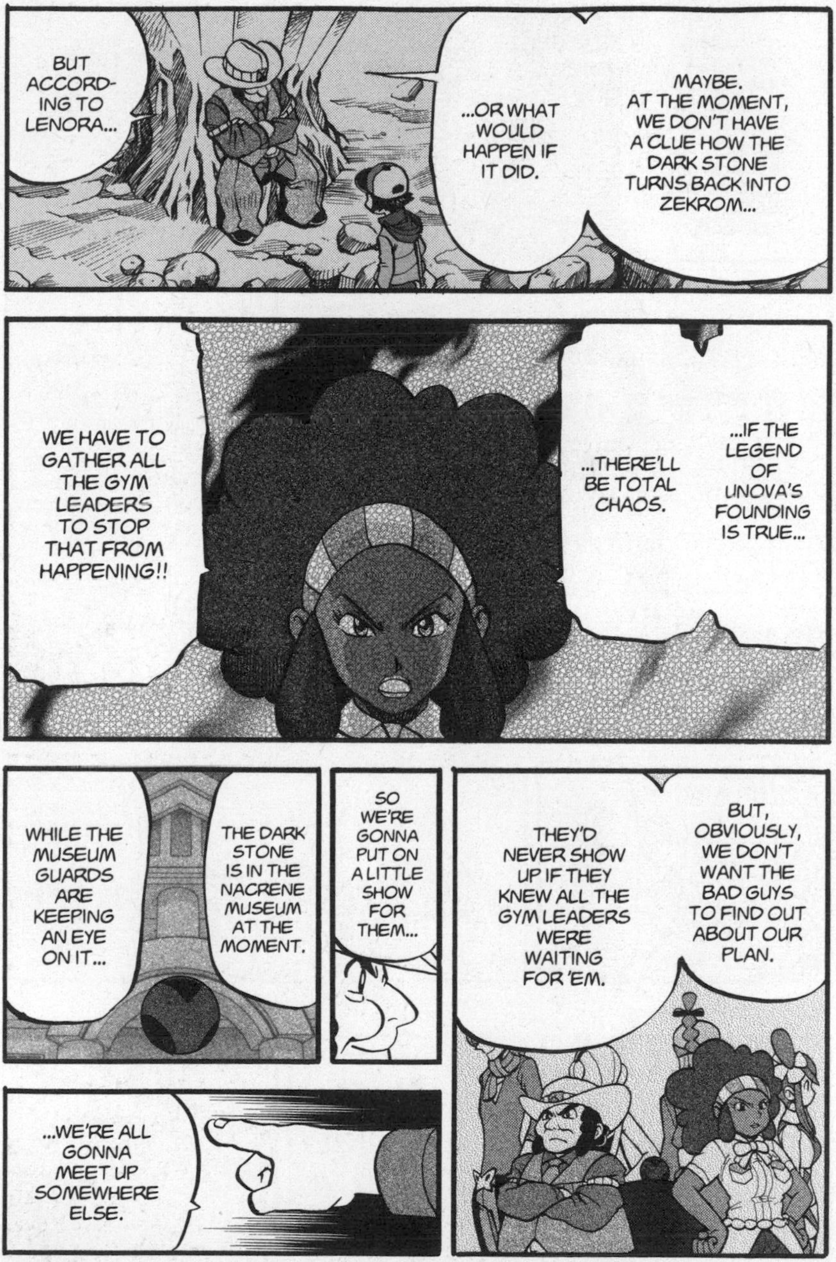
MAYBE. AT THE MOMENT, WE DON'T HAVE A CLUE HOW THE DARK STONE TURNS BACK INTO ZEKROM...
...OR WHAT WOULD HAPPEN IF IT DID.
BUT ACCORDING TO LENORA...
...IF THE LEGEND OF UNOVA'S FOUNDING IS TRUE...
...THERE'LL BE TOTAL CHAOS.
WE HAVE TO GATHER ALL THE GYM LEADERS TO STOP THAT FROM HAPPENING!!
BUT, OBVIOUSLY, WE DON'T WANT THE BAD GUYS TO FIND OUT ABOUT OUR PLAN.
THEY'D NEVER SHOW UP IF THEY KNEW ALL THE GYM LEADERS WERE WAITING FOR 'EM.
SO WE'RE GONNA PUT ON A LITTLE SHOW FOR THEM...
THE DARK STONE IS IN THE NACRENE MUSEUM AT THE MOMENT.
WHILE THE MUSEUM GUARDS ARE KEEPING AN EYE ON IT...
...WE'RE ALL GONNA MEET UP SOMEWHERE ELSE.

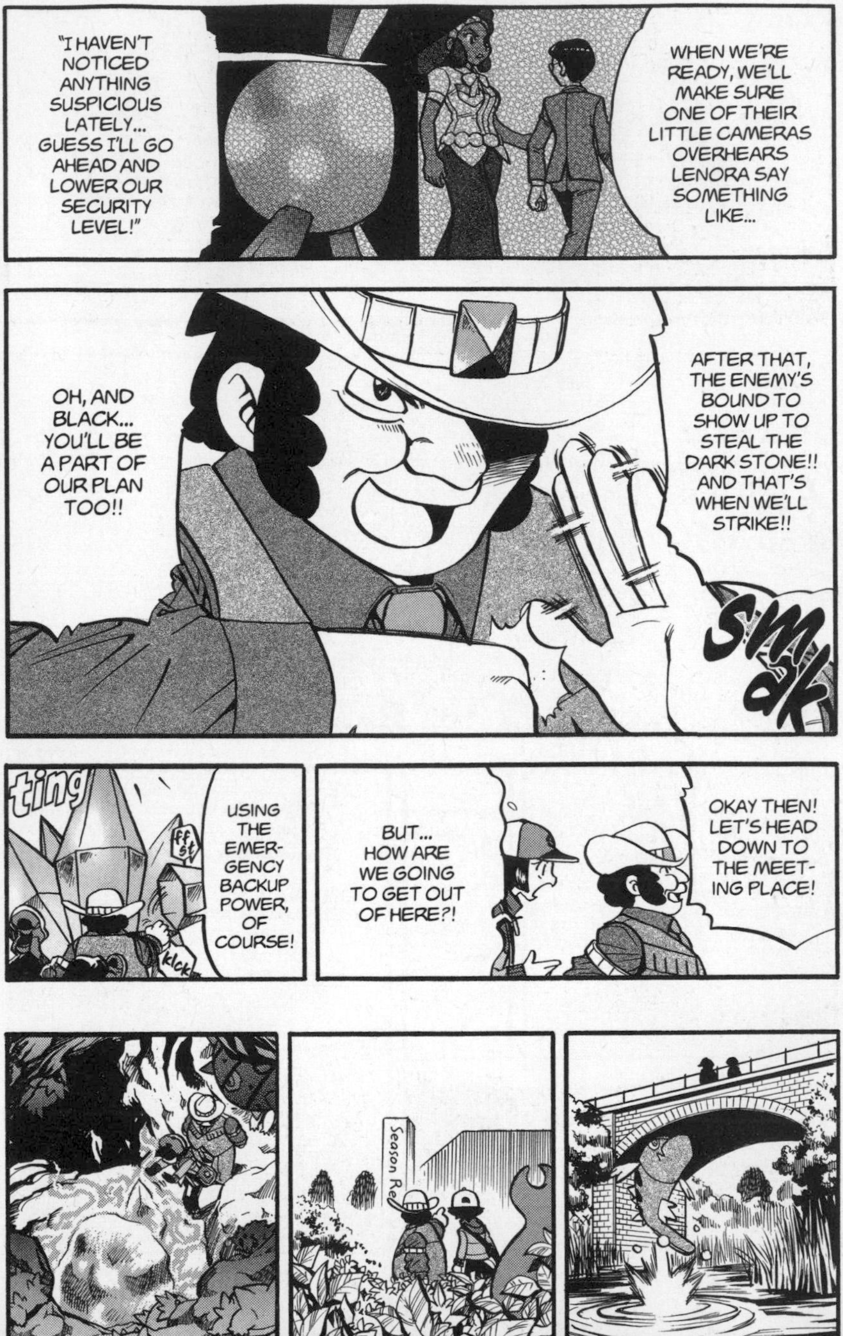
WHEN WE'RE READY, WE'LL MAKE SURE ONE OF THEIR LITTLE CAMERAS OVERHEARS LENORA SAY SOMETHING LIKE...
"I HAVEN'T NOTICED ANYTHING SUSPICIOUS LATELY... GUESS I'LL GO AHEAD AND LOWER OUR SECURITY LEVEL!"
AFTER THAT, THE ENEMY'S BOUND TO SHOW UP TO STEAL THE DARK STONE!! AND THAT'S WHEN WE'LL STRIKE!!
SMAK
OH, AND BLACK... YOU'LL BE A PART OF OUR PLAN TOO!!
OKAY THEN! LET'S HEAD DOWN TO THE MEET-ING PLACE!
BUT... HOW ARE WE GOING TO GET OUT OF HERE?!
ting
ffst
USING THE EMER-GENCY BACKUP POWER, OF COURSE!
klck
Season Re

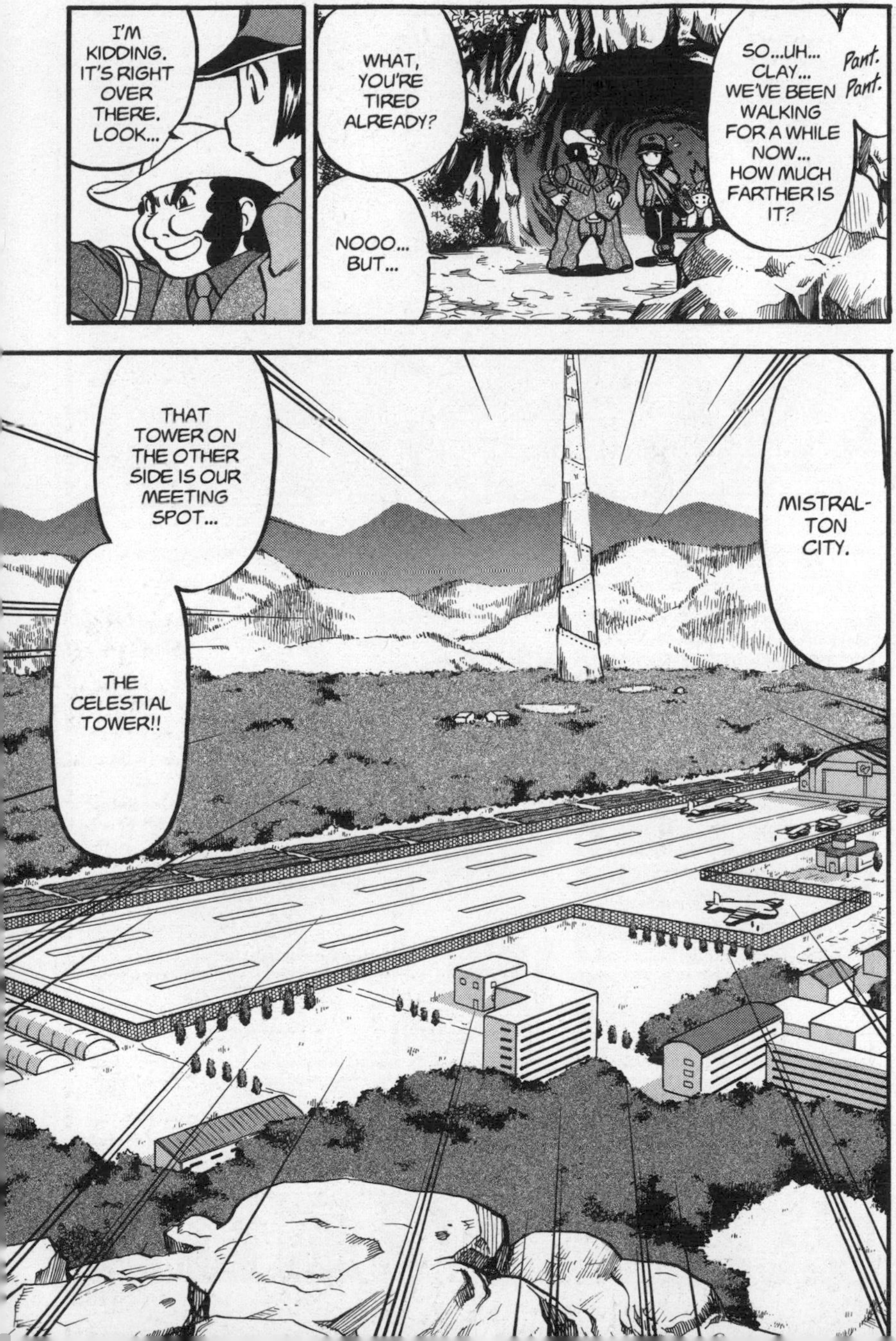
SO...UH... CLAY... WE'VE BEEN WALKING FOR A WHILE NOW... HOW MUCH FARTHER IS IT?
Pant. Pant.
WHAT, YOU'RE TIRED ALREADY?
NOOO... BUT...
I'M KIDDING. IT'S RIGHT OVER THERE. LOOK...
MISTRAL-TON CITY.
THAT TOWER ON THE OTHER SIDE IS OUR MEETING SPOT...
THE CELESTIAL TOWER!!

ADVENTURE MAP

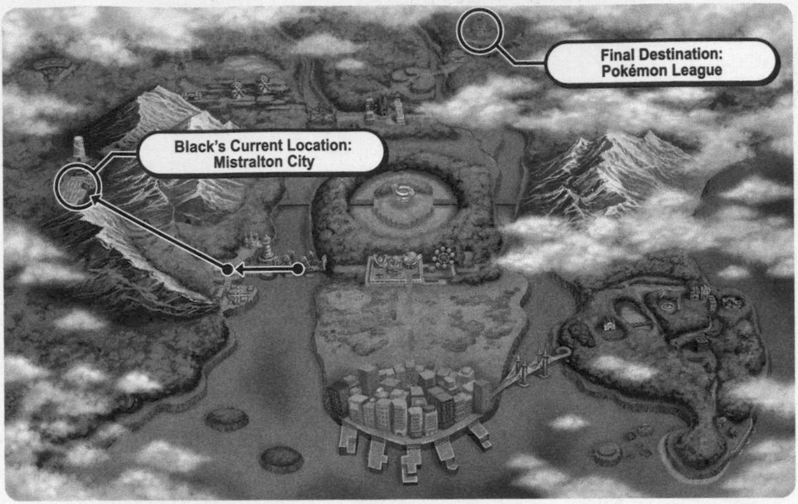

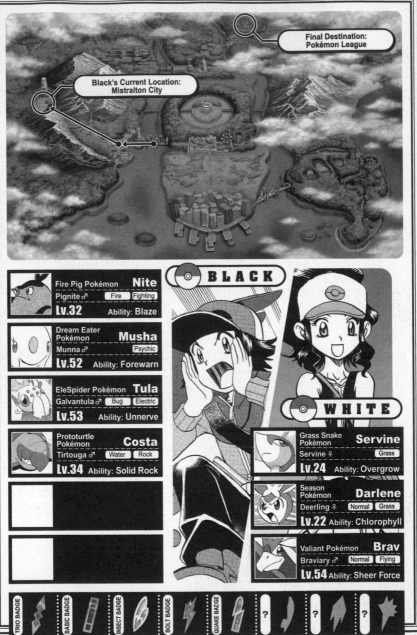

Final Destination:
Pokémon League
Black's Current Location:
Mistralton City

BLACK

Nite
Fire Pig Pokémon
Pignite ♂ | Fire | Fighting
Lv.32 Ability: Blaze

Musha
Dream Eater Pokémon
Munna ♂ | Psychic
Lv.52 Ability: Forewarn

Tula
EleSpider Pokémon
Galvantula ♂ | Bug | Electric
Lv.53 Ability: Unnerve

Costa
Prototurtle Pokémon
Tirtouga ♂ | Water | Rock
Lv.34 Ability: Solid Rock

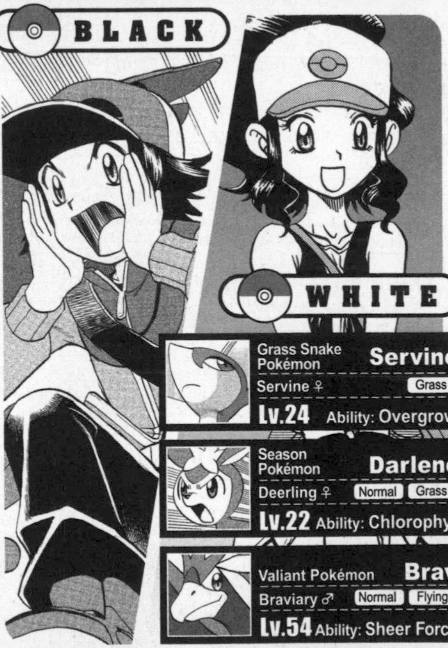

WHITE

Servine
Grass Snake Pokémon
Servine ♀ | Grass
Lv.24 Ability: Overgrow

Darlene
Season Pokémon
Deerling ♀ | Normal | Grass
Lv.22 Ability: Chlorophyll

Brav
Valiant Pokémon
Braviary ♂ | Normal | Flying
Lv.54 Ability: Sheer Force

TRIO BADGE | BASIC BADGE | INSECT BADGE | BOLT BADGE | QUAKE BADGE | ? | ? | ?

Pokémon™

Adventures

Black & White

SWOOBAT

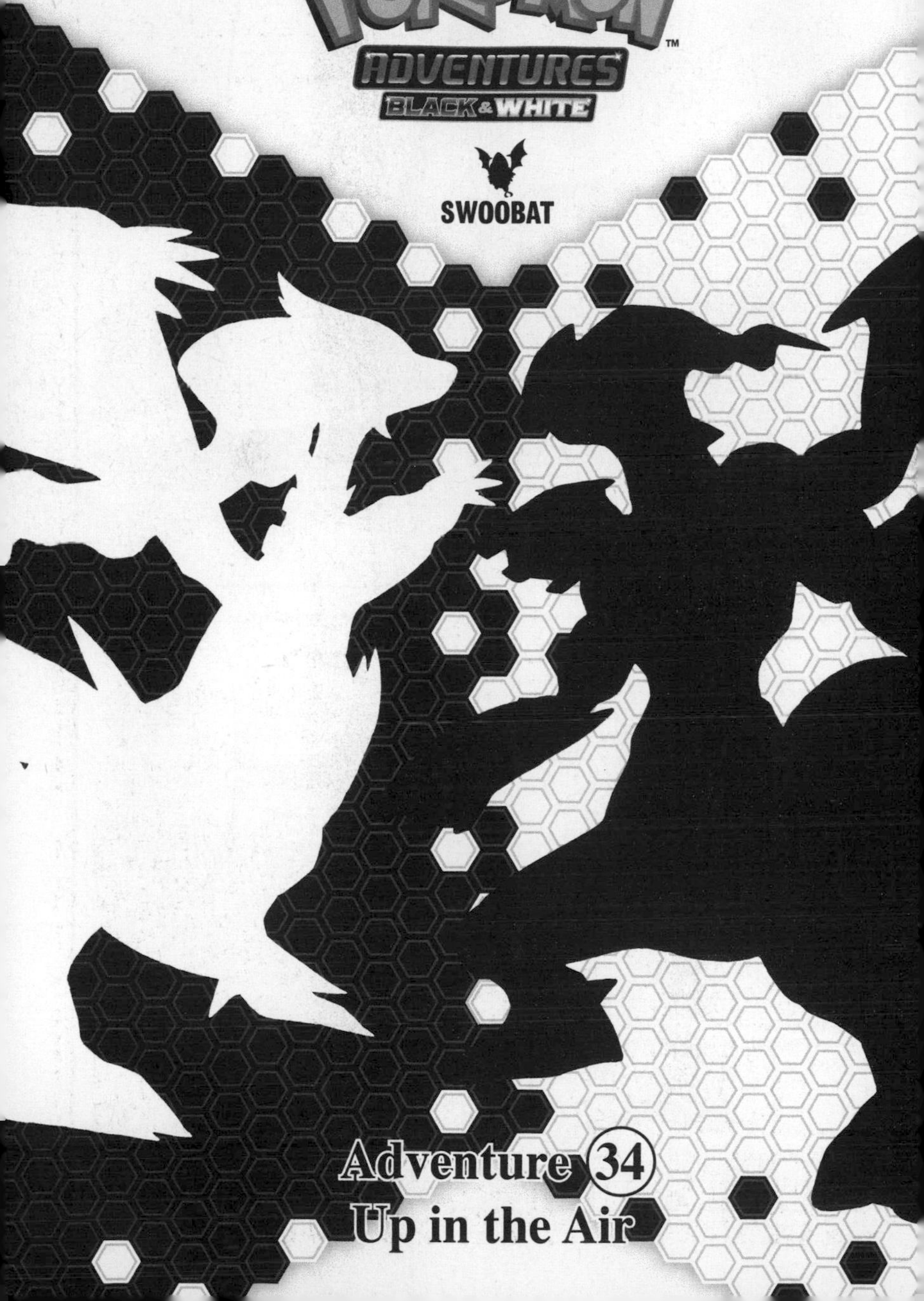

Adventure 34
Up in the Air

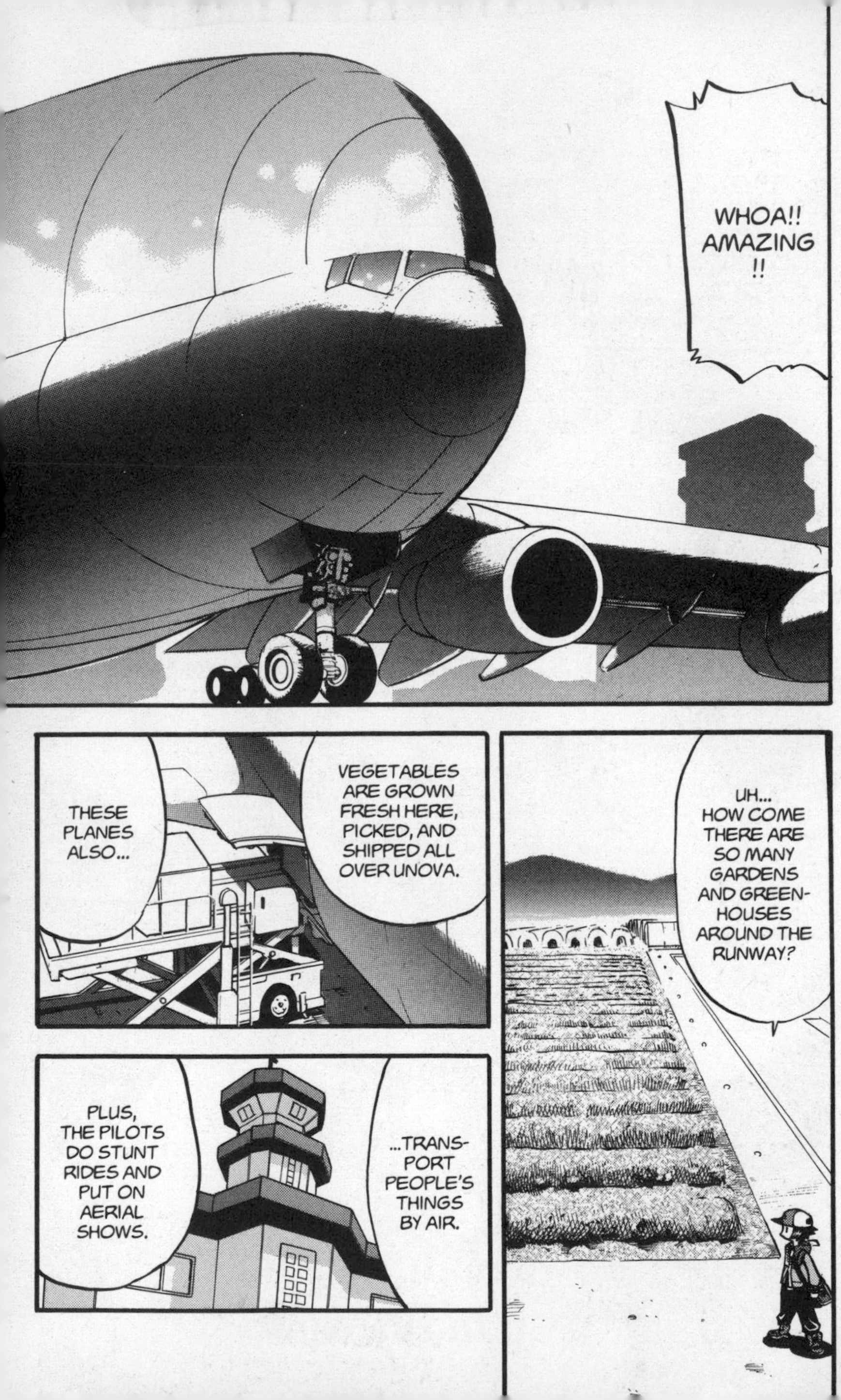
WHOA!! AMAZING !!
UH... HOW COME THERE ARE SO MANY GARDENS AND GREEN-HOUSES AROUND THE RUNWAY?
VEGETABLES ARE GROWN FRESH HERE, PICKED, AND SHIPPED ALL OVER UNOVA.
THESE PLANES ALSO...
...TRANS-PORT PEOPLE'S THINGS BY AIR.
PLUS, THE PILOTS DO STUNT RIDES AND PUT ON AERIAL SHOWS.

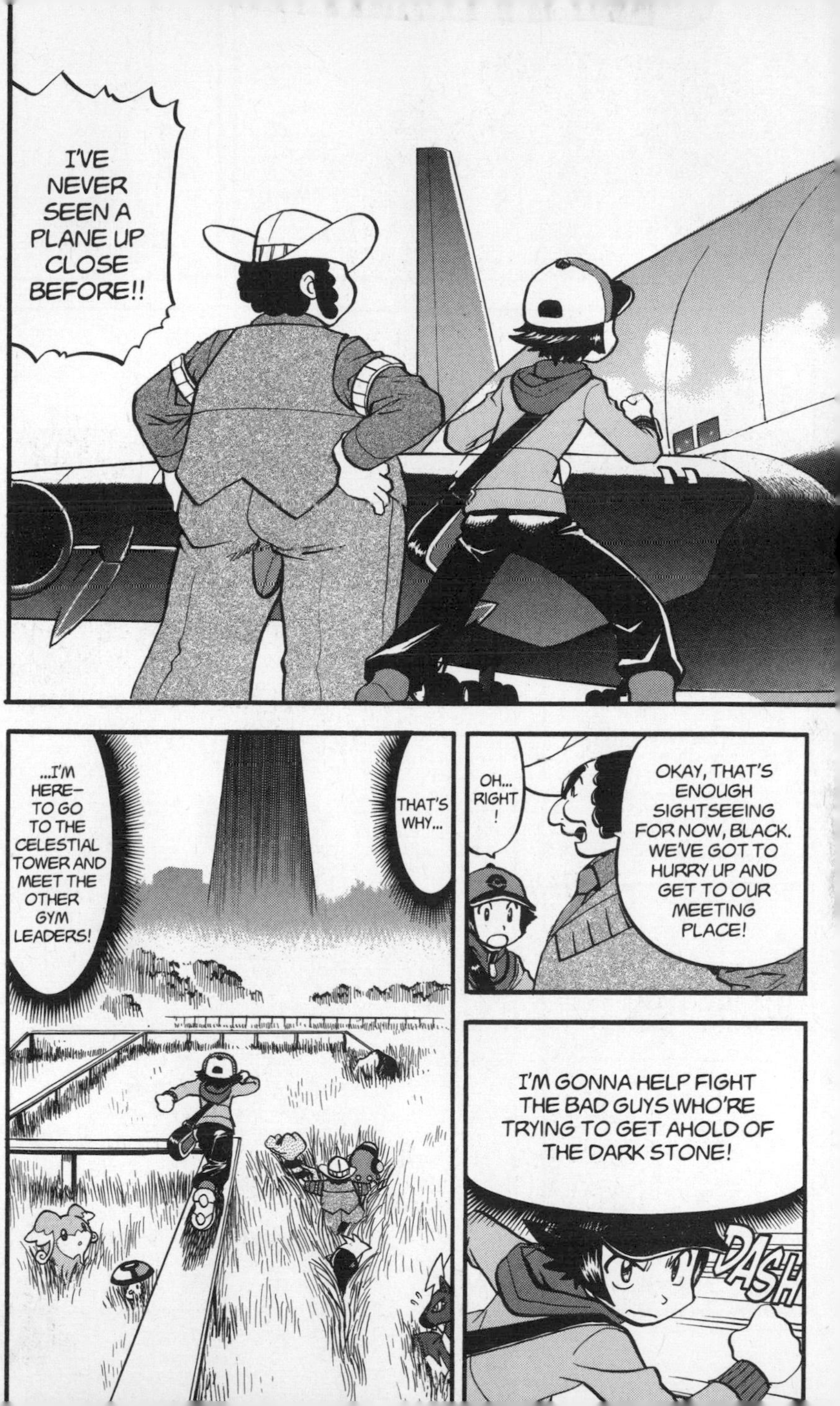
I'VE NEVER SEEN A PLANE UP CLOSE BEFORE!!
OKAY, THAT'S ENOUGH SIGHTSEEING FOR NOW, BLACK. WE'VE GOT TO HURRY UP AND GET TO OUR MEETING PLACE!
OH... RIGHT!
I'M GONNA HELP FIGHT THE BAD GUYS WHO'RE TRYING TO GET AHOLD OF THE DARK STONE!
DASH
THAT'S WHY...
...I'M HERE— TO GO TO THE CELESTIAL TOWER AND MEET THE OTHER GYM LEADERS!

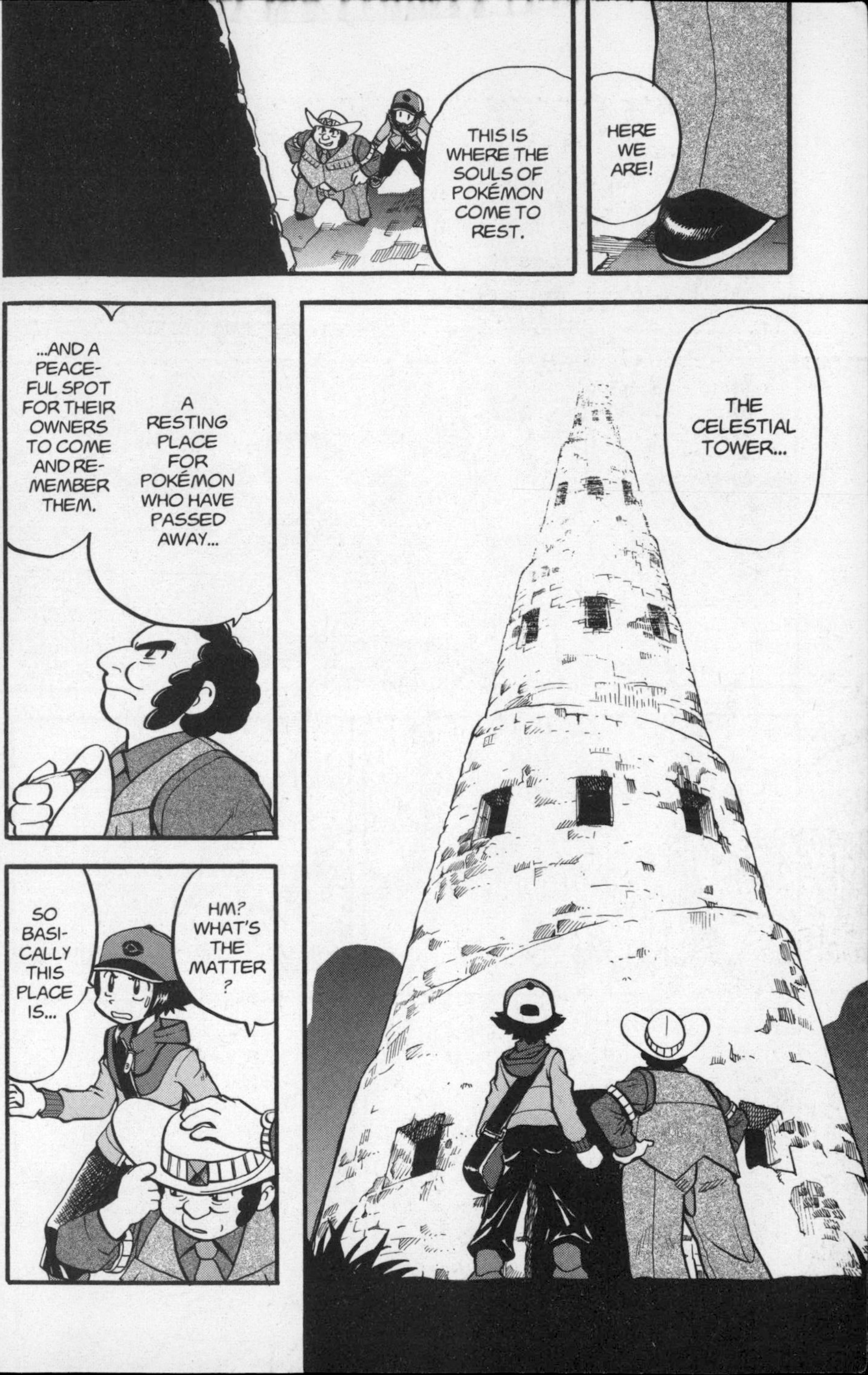
HERE WE ARE!
THIS IS WHERE THE SOULS OF POKÉMON COME TO REST.
THE CELESTIAL TOWER...
A RESTING PLACE FOR POKÉMON WHO HAVE PASSED AWAY...
...AND A PEACE-FUL SPOT FOR THEIR OWNERS TO COME AND RE-MEMBER THEM.
HM? WHAT'S THE MATTER?
SO BASI-CALLY THIS PLACE IS...

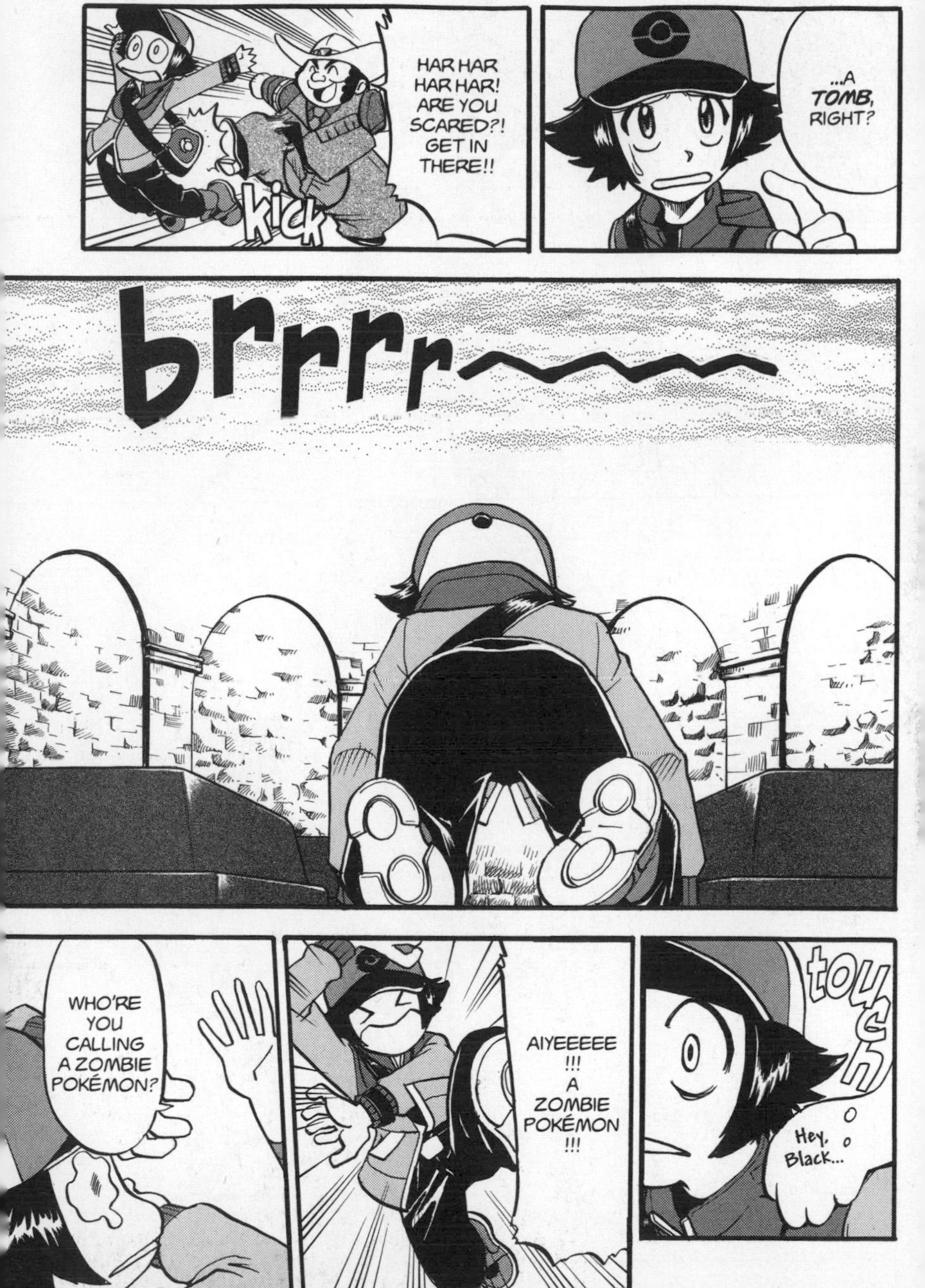
...A TOMB, RIGHT?
HAR HAR HAR HAR! ARE YOU SCARED?! GET IN THERE!!
kick
brrrr~~~
touch
Hey, Black...
AIYEEEE!!! A ZOMBIE POKÉMON!!!
WHO'RE YOU CALLING A ZOMBIE POKÉMON?

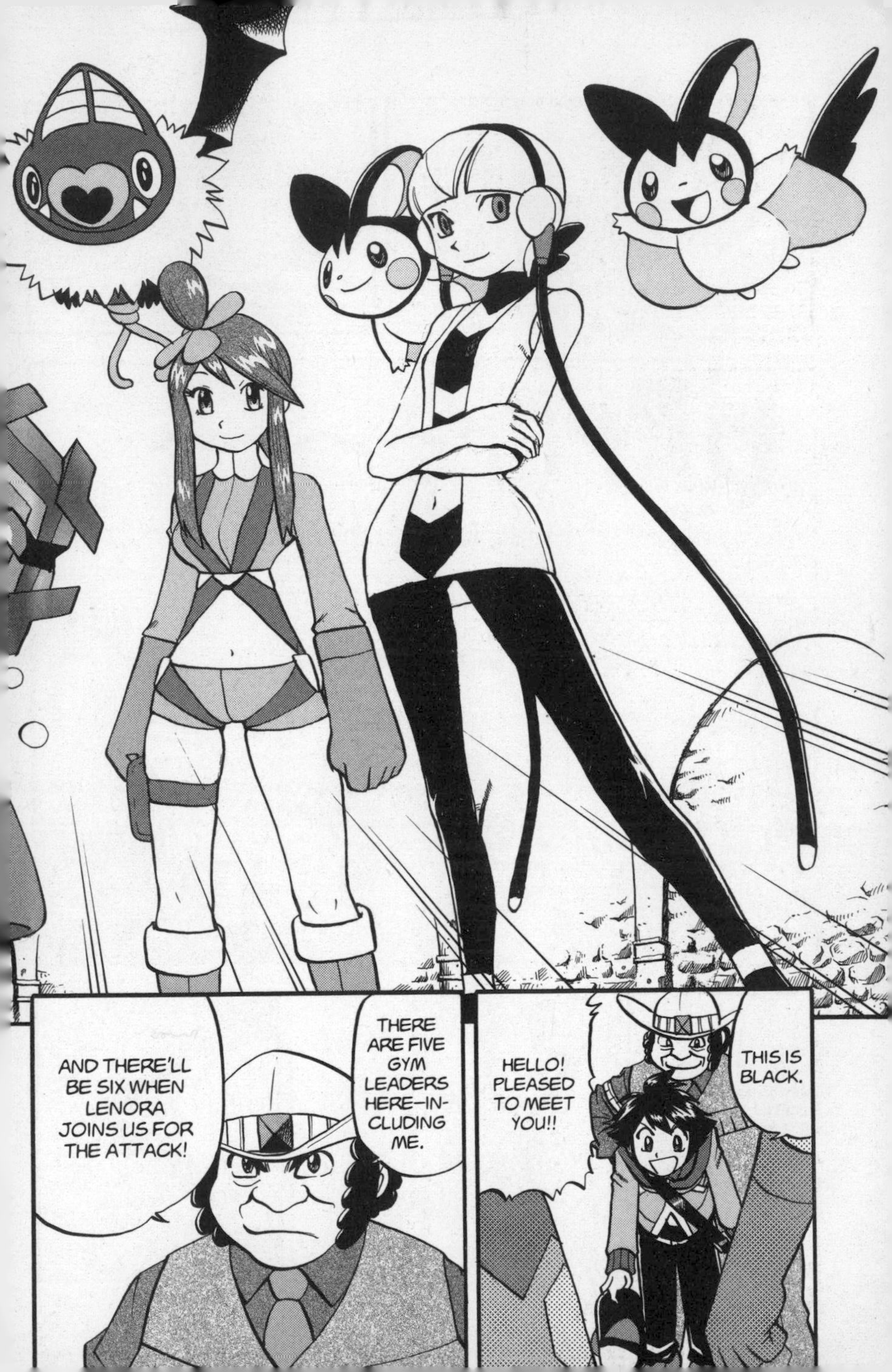
THIS IS BLACK.
HELLO! PLEASED TO MEET YOU!!
THERE ARE FIVE GYM LEADERS HERE—INCLUDING ME.
AND THERE'LL BE SIX WHEN LENORA JOINS US FOR THE ATTACK!

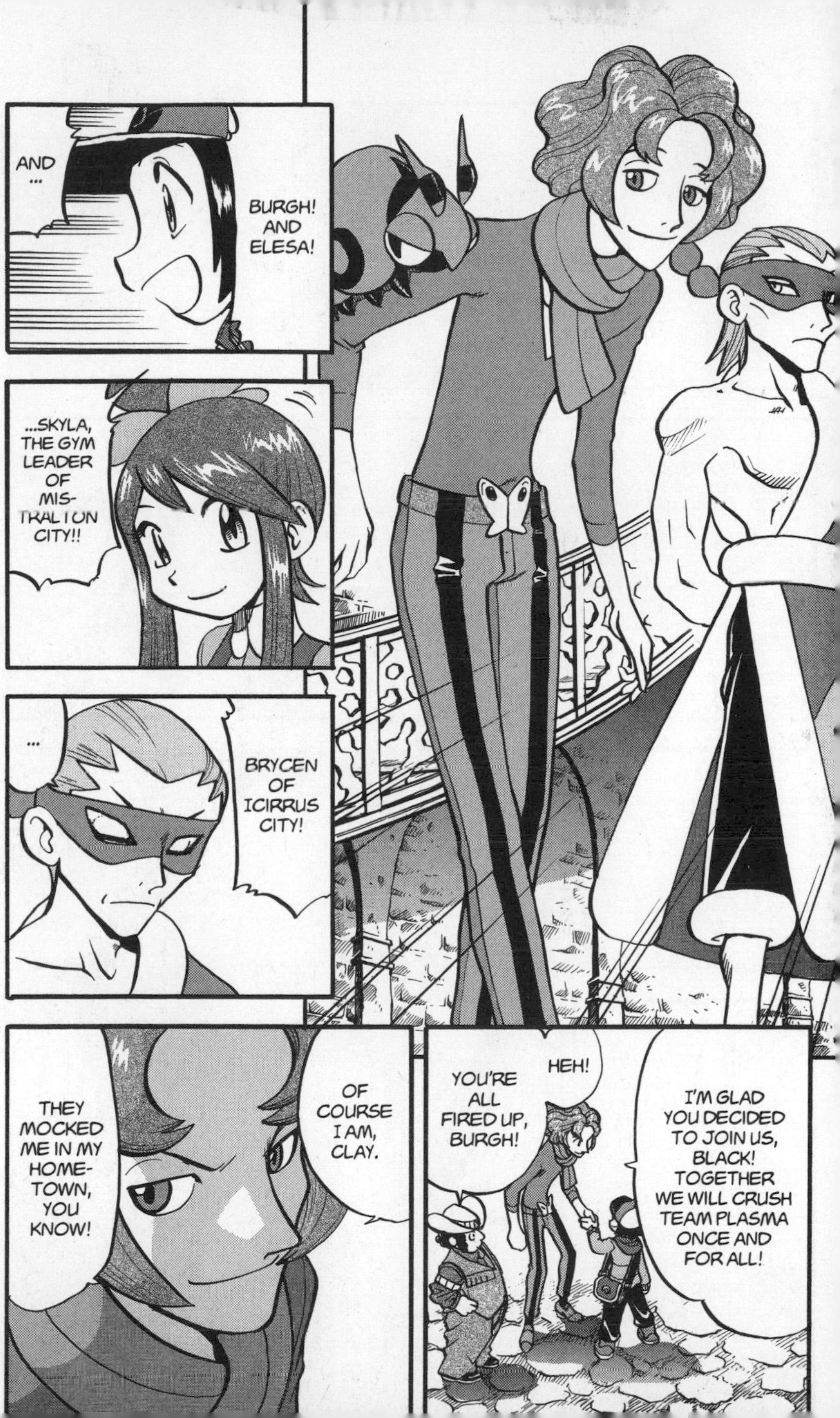
AND ...
BURGH! AND ELESA!
...SKYLA, THE GYM LEADER OF MISTRALTON CITY!!
...
BRYCEN OF ICIRRUS CITY!
I'M GLAD YOU DECIDED TO JOIN US, BLACK! TOGETHER WE WILL CRUSH TEAM PLASMA ONCE AND FOR ALL!
HEH!
YOU'RE ALL FIRED UP, BURGH!
OF COURSE I AM, CLAY.
THEY MOCKED ME IN MY HOME-TOWN, YOU KNOW!

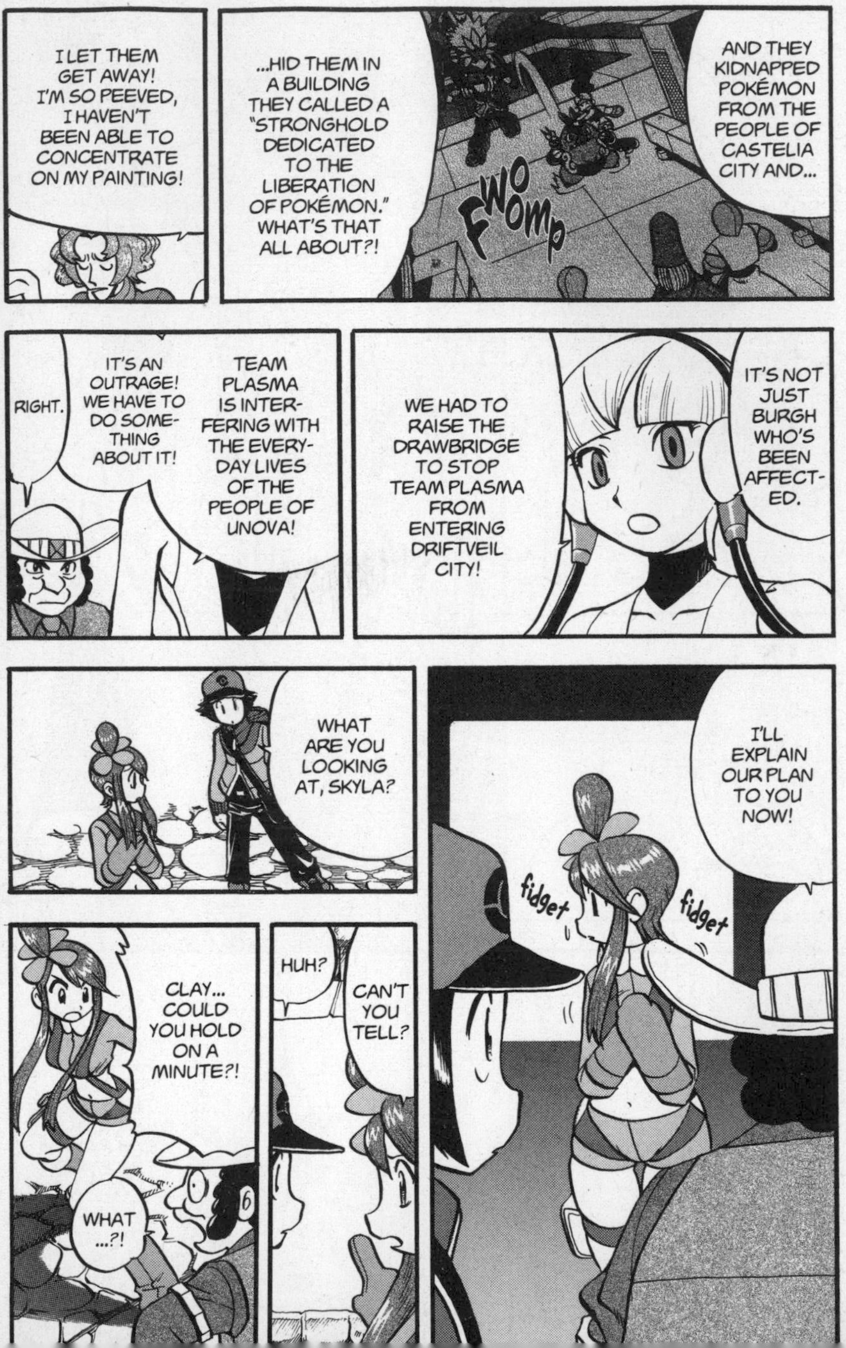
AND THEY KIDNAPPED POKÉMON FROM THE PEOPLE OF CASTELIA CITY AND...
...HID THEM IN A BUILDING THEY CALLED A "STRONGHOLD DEDICATED TO THE LIBERATION OF POKÉMON." WHAT'S THAT ALL ABOUT?!
FWOOMP
I LET THEM GET AWAY! I'M SO PEEVED, I HAVEN'T BEEN ABLE TO CONCENTRATE ON MY PAINTING!
IT'S NOT JUST BURGH WHO'S BEEN AFFECTED.
WE HAD TO RAISE THE DRAWBRIDGE TO STOP TEAM PLASMA FROM ENTERING DRIFTVEIL CITY!
TEAM PLASMA IS INTERFERING WITH THE EVERYDAY LIVES OF THE PEOPLE OF UNOVA!
IT'S AN OUTRAGE! WE HAVE TO DO SOMETHING ABOUT IT!
RIGHT.
I'LL EXPLAIN OUR PLAN TO YOU NOW!
fidget
fidget
WHAT ARE YOU LOOKING AT, SKYLA?
HUH?
CAN'T YOU TELL?
CLAY... COULD YOU HOLD ON A MINUTE?!
WHAT ...?!

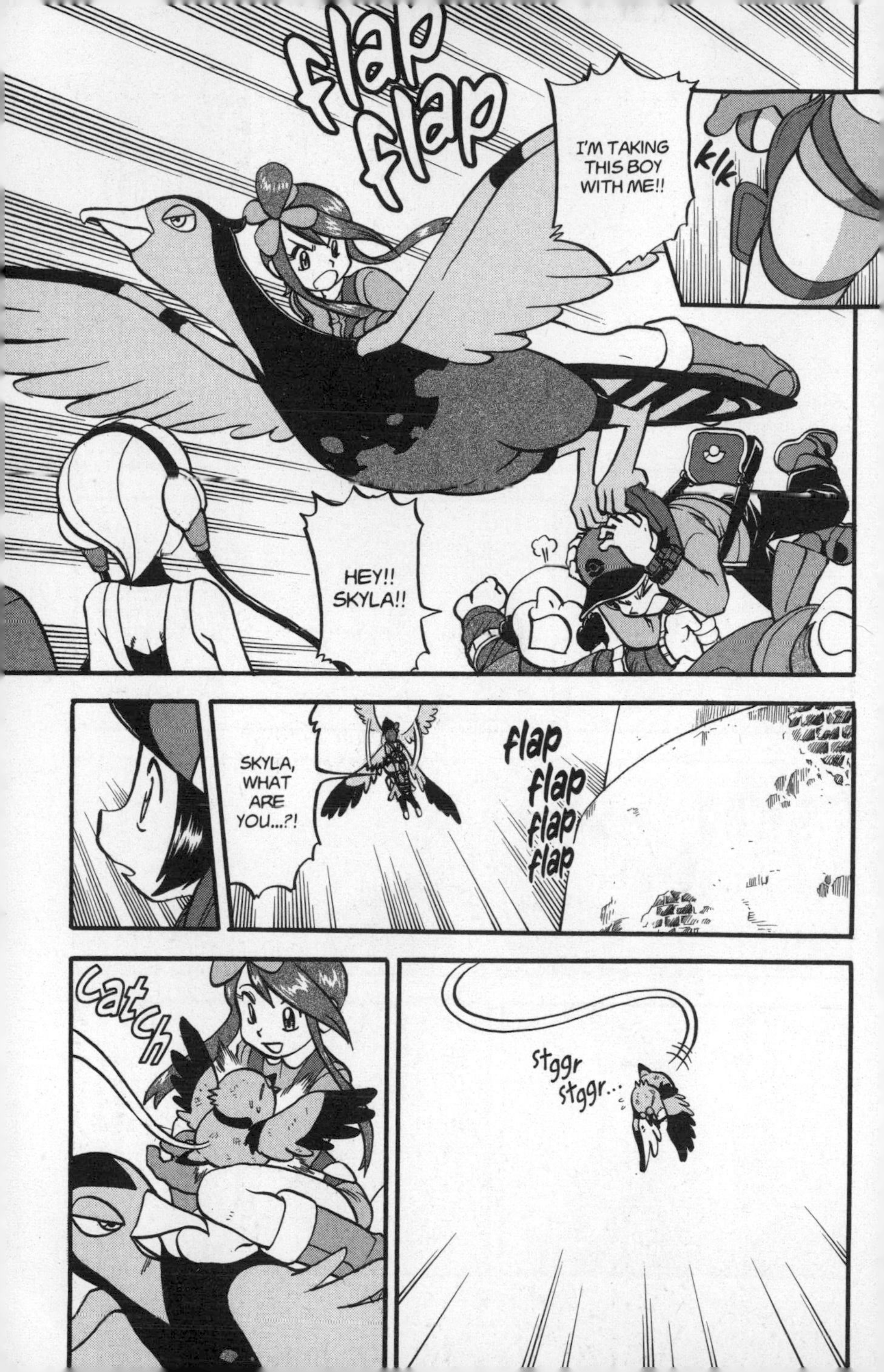
klk
I'M TAKING THIS BOY WITH ME!!
flap flap
HEY!! SKYLA!!
flap flap flap flap
SKYLA, WHAT ARE YOU...?!
stggr stggr...
catch

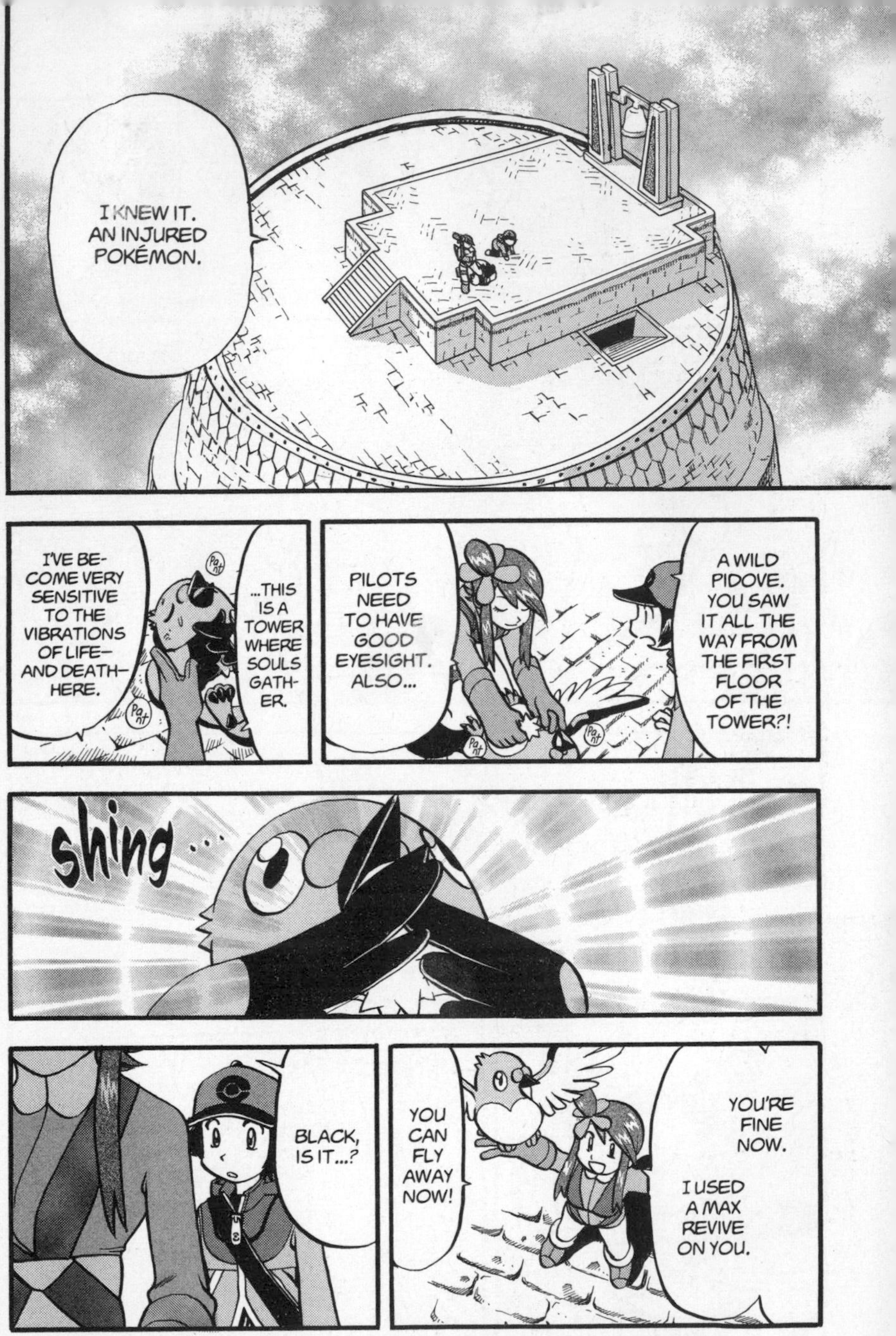
I KNEW IT. AN INJURED POKÉMON.
A WILD PIDOVE. YOU SAW IT ALL THE WAY FROM THE FIRST FLOOR OF THE TOWER?!
Pant
PILOTS NEED TO HAVE GOOD EYESIGHT. ALSO...
Pant
...THIS IS A TOWER WHERE SOULS GATH-ER.
I'VE BE-COME VERY SENSITIVE TO THE VIBRATIONS OF LIFE—AND DEATH—HERE.
Pant
Pant
shing...
YOU'RE FINE NOW.
I USED A MAX REVIVE ON YOU.
YOU CAN FLY AWAY NOW!
BLACK, IS IT...?

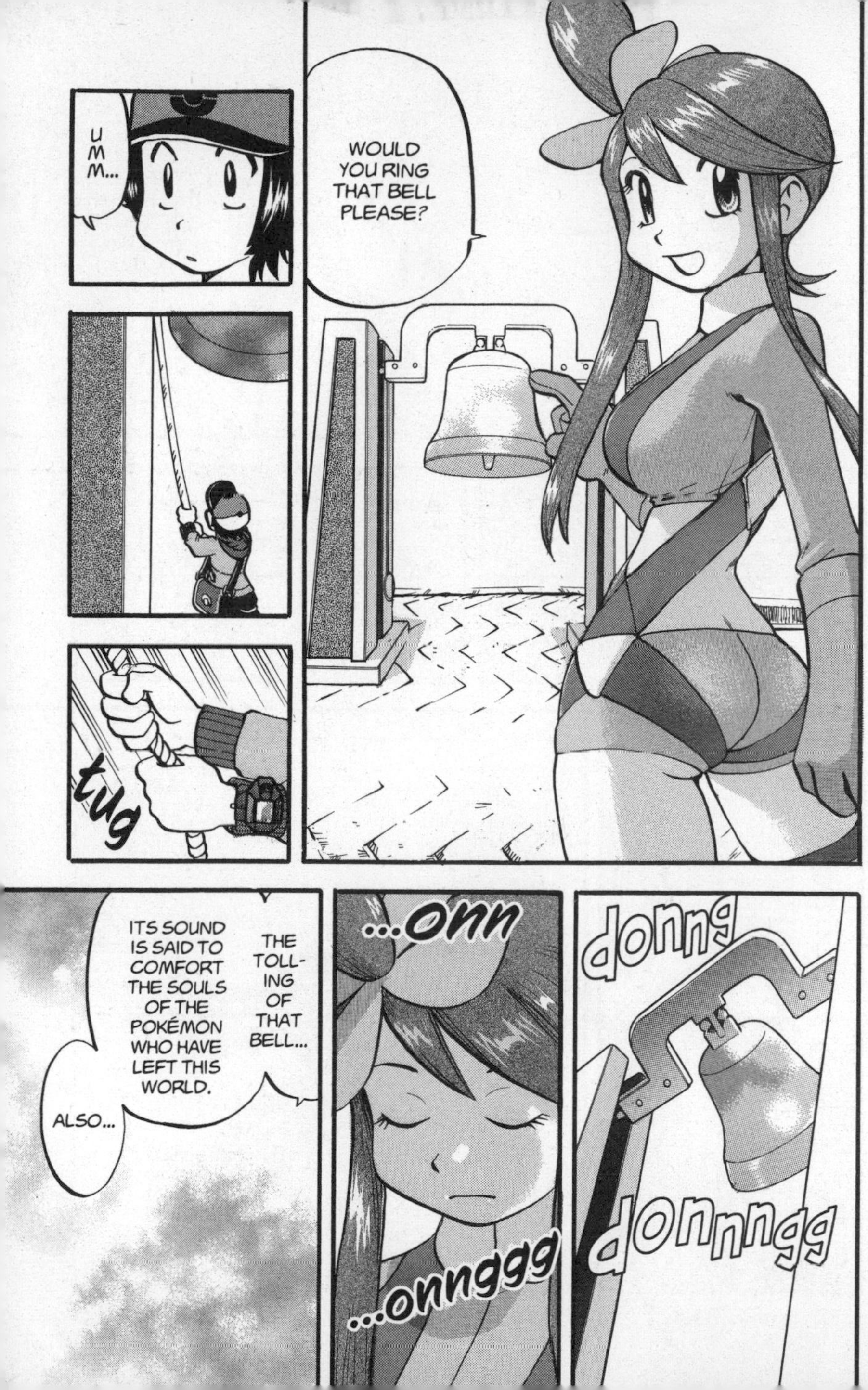
WOULD YOU RING THAT BELL PLEASE?
UMM...
tug
donng
donnngg
...onn
...onnggg
THE TOLL-ING OF THAT BELL...
ITS SOUND IS SAID TO COMFORT THE SOULS OF THE POKÉMON WHO HAVE LEFT THIS WORLD.
ALSO...

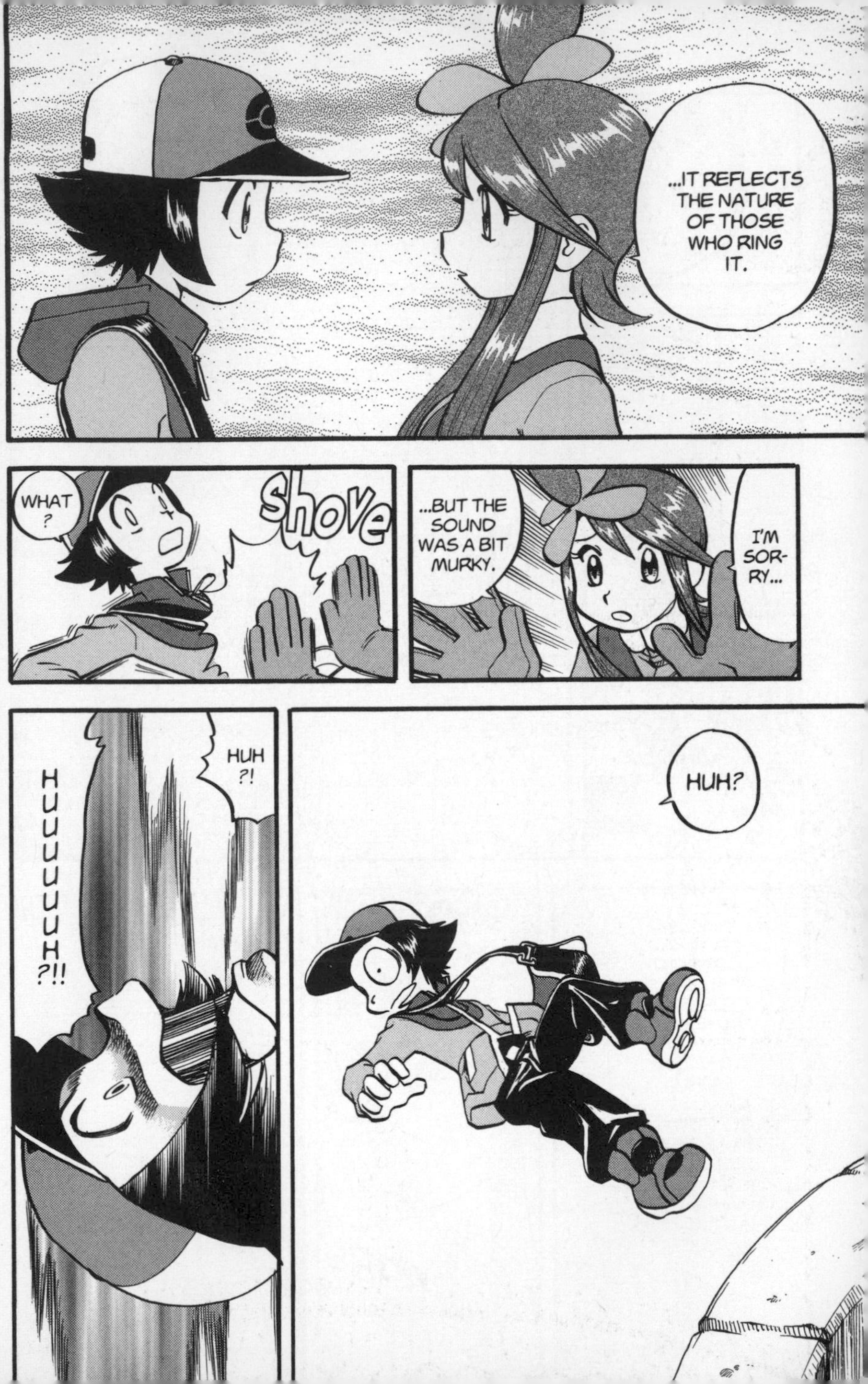
...IT REFLECTS THE NATURE OF THOSE WHO RING IT.
I'M SOR-RY...
...BUT THE SOUND WAS A BIT MURKY.
shove
WHAT?
HUH?
HUH?!
HUUUUUUH?!!

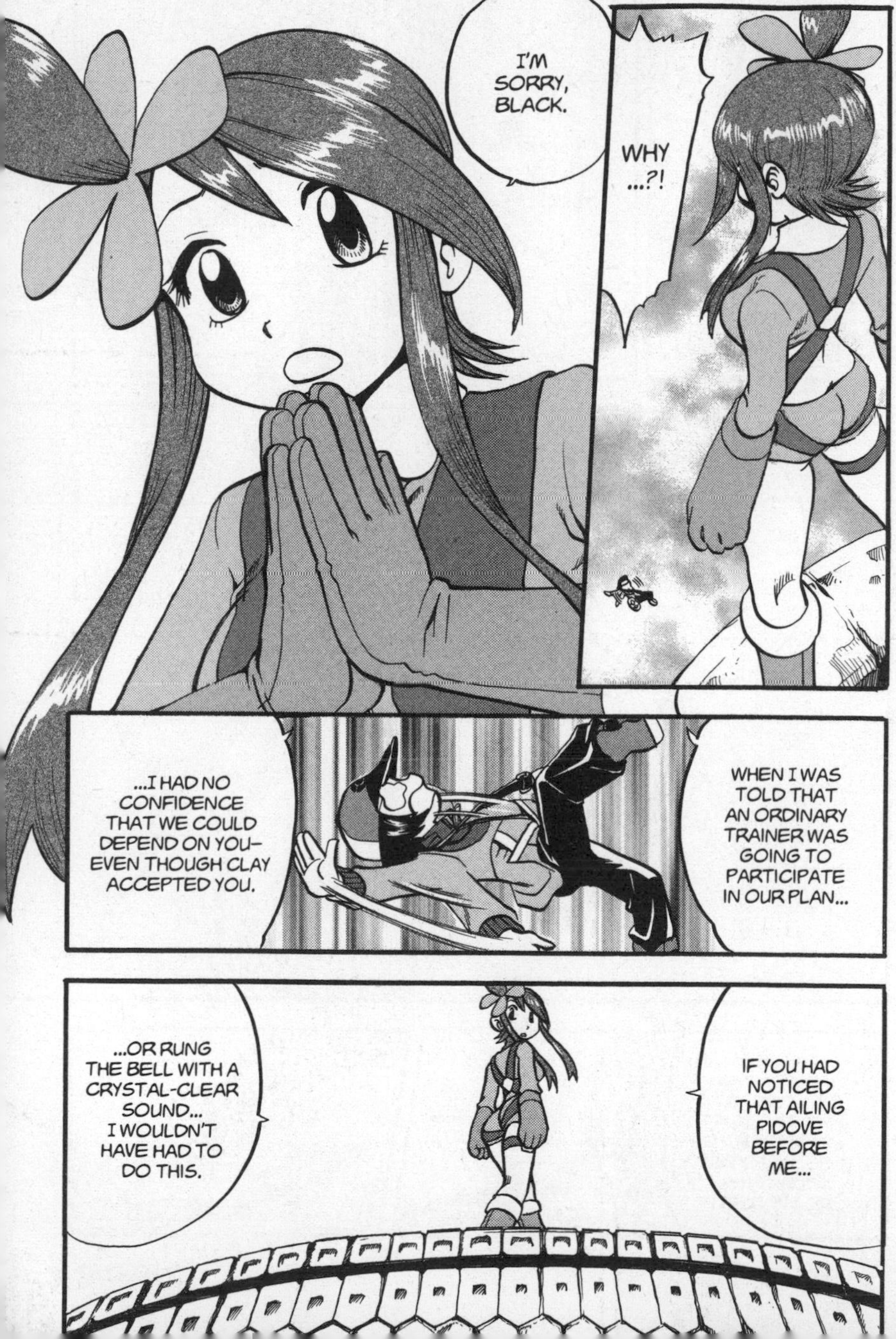
WHY ...?!
I'M SORRY, BLACK.
WHEN I WAS TOLD THAT AN ORDINARY TRAINER WAS GOING TO PARTICIPATE IN OUR PLAN...
...I HAD NO CONFIDENCE THAT WE COULD DEPEND ON YOU—EVEN THOUGH CLAY ACCEPTED YOU.
IF YOU HAD NOTICED THAT AILING PIDOVE BEFORE ME...
...OR RUNG THE BELL WITH A CRYSTAL-CLEAR SOUND... I WOULDN'T HAVE HAD TO DO THIS.

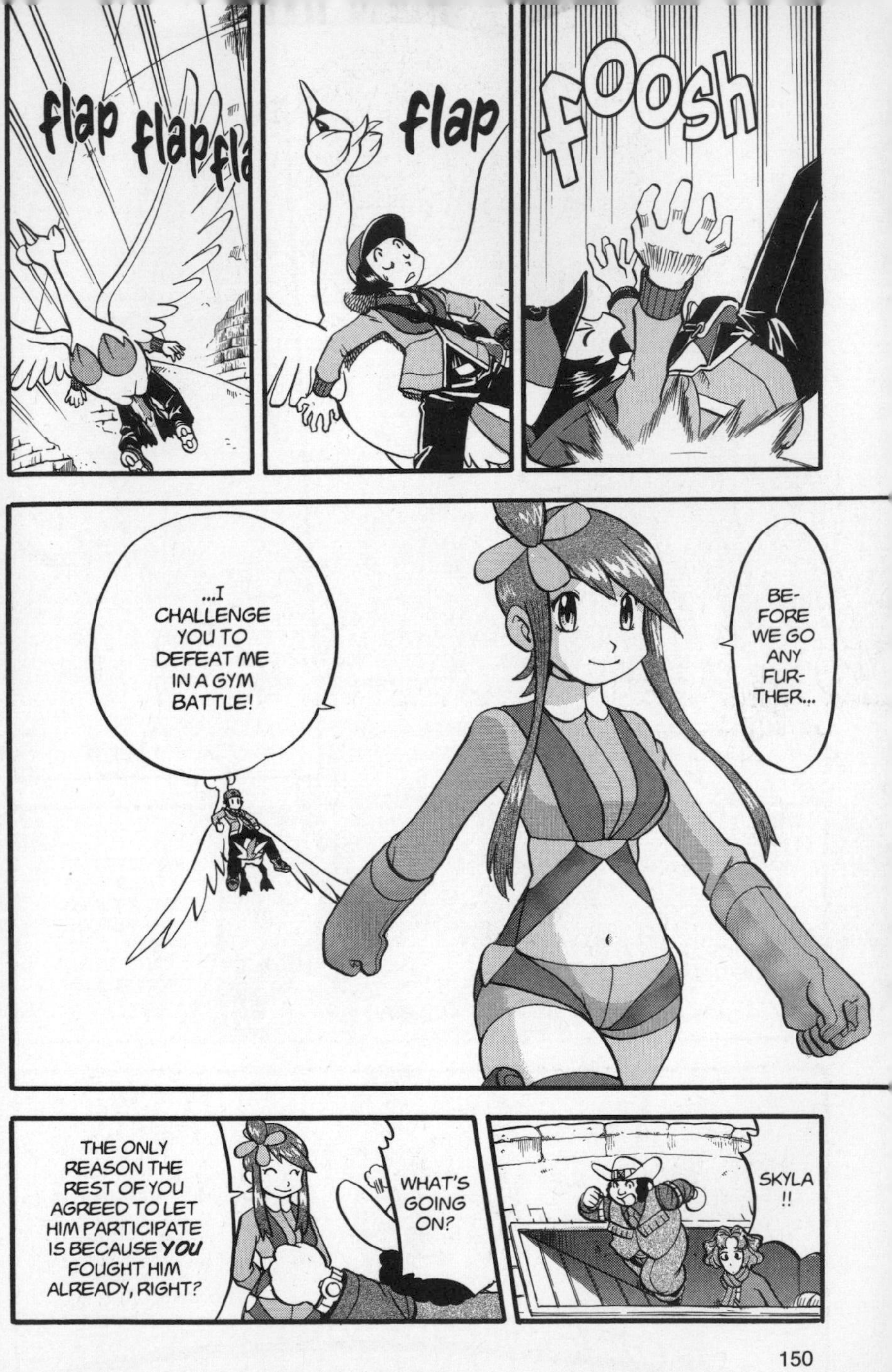
fOOsh
flap
flap flap fla
BE-FORE WE GO ANY FUR-THER...
...I CHALLENGE YOU TO DEFEAT ME IN A GYM BATTLE!
SKYLA !!
WHAT'S GOING ON?
THE ONLY REASON THE REST OF YOU AGREED TO LET HIM PARTICIPATE IS BECAUSE ***YOU*** FOUGHT HIM ALREADY, RIGHT?

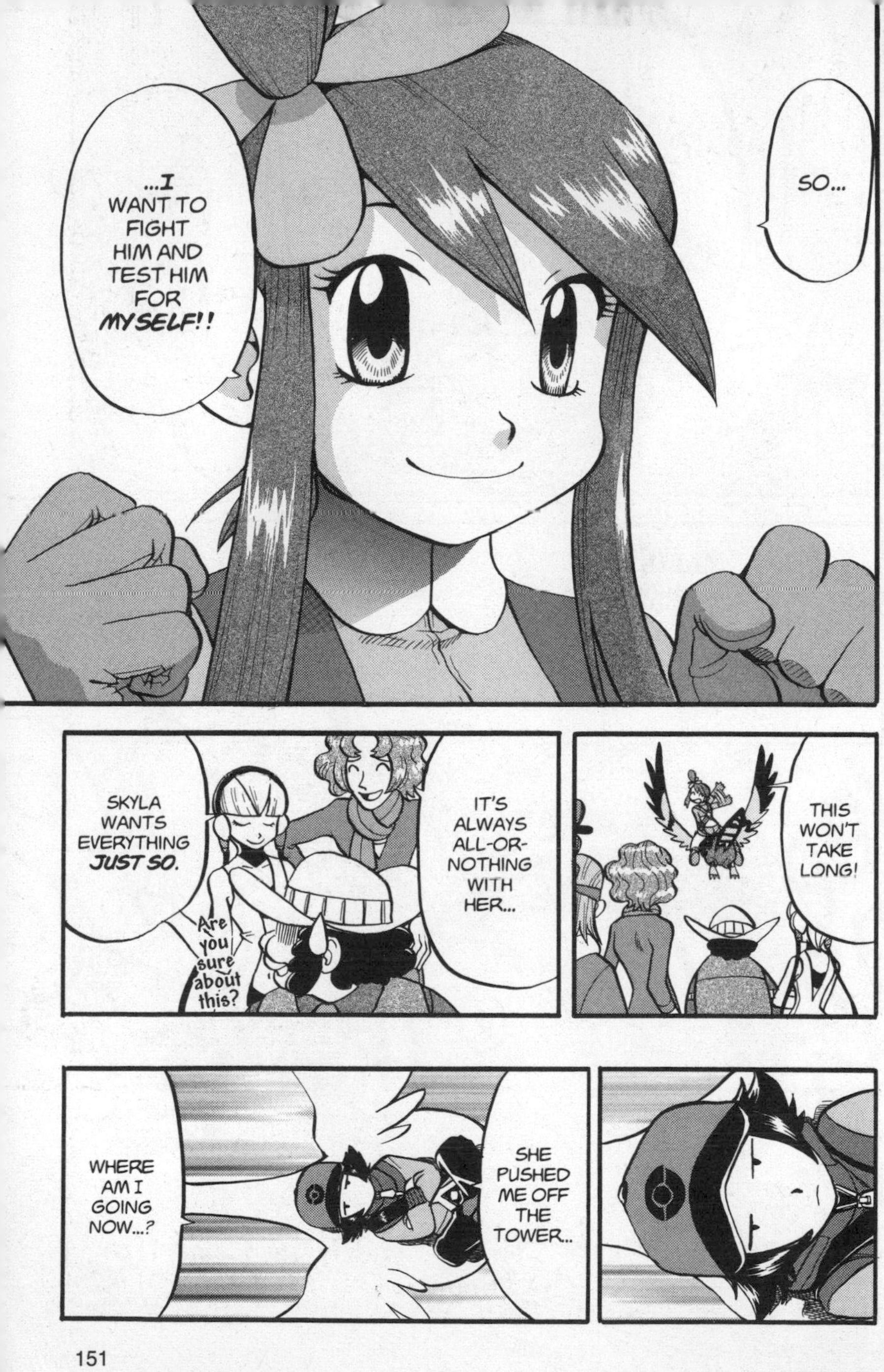
SO...
...I WANT TO FIGHT HIM AND TEST HIM FOR MYSELF!!
THIS WON'T TAKE LONG!
IT'S ALWAYS ALL-OR-NOTHING WITH HER...
SKYLA WANTS EVERYTHING JUST SO.
Are you sure about this?
SHE PUSHED ME OFF THE TOWER..
WHERE AM I GOING NOW...?

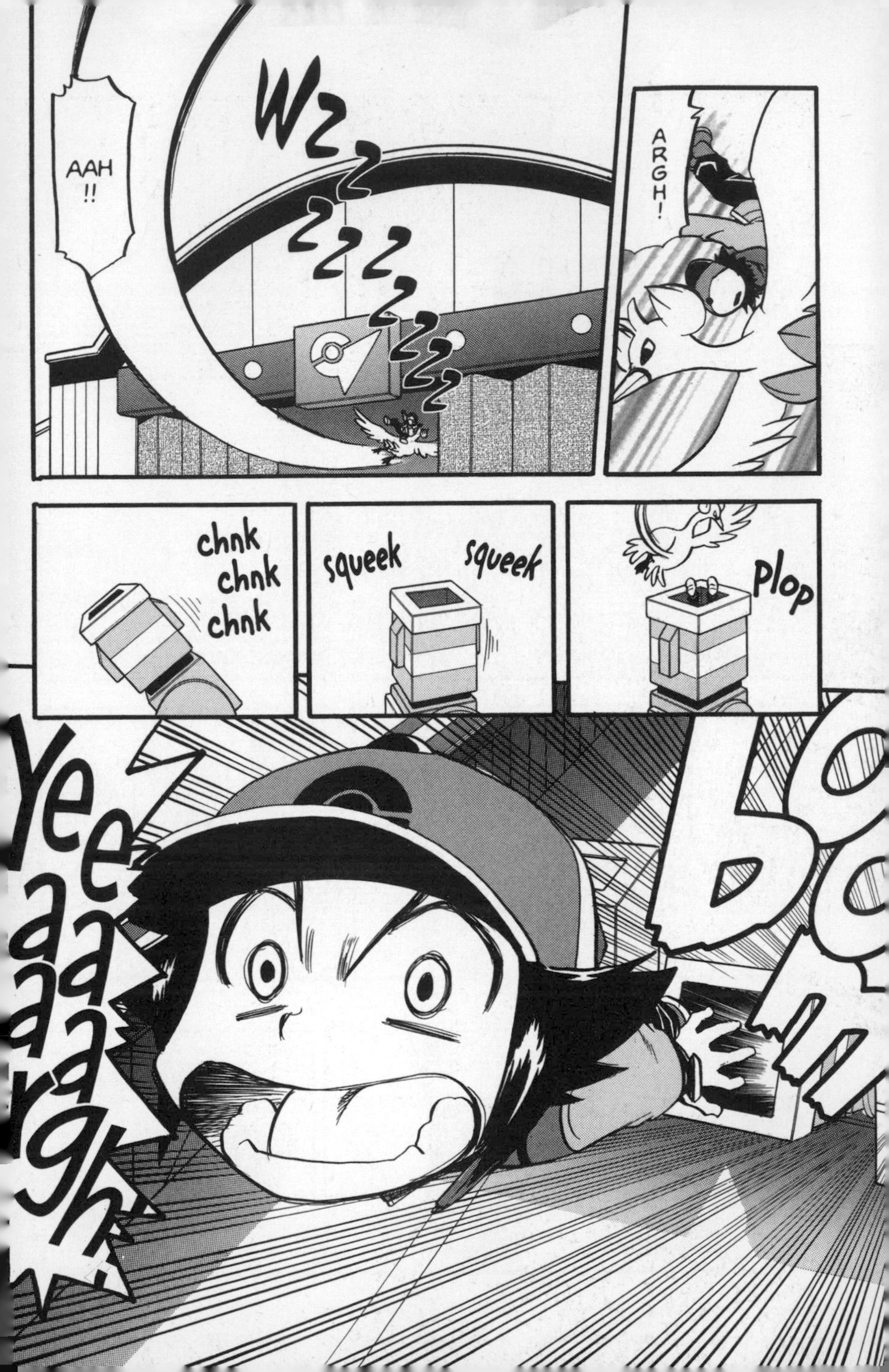
ARGH!
Wzzzzzzzz
AAH!!
plop
squeek
squeek
chnk
chnk
chnk
Yeeaaaargh!!

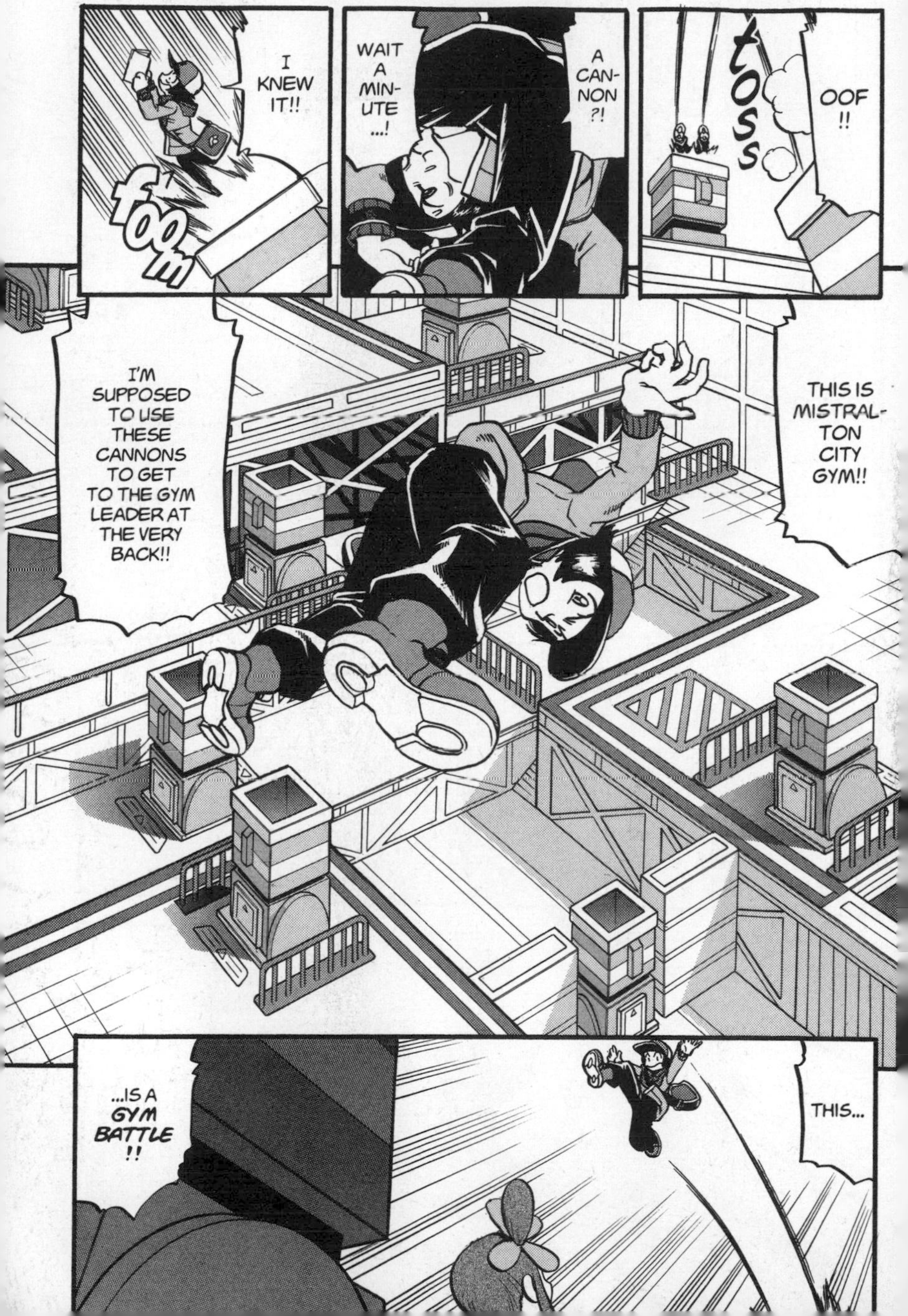
toss
OOF !!
A CAN-NON ?!
WAIT A MIN-UTE ...!
I KNEW IT!!
foom
THIS IS MISTRAL-TON CITY GYM!!
I'M SUPPOSED TO USE THESE CANNONS TO GET TO THE GYM LEADER AT THE VERY BACK!!
THIS...
...IS A GYM BATTLE !!

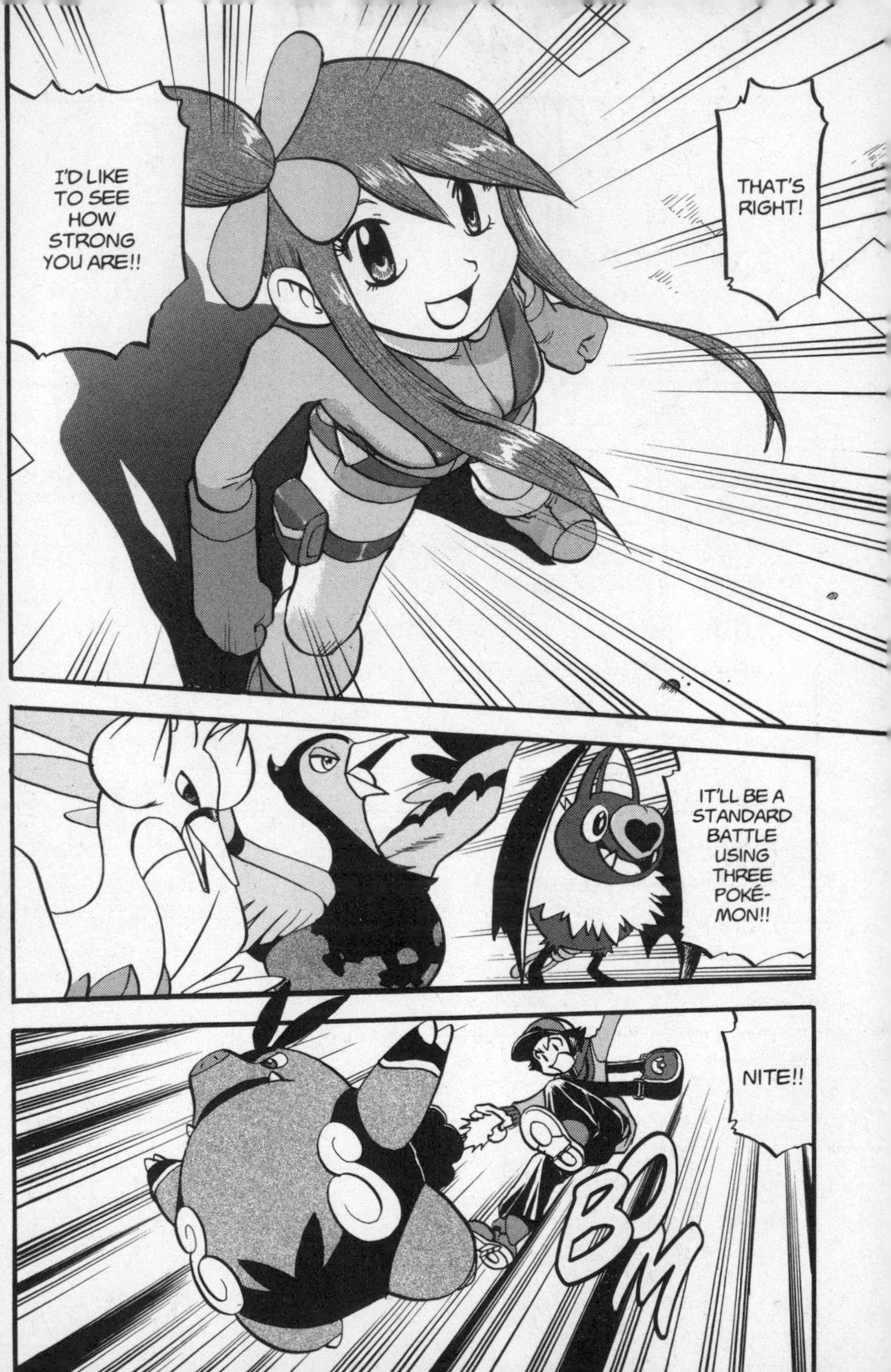
THAT'S RIGHT!
I'D LIKE TO SEE HOW STRONG YOU ARE!!
IT'LL BE A STANDARD BATTLE USING THREE POKÉ-MON!!
NITE!!
BOM

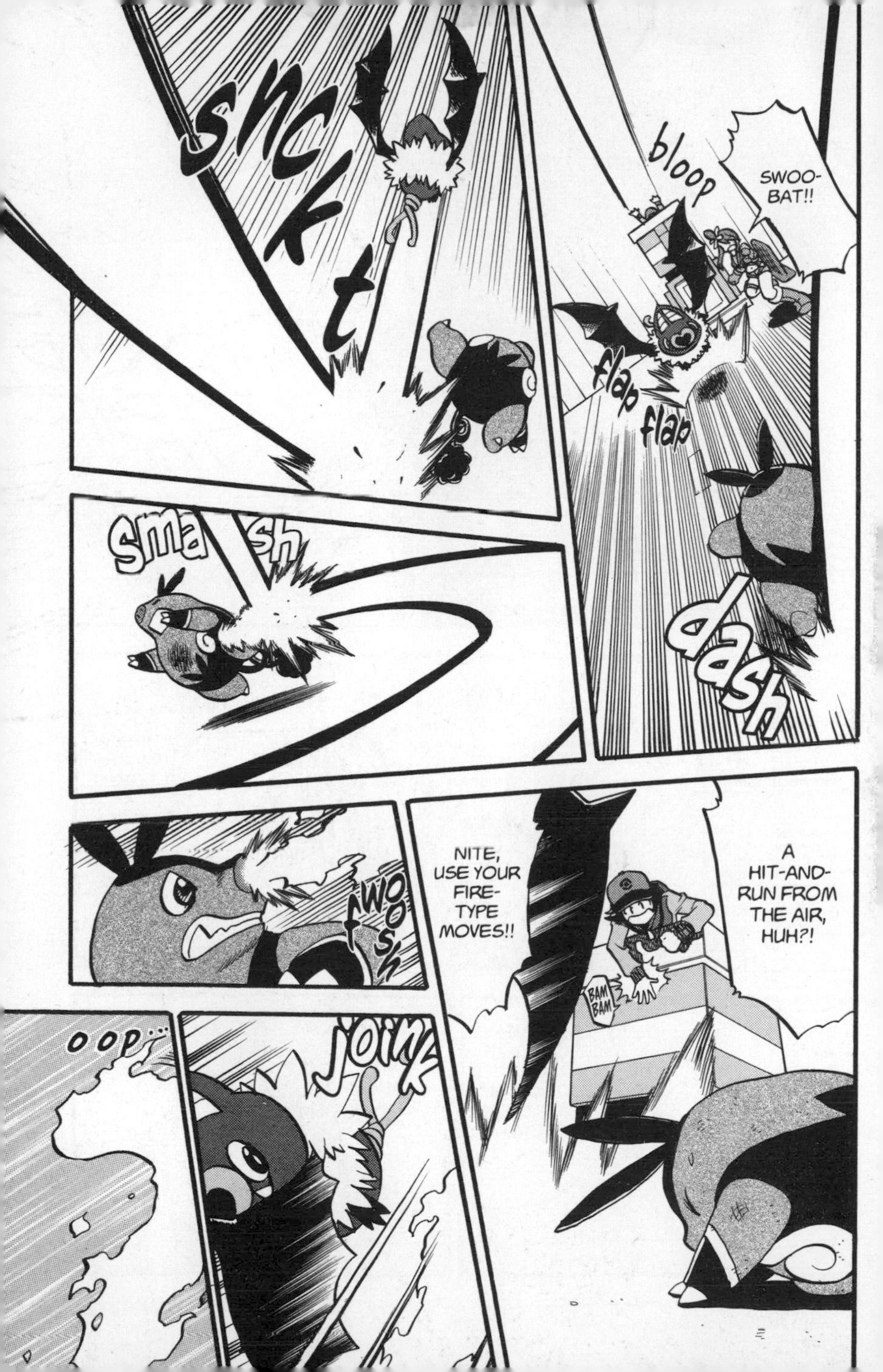
bloop
SWOO-BAT!!
flap
flap
dash
snckt
smash
A HIT-AND-RUN FROM THE AIR, HUH?!
NITE, USE YOUR FIRE-TYPE MOVES!!
BAM BAM
fwoosh
yoink
oop...

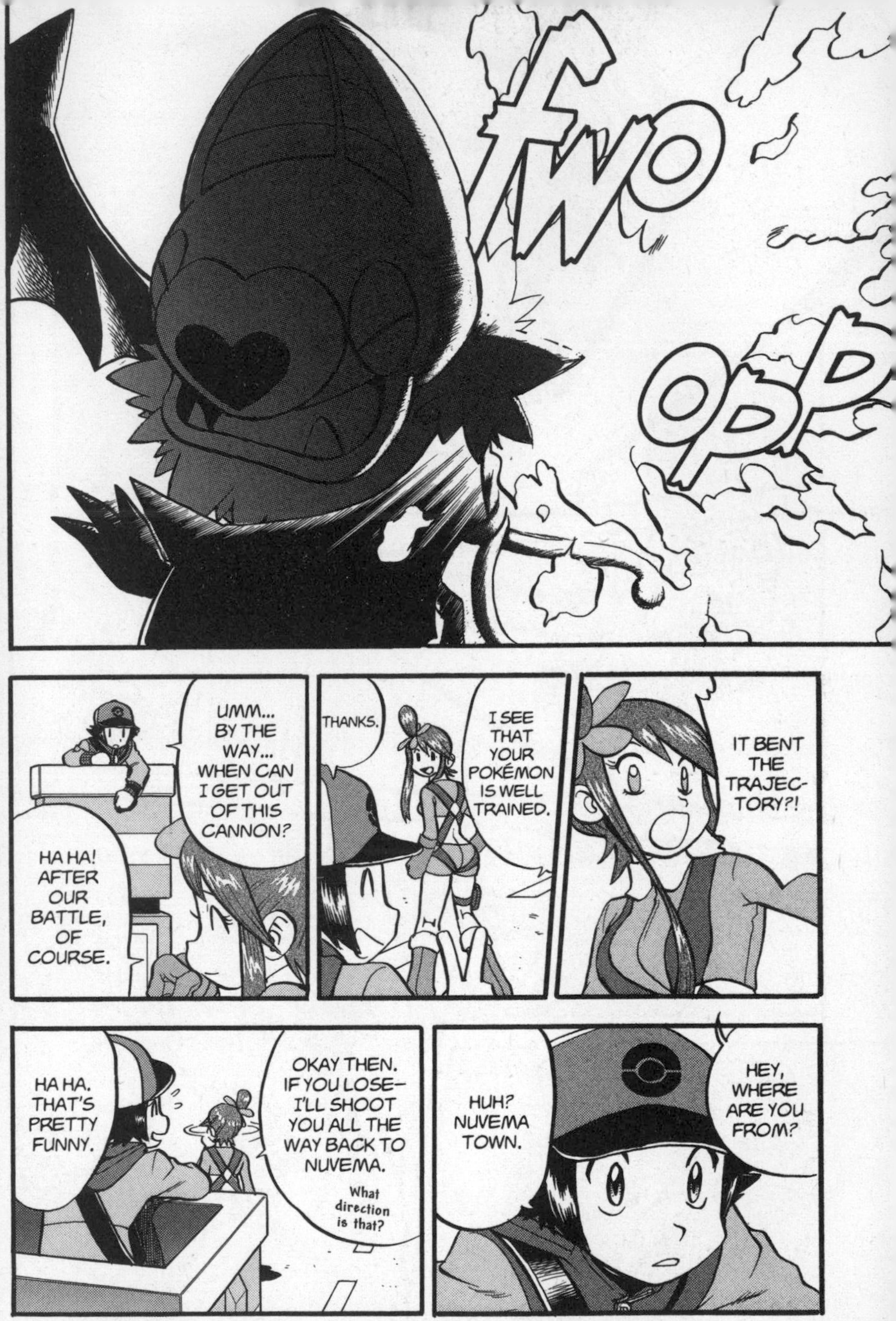
fwo
OPP
IT BENT THE TRAJECTORY?!
I SEE THAT YOUR POKÉMON IS WELL TRAINED.
THANKS.
UMM... BY THE WAY... WHEN CAN I GET OUT OF THIS CANNON?
HA HA! AFTER OUR BATTLE, OF COURSE.
HEY, WHERE ARE YOU FROM?
HUH? NUVEMA TOWN.
OKAY THEN. IF YOU LOSE— I'LL SHOOT YOU ALL THE WAY BACK TO NUVEMA.
What direction is that?
HA HA. THAT'S PRETTY FUNNY.

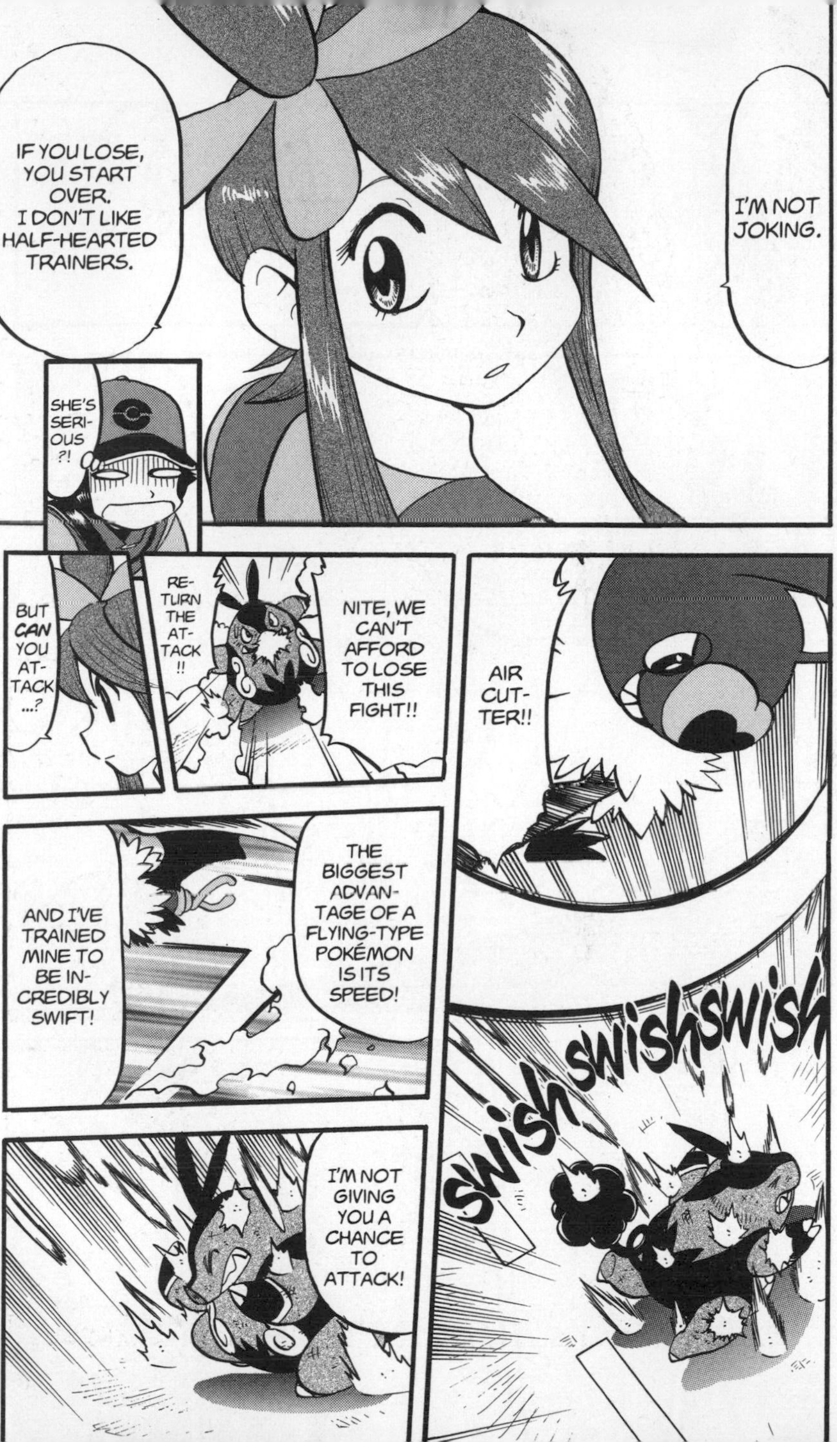
I'M NOT JOKING.
IF YOU LOSE, YOU START OVER. I DON'T LIKE HALF-HEARTED TRAINERS.
SHE'S SERIOUS?!
AIR CUTTER!!
SWISH SWISH SWISH
NITE, WE CAN'T AFFORD TO LOSE THIS FIGHT!!
RETURN THE ATTACK!!
BUT **CAN** YOU ATTACK...?
THE BIGGEST ADVANTAGE OF A FLYING-TYPE POKÉMON IS ITS SPEED!
AND I'VE TRAINED MINE TO BE INCREDIBLY SWIFT!
I'M NOT GIVING YOU A CHANCE TO ATTACK!

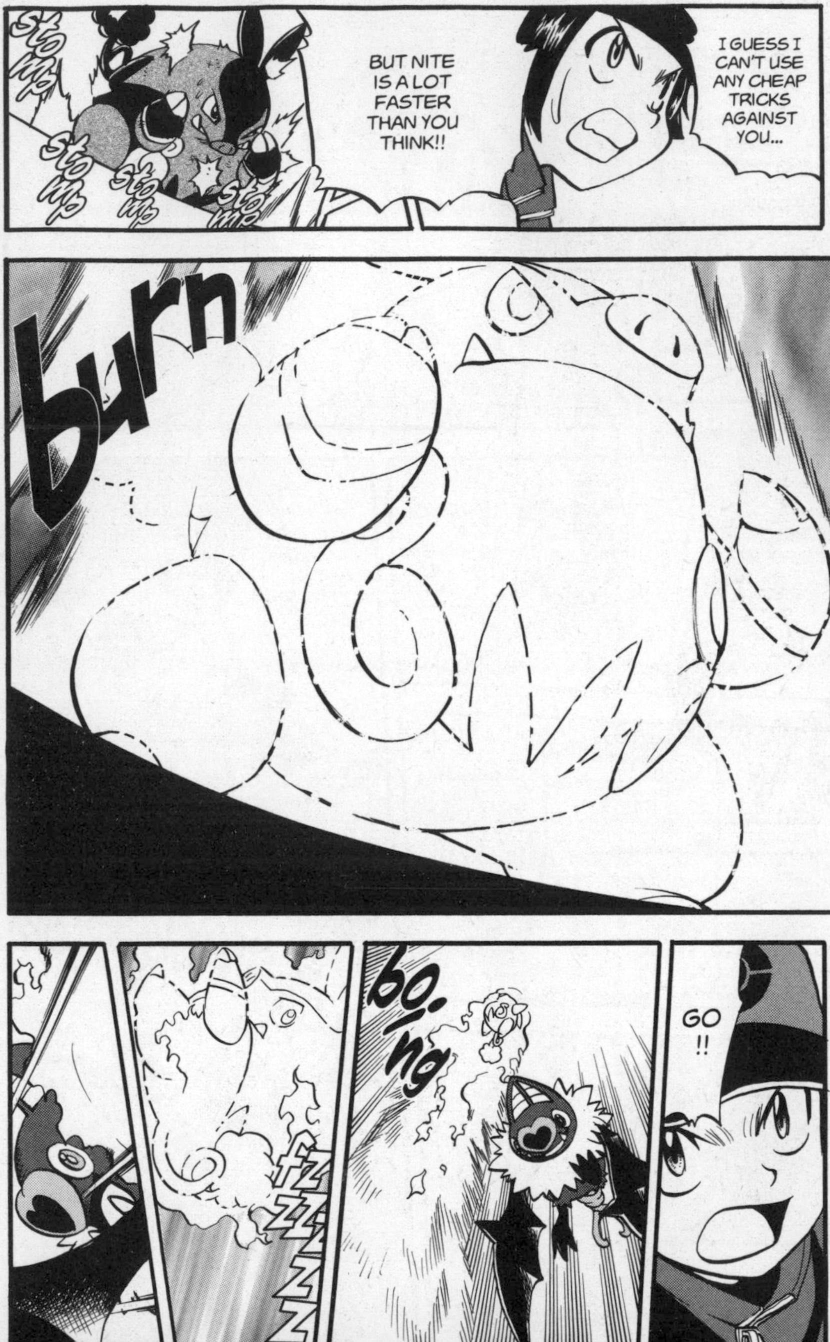
I GUESS I CAN'T USE ANY CHEAP TRICKS AGAINST YOU...
BUT NITE IS A LOT FASTER THAN YOU THINK!!
stomp
stomp
stomp
stomp
burn
GO !!
boing
fzzzz

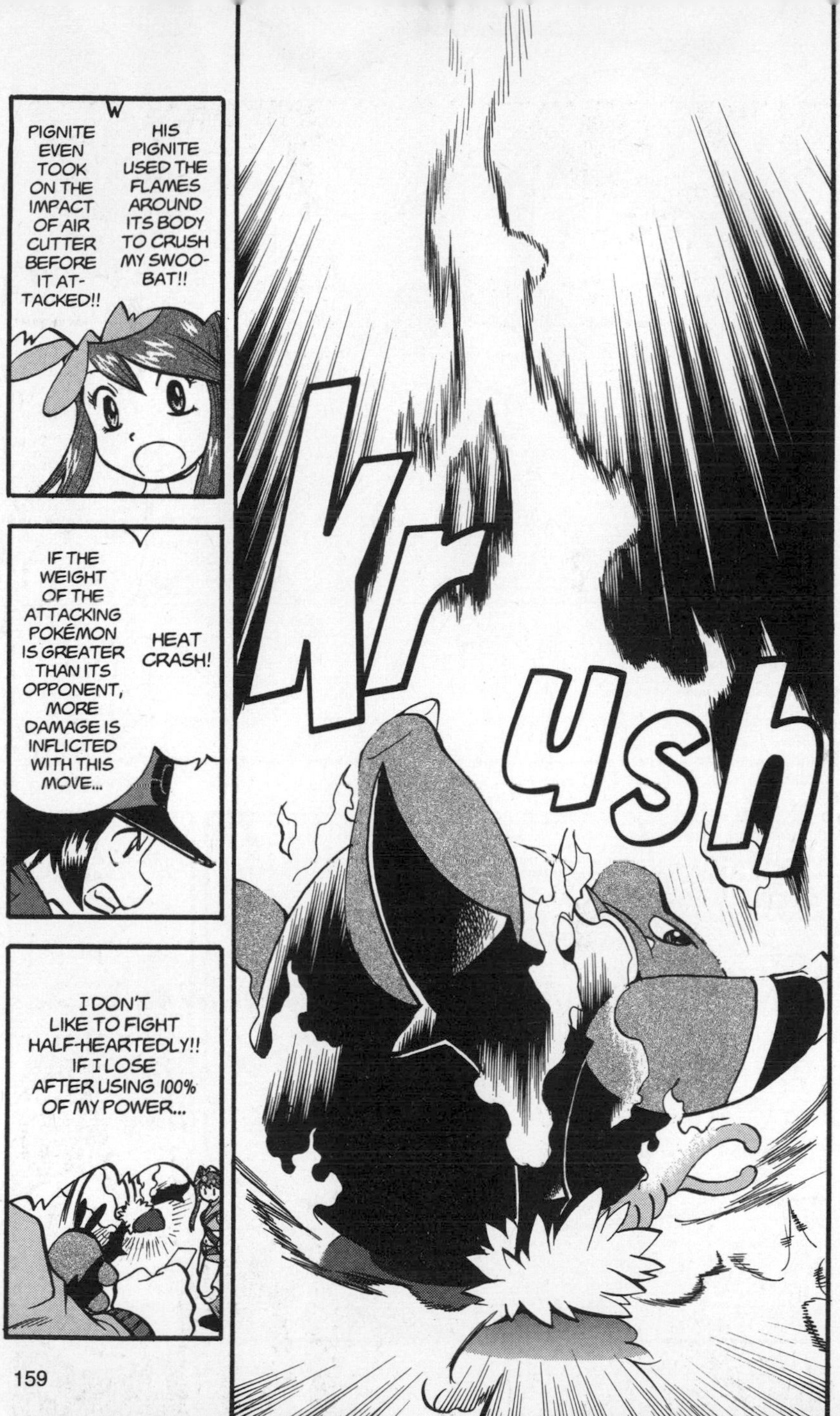
Krush
HIS PIGNITE USED THE FLAMES AROUND ITS BODY TO CRUSH MY SWOO-BAT!!
PIGNITE EVEN TOOK ON THE IMPACT OF AIR CUTTER BEFORE IT AT-TACKED!!
HEAT CRASH!
IF THE WEIGHT OF THE ATTACKING POKÉMON IS GREATER THAN ITS OPPONENT, MORE DAMAGE IS INFLICTED WITH THIS MOVE...
I DON'T LIKE TO FIGHT HALF-HEARTEDLY!! IF I LOSE AFTER USING 100% OF MY POWER...

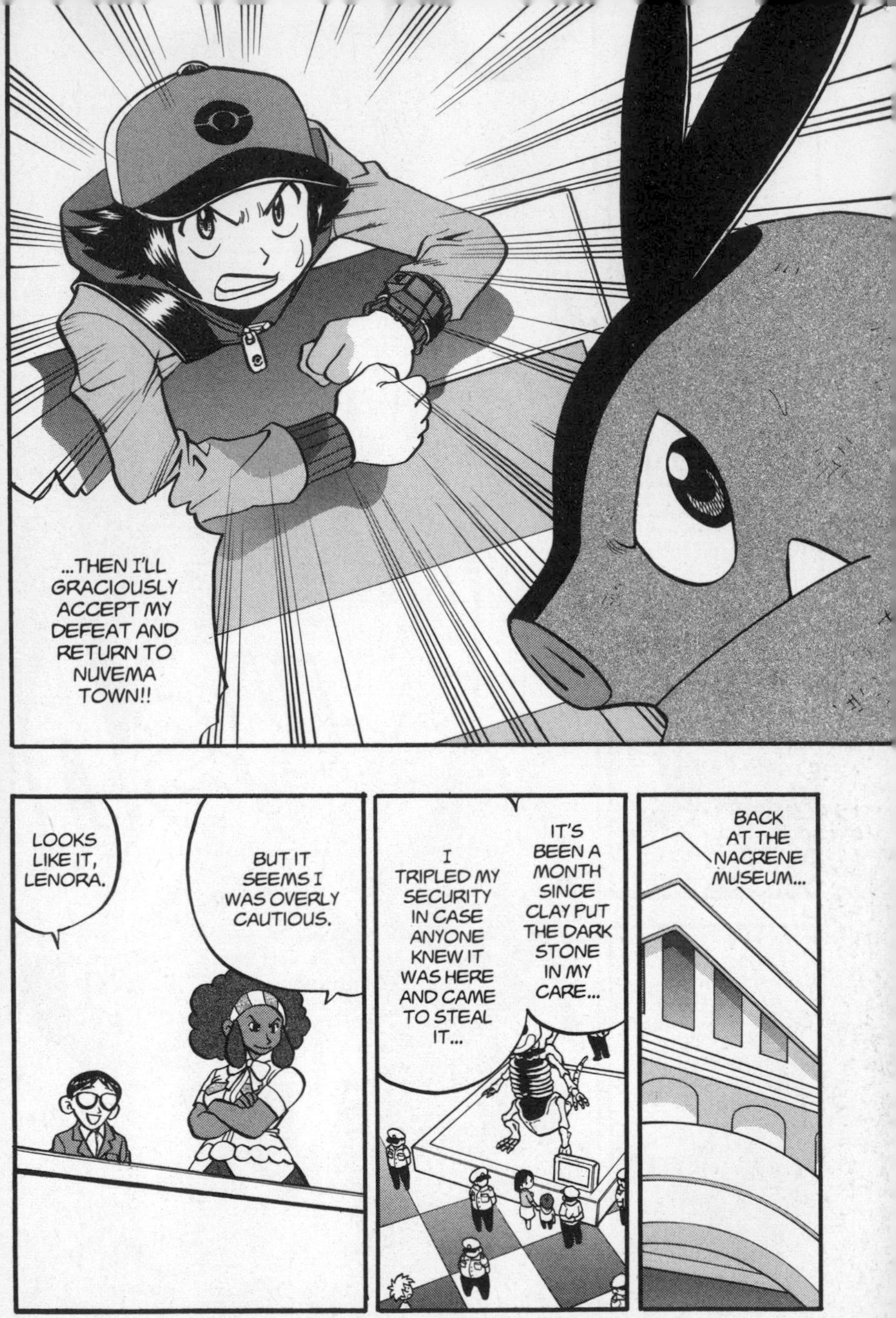
...THEN I'LL GRACIOUSLY ACCEPT MY DEFEAT AND RETURN TO NUVEMA TOWN!!
BACK AT THE NACRENE MUSEUM...
IT'S BEEN A MONTH SINCE CLAY PUT THE DARK STONE IN MY CARE...
I TRIPLED MY SECURITY IN CASE ANYONE KNEW IT WAS HERE AND CAME TO STEAL IT...
BUT IT SEEMS I WAS OVERLY CAUTIOUS.
LOOKS LIKE IT, LENORA.

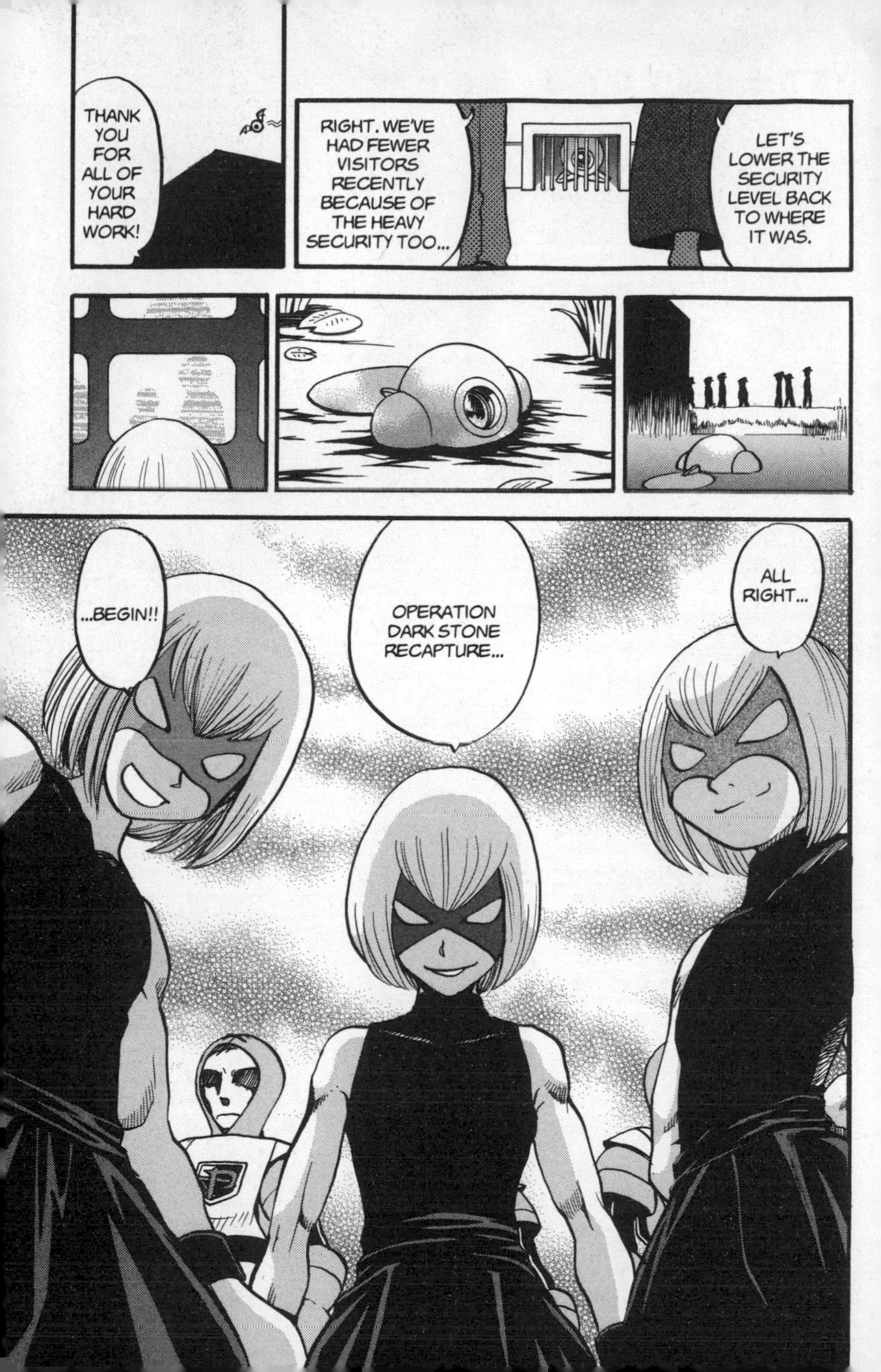
LET'S LOWER THE SECURITY LEVEL BACK TO WHERE IT WAS.
RIGHT. WE'VE HAD FEWER VISITORS RECENTLY BECAUSE OF THE HEAVY SECURITY TOO...
THANK YOU FOR ALL OF YOUR HARD WORK!
ALL RIGHT...
OPERATION DARK STONE RECAPTURE...
...BEGIN!!

ADVENTURE MAP

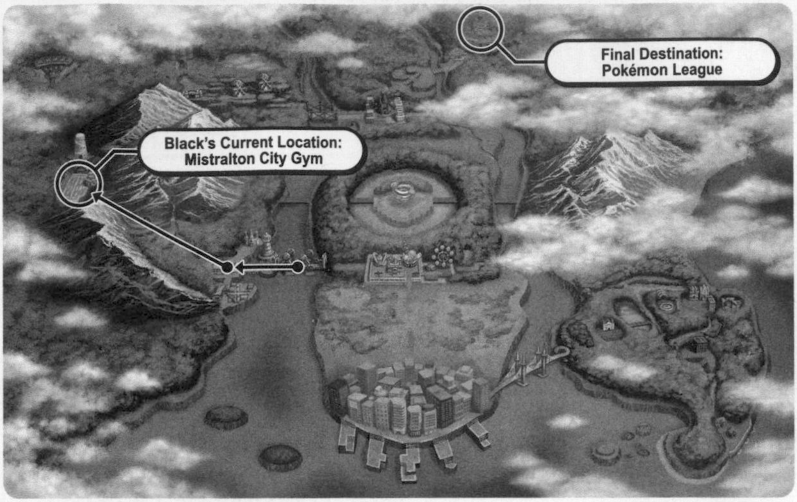

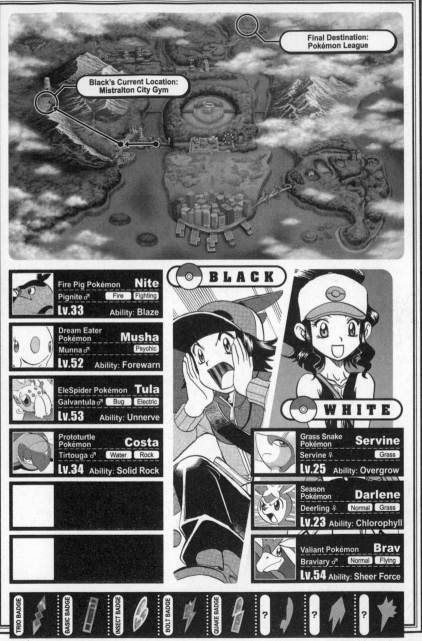

Final Destination:
Pokémon League
Black's Current Location:
Mistralton City Gym

BLACK

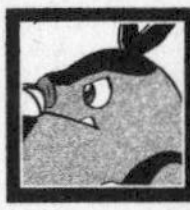
Fire Pig Pokémon **Nite**
Pignite ♂ Fire Fighting
Lv.33 Ability: Blaze

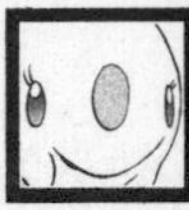
Dream Eater Pokémon **Musha**
Munna ♂ Psychic
Lv.52 Ability: Forewarn

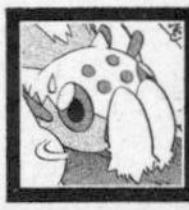
EleSpider Pokémon **Tula**
Galvantula ♂ Bug Electric
Lv.53 Ability: Unnerve

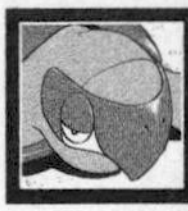
Prototurtle Pokémon **Costa**
Tirtouga ♂ Water Rock
Lv.34 Ability: Solid Rock

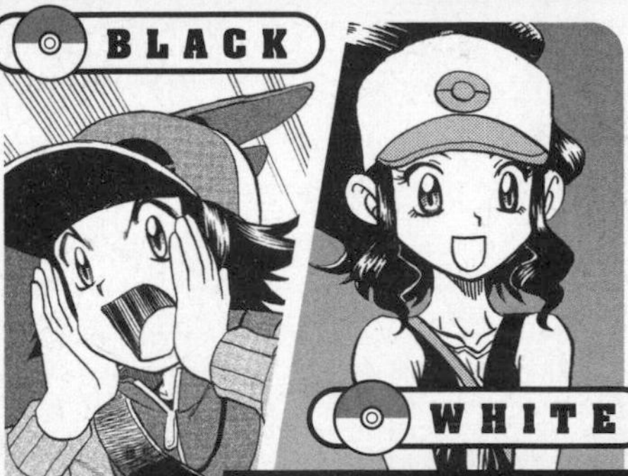

WHITE

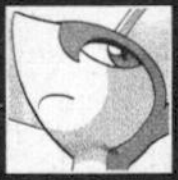
Grass Snake Pokémon **Servine**
Servine ♀ Grass
Lv.25 Ability: Overgrow

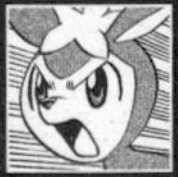
Season Pokémon **Darlene**
Deerling ♀ Normal Grass
Lv.23 Ability: Chlorophyll

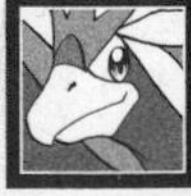
Valiant Pokémon **Brav**
Braviary ♂ Normal Flying
Lv.54 Ability: Sheer Force

TRIO BADGE | BASIC BADGE | INSECT BADGE | BOLT BADGE | QUAKE BADGE | ? | ? | ?

Pokémon™ Adventures Black & White

SWANNA

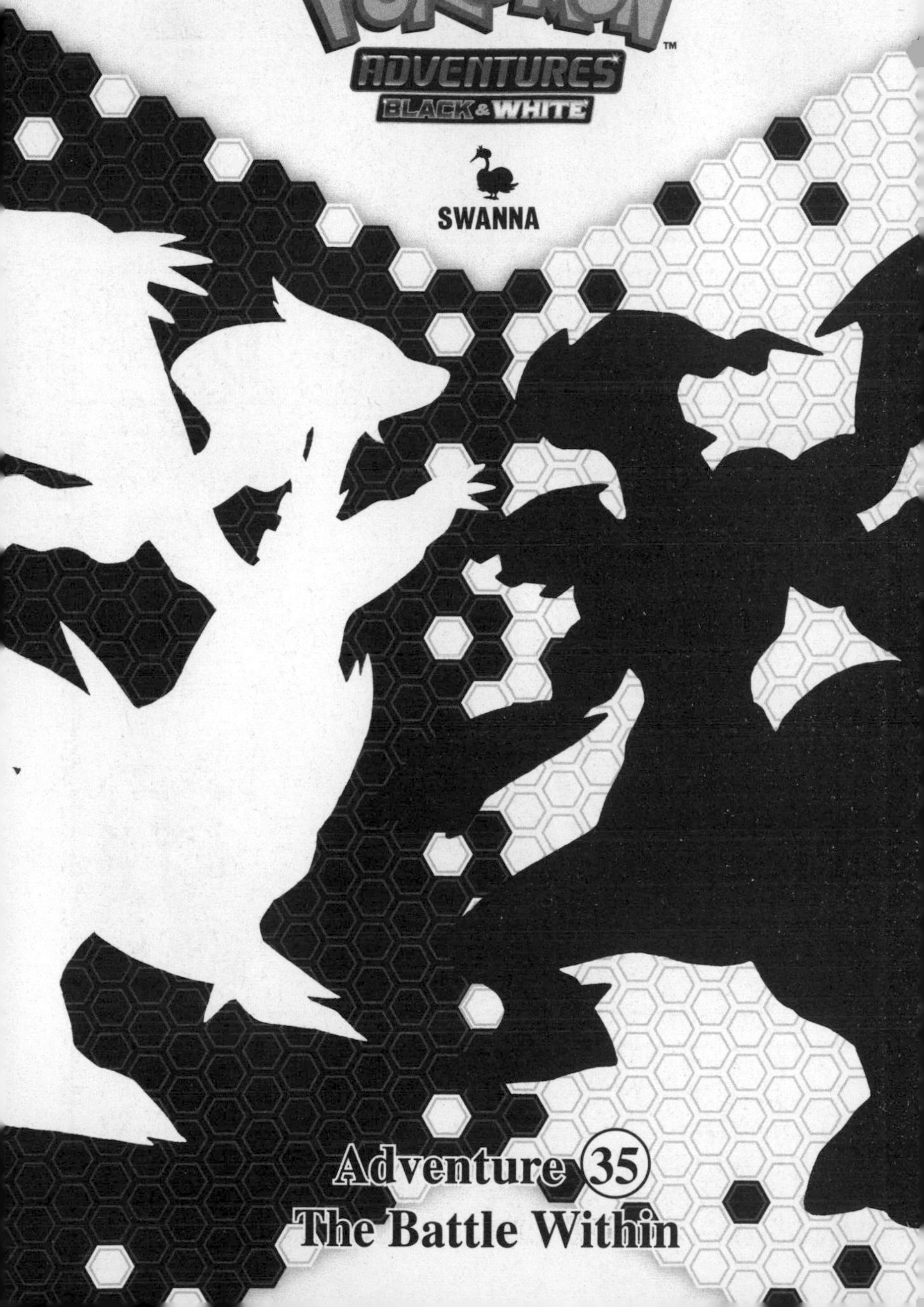

Adventure 35

The Battle Within

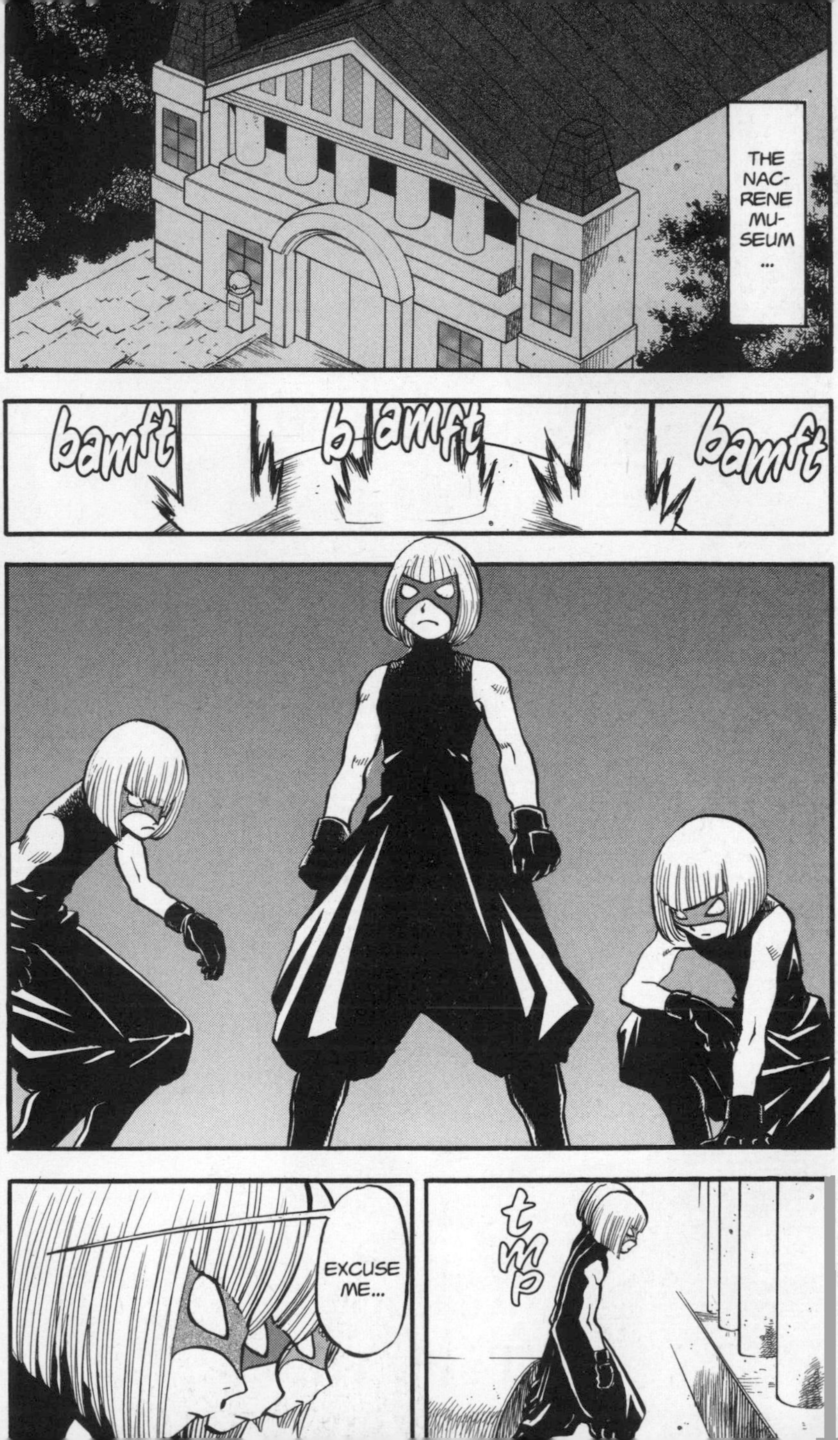
THE NACRENE MUSEUM...
bamft
b amft
bamft
tmp
EXCUSE ME...

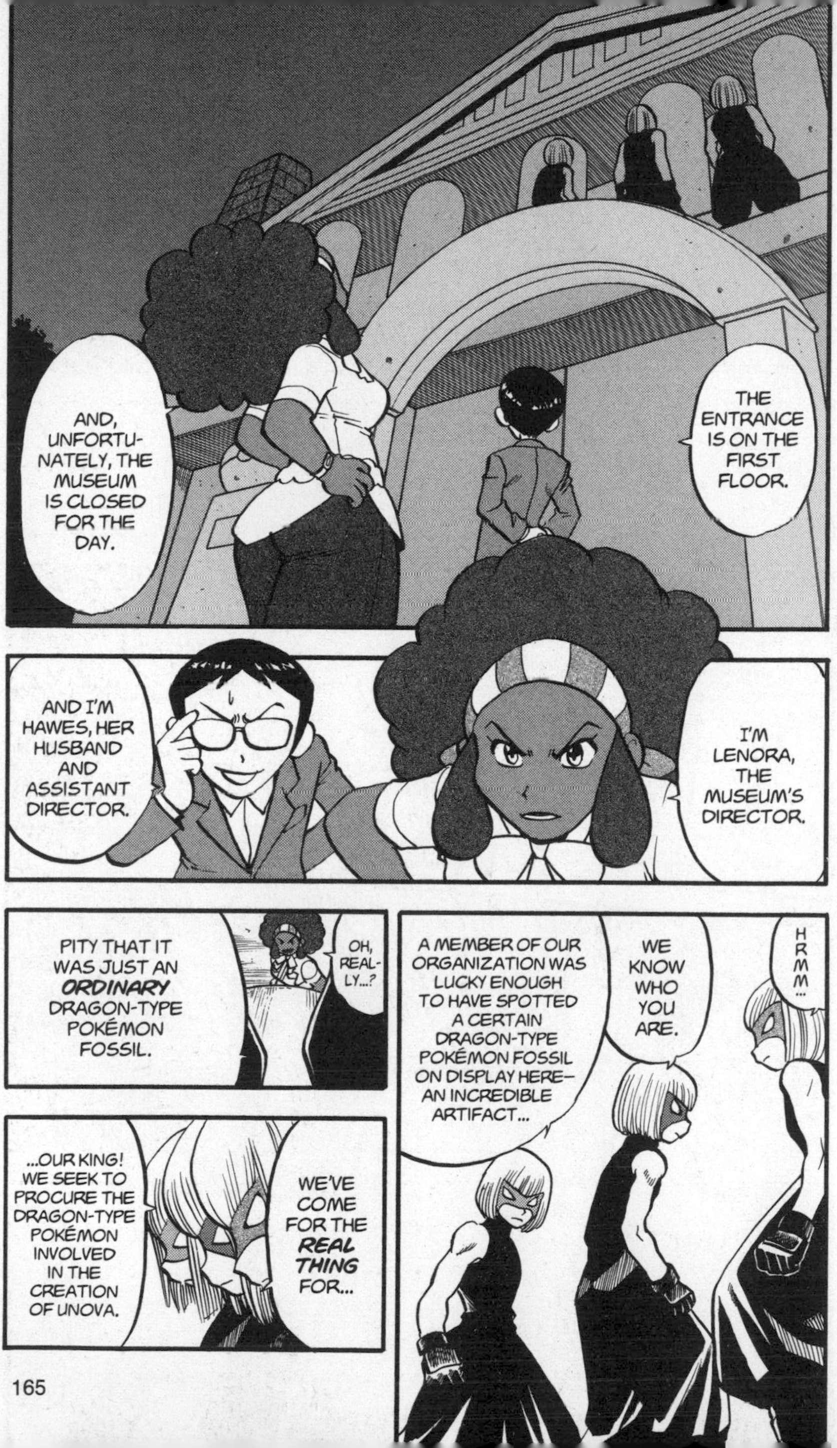
THE ENTRANCE IS ON THE FIRST FLOOR.
AND, UNFORTUNATELY, THE MUSEUM IS CLOSED FOR THE DAY.
I'M LENORA, THE MUSEUM'S DIRECTOR.
AND I'M HAWES, HER HUSBAND AND ASSISTANT DIRECTOR.
HRMM...
WE KNOW WHO YOU ARE.
A MEMBER OF OUR ORGANIZATION WAS LUCKY ENOUGH TO HAVE SPOTTED A CERTAIN DRAGON-TYPE POKÉMON FOSSIL ON DISPLAY HERE—AN INCREDIBLE ARTIFACT...
OH, REALLY...?
PITY THAT IT WAS JUST AN ***ORDINARY*** DRAGON-TYPE POKÉMON FOSSIL.
WE'VE COME FOR THE ***REAL THING*** FOR...
...OUR KING! WE SEEK TO PROCURE THE DRAGON-TYPE POKÉMON INVOLVED IN THE CREATION OF UNOVA.

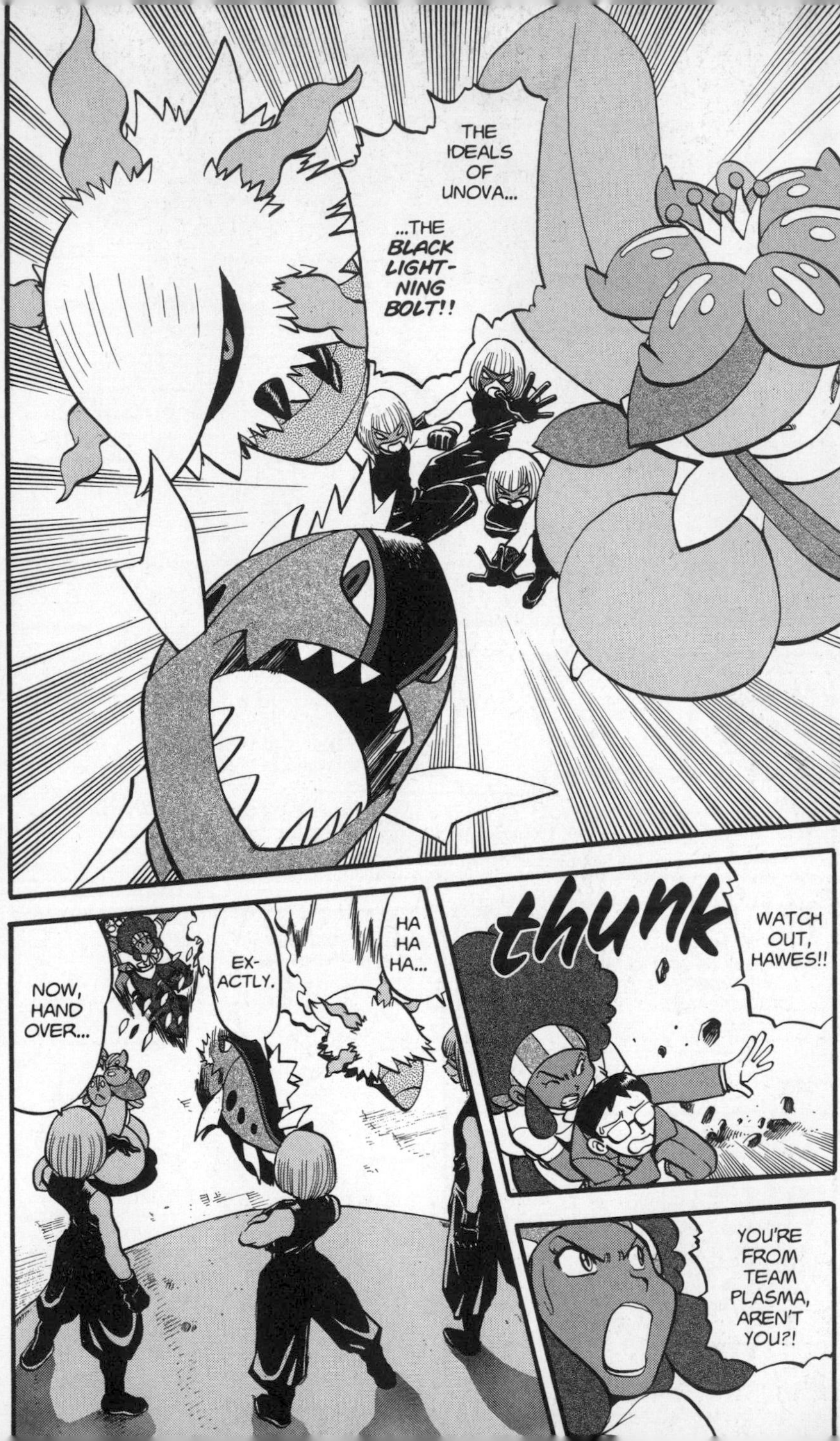
THE IDEALS OF UNOVA...
...THE *BLACK LIGHTNING BOLT*!!
thunk
WATCH OUT, HAWES!!
YOU'RE FROM TEAM PLASMA, AREN'T YOU?!
HA HA HA...
EX-ACTLY.
NOW, HAND OVER...

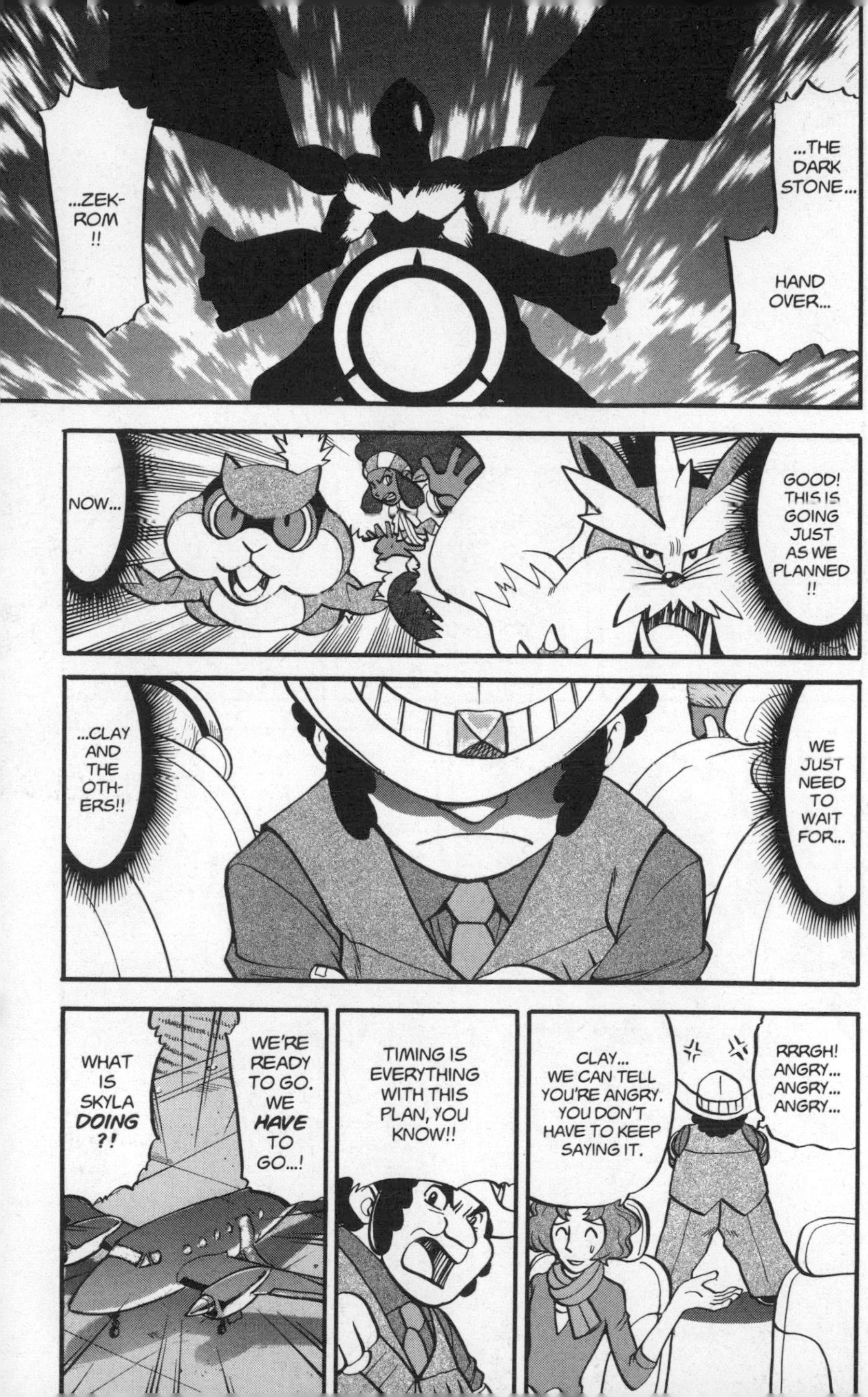
...THE DARK STONE...
HAND OVER...
...ZEK-ROM!!
GOOD! THIS IS GOING JUST AS WE PLANNED!!
NOW...
WE JUST NEED TO WAIT FOR...
...CLAY AND THE OTH-ERS!!
RRRGH! ANGRY... ANGRY... ANGRY...
CLAY... WE CAN TELL YOU'RE ANGRY. YOU DON'T HAVE TO KEEP SAYING IT.
TIMING IS EVERYTHING WITH THIS PLAN, YOU KNOW!!
WE'RE READY TO GO. WE *HAVE* TO GO...!
WHAT IS SKYLA *DOING*?!

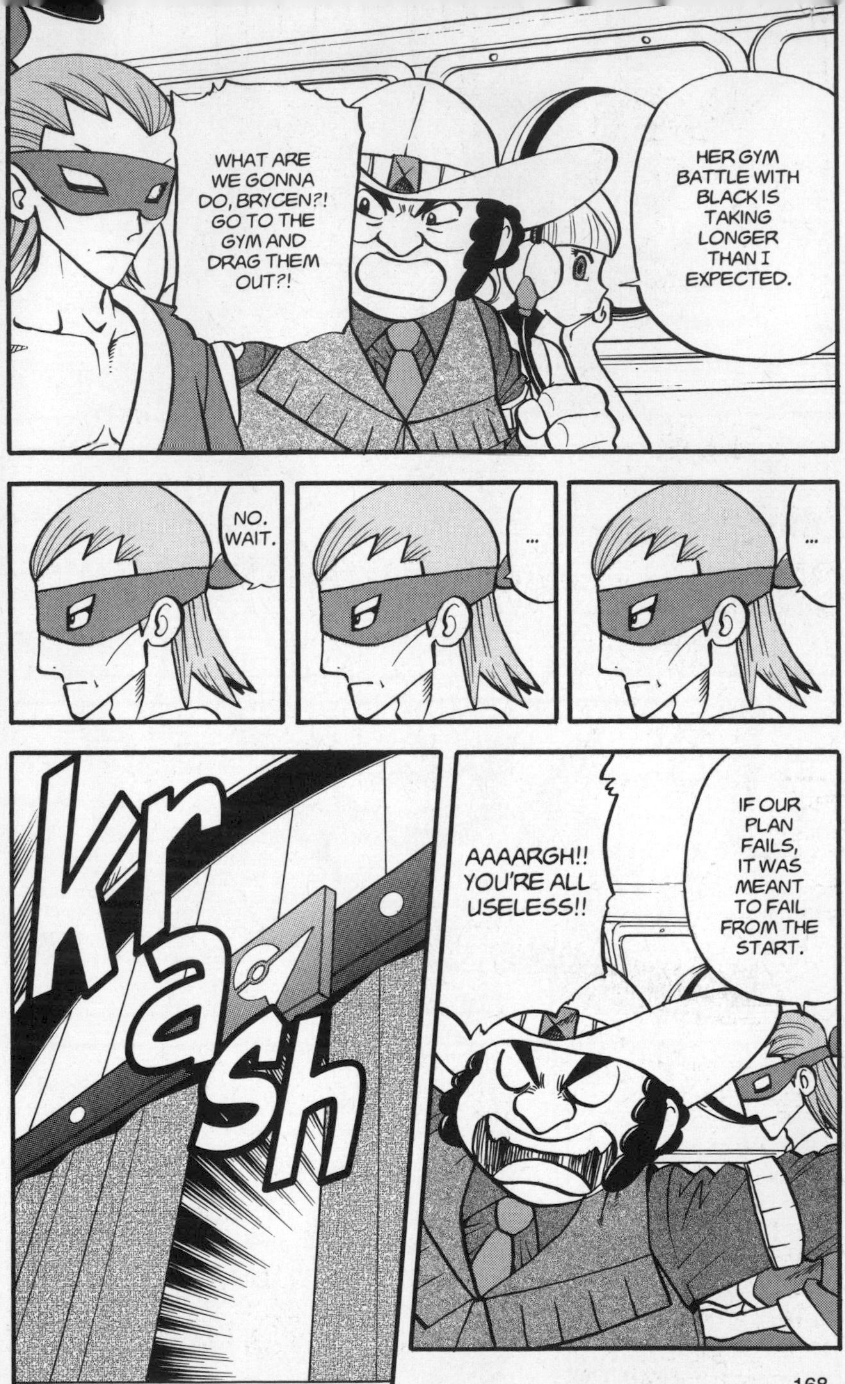
HER GYM BATTLE WITH BLACK IS TAKING LONGER THAN I EXPECTED.
WHAT ARE WE GONNA DO, BRYCEN?! GO TO THE GYM AND DRAG THEM OUT?!
...
...
NO. WAIT.
IF OUR PLAN FAILS, IT WAS MEANT TO FAIL FROM THE START.
AAAARGH!! YOU'RE ALL USELESS!!
Krash

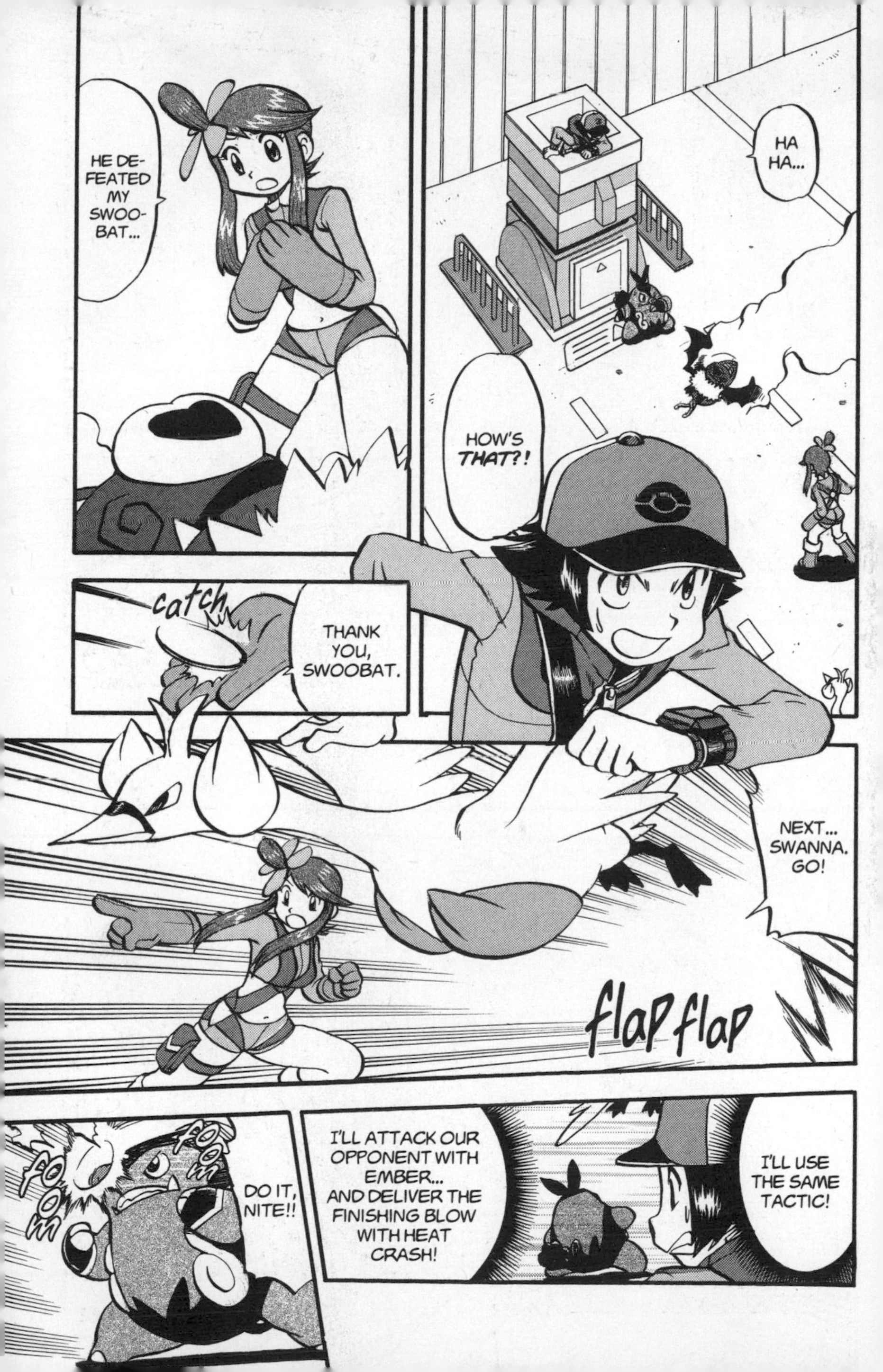
HA HA...
HOW'S THAT?!
HE DE-FEATED MY SWOO-BAT...
catch
THANK YOU, SWOOBAT.
NEXT... SWANNA. GO!
flap flap
I'LL USE THE SAME TACTIC!
I'LL ATTACK OUR OPPONENT WITH EMBER... AND DELIVER THE FINISHING BLOW WITH HEAT CRASH!
FOOM
FOOM
DO IT, NITE!!

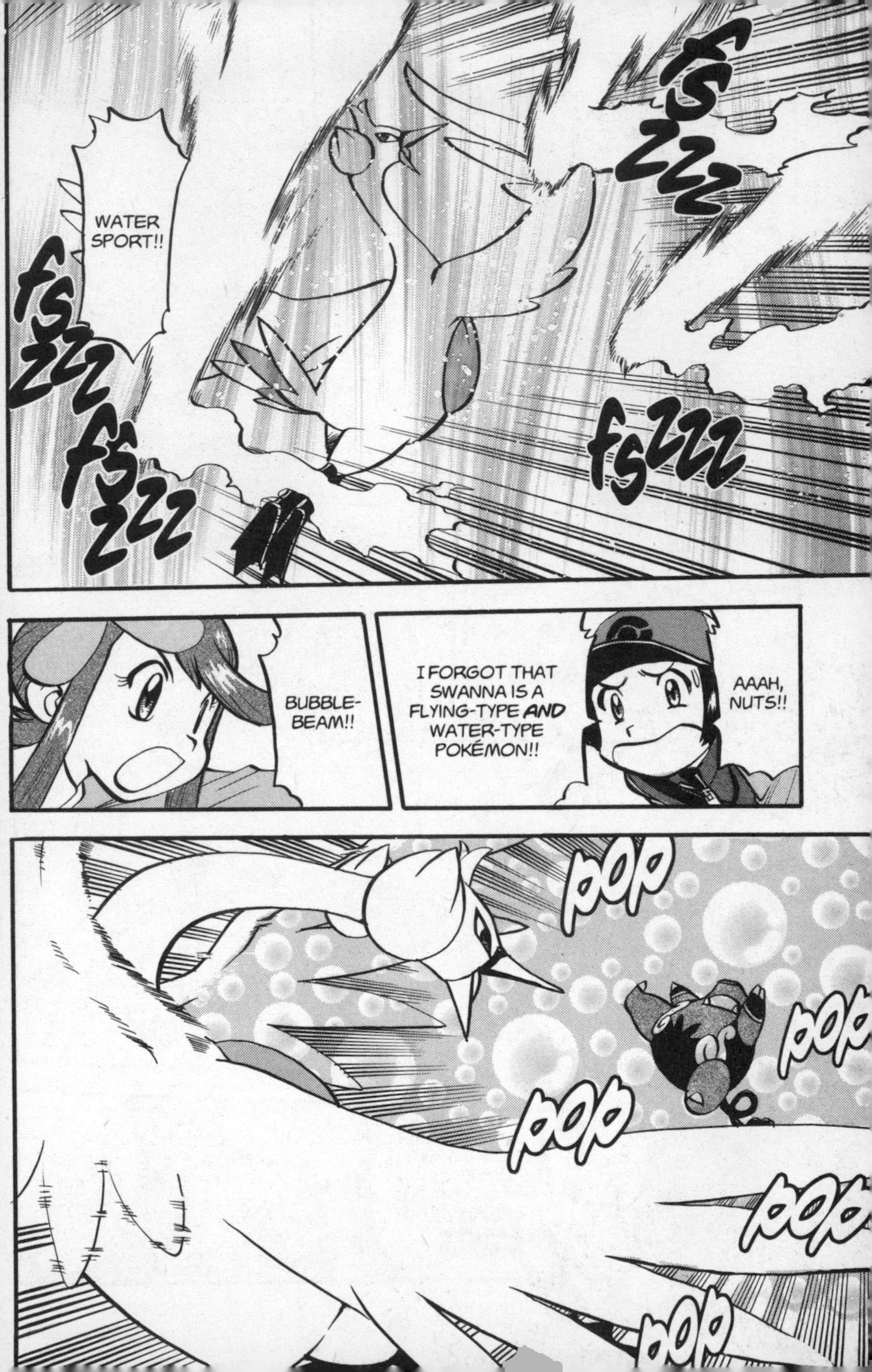

FSZZZ
WATER SPORT!!
FSZZZ
FSZZZ
FSZZZ
AAAH, NUTS!!
I FORGOT THAT SWANNA IS A FLYING-TYPE AND WATER-TYPE POKÉMON!!
BUBBLE-BEAM!!
POP
POP
POP
POP
POP

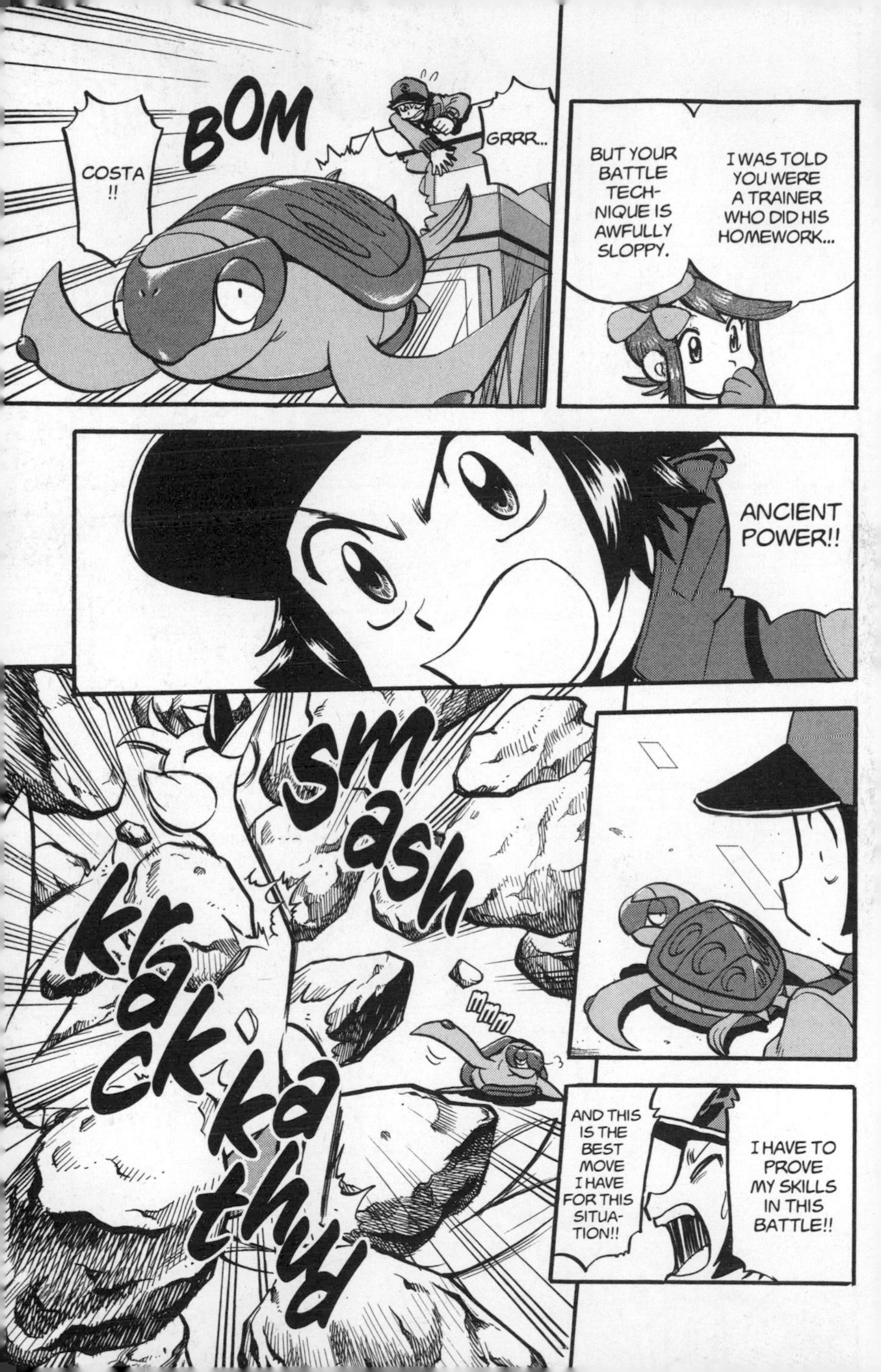
I WAS TOLD YOU WERE A TRAINER WHO DID HIS HOMEWORK...
BUT YOUR BATTLE TECH-NIQUE IS AWFULLY SLOPPY.
GRRR...
BOM
COSTA !!
ANCIENT POWER!!
I HAVE TO PROVE MY SKILLS IN THIS BATTLE!!
AND THIS IS THE BEST MOVE I HAVE FOR THIS SITUA-TION!!
smash
krackkathud
mmm

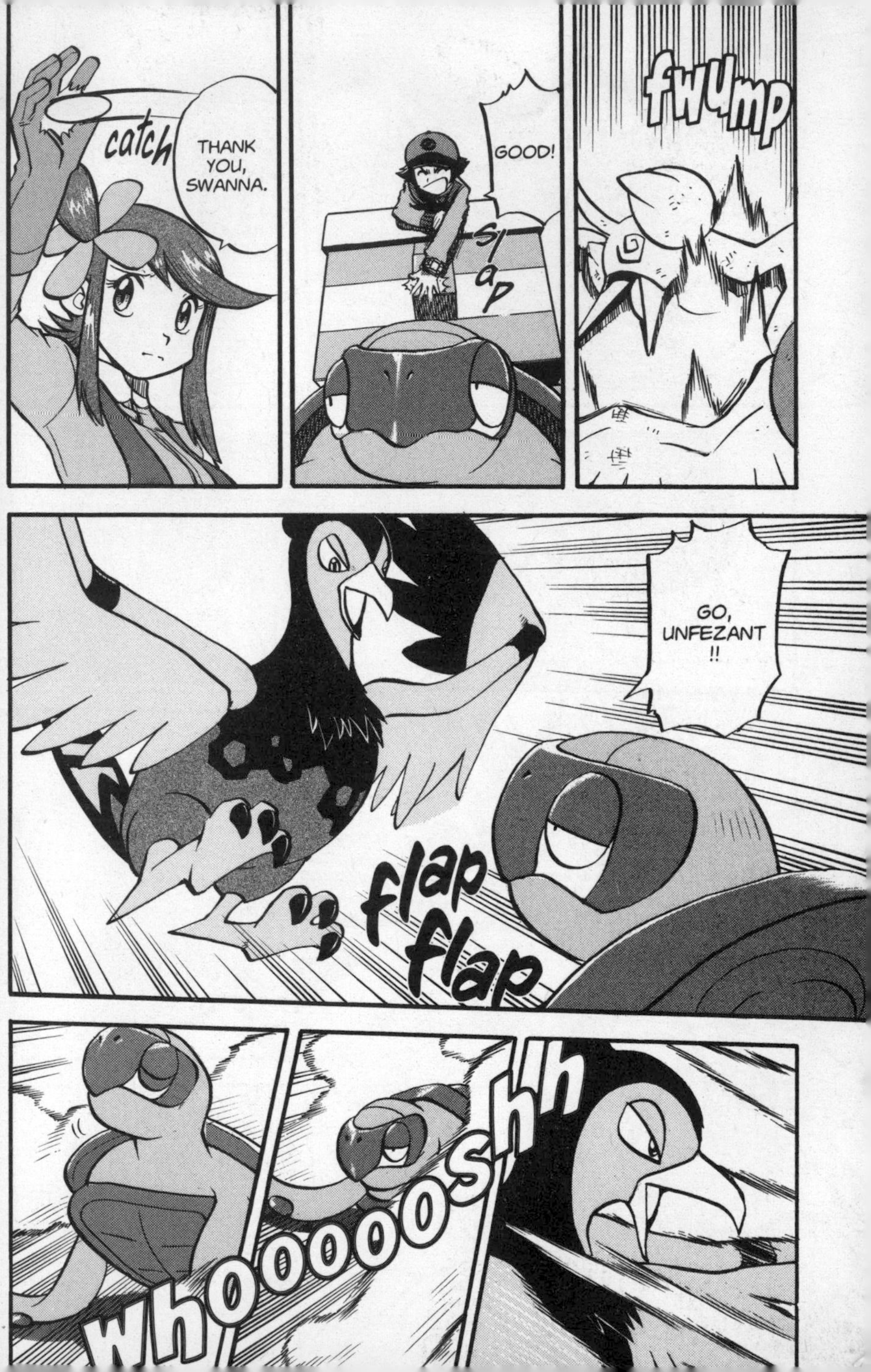
fwump
GOOD!
slap
THANK YOU, SWANNA.
catch
GO, UNFEZANT !!
flap flap
whoooooosshh

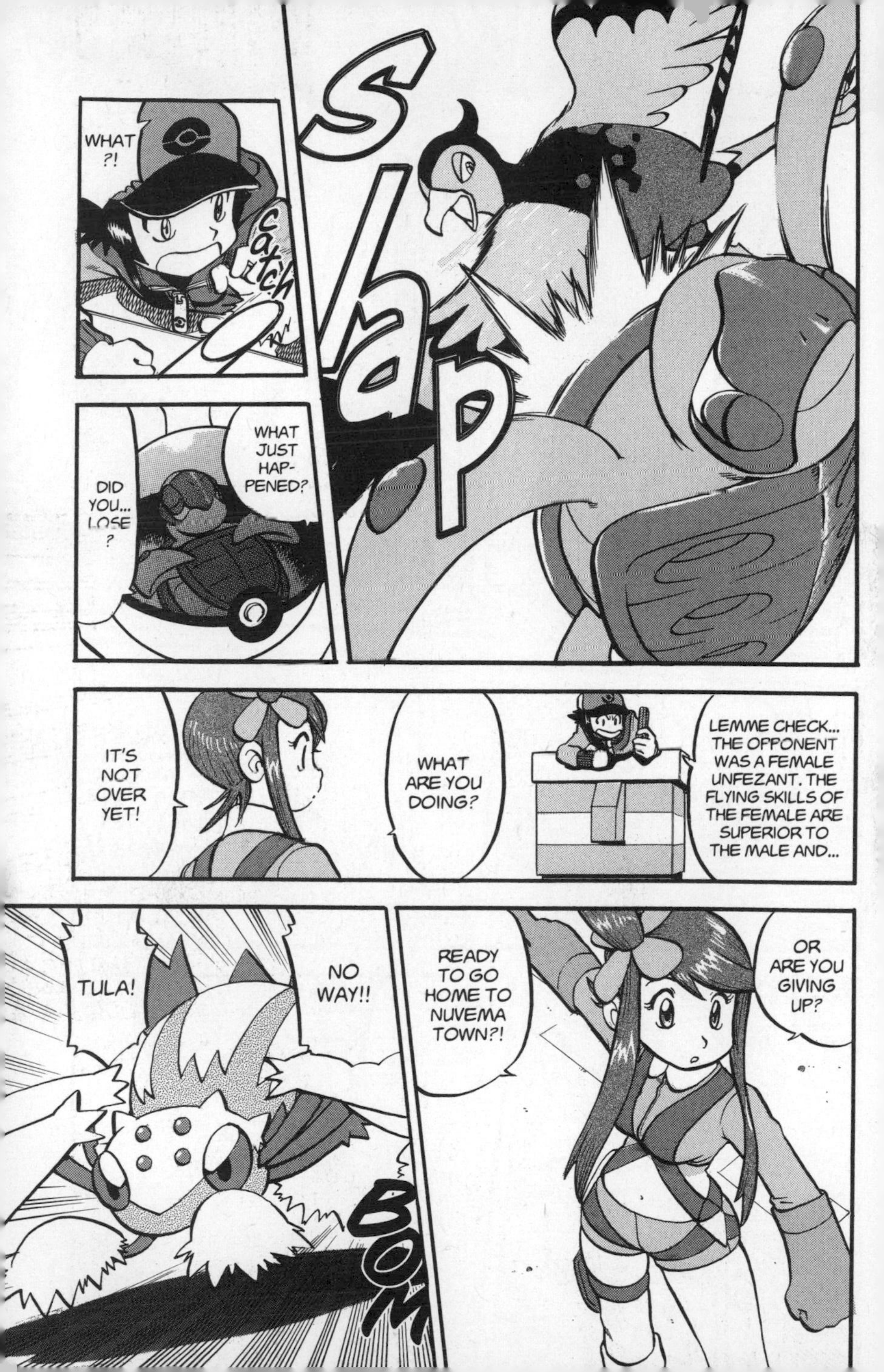
SLAP
WHAT ?!
CATCH
WHAT JUST HAPPENED?
DID YOU... LOSE?
LEMME CHECK... THE OPPONENT WAS A FEMALE UNFEZANT. THE FLYING SKILLS OF THE FEMALE ARE SUPERIOR TO THE MALE AND...
WHAT ARE YOU DOING?
IT'S NOT OVER YET!
OR ARE YOU GIVING UP?
READY TO GO HOME TO NUVEMA TOWN?!
NO WAY!!
TULA!
BOOM

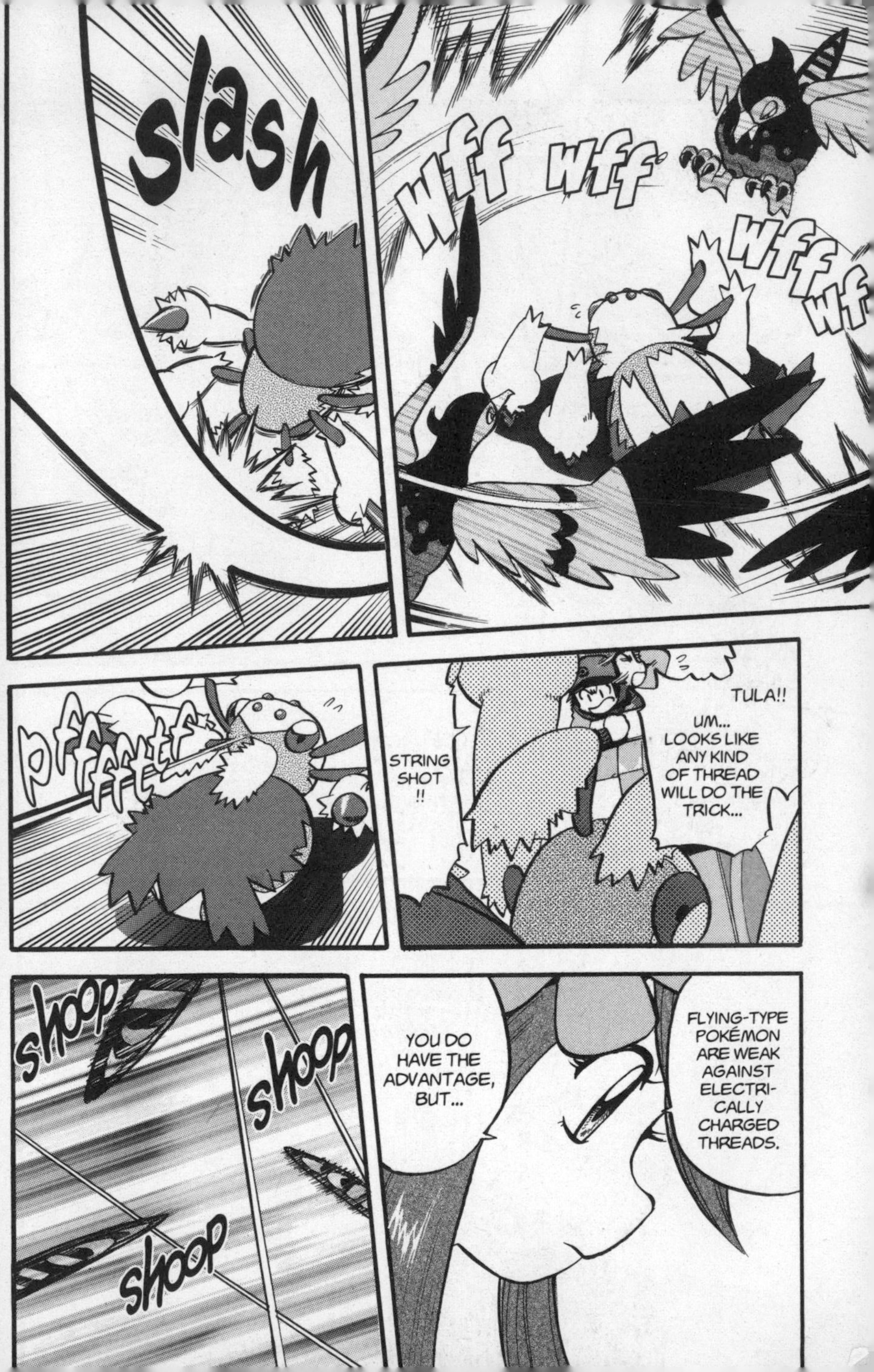
wff
wff
wff
wf
slash
TULA!!
UM... LOOKS LIKE ANY KIND OF THREAD WILL DO THE TRICK...
STRING SHOT !!
pffftf
ffft
FLYING-TYPE POKÉMON ARE WEAK AGAINST ELECTRICALLY CHARGED THREADS.
YOU DO HAVE THE ADVANTAGE, BUT...
shoop
shoop
shoop

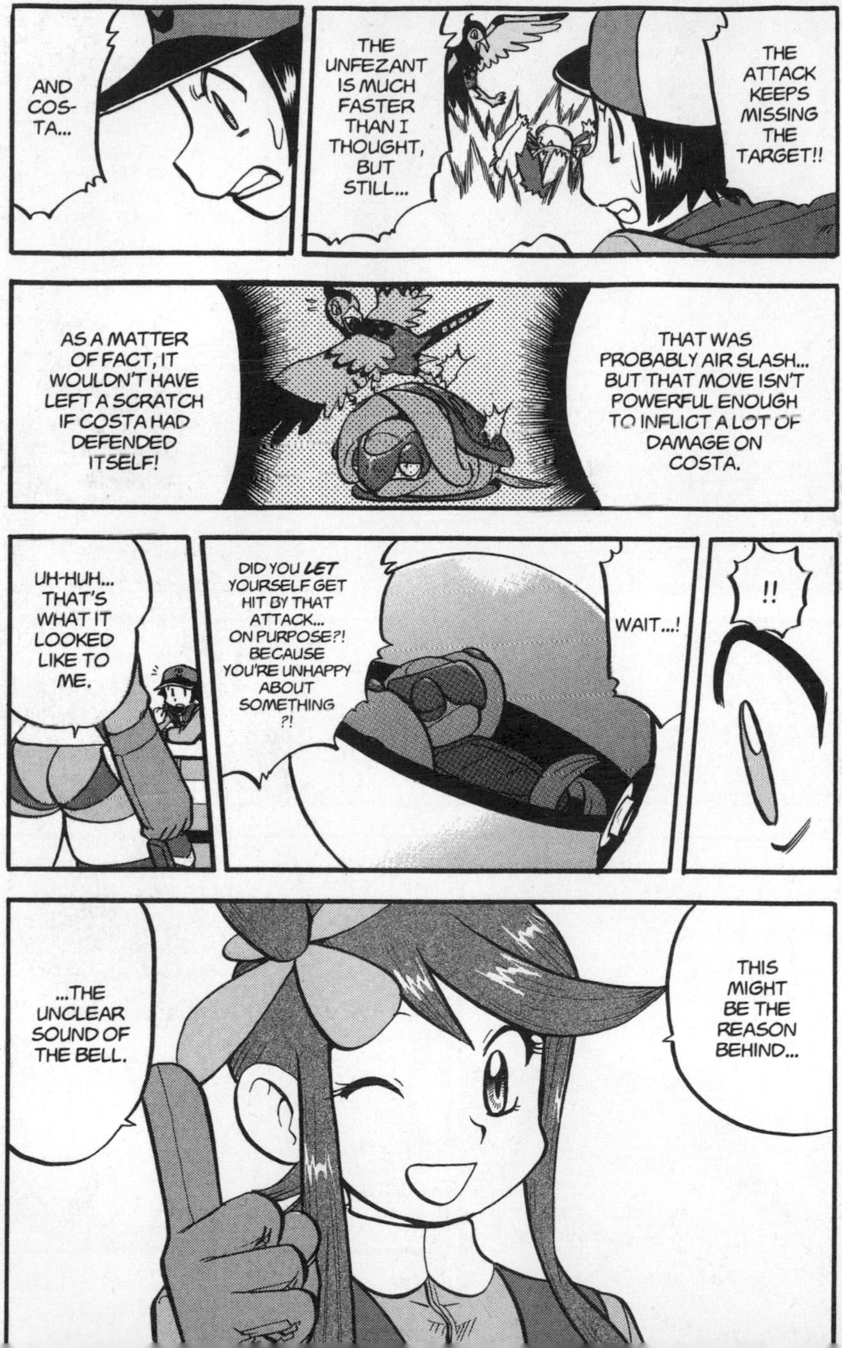
THE ATTACK KEEPS MISSING THE TARGET!!
THE UNFEZANT IS MUCH FASTER THAN I THOUGHT, BUT STILL...
AND COS-TA...
THAT WAS PROBABLY AIR SLASH... BUT THAT MOVE ISN'T POWERFUL ENOUGH TO INFLICT A LOT OF DAMAGE ON COSTA.
AS A MATTER OF FACT, IT WOULDN'T HAVE LEFT A SCRATCH IF COSTA HAD DEFENDED ITSELF!
!!
WAIT...!
DID YOU *LET* YOURSELF GET HIT BY THAT ATTACK... ON PURPOSE?! BECAUSE YOU'RE UNHAPPY ABOUT SOMETHING?!
UH-HUH... THAT'S WHAT IT LOOKED LIKE TO ME.
THIS MIGHT BE THE REASON BEHIND...
...THE UNCLEAR SOUND OF THE BELL.

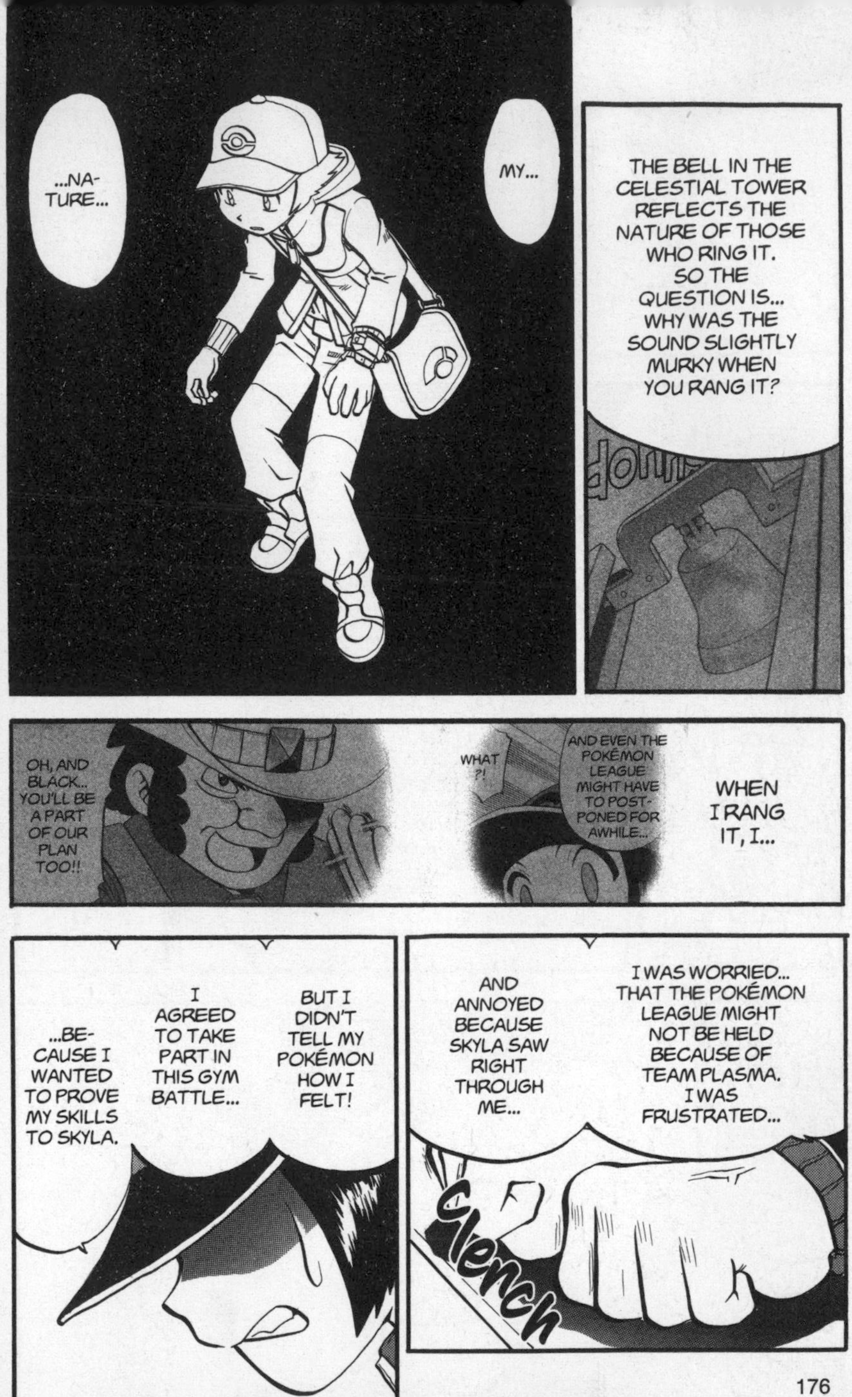
THE BELL IN THE CELESTIAL TOWER REFLECTS THE NATURE OF THOSE WHO RING IT. SO THE QUESTION IS... WHY WAS THE SOUND SLIGHTLY MURKY WHEN YOU RANG IT?
MY...
...NA-TURE...
WHEN I RANG IT, I...
AND EVEN THE POKÉMON LEAGUE MIGHT HAVE TO POST-PONED FOR AWHILE...
WHAT?!
OH, AND BLACK... YOU'LL BE A PART OF OUR PLAN TOO!!
I WAS WORRIED... THAT THE POKÉMON LEAGUE MIGHT NOT BE HELD BECAUSE OF TEAM PLASMA. I WAS FRUSTRATED...
AND ANNOYED BECAUSE SKYLA SAW RIGHT THROUGH ME...
Clench
BUT I DIDN'T TELL MY POKÉMON HOW I FELT!
I AGREED TO TAKE PART IN THIS GYM BATTLE...
...BE-CAUSE I WANTED TO PROVE MY SKILLS TO SKYLA.

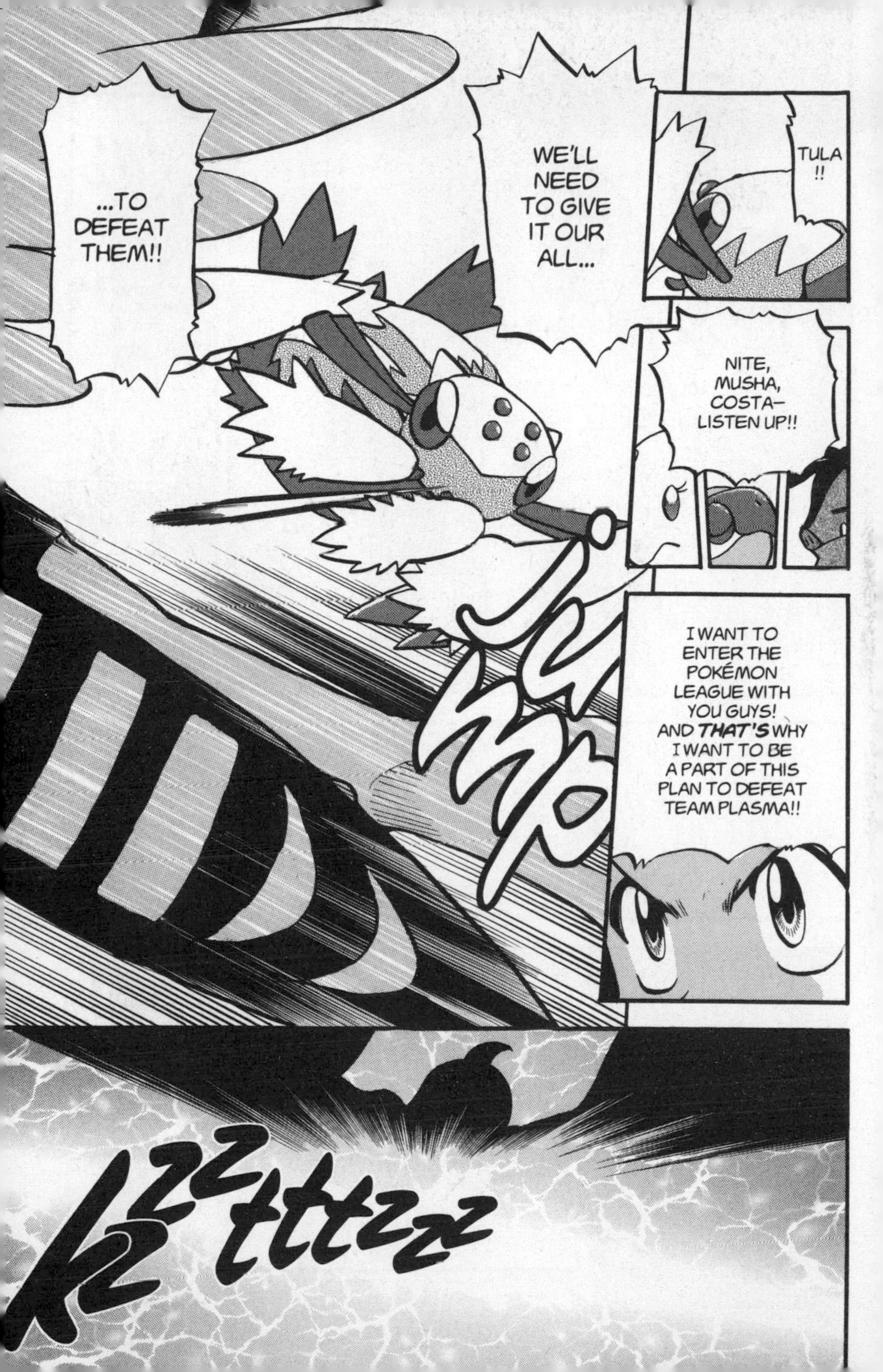
TULA!!
NITE, MUSHA, COSTA— LISTEN UP!!
I WANT TO ENTER THE POKÉMON LEAGUE WITH YOU GUYS! AND ***THAT'S*** WHY I WANT TO BE A PART OF THIS PLAN TO DEFEAT TEAM PLASMA!!
WE'LL NEED TO GIVE IT OUR ALL...
...TO DEFEAT THEM!!
JUMP
kzzztttzzz

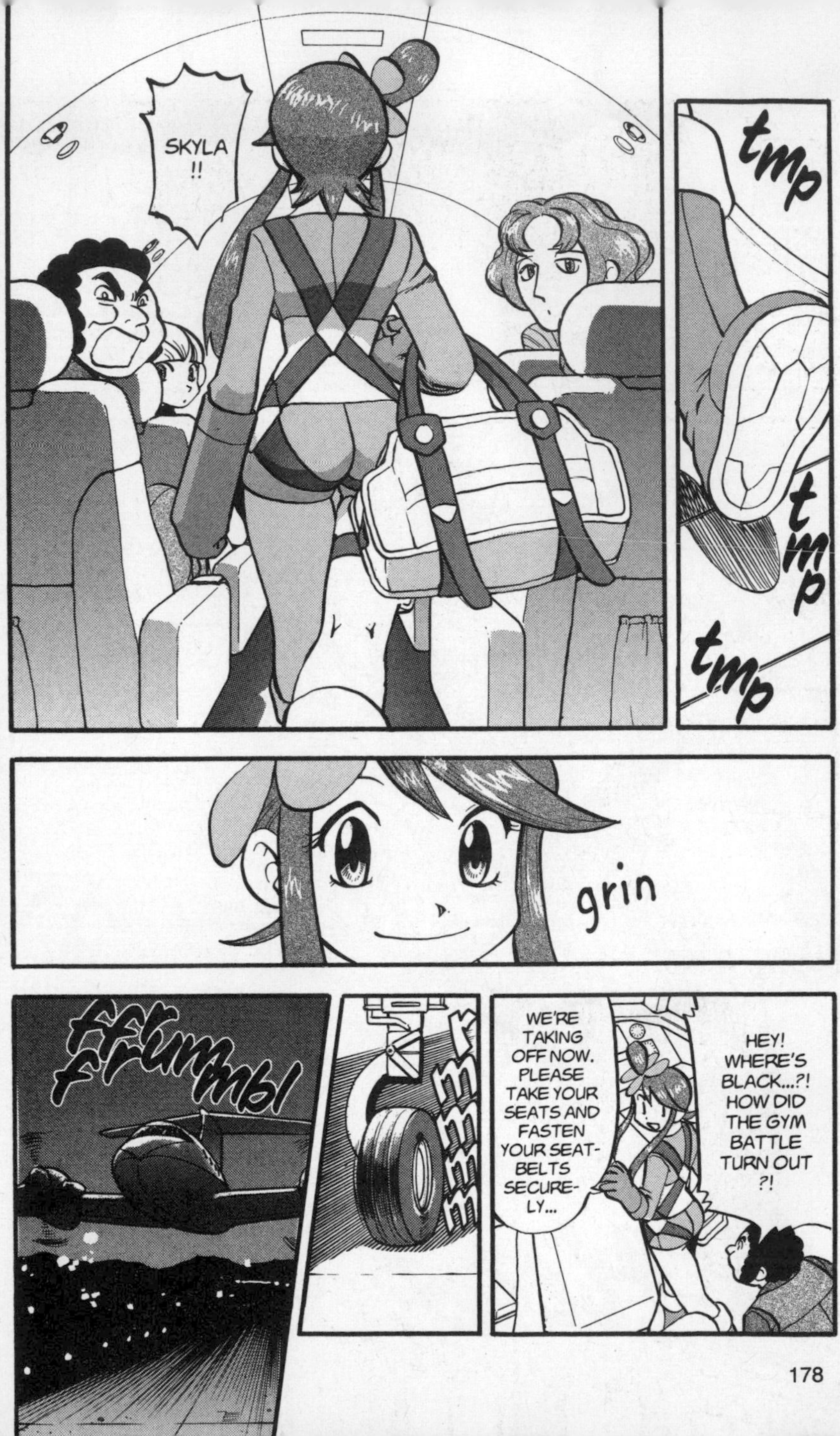
tmp
tmp
tmp
SKYLA !!
grin
HEY! WHERE'S BLACK...?! HOW DID THE GYM BATTLE TURN OUT ?!
WE'RE TAKING OFF NOW. PLEASE TAKE YOUR SEATS AND FASTEN YOUR SEAT-BELTS SECURE-LY...
frummbl

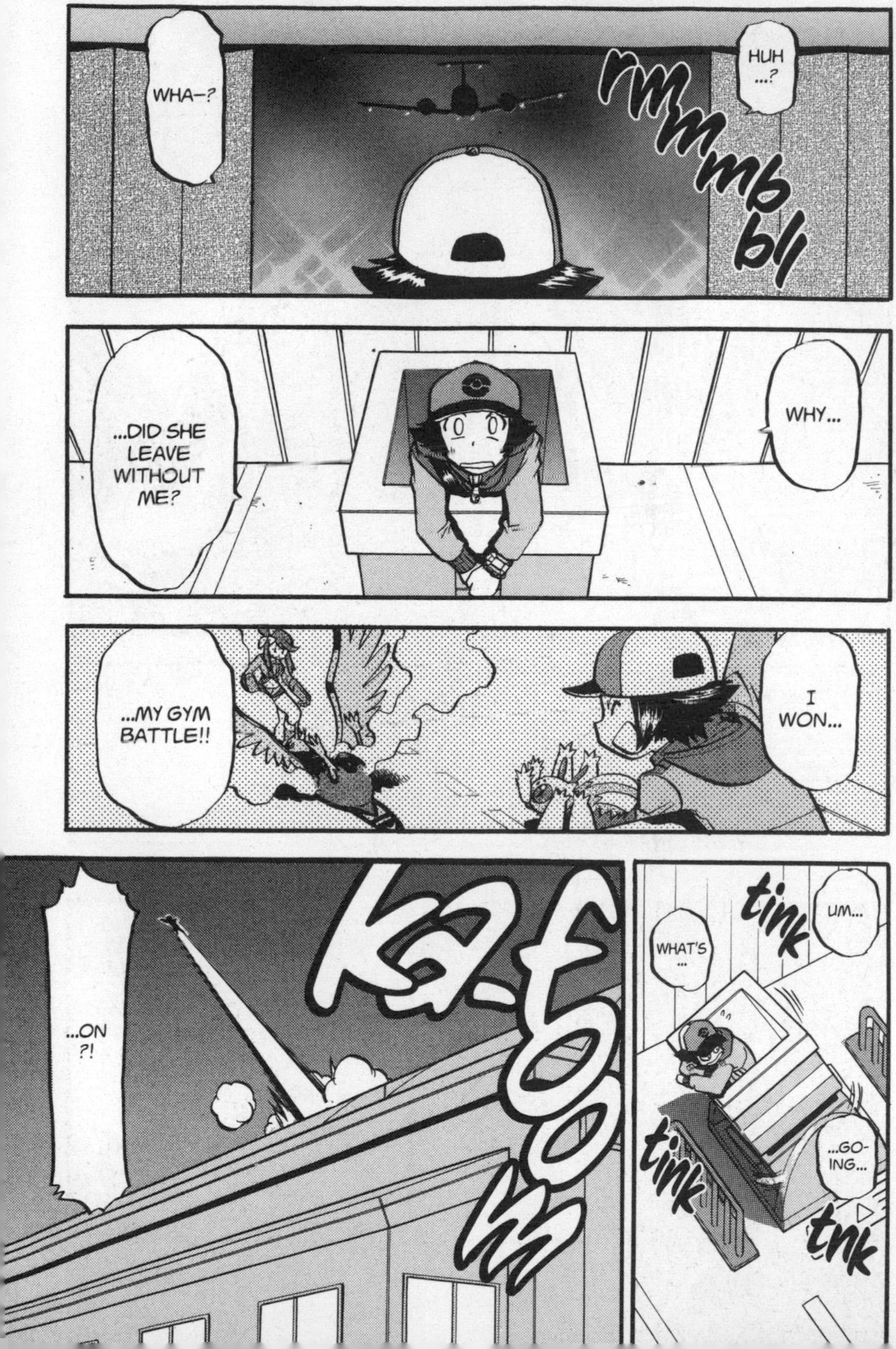
HUH ...?
WHA–?
rmmmbll
WHY...
...DID SHE LEAVE WITHOUT ME?
I WON...
...MY GYM BATTLE!!
tink
UM...
WHAT'S ...
...GO-ING...
tink
tnk
ka-booom
...ON ?!

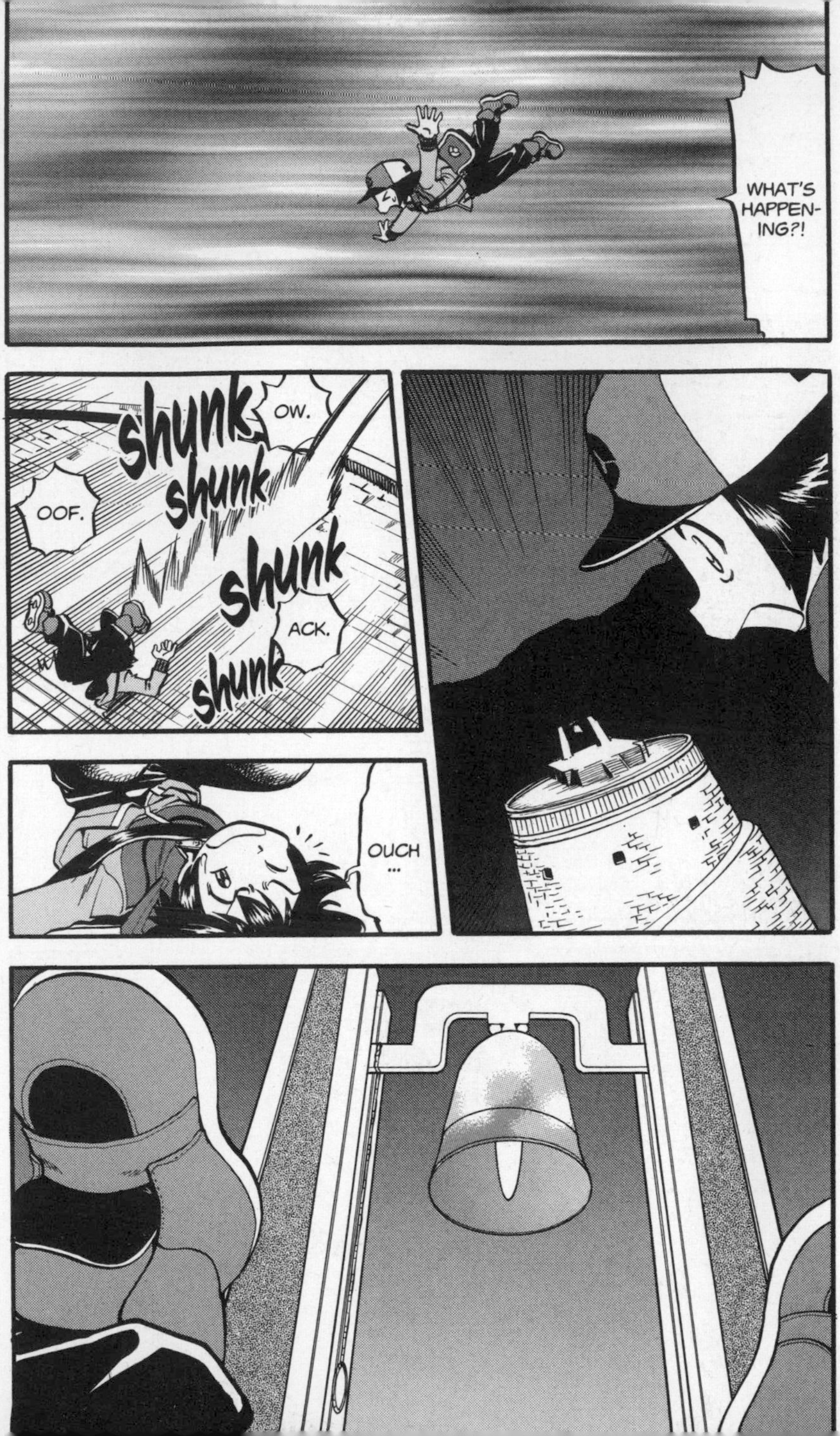
WHAT'S HAPPENING?!
OW.
shunk
shunk
OOF.
shunk
ACK.
shunk
OUCH...

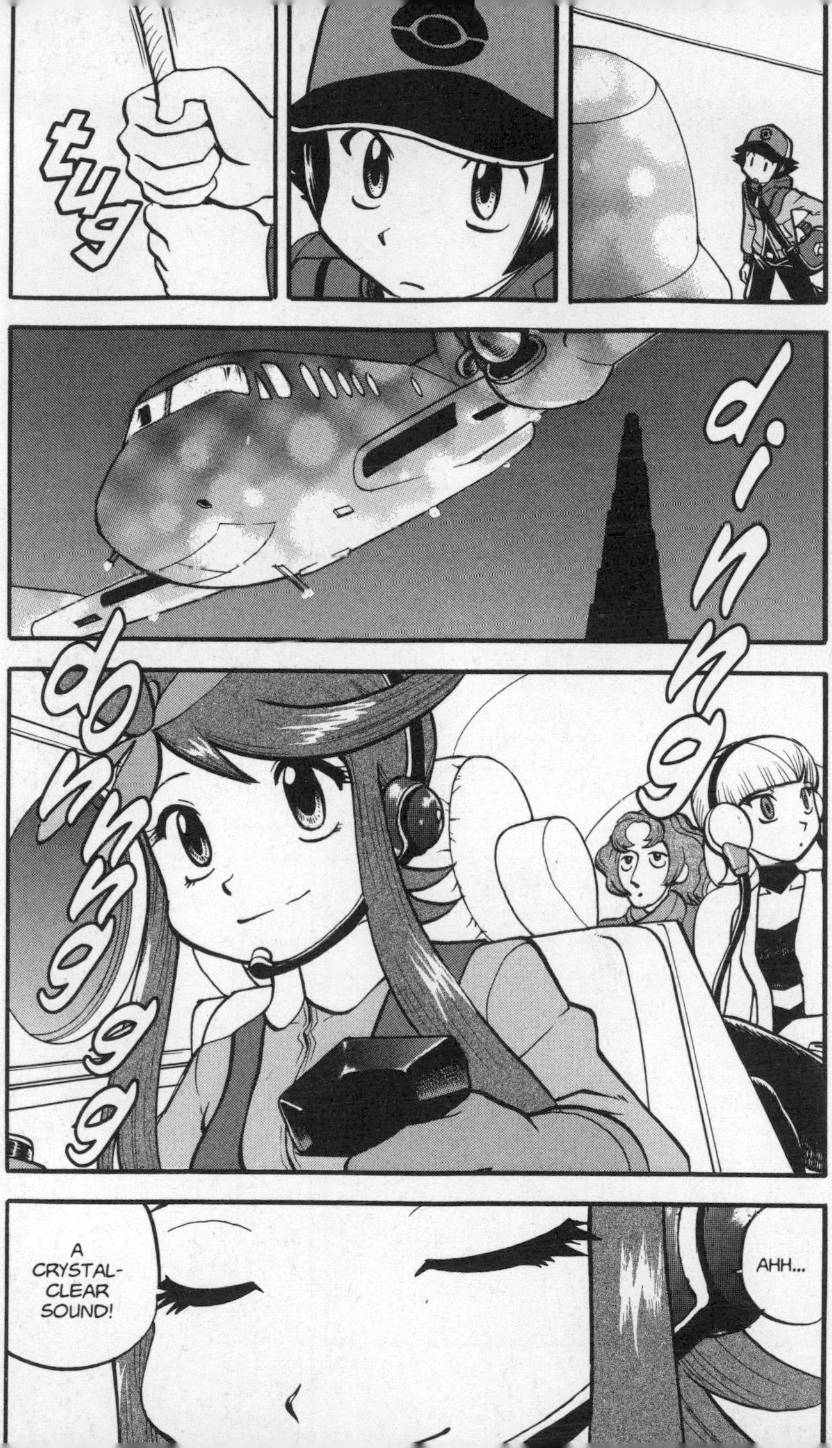
tug
dinng
donnnggg
AHH...
A CRYSTAL-CLEAR SOUND!

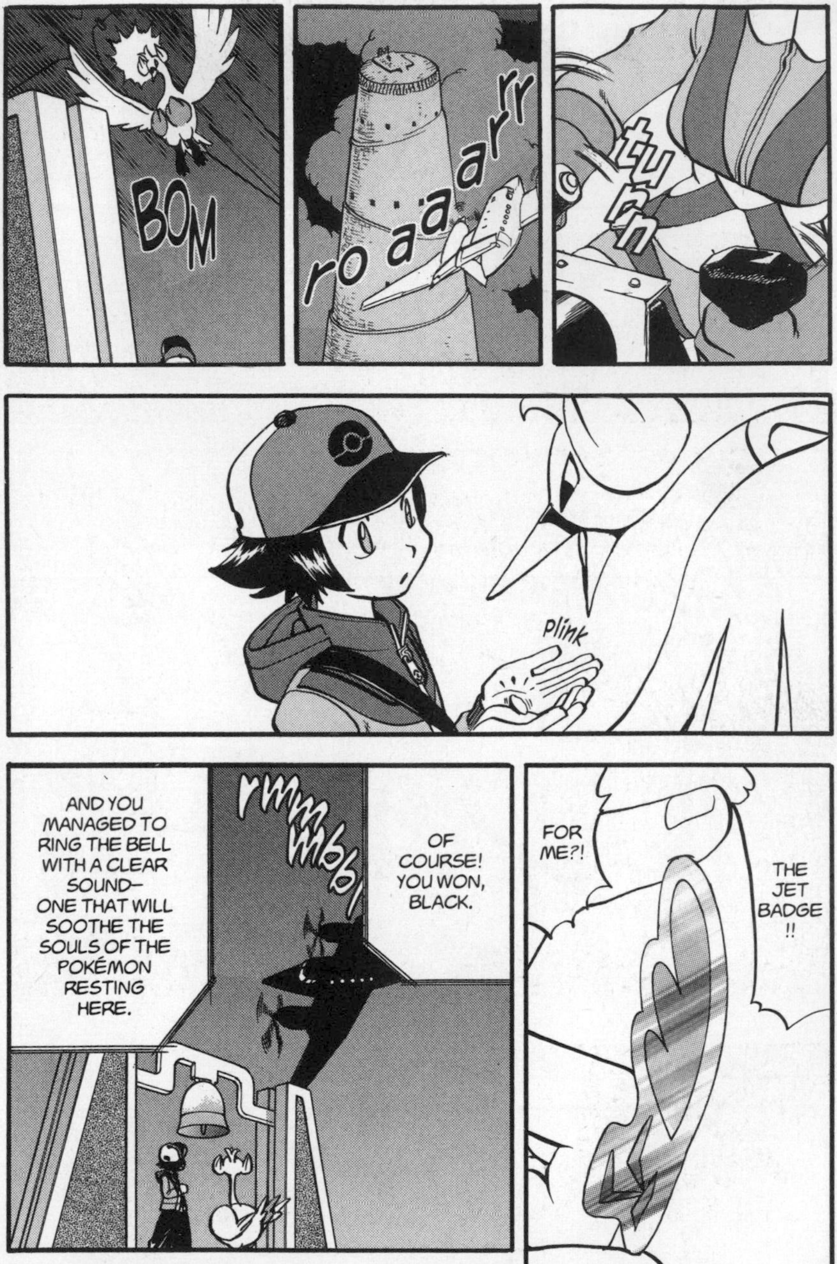
turn
roaaaarrr
BOM
plink
THE JET BADGE !!
FOR ME?!
OF COURSE! YOU WON, BLACK.
rmmmbbl
AND YOU MANAGED TO RING THE BELL WITH A CLEAR SOUND— ONE THAT WILL SOOTHE THE SOULS OF THE POKÉMON RESTING HERE.

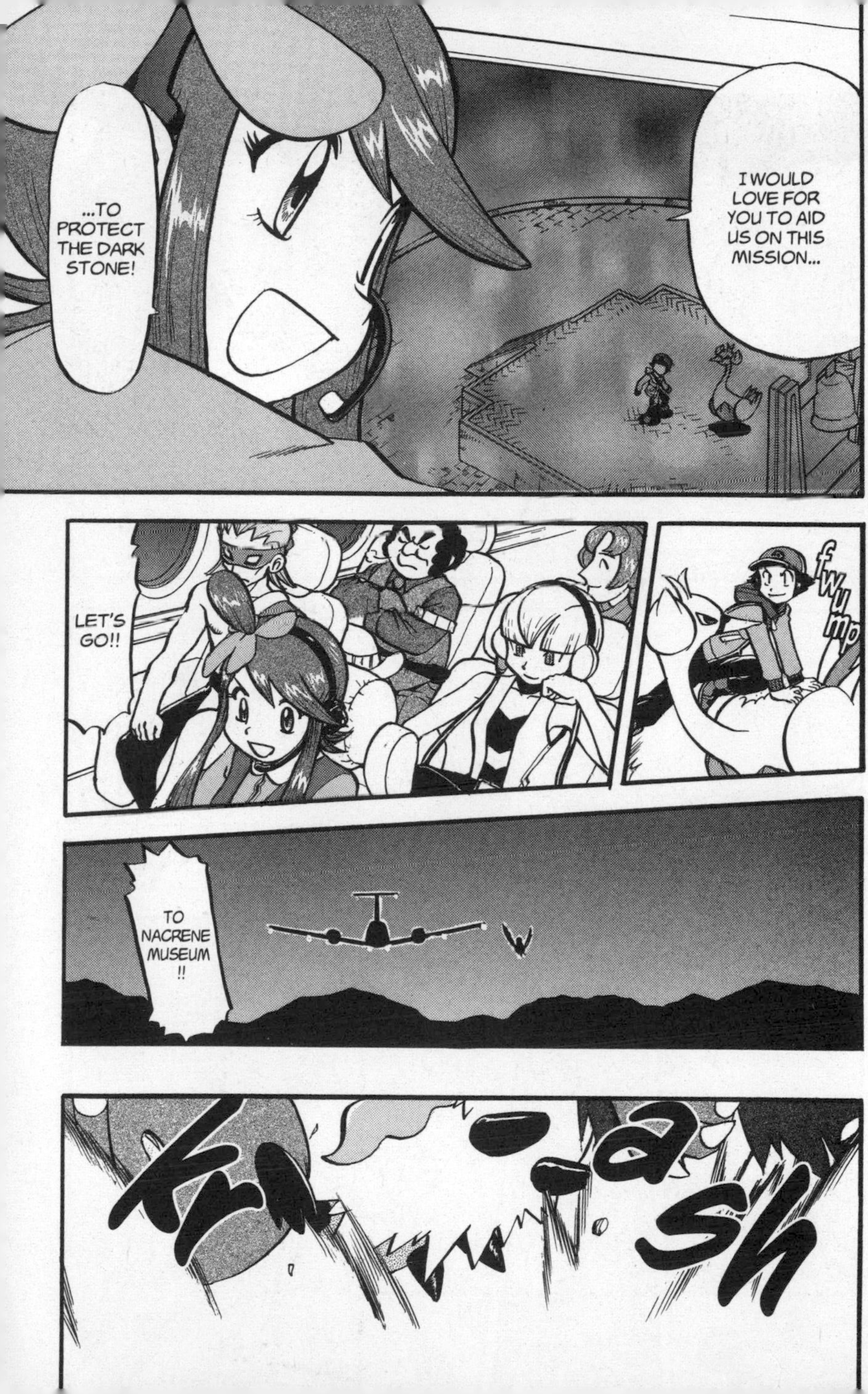
I WOULD LOVE FOR YOU TO AID US ON THIS MISSION...
...TO PROTECT THE DARK STONE!
fwump
LET'S GO!!
TO NACRENE MUSEUM !!
kr-a-sh

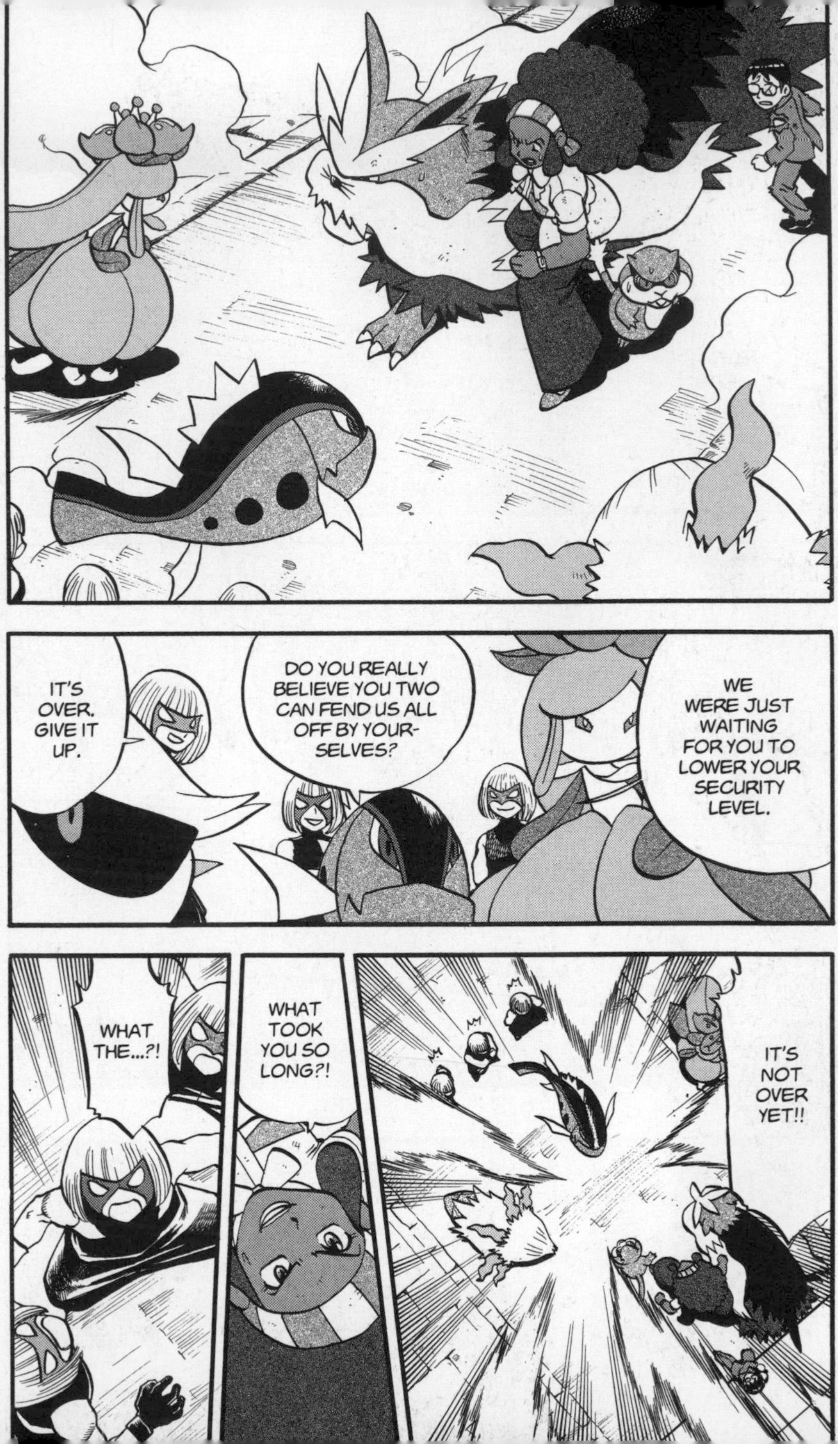
WE WERE JUST WAITING FOR YOU TO LOWER YOUR SECURITY LEVEL.
DO YOU REALLY BELIEVE YOU TWO CAN FEND US ALL OFF BY YOUR-SELVES?
IT'S OVER. GIVE IT UP.
IT'S NOT OVER YET!!
WHAT TOOK YOU SO LONG?!
WHAT THE...?!

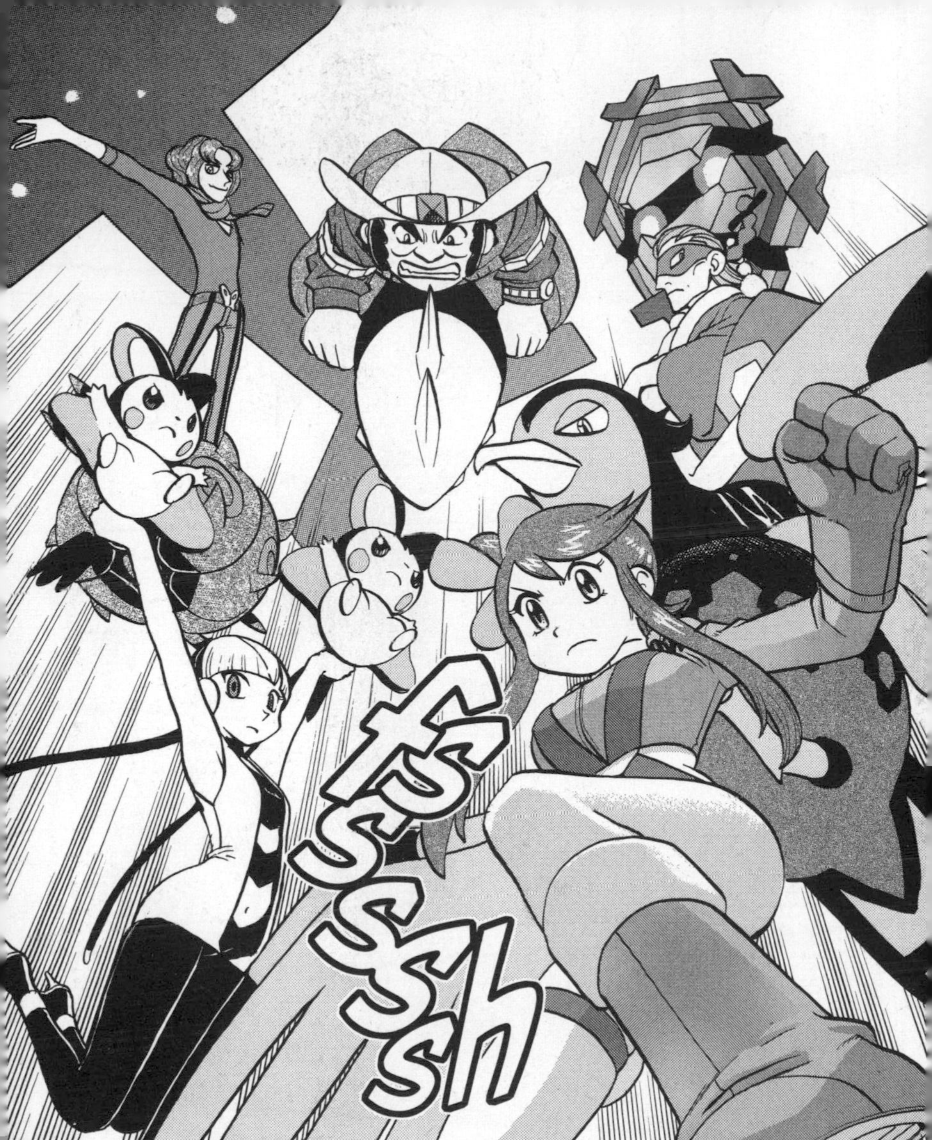
fsssh
tmp
tmp
tmp
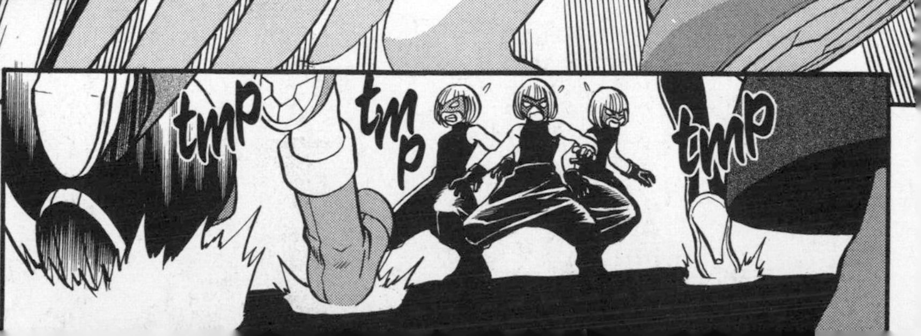

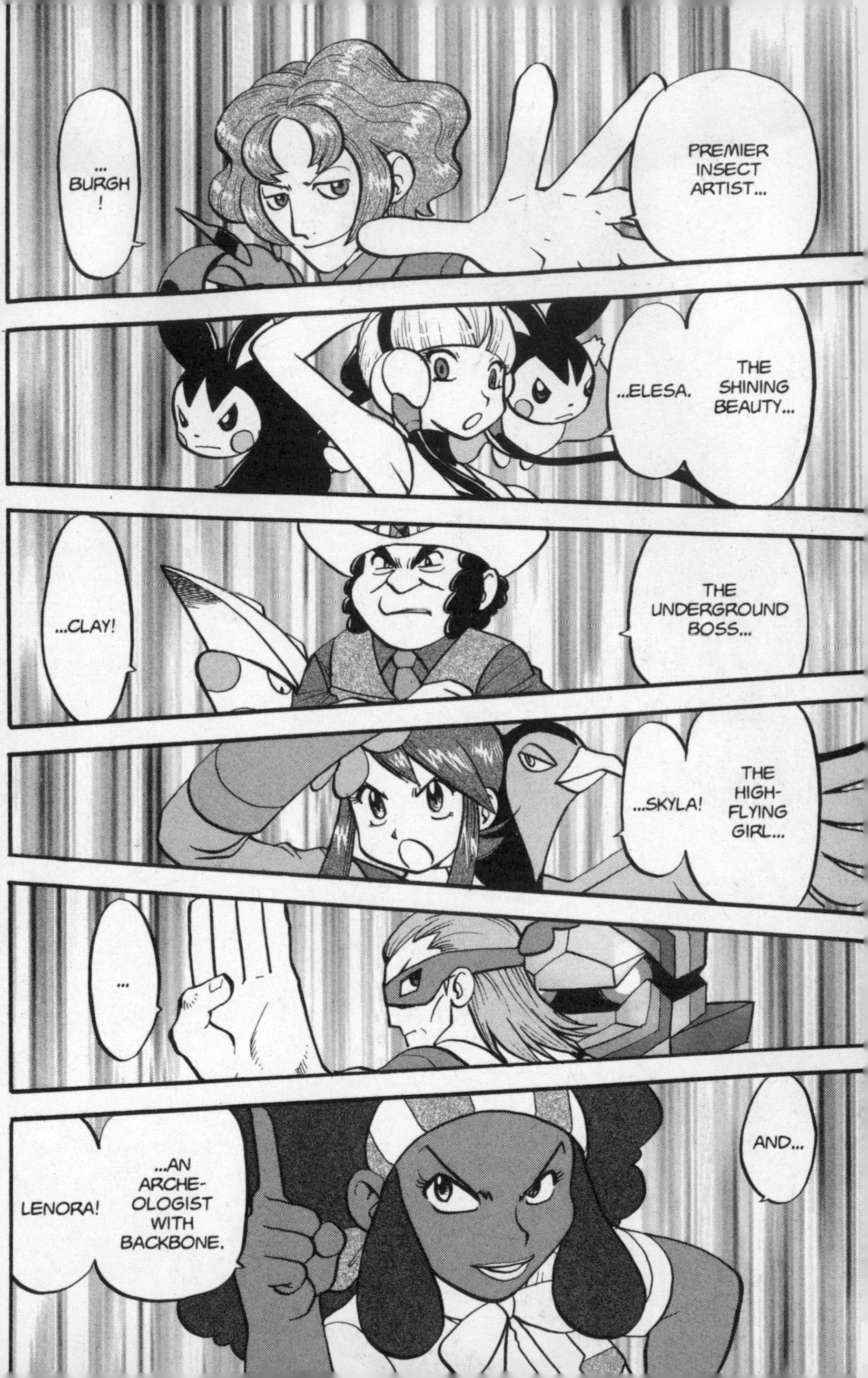
PREMIER INSECT ARTIST...
...BURGH!
THE SHINING BEAUTY...
...ELESA.
THE UNDERGROUND BOSS...
...CLAY!
THE HIGH-FLYING GIRL...
...SKYLA!
...
AND...
...AN ARCHE-OLOGIST WITH BACKBONE.
LENORA!

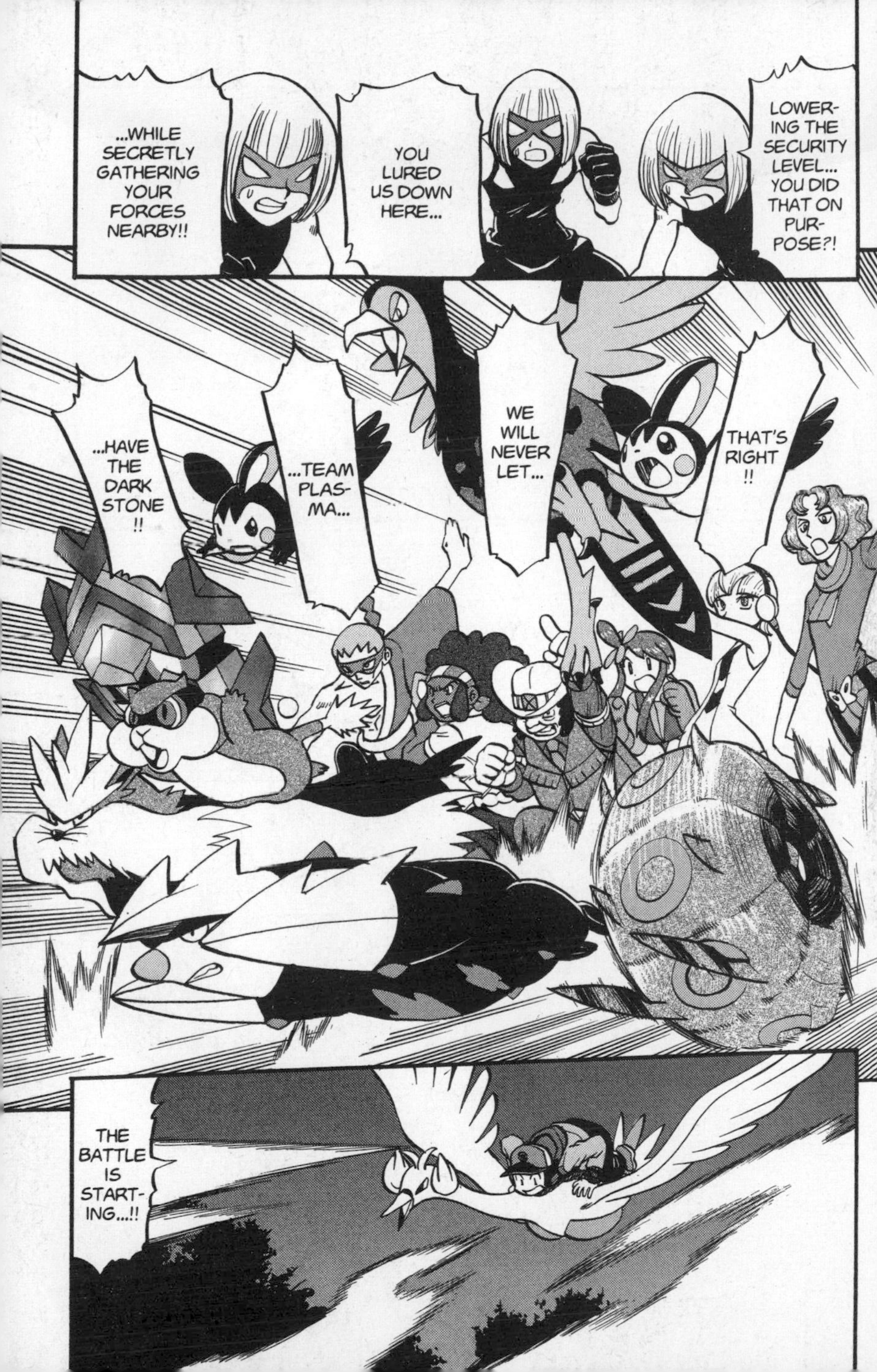
LOWERING THE SECURITY LEVEL... YOU DID THAT ON PURPOSE?!
YOU LURED US DOWN HERE...
...WHILE SECRETLY GATHERING YOUR FORCES NEARBY!!
THAT'S RIGHT!!
WE WILL NEVER LET...
...TEAM PLASMA...
...HAVE THE DARK STONE!!
THE BATTLE IS STARTING...!!

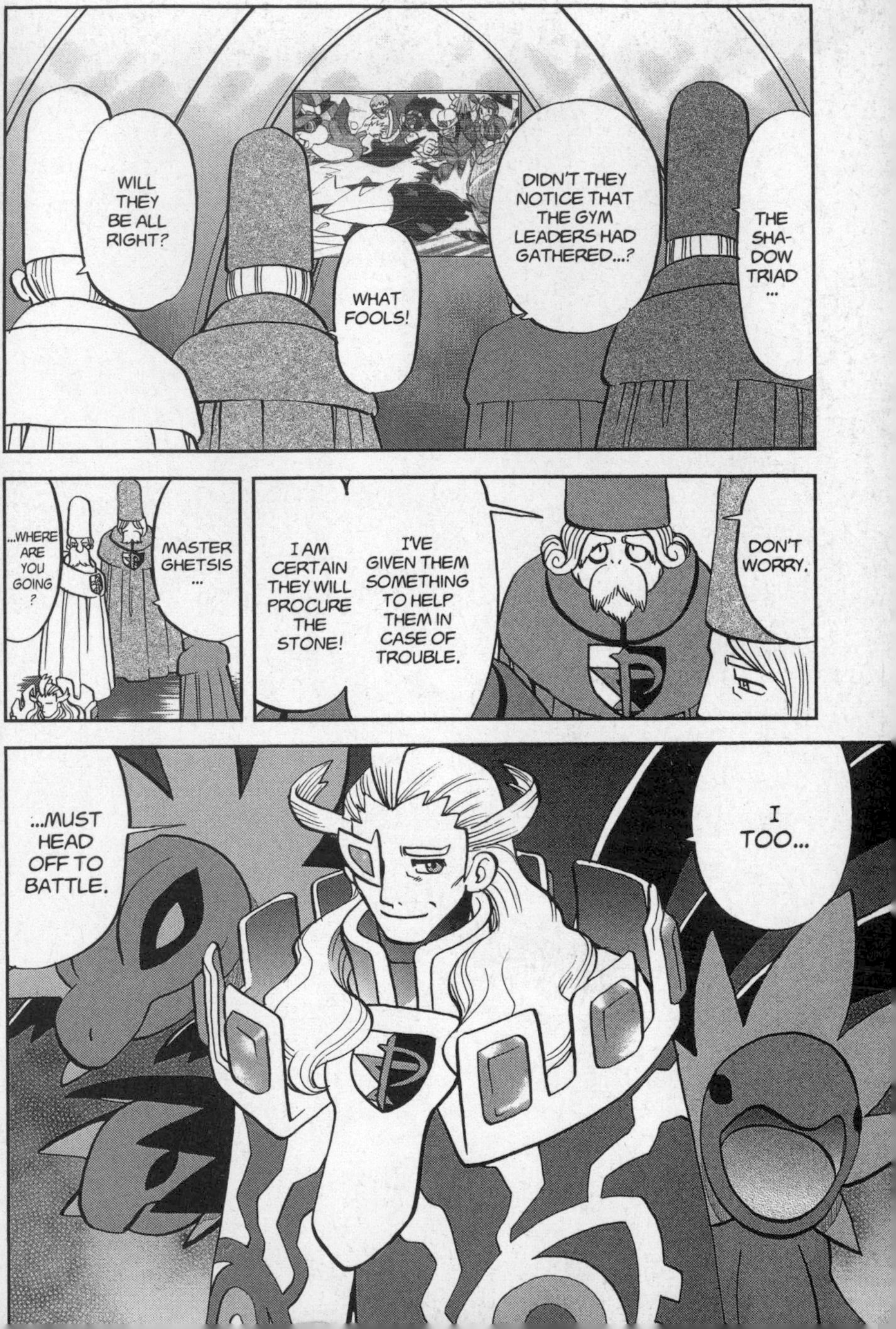
THE SHADOW TRIAD...
DIDN'T THEY NOTICE THAT THE GYM LEADERS HAD GATHERED...?
WHAT FOOLS!
WILL THEY BE ALL RIGHT?
DON'T WORRY.
I'VE GIVEN THEM SOMETHING TO HELP THEM IN CASE OF TROUBLE.
I AM CERTAIN THEY WILL PROCURE THE STONE!
MASTER GHETSIS...
...WHERE ARE YOU GOING?
I TOO...
...MUST HEAD OFF TO BATTLE.

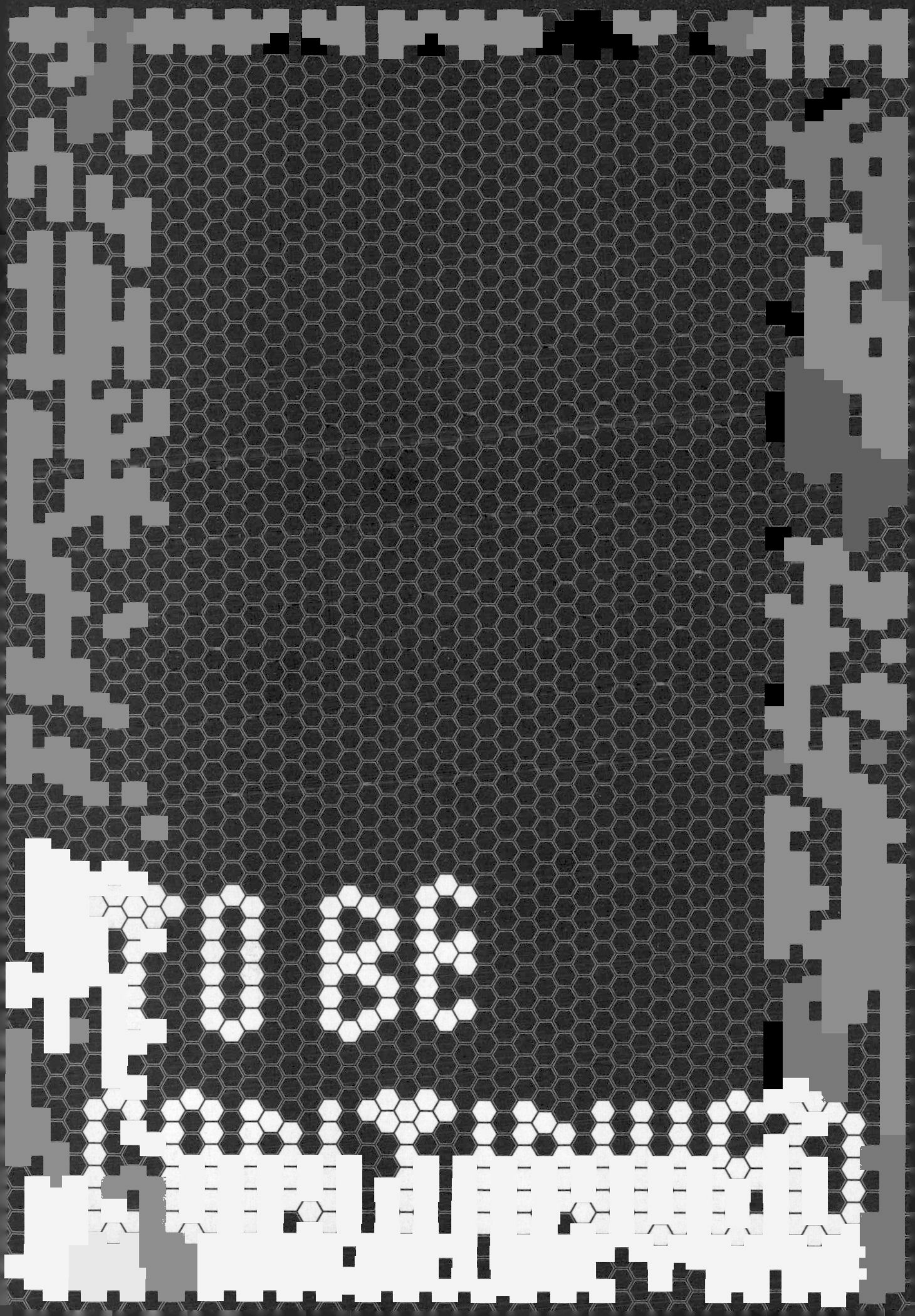
TO BE

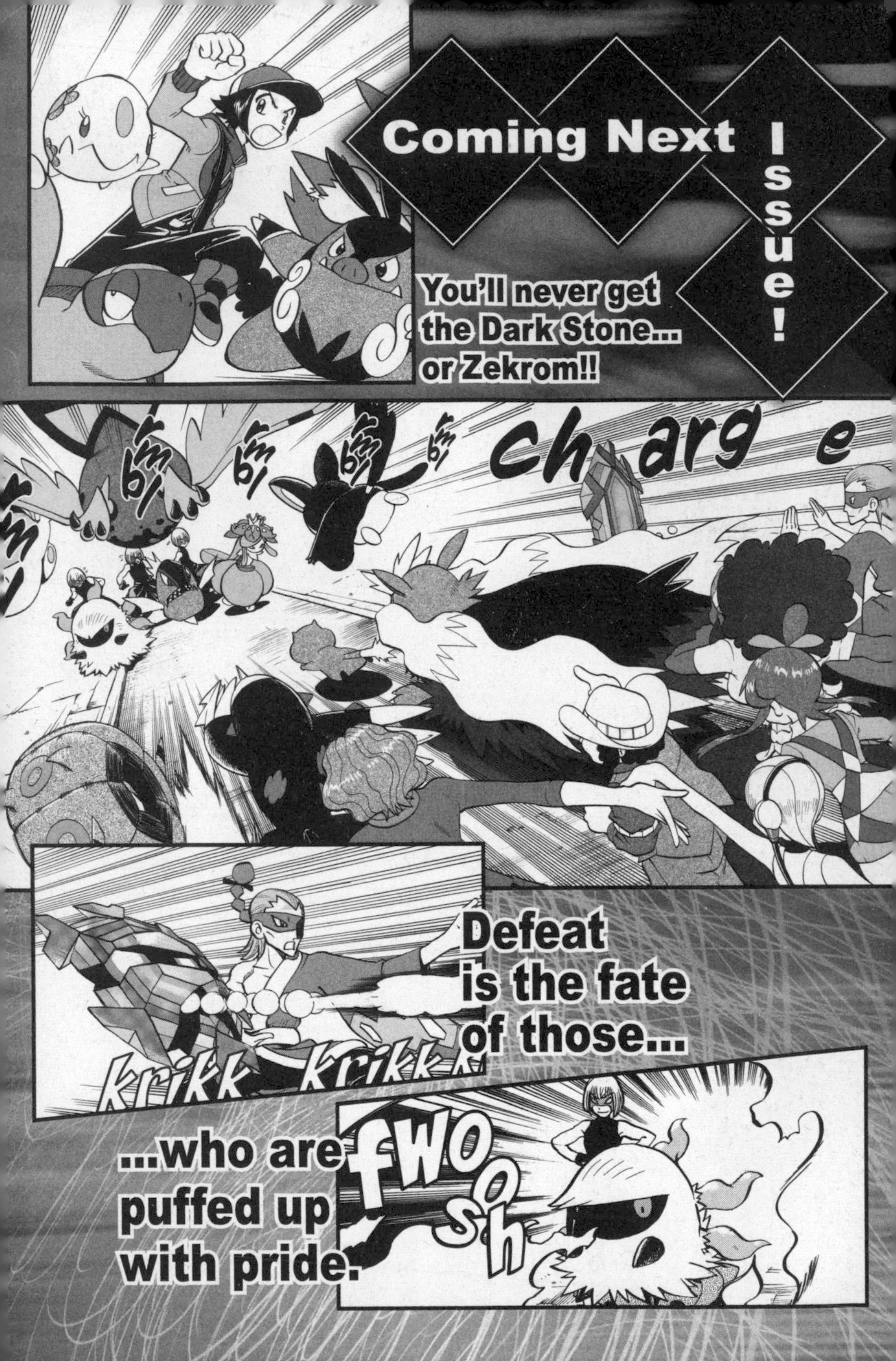
Coming Next Issue!
You'll never get the Dark Stone... or Zekrom!!
charge
Defeat is the fate of those...
krikk krikk
...who are puffed up with pride.
fwoosh

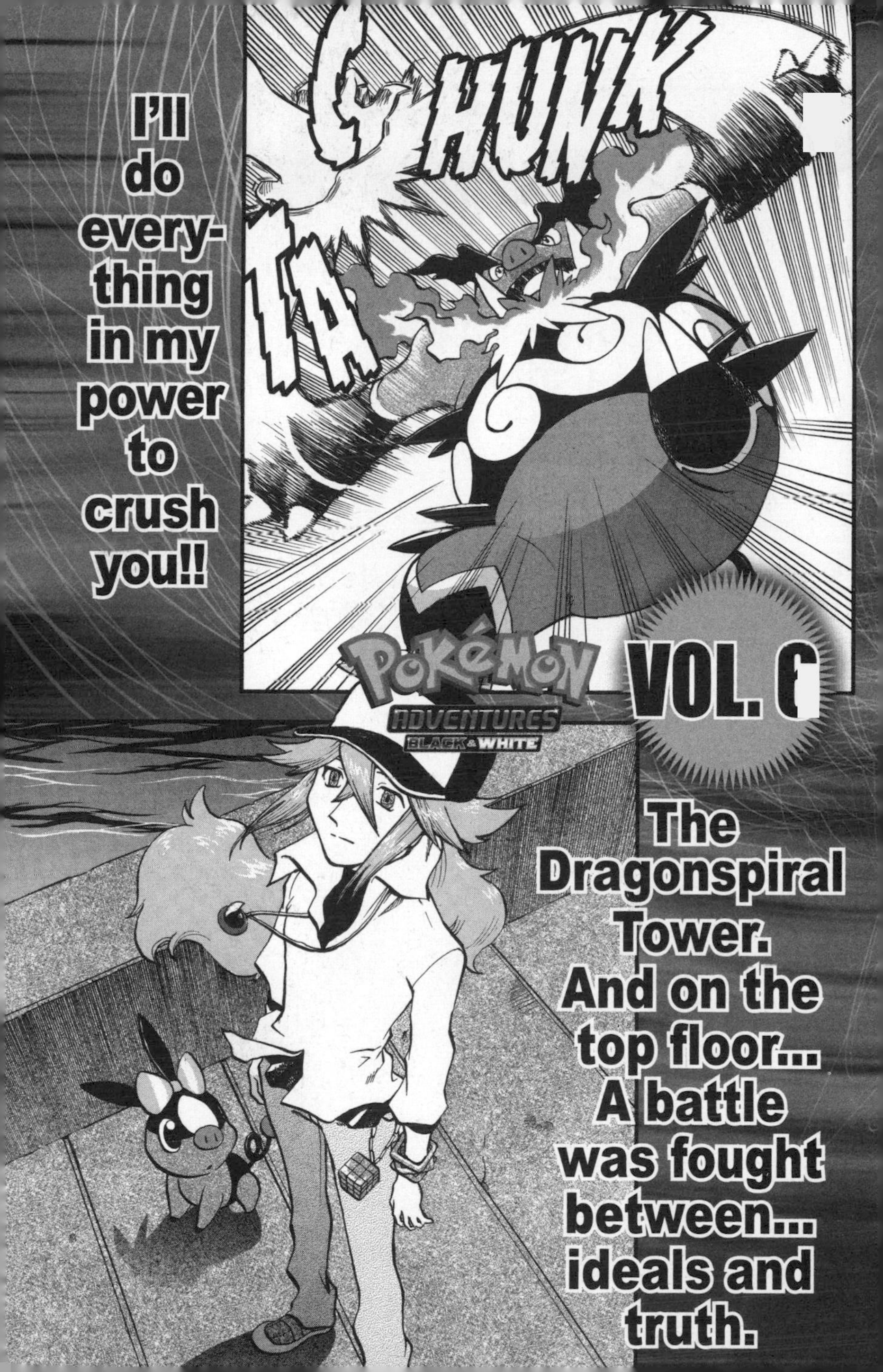
I'll do every-thing in my power to crush you!!
CHUNK
TA
POKÉMON ADVENTURES BLACK & WHITE
VOL. 6
The Dragonspiral Tower. And on the top floor... A battle was fought between... ideals and truth.

Chapter Title Page Illustration Collection

Presenting title page illustrations
originally drawn for some of
the chapters of *Pokémon Black
& White* when they were first
published in Japanese children's
magazines *Pokémon Fan* and
Corocoro Ichiban!

Let's take a look back at Black and
White's journey in pictures...

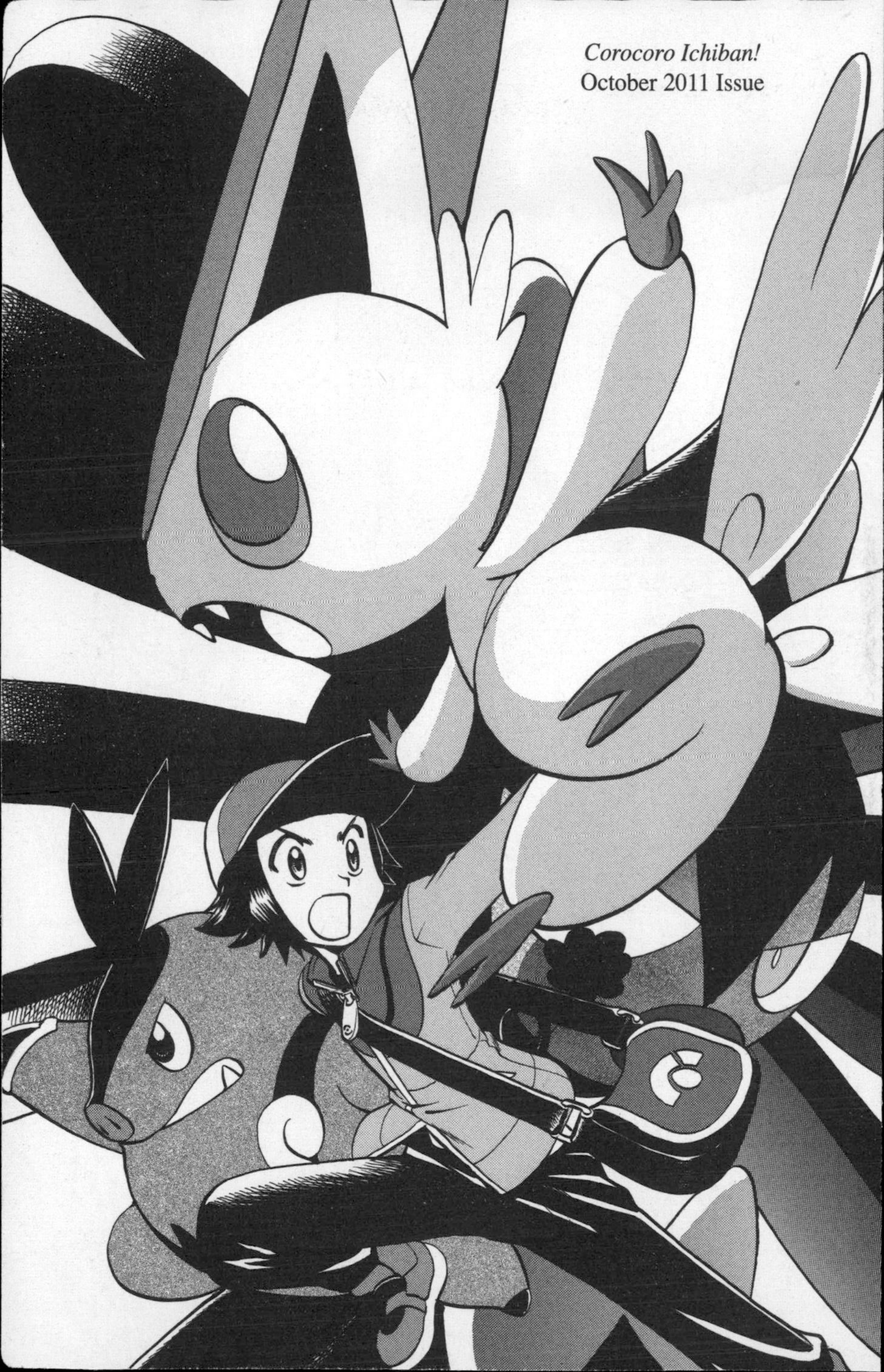

Corocoro Ichiban!
October 2011 Issue

Corocoro Ichiban!
November 2011 Issue

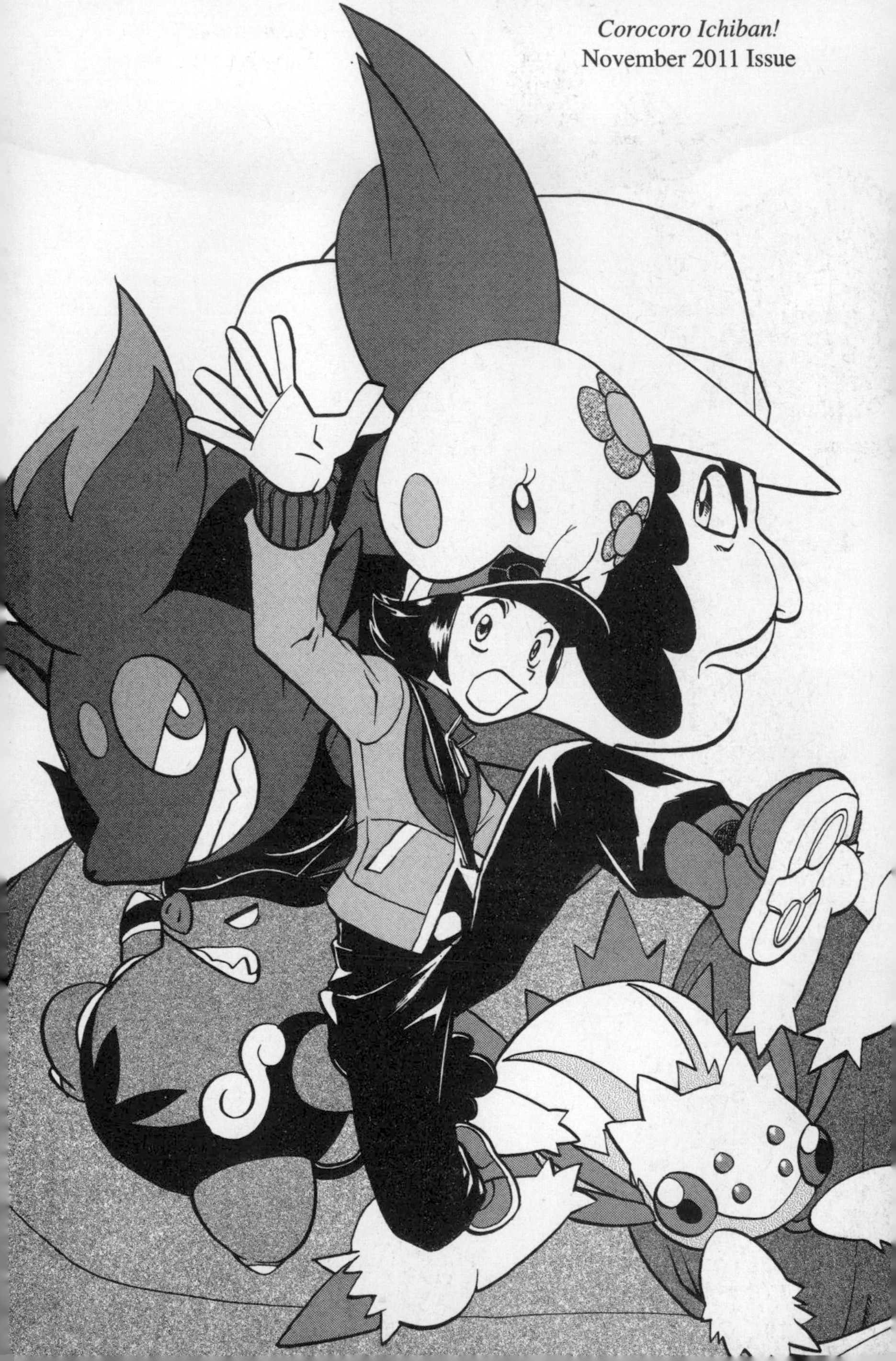

Pokémon Fan
Issue 20

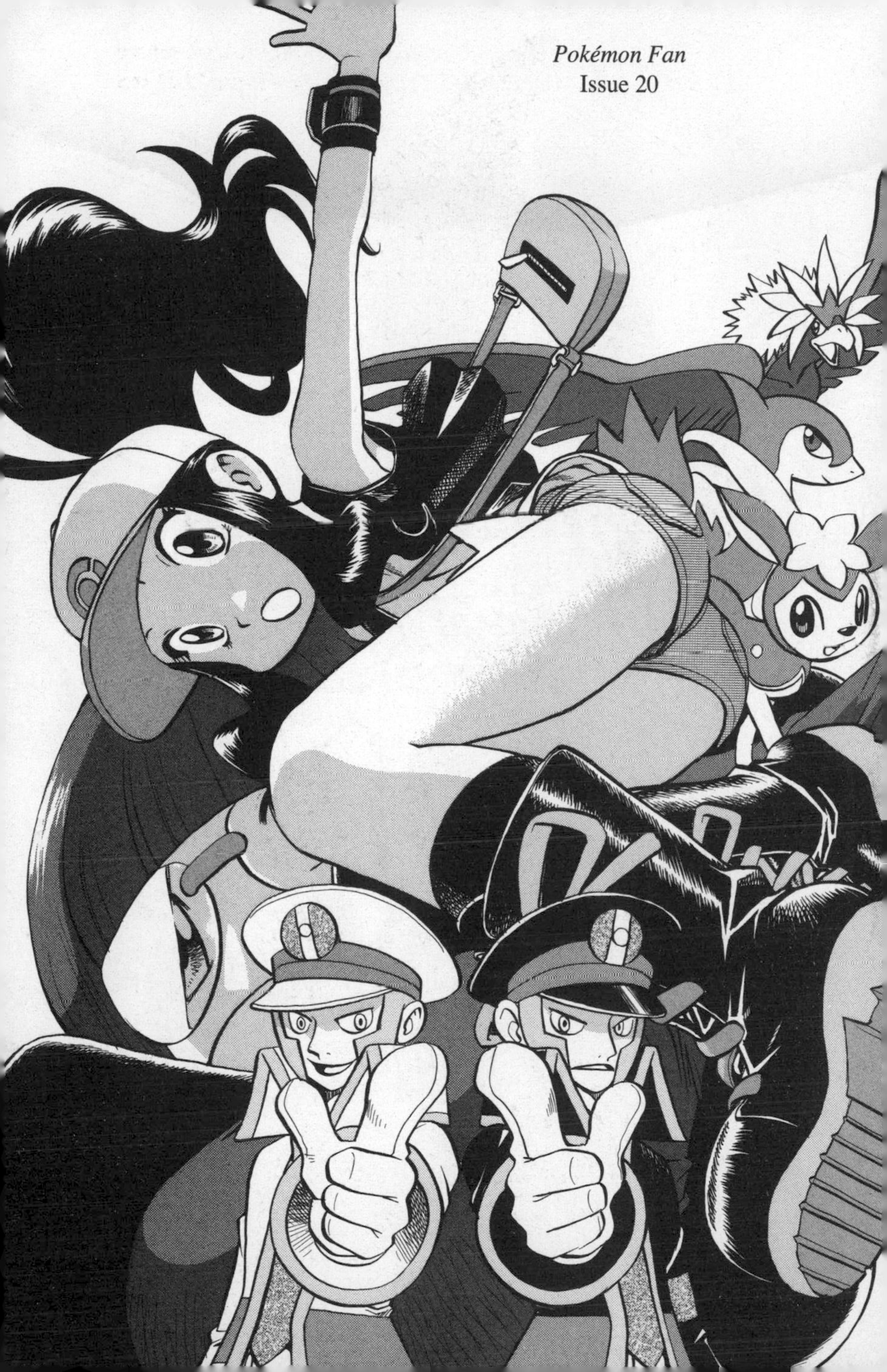

Corocoro Ichiban!
December 2011 Issue

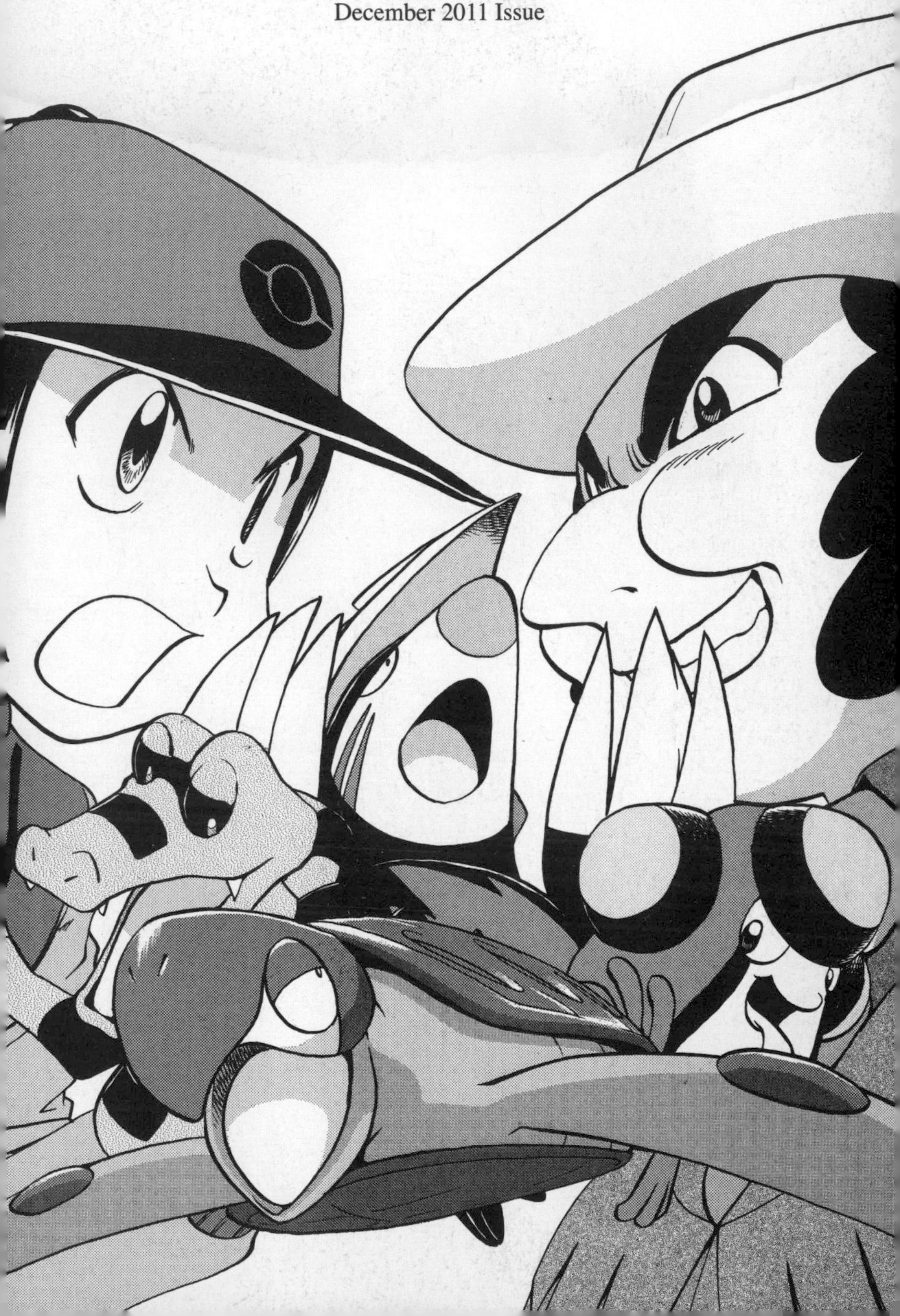

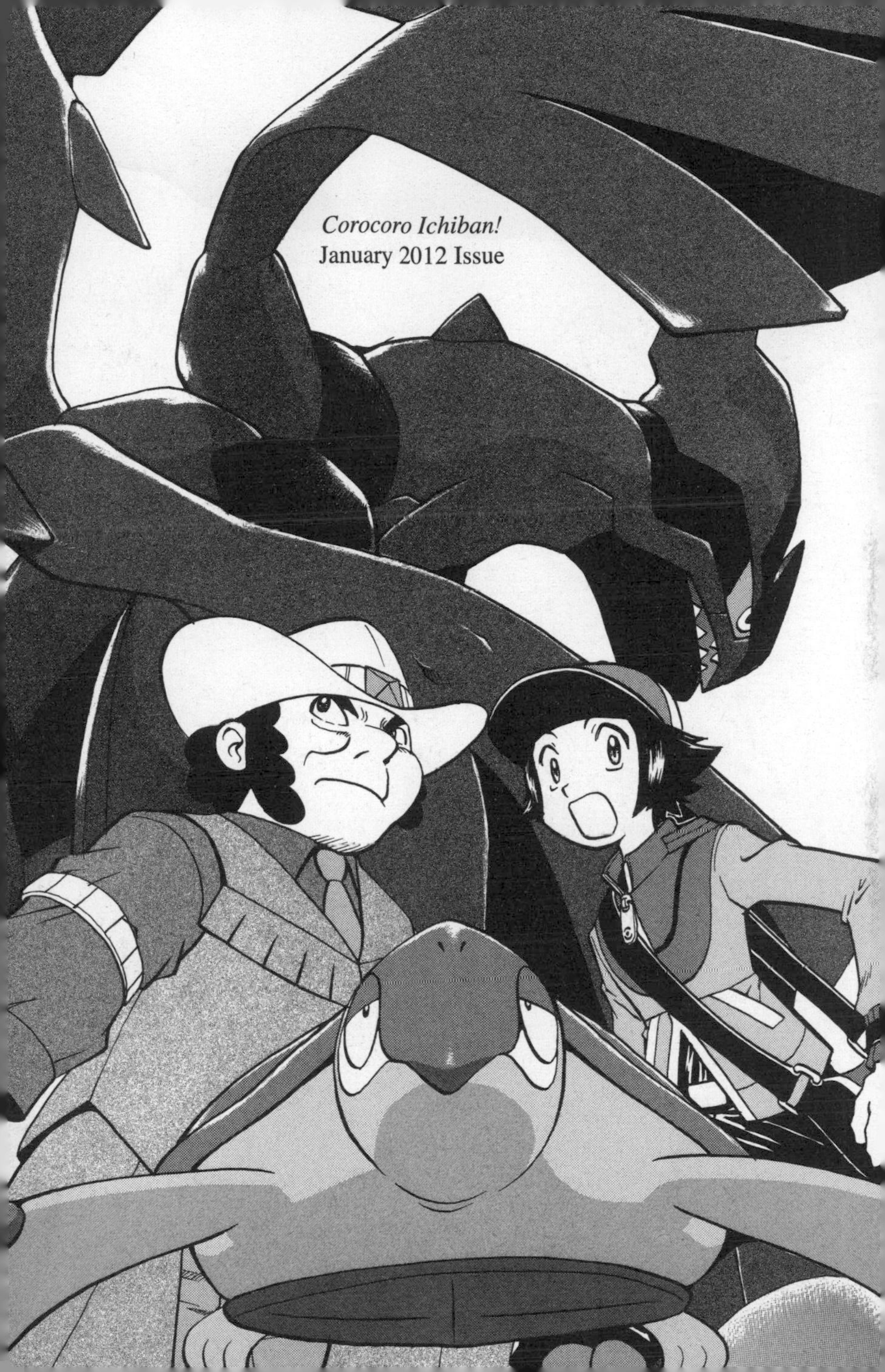
Corocoro Ichiban!
January 2012 Issue

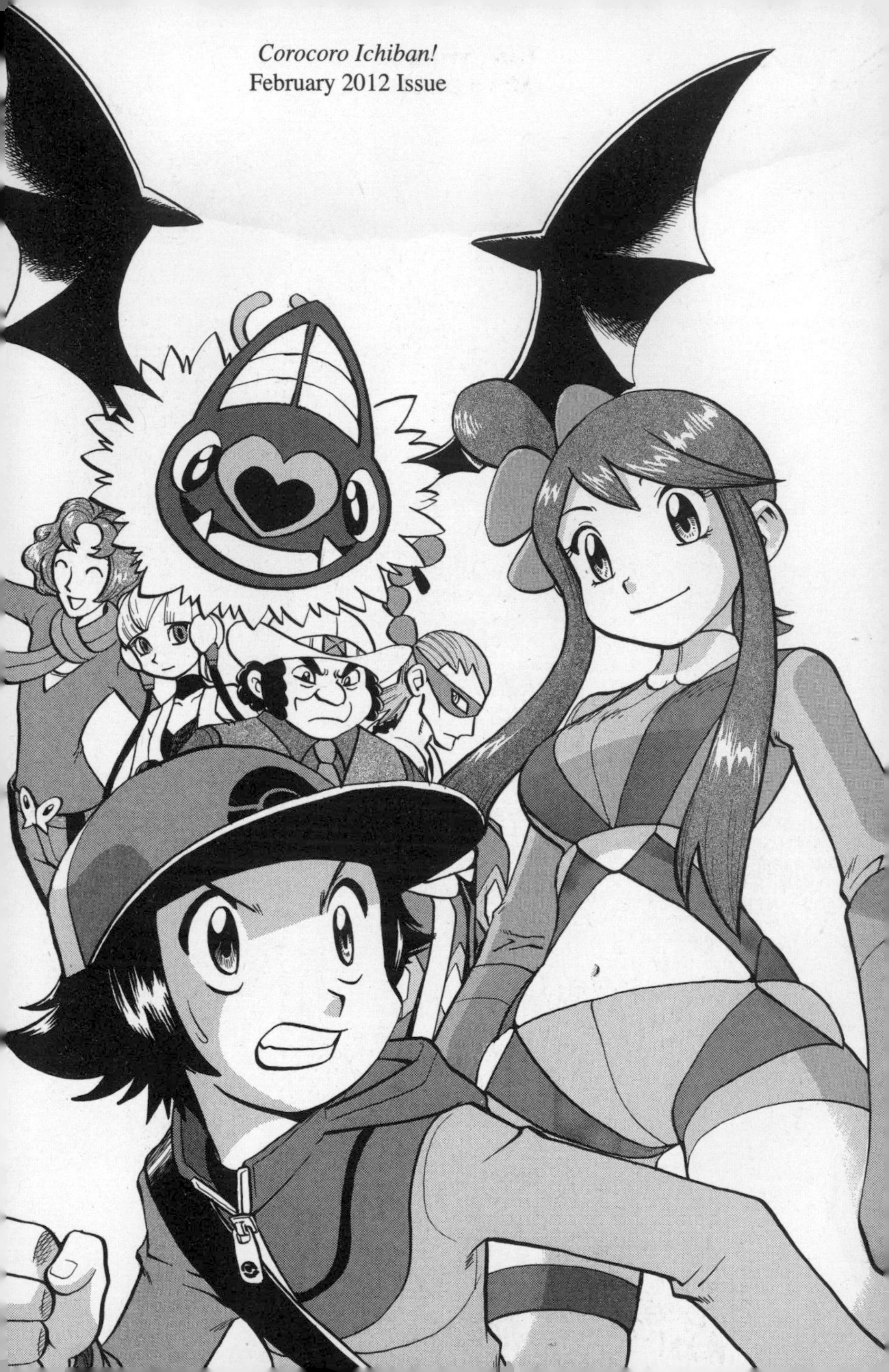

Corocoro Ichiban!
February 2012 Issue

Corocoro Ichiban!
March 2012 Issue

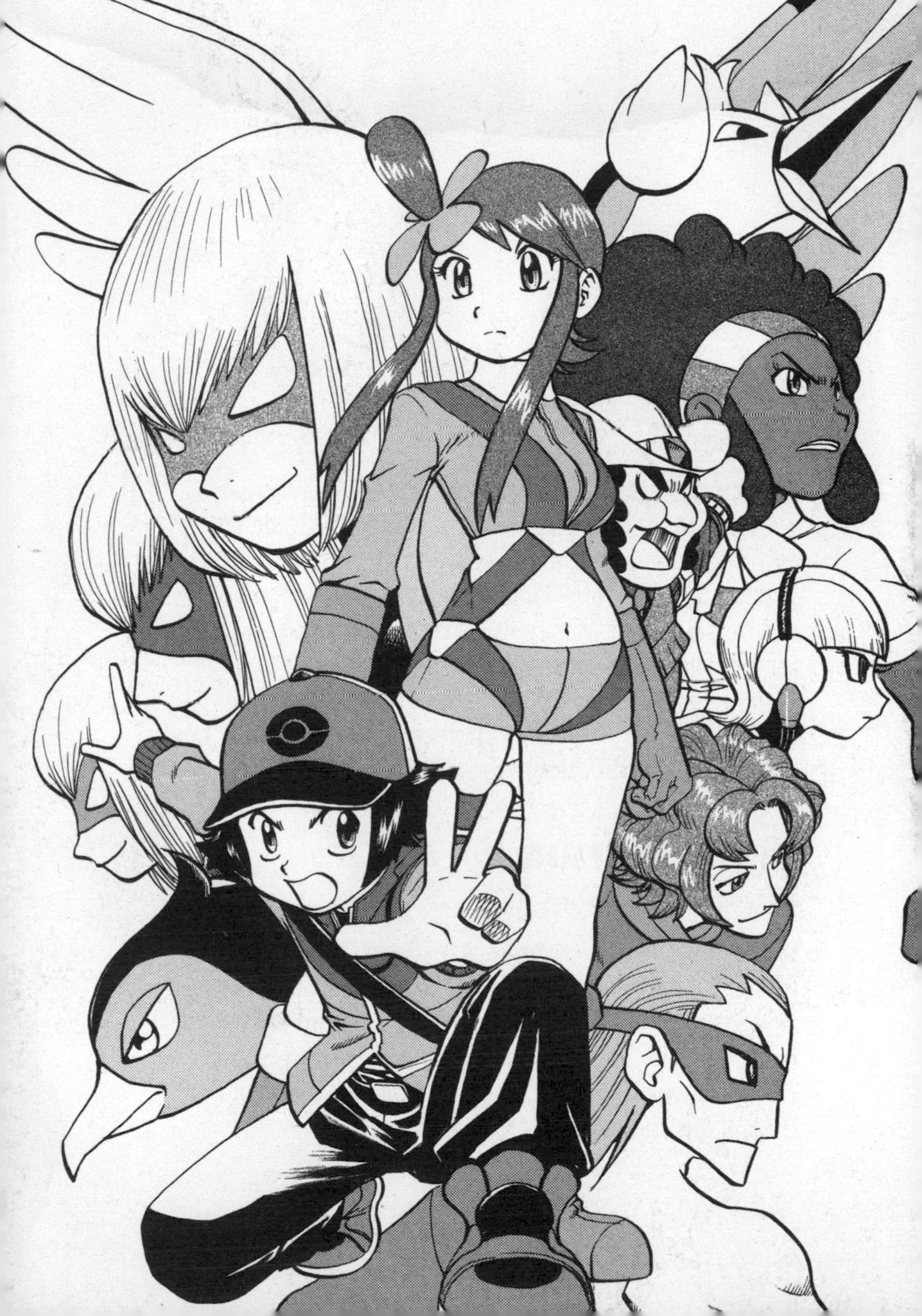

Message from
Hidenori Kusaka

I like suits, so whenever I drop by a store I always pay attention to the dress clothes. Shirts, ties, belts, tie pins, cuff links... I'm interested in suit accessories as well. In particular, I've been collecting Pokémon-patterned ties for seventeen years now. I have quite a collection! But my favorite Pokémon aren't always chosen for tie patterns, so, recently, I've been creating my own original ties using iron-on transfers I bought at the Pokémon Center! (*laugh*) Yes, I'm going all out! ♪ (´ ε `)

Message from
Satoshi Yamamoto

When I designed the members of Team Plasma, I tried to make them look like ordinary people. I imagined the reasons they might have joined up, what kind of life they led up to that point, etc. The result is the Team Plasma members who appear at the Cold Storage; every one of them has a unique story...to me. (*laugh*)

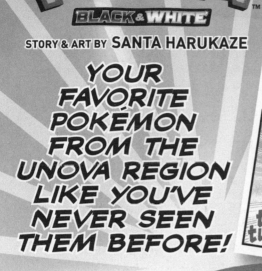

PERFECT SQUARE

viz media
www.viz.com

RATED A ALL AGES ratings.viz.com

Pokémon

DIAMOND AND PEARL ADVENTURE!

A BRAND NEW QUEST

Can a new trainer and his friends track down the legendary Pokémon Dialga before it's too late?

vizkids

Pokémon
DIAMOND AND PEARL ADVENTURE!
1

Story and Art by
Shigekatsu Ihara

Find out in the *Pokémon Diamond and Pearl Adventure* manga—buy yours today!

On sale at store.viz.com
Also available at your local bookstore or comic store.

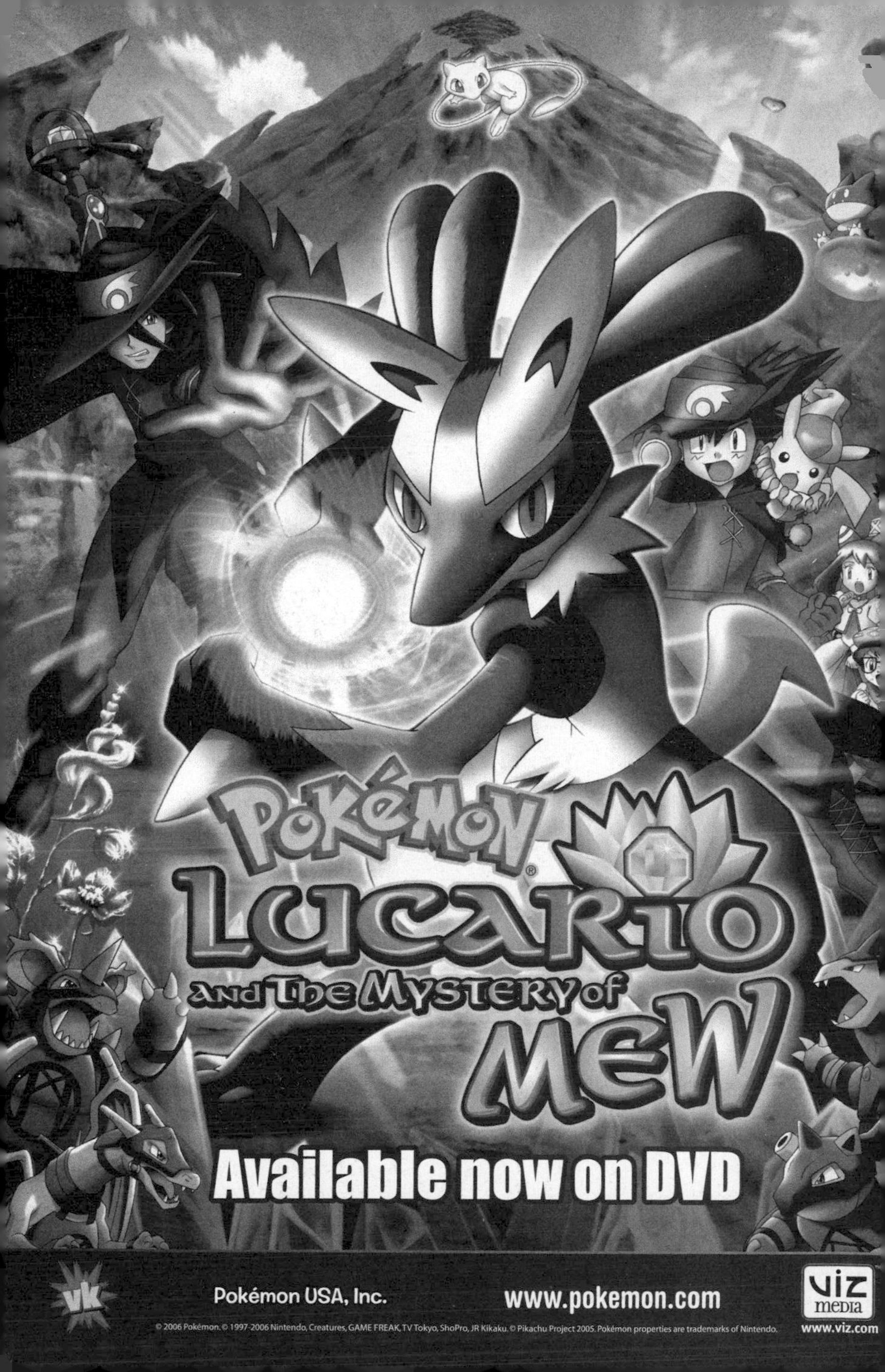
POKéMON®
LUCARIO
AND THE MYSTERY OF
MEW
Available now on DVD
vk
Pokémon USA, Inc.
www.pokemon.com
VIZ MEDIA
www.viz.com
© 2006 Pokémon. © 1997-2006 Nintendo, Creatures, GAME FREAK, TV Tokyo, ShoPro, JR Kikaku. © Pikachu Project 2005. Pokémon properties are trademarks of Nintendo.

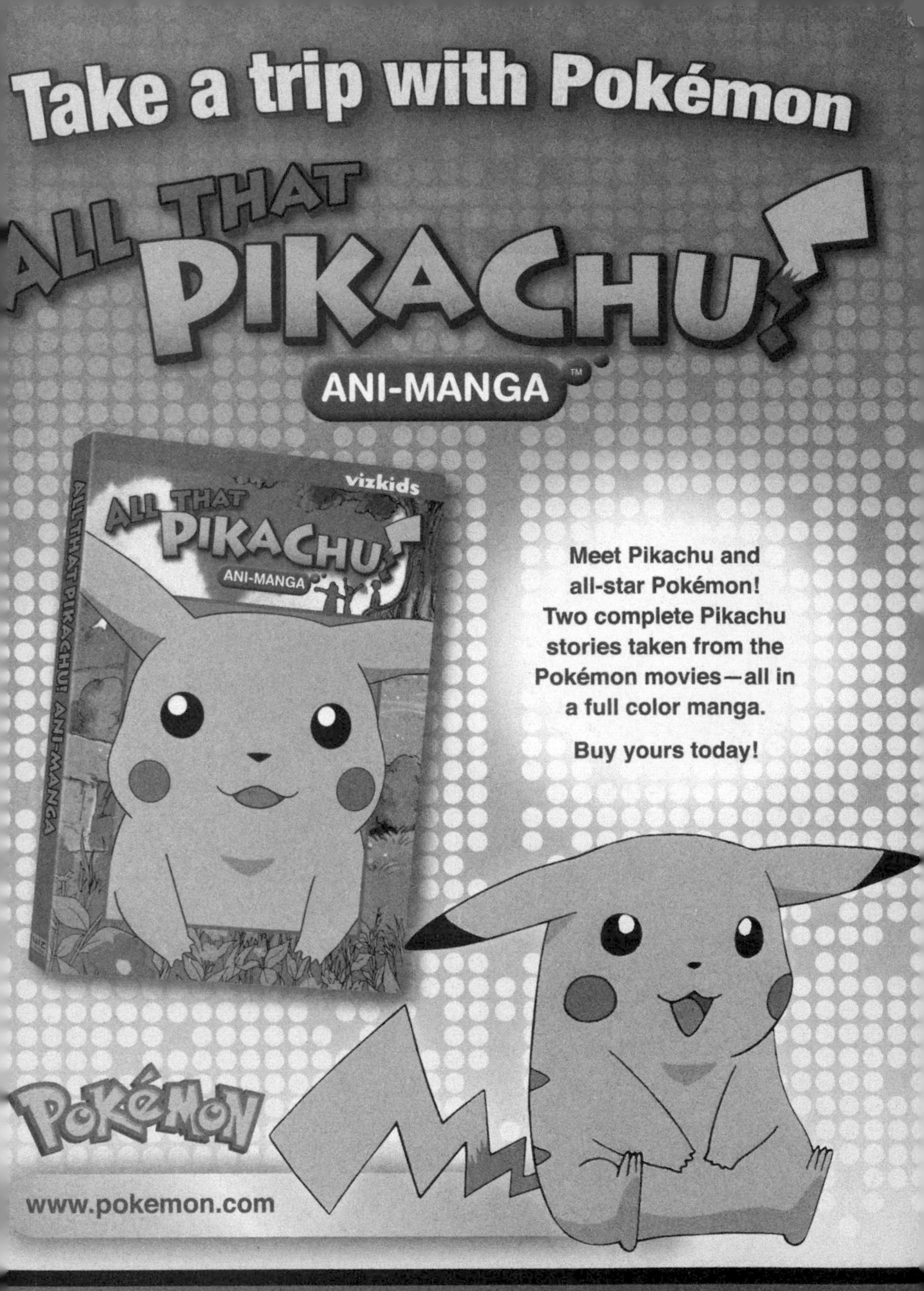
Take a trip with Pokémon
ALL THAT PIKACHU!
ANI-MANGA™
vizkids
ALL THAT PIKACHU!
ANI-MANGA
ALL THAT PIKACHU! ANI-MANGA
Meet Pikachu and all-star Pokémon! Two complete Pikachu stories taken from the Pokémon movies—all in a full color manga.
Buy yours today!
POKéMON
www.pokemon.com

The Struggle for Time and Space Begins Again!

Pokémon Trainer Ash and his Pikachu must find the Jewel of Life and stop Arceus from devastating all existence! The journey will be both dangerous and uncertain: even if Ash and his friends can set an old wrong right again, will there be time to return the Jewel of Life before Arceus destroys everything and everyone they've ever known?

Manga edition also available from VIZ Media

POKÉMON

ARCEUS
JEWEL OF LIFE
A TALE UNTOLD. A LEGEND UNLEASHED.

POKÉMON
ARCEUS
AND THE JEWEL OF LIFE

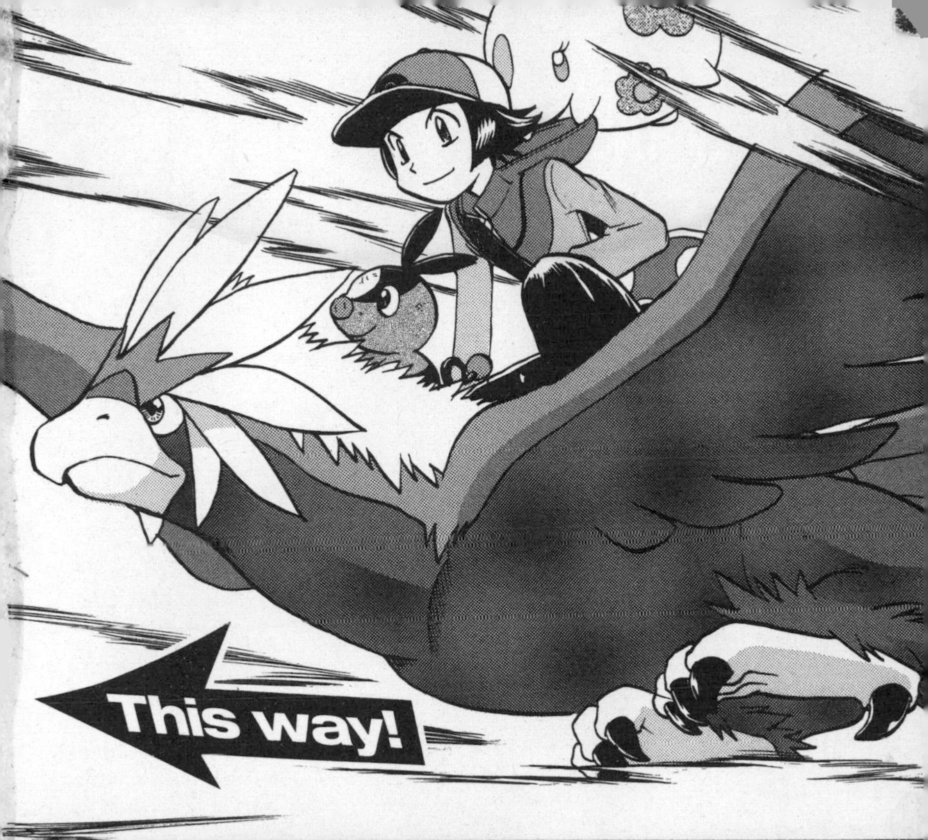
This way!

THIS IS THE END OF THIS GRAPHIC NOVEL!

To properly enjoy this VIZ Media graphic novel, please turn it around and begin reading from right to left.

This book has been printed in the original Japanese format in order to preserve the orientation of the original artwork.

Have fun with it!

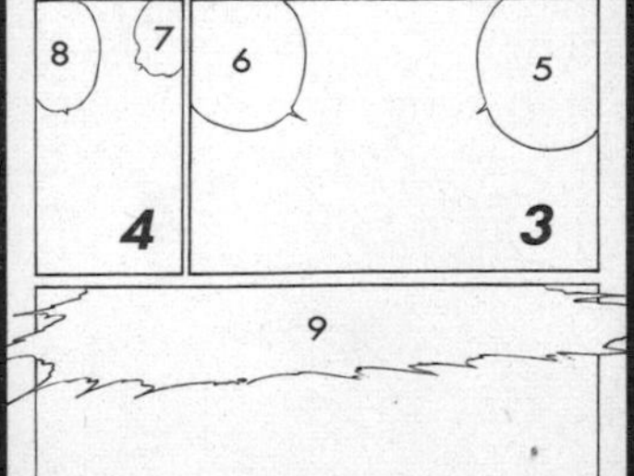
1
2
3
4
5
6
7
8
9
1
2
3
4
5

FOLLOW THE ACTION THIS WAY.

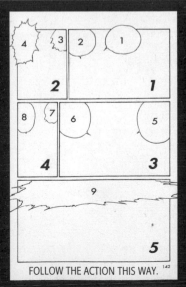